W9-ANW-913

SONS OF WAR 3
SINNERS

OTHER BOOKS BY NICHOLAS SANSBURY SMITH

Blackstone Publishing

THE SONS OF WAR SERIES

Sons of War

Sons of War 2: Saints

Sons of War 3: Sinners

THE HELL DIVERS SERIES

Hell Divers

Hell Divers II: Ghosts

Hell Divers III: Deliverance

Hell Divers IV: Wolves

Hell Divers V: Captives

Hell Divers VI: Allegiance

Hell Divers VII: Warriors

Orbit

THE EXTINCTION CYCLE SERIES (SEASON ONE)

Extinction Horizon

Extinction Edge

Extinction Age

Extinction Evolution

Extinction End

Extinction Aftermath

Extinction Lost (A Team Ghost short story)

Extinction War

Great Wave Ink Publishing

THE EXTINCTION CYCLE: DARK AGE SERIES (SEASON TWO)

Extinction Shadow

Extinction Inferno

Extinction Ashes

Extinction Darkness

THE TRACKERS SERIES

Trackers

Trackers 2: The Hunted

Trackers 3: The Storm

Trackers 4: The Damned

THE ORBS SERIES

Solar Storms (An Orbs Prequel)

White Sands (An Orbs Prequel)

Red Sands (An Orbs Prequel)

Orbs

Orbs II: Stranded

Orbs III: Redemption

Orbs IV: Exodus

NICHOLAS SANSBURY SMITH

Published in 2021 by Blackstone Publishing
Cover and book design by K. Jones

The characters and events in this book are fictitious. Any similarity to real persons, living or dead, is coincidental and not intended by the author.

Printed in the United States of America

First edition: 2021
ISBN 978-1-5385-5707-5
Science Fiction / Apocalyptic & Post-Apocalyptic

1 3 5 7 9 10 8 6 4 2

CIP data for this book is available
from the Library of Congress

Blackstone Publishing
31 Mistletoe Rd.
Ashland, OR 97520

www.BlackstonePublishing.com.

To Don Winslow, who inspires me every day,
and Ray Porter, who brought this series to life with his talented voice.

“Do not underestimate these men. They are not sheep like the other cops in this city. These men are wolves.”

—Don Antonio Moretti

“Sometimes, it feels like we’re the only soldiers fighting for justice. My father told me before I left with Ronaldo that justice was a rare thing in this new world.”

—Saint Namid Mata

-PROLOGUE-

The raiders hunting refugees in the deserts tonight would have a hard time spotting the Toyota pickup covered by a tarp the color of the sand.

To further protect their camp's location, the three men had nestled the truck against a rock outcropping. Anyone searching the terrain would see just another rusty-hued boulder under the jeweled sky.

But the raiders weren't the only hunters. The real hunters were undercover officers Dominic Salvatore, Andre "Moose" Clarke, and their guide, Namid Mata, a Mojave Indian from a reservation forty miles away.

Darkness had fallen an hour ago, ending the hunt for the day. Now Dom sat on the truck bed while Namid cooked dinner and Moose held watch on the other side of the jumbled rocks.

A shooting star blazed across the sky, faded, and vanished.

Dom jumped down to the dirt, where his three-legged red-nosed pit bull, Cayenne, watched Namid pinch seasoning into a boiling pot. She hardly even looked up when Dom rubbed her muscular neck.

Cayenne didn't seem worried about the raiders they had tracked earlier today. Her attention was on food, and Dom's was on something that happened out here three years ago.

"Do you think you could find where my father died?" Dom asked.

Namid looked up from the stew pot. "All due respect, but why would you want to see where he fell in battle?"

Dom wasn't sure exactly.

"Your father put up a hell of a fight that day, like he did every time we did battle with evil men," Namid said. "He was as great a warrior as I've ever had the honor of fighting with. My father saw it in him. That's why he sent me with the Desert Snakes before he, too, was killed."

"I'm sorry about your father."

Dom never met Tomson, but he had raised an honorable son in Namid, and the two had formed a strong bond over the past few years.

"We should remember not how our fathers died, but how they lived," Namid said.

Dom nodded. Normally, he did remember his dad for the man he was before he died. But he had always wondered about that fateful day when Vega sicarios gunned Ronaldo down in the desert.

Namid looked at the sky and let out a sigh, no doubt reliving a painful memory of the day he lost his father to raiders on the reservation.

The two men shared more than the loss of their fathers. They each had lost a sister too. In a cruel twist of fate, their losses had brought them together in a fight against evil.

"Regrets will eat us alive," Dom admitted. "You're right about remembering our loved ones for who they were, and honoring them by fighting for justice."

Dom pulled out a flask of vodka, welcoming the burn. He offered it to Namid, who declined.

"Sometimes, it feels like we're the only soldiers fighting for justice," Namid said. He crouched back to the fire and stirred the broth. "My father told me before I left with Ronaldo that justice was a rare thing in this new world."

The three years since he lost his father were a whirlwind. He had led the Saints, a small task force of brave men and women, to do what the LAPD couldn't—or *wouldn't*—do: fight back against the crime families and gangs. And to take down the Vega brothers, who were responsible for killing his dad and probably for taking his sister in their trafficking network known as the Shepherds.

Dom had their attention now. The narcos had their own nickname for the Saints: *las ratas*—the rats.

He had the attention of the Italian mafiosi too. The mobsters called them rabbits, or *conigli*, which basically meant they were cowards.

Dom understood the irony better than anyone in the city. The real rats and rabbits were the crime families and the cops on their payroll.

"We will find justice, in this life or the next," Namid said.

Dom thought about raising a toast to that too, but he saw Namid watching. Twisting the top back on, he stuffed the flask back in his vest, and Namid went back to stirring the soup.

"Your father would be proud of you," he said. "You've done a heck of a job poking the hornets' nest without bringing the entire swarm down on us."

It was a balancing act, fighting the crime families without drawing too much attention, but so far, he had kept his team alive. Lieutenant Zed Marks had certainly helped by keeping their identities protected and giving them fake jobs at Refugee Processing Center 4, a facility under the umbrella of the Los Angeles County Sheriff's Department.

But Dom knew that it was only a matter of time before their luck ran out.

For every gangster they took off the streets, three more would step up to take his place, eager to make money and feed their families. And every time the Saints destroyed a shipment of drugs, more would come flooding into the city.

Using their guerrilla tactics, they won battle after battle, but they weren't any closer to winning the war.

He had needed a vacation from fighting in the city, so he headed to the desert after Namid agreed to lead them to the same black hole that swallowed his sister years ago.

This trip to Las Vegas wasn't a vacation. It was a continuation of the search for Monica. And this time, he had a faint lead that Lieutenant Marks had given them after interrogating two Vega sicarios. There was a small chance his sister had been taken to a place in Sin City that he couldn't even bear to think about.

While he went there to search with Namid and Moose, the rest of their small undercover task force waited back in Los Angeles. Dom had left William

Bettis in charge of the team, with Camilla Santiago second in command. Thanks to his former high school Spanish partner turned cop, they knew the best routes to Las Vegas, and how to stay alive once they got there.

"You got the map? I want to take a look," Dom said.

Namid reached into his vest and pulled out the map Camilla had given them—a present from her uncle Álvaro, who ran a smuggling operation.

Unlike the Shepherds and other human traffickers, Álvaro helped people get across the desert to safety, not into slavery. And the man had memorized all the good roads and most of the bad ones.

"Glad we have this," Namid said, handing the map over. "A lot's changed since I was out here last."

Cayenne hopped over to the soup, sniffed the air, and whined. Dom looked up from the chart, unable to see much by the thin moonlight.

"Okay, okay," he said to the dog. "I'll feed you."

Tail whipping back and forth, she followed Dom to the back of the truck, where he rummaged through his gear until he found her food. She wedged her massive head between his arms as he lowered the plastic bowl, and was eating before it touched the ground.

Her tail suddenly dropped as she chewed, and instead of going back in for another bite, she growled.

"What is it?" he whispered.

Dom unholstered the SIG Sauer 1911 Nightmare that had belonged to his father, then relaxed when he saw it was just Moose.

Cradling his shotgun, he stepped from behind a Joshua tree with branches jutting out like the spiky dreadlocks on his head.

"Something smells dope, and I'm starving, baby," he said. "Hope the raiders can't smell it."

"That's why you're supposed to be on watch," Dom said.

"I'll return to my post with a bowl, boss, don't worry."

Namid laughed. "Help yourself. I'll take your place. I'm not really hungry."

He grabbed his rifle and set off. Moose didn't complain. He filled a bowl and sucked the hot soup down. Dom filled a bowl too, taking his time and admiring the dazzling star-filled sky as he ate.

He took solace in the vastness of space. It reminded him how precious and transitory life was, and the beautiful view brought questions to mind. He couldn't help wondering whether there was something else out there, beyond this life—a heaven where you could see your loved ones again.

"Nice out here, right?" Moose said, cheerful as ever. "Never thought I'd be in the desert camping with you, bro. Then again, I never thought I'd be married with a kid at twenty-two."

He scraped at his bowl, then looked covetously at Dom's. "Help yourself, man."

"You sure?" Moose asked.

"I'm not really hungry, either."

Dom took out his flask again and swished the vodka around in his mouth. He was happy for Moose and his brother Ray for moving on, marrying, and starting families, just as Namid had done. But Dom couldn't bring himself to move on. He had spent the past three years doing everything he could to bring his mother back from the darkness, but their relationship continued to deteriorate. There was nothing he could do to help her.

Moose spooned food into his mouth. "Did I tell you Ray and his wife are talking about having a third kid?" he asked. "Not sure how he's going to pay for another mouth to feed."

Dom shrugged. He didn't want to approach the subject of Moose's detective brother, who had been skimming off the top for years. Probably working with the same people the Saints were trying to bring down.

"Crazy," Dom said.

He got up, and Moose lowered his bowl. "Where you going?"

"To get Namid," Dom replied. "He should eat. I'll hold watch." He whistled at Cayenne, and she hopped after him to another cluster of rocks that would give them a panoramic view of the area.

Nearing the top, he heard Namid's low whistle.

"Go back and eat before Moose polishes off that entire pot," Dom said.

Namid chuckled on his way down.

As soon as Dom was alone with his dog, a sense of dread washed over him. Being out here, not far from where his father had died, affected him in a way he hadn't expected.

"I miss you, Dad," he said. "I wish you were here."

He wondered whether his father would be proud of him, as Namid had said. Would Ronaldo approve of the way he led the Saints?

Dom idolized his father, not just because he was a warrior, but because he never gave up. He still didn't know exactly what had happened to his dad in the desert before he died, and part of him had never wanted to know.

But tonight, he wanted more than ever to know where his father had taken his last breaths. He wanted to see where the warrior had fallen, where he had handed Tooth and Bettis the note.

Dom took another drink of vodka and put it away. Then he pulled out a plastic sleeve protecting the crinkled note stained brown with blood.

If you're reading this, I failed. I failed you both. But you must go on, Dominic. You must find your sister no matter how long it takes you. I will be there with you in spirit, fighting in your heart.

With love,
your father

Dom put the note away.

Cayenne pressed against his leg, sensing his anguish. She knew him better than anyone besides Moose. And tonight, she could feel his heart hurt.

He bent down, and she licked his face.

Dom still couldn't believe how mild-mannered the dog was after the trauma of being torn up in a fighting ring and thrown in the street to die.

She was the kindest animal Dom had ever known, but when someone messed with either of them, she could be ferocious, even on three legs.

"I love you too, girl," Dom said.

Standing, he scanned the terrain.

Cayenne got up too, and after a few minutes, he gestured for her to follow him back to camp.

By the time he got back, Namid and Moose were both in their sleeping bags, but neither was asleep.

"Something wrong?" Moose asked, sitting up.

Namid reached for his rifle.

"No, just wanted to let you know we're taking a detour in the morning," Dom said. "Namid, I want you to show me where my father died."

* * *

The next morning, fingers of smoke rose with the sun.

Dom and his men had packed up camp and set off for the place his father died fighting the Vega traffickers. But it was the sight of another battle that made Dom pause.

Not a battle—a slaughter.

The raiders had attacked a caravan of refugees heading west to California. The travelers had camped in an abandoned gas station not far from Sandy Valley and only miles from the California line, not far from where his father died.

"Should we check for survivors? Moose asked.

Namid looked at Dom for orders. Cayenne tilted her head.

"Yeah," Dom said.

They drove within a mile of the smoke. Buzzards had found the grisly scene, circling over the smoldering gas station and surrounding buildings.

Moose parked and killed the engine.

"Stay here, girl," Dom said. He put Cayenne on the floor in front of the passenger seat. Then he grabbed his M1A SOCOM 16 rifle and hopped out. The wind whistled through his fatigues, sandblasting any exposed skin.

He closed the door and glassed the area for signs of life. Bodies lay in the dirt and sand, burned to charcoal. A skinned, limbless corpse was nailed to a shed wall. The sight told Dom the raiders were the worst kind: the kind that ate human flesh.

Cannibalism had started to spread a few years back, when things got really bad in other states. Desperation changed people.

Namid joined Dom. "I've seen this before," he said.

A buzzard flew down to peck at charred flesh.

"Maybe we should bury them," Dom said.

"Too dangerous," Namid said. "We should go see where your dad fell in battle."

Dom shook his head. “Not now. If there are raiders close by, that could be dangerous too. I don’t want to put us at risk if it doesn’t get us closer to Monica. My dad would want me to do what we came here for.”

Namid put a hand on his shoulder. “Good decision.”

They sped away from the grisly but not uncommon scene in the wastes. Dom put his dad out of mind, and their mission in focus. He pulled out the map to make sure they stayed off the worst of the roads. The journey to Vegas from LA was only five or six hours if you took the highway and avoided the raiders. But travelers who did cross their path seldom lived to tell the tale.

Some, like the caravan they had just seen, did everything right but were still murdered. It was a gamble either way.

Fortunately, Dom had the map from Camilla’s uncle Álvaro. He was going to owe the old man a few beers when they got back to Los Angeles.

Three hours into the second day of their journey, the pickup crested a hill overlooking the outskirts of what was once an oasis in the desert. Derelict communities surrounded the gambling mecca, and a graffitied sign pocked with bullet holes greeted them: “Sinners welcome.”

The strip flickered in the distance. The pyramid-shaped Sphinx Hotel reminded Dom of the Vega-controlled Angel Pyramids in Los Angeles, and the Excalibur resort looked much like the Commerce Hotel after Antonio Moretti turned it into his personal castle.

The mini Eiffel Tower reached for the sky in the center of the lavish resorts that once attracted millions of visitors each year.

“Always wanted to see this place,” Moose said.

Namid stared silently ahead, probably thinking about his sister now.

Cayenne slept on the floor, uninterested in the boarded-up mansions in the burbs, or the blocks of houses burned to their foundations. Unsurprisingly, a few appeared occupied. The former methadone capital of the world had problems with junkies and squatters long before the apocalypse.

Eventually, the LA crime families would move in when they were strong enough to defeat the organizations that controlled this city. For now, men like Antonio Moretti and Esteban Vega were only bringing their product here: both drugs and slaves.

"Where first? Bellagio?" Moose asked.

Dom flattened the map. "Yeah, Marks said there's a pimp the sicarios spoke of—guy who specializes in girls my sister's age."

He had a hard time saying it, but he had to be strong. Stroking Cayenne helped ease his anxiety as they entered traffic on the highway to the strip.

A plane touched down at the airport, and traffic increased as they made their way into the city. The wealthy few still flocked here with entourages of former soldiers, to play poker against other rounders. Even with bodyguards, some still ended up with empty pockets and a bullet in the head.

This was the Wild West, where a man could fulfill any desire, even those that once would have landed him in federal prison.

"Is that a . . ." Moose said.

On the shoulder of the road, a man led a donkey with a cart full of junk. Cayenne barked when she saw the donkey.

At the strip, they weren't greeted with the flashing lights and half-naked women Dom remembered seeing in the movies.

Most of the businesses were boarded up like the houses in the surrounding communities. But there were a few exceptions. Caesar's Palace, the Bellagio, the Wynn, and the Venetian had reopened and were humming along.

Cars waited under the porte cocheres, and pedestrians loitered outside, smoking cigarettes and surrounded by their bags.

Moose passed a dry pool where the Bellagio's fountains once shot a hundred feet into the air. They drove to an aboveground parking garage.

"Namid, you stay here with Cayenne for this first check," Dom said. "Watch the truck and our gear. We'll call if we need help."

"You got it," Namid said. "Be careful."

Cayenne tried to follow Dom, but he snapped his fingers. She sat next to Namid, letting out a low whine as Moose and Dom walked away.

Wearing jeans and T-shirts, with face masks around their necks, they entered the casino carrying two bags. Thick clouds of cigar smoke greeted them.

Men wearing suits sat around card tables, smoking and drinking. Dolled-up women in tight dresses watched their husbands or dates.

It wasn't hard to distinguish the tourists from their bodyguards. Most of the tourists appeared to have plenty of money, and Dom suddenly felt underdressed. Still, he didn't bother placing any bets to blend in.

The pimps were scattered about the casino floor, and it didn't take Dom long to find the one who fit the description Marks had given.

A tall, pale man leaned back against a bar, watching old horse races on massive flat-screens. His red suit jacket, red cowboy hat, silver rings, and watch weren't what gave him away. It was the cane with a silver grip.

"Hey," Dom said.

The guy turned slightly, holding a cigarette to his lips.

"Whattya want?" he asked in a Southern drawl.

"A fucking unicorn and a billion bucks," Dom said. "What the fuck you think we want?"

The man lowered his wing-tip shoe to the floor and stiffened. He was much taller than Dom originally thought.

Pushing up his mirrored sunglasses, he looked each of them up and down.

"You got coin?" he asked.

Dom set his bag down and pulled a black bag from his pocket. "Don't mistake my clothes for my bank balance."

The guy leaned forward to look in the bag.

"And don't play me or my buddy for a fool," Dom added. "There are plenty of other businessmen in this casino."

Moose folded his muscular arms over his chest.

The man tapped the spiked silver tip of his cane on the stained carpet once, twice.

"Type of girls you boys looking for?" he said.

"He likes 'em young," Moose said with a laugh. "Fifteen or so. Italian roots if you got any."

"You came to the right guy, my friends. I'm Jimmy Two Shoes." Reaching out, he put his hands around both men's shoulders, but Dom pulled away.

"Easy there, partner. I don't bite, but I got girls that will. Boys too, if that's your thing." Jimmy flashed Moose a glance, and Moose grunted back.

"Not my thing, bro."

"Fair enough." Jimmy stopped under a chandelier that emphasized the mascara he wore. He pulled out a cell phone and turned his back to them.

Dom and Moose exchanged a glance.

A few feet away, an attendant opened the doors to the Bellagio Theater, exposing a stage and arena that once attracted hundreds of patrons to water shows featuring talented gymnasts.

Now the stage was used for strippers and sex shows.

Jimmy turned and grinned as he lowered his phone. "I think I have what you're looking for, but it's going to cost you."

"Let's see her first," Dom said.

The pimp hesitated.

"You saw the coin; now let's see the merchandise, or I'll go elsewhere."

"Okay, okay, follow me." Jimmy swung his cane and led the way across the casino floor. They passed roulette and blackjack tables, most of them empty. Then they passed what was once a sushi bar, now a pub with peanut shells crushed on the floor.

The pimp led them through the lobby, but instead of going to the elevators that would take them to any of thousands of suites, he took them to the pools.

Dom remained patient, following without uttering a word, eyes roving for threats. Most of the people here were just tourists with their bodyguards, and casino staff. He didn't see any gangbangers like those who hung out at LA's biggest casino—the Golden Oyster, another Moretti property.

Outside, tourists lounged and swam in two large pools while bikini-clad women served cocktails and beers. One of the girls nodded at Jimmy, and he flashed her a cocky grin that she did not return.

When they got to the smaller tables, he pointed his cane at lounges with drapes for privacy. Dom and Moose took a seat on the comfortable couches inside.

Someone was having fun a few lounges down, but the fun didn't sound entirely mutual. Dom tried to block out the sounds.

A woman in a bikini brought them beers, and a few minutes later, Jimmy returned with two muscular men. Both had flames tattooed on their bald scalps. They flanked a high-school-age girl with a short black dress and skimpy top. Not Monica.

Dom shook his head. "Too skinny."

The pimp brought out more women, and each time, Dom gave some excuse for not liking them.

Thirty minutes later, Jimmy was growing frustrated. He narrowed his eyes and said, "I get the sense you're looking for *someone*, not for a good time."

"You'd be wrong," Dom said, getting up from the couch.

Jimmy stood, rising a good six inches over Dom. Moose stood and matched the pimp's height.

"Is there a problem, boss?" asked one of the guards outside the open drapes.

Both men stepped up, but he waved them back.

"Not yet," Jimmy said.

He brought four more girls, none of them Monica.

Dom sighed and got off the couch when he realized he had pushed his luck. Though he really wanted to shove the cane where it belonged, he gave Jimmy a silver coin for his time. He couldn't afford to create trouble just yet.

"You boys sure you don't want to go younger?" Jimmy called out as they walked away from the lounge. "Maybe that's the problem. I got a girl that's twelve, fits your description."

Dom stopped with his back to Jimmy.

Monica was only thirteen when she was taken, and imagining her working for this powdery fuck boiled his blood.

"Don't," Moose said.

"Sorry, can't let it slide."

Moose sighed and followed Dom as he rushed back toward the draped-off lounge. Jimmy looked surprised and held up his cane.

"Hey, what the fuck?" he shouted.

Both bodyguards moved to intercept Dom. He ducked one guy's punch, then elbowed the guy in the back of the head, bringing him to his knees. Moose took the other guy.

These two bozos were nothing to the opponents Dom had faced in the underground cage bouts when he was trying to catch the Vega brothers.

He took the big man down with a punch to the throat, then a knee to the face.

Jimmy backed up, swinging his cane. Dom ripped it from his hand and smacked Jimmy in the face with the silver handle. A tooth flew out and clattered on the floor tiles.

A familiar deep growl came from behind Dom.

He almost smiled when he saw Namid walking—or rather, being walked by—Cayenne. Straining at the leash, she snapped the air near the downed second guard while Moose finished neutralizing the first.

A final blow to the face sent him to dreamland.

Jimmy watched in shock, a hand to his jaw, blood dripping from his lips.

"Come on, guys," he said, holding up his other hand. "No need for such—"

Cayenne growled at him, shutting him up.

He took a step backward, tripped, and fell.

"Cayenne," Dom said, patting his thigh.

Namid let go of the leash, and she hopped over to Dom, still snarling at Jimmy, who held up both hands defensively. "Please," he begged. "Please, call it off."

"I'll be right back," Dom said.

Namid and Moose turned to give him privacy and watch for more trouble.

After pulling the drapes closed, Dom snapped his fingers at Cayenne. She sat and panted, eyes pinned on Jimmy.

Dom bent down, studying the pimp like his dog. Then he reached out quickly, making Jimmy flinch.

"Relax," Dom said. He fished inside the red jacket, pulling out the silver coin he had tossed Jimmy only a minute before.

"I'd let my dog rip your nuts off, but I'm afraid she'd get sick." He patted Jimmy on the shoulder. "But I've got a better idea anyway."

Dom stood and picked up the cane, holding it like a golf club. Then he took a nice-looking backswing and teed off on two balls at once.

Cayenne tilted her head as Jimmy howled.

Moose waited outside, both bodyguards limp at his feet. Namid had stepped outside the drape to keep the gathering crowd back.

Dom tossed a coin to the first staff member who arrived—a woman in her twenties. The same one Jimmy had grinned at earlier. She smiled and then surprised Dom.

"Thanks for taking care of that asshole, mister."

The Saints hurried out of the casino without facing any resistance. Apparently, Jimmy wasn't all that popular. When they got back to their truck, they were out of breath and Moose was panting like Cayenne.

Dom clapped his friend on the back. "Get it together, brother. The hunt has just begun."

This time, Dom got behind the wheel. If his sister was here, he would find her, even if he had to beat down every pimp and search every dive and flophouse in town.

-1-

FIVE YEARS LATER . . .

"We can't get to Esteban or Miguel," said Chief of Police Brian Stone. Slouched in his chair, he looked like a dog anticipating a beating. "They've gone underground after our last raid."

And here Antonio Moretti was, standing behind the bulletproof office windows of his casino overlooking the hills of Hollywood. Right out in the open, while his enemies cowered out there.

Come and get me, you cockroach motherfuckers, Antonio thought.

It would be no easy task. He was surrounded by a small army, and the Golden Oyster, like his office at his compound, was as secure as the White House had once been.

He had escape routes, security everywhere, and multiple getaway cars if he ever needed to flee to a safe location.

"Sir," said a voice much smoother than the chief's two-pack-a-day rasp. This was the voice of a politician.

Antonio looked at Mayor Buren's reflection in the window. The mayor had aged over the years—his hair gray and thinning, his athletic frame a little thicker in the middle—but he still had that smooth voice and business smile.

All the men in this room looked older.

Wars always aged those lucky enough to survive them.

Antonio had a receding hairline, more wrinkles from a constantly furrowed brow, and worst of all, weakening vision. He wore contacts in public, glasses when he was by himself.

But it wasn't just his physical form that had taken a beating. The losses had softened his heart. It was odd. War broke some men and hardened the rest. But war had made Antonio more empathetic to the plight of the less fortunate. That was part of the reason he donated so much of his profits back to the city.

The mayor stepped up to the window and adjusted his tie. "Looks like a bad one brewing," he said.

Chief Stone remained back in a leather chair, drinking the glass of whiskey that Lino De Caro had just brought him.

Zachary "Yellowtail" Moretti was also here, wearing a black tank top that showed off his gold cross and thick muscles. Unlike Buren, he had lost some weight.

The wind blasted the window with grit. The mayor stepped back.

"Don't worry, nothing short of an armor-piercing round is going to break this glass," Antonio said. "Why don't you have a seat while we wait for my brother."

Buren went back to the chairs and sat next to Stone, but Antonio remained here, admiring the view from the fifteenth floor of the Golden Oyster. The dust storm was gathering strength.

Soon he wouldn't be able to see the Hollywood Hills. He could still make out what remained of the iconic Hollywood sign up on Mount Lee. Most of the letters had tumbled away in previous storms, leaving only "H" and "OOD."

Hood.

Almost the entire city was the hood, not controlled by the dirty politician or the crooked cop sitting beside him—although Antonio sometimes found it convenient to make the mayor and the chief *think* they were in charge. Everyone knew that it was really the Vegas, the Morettis, the Nevsky crime family, and a few hardcore street gangs who were in control of the four zones.

Antonio had always considered himself a patient man. But eight years had passed since the old war ended and his war for the city began.

Sometimes, you have to do things yourself—his own cold words from the night his crew ambushed the Vega brothers and an LAPD task force. The same night the Vega brothers used a drone to attack the wedding ceremony of Raffaello Tursi and his bride.

Antonio gritted his teeth at the painful memories. He would have his revenge.

In war, patience wasn't just a virtue; it was a strategy. Now it was time to cash in on that patience.

The office door finally opened, and Christopher Moretti stepped inside, dressed in a black suit with a tie and pocket square that matched the silver-gray in his goatee and slicked-back hair.

Two guards, both armed with automatic rifles, closed the door behind him.

"Sorry for the delay," Christopher said. He went straight to the table overlooking the carmine sky.

Antonio remained standing.

"I called this meeting to discuss a new strategy to destroy the Vegas, and to discuss the upcoming election," he said.

The cops weren't getting the job done, his men weren't getting the job done, and the Vegas weren't leaving their hideouts. He had to draw them out. There was only one way he could think of to do that.

"I want Mariana López," Antonio said.

Stone swallowed. "What do you mean, you *want* her?" he asked.

"I want you to deliver her to me."

"I can't give her to you—she's in County, under the watch of Sheriff Benson. But I can request she be transferred for medical care. If something should happen to her en route, well . . ." He shrugged a shoulder.

"That will do," Antonio replied. "How fast can you make this happen?"

"I don't know. I have to make some calls."

Antonio paced in front of the desk, considering this plan.

The wind howled outside, flinging grit against the window. It sounded like a hundred little fingernails. He enjoyed the sound of the storm and thought the foreshadowing apt.

"Open the safe, Chrissy," Antonio said.

Christopher walked over to a door in the expansive office and started twisting the wheel on the massive vault.

"Make your calls," Antonio said to Stone.

The chief pulled out a phone and walked to the corner while Antonio pulled a chair in front of Buren.

"About that election in a few months, Mr. Mayor," Antonio said. "You've got some major competition this time."

"I'll win," Buren said.

He was a confident man. Antonio was too, but confidence could also be victory's assassin.

"Don't bank on it," Antonio said. "Times are changing. We're seeing an influx of refugees from other cities, and while we have the water, we don't have the food."

"I've got a plan."

"You'll need my financial support." Antonio looked over as Christopher opened the vault door.

Inside were shelves of silver, gold, and foreign currencies.

Antonio got up and entered the walk-in safe as Stone hung up the phone. He had over twenty million dollars in here alone, and he wanted the mayor and the chief to see it.

They looked in, wide-eyed as country boys in a strip club.

Antonio picked up a gold bar, hefted the weight, and returned it to the stack. *Thank you, Yamazakis.* Much of the gold had gone to Eduardo Nina, but Antonio was now paying in silver.

The wind shook the window as he closed the vault and secured it.

Christopher stood by his side, hands over the front of his suit.

"Well?" Antonio asked.

"They'll move her at dusk tomorrow," Stone said. "Storm or no storm."

Antonio scrutinized the two men who had been partners since near the beginning of his rise to power.

"Join me," he said.

They stepped up to the window. Antonio couldn't see the Hollywood Bowl, but he remembered every detail from the night Carmine assassinated Chief Walt Diamond.

"I really hope we don't have another Hollywood Bowl event," he said.

"What's that supposed to mean?" Stone said.

"You promised me the heads of the Vegas *eight years ago*," Antonio said. "If something goes wrong with the Mariana transfer . . ."

He didn't need to complete the thought.

Stone and Buren had helped Antonio become a rich man over the years, and they, too, had become very wealthy. But his patience with them was wearing thin.

"I want you to personally make sure your men are part of that caravan to transfer her," he said.

"I will, Don Antonio," Stone said. "Don't worry."

"Good."

The mayor took a sip of whiskey, placed it on the table, and stood, indicating that the meeting was over. But Antonio shook his head, reminding him who was in charge.

"Schedule a ribbon-cutting ceremony for the new water infrastructure announcement," Antonio said. "And invite the other candidates for mayor. Show them who's boss."

Buren smiled. "I like how you think, Don Antonio."

"Leave me," he said.

Antonio turned back to the window as the chief and the mayor left. He clasped his hands behind his back and looked out at the storm engulfing the city.

In a few nights, he would receive the biggest drug shipment yet from Eduardo Nina, and he would have the fallen narco queen to use as bait, to draw out the only remaining threat to the Moretti organization.

Soon, the Vega brothers would be gone, and he would be king.

* * *

Ray Clarke was a dirty cop with a good heart. Not uncommon for officers working in a city controlled by gangsters, narcos, and bangers.

He had watched the city become a third world country after the Second Civil War tore the United States of America to shreds.

There were exceptions to the rule, of course. Men like his younger brother, Andre.

They sat together at the Flying Crow, a bar just two blocks from Memorial Coliseum, where the Dodgers used to play. The stadium was now a modern gladiatorial fighting ground called the Diamond Arena.

Moose was one of those lawmen who risked their lives every day to keep the city safe yet never took bribes.

Ray had always thought of his younger brother as a larger-than-life beast, like his namesake animal.

He was the kind of man Ray had always wanted to be. A man who fought against the evil instead of helping it poison one of the last cities standing in America. A man who loved as passionately as he fought.

But Moose had only two kids. Ray had four. It was a lot of mouths to feed, especially when half his money went to the antiradiation doses that his youngest required to survive. It didn't help that he also had more expensive tastes than his brother. Things he couldn't do without, like his black Audi A8 with red leather seats and a sound system that turned heads and rattled windows.

And Ray couldn't help that he liked to drink and smoke. He worked hard, and this was how he unwound.

He held a filthy glass up to the dangling yellow light bulb. Most bars in Los Angeles were dives—holes in the wall that most people wouldn't have set foot in before the war. But things had changed drastically, and shitholes like this were gathering places for cops, gangsters, and locals.

"I miss American beer," Ray said.

Moose laughed on the stool next to him. "Let's not start with the 'I miss shit' game. 'Cause I could play it all damn night." He took a slug of Negra Modelo and wiped his lips. "Mexican beer ain't so bad, though. Japanese too."

Ray watched the bubbles rising in his Guinness and thought about something they rarely discussed. They never did find the bastards responsible for killing their parents.

"Yeah, not *bad*," Ray said, taking another drink. "But it's not American beer. I can still remember what a Bud tastes like."

He took another gulp and scooted his stool closer to his brother. "So how are things at Refugee Processing Four and patrolling the borders?" he asked.

"Been a bad week, bro. Raiders hit a roadblock with a convoy of six vehicles. We lost three deputies. The attacks are becoming more coordinated. Eventually, they're going to happen in the city. Just a matter of time."

"Then they get to face the crime families—and me," Ray said. He fingered out the speck floating in his beer, then took a long pull as he considered what his brother had just said.

In a few nights, Ray was headed outside the walls to do a drop-off and pickup for the Morettis, but first he had another mission that came straight from the top.

"You hear about Portland and Salem?" Moose asked.

Ray belched. "Yeah. You bracing for refugees?"

"Hard to believe there are so few cities left," Moose said. He lowered his head, wagging his antler-styled dreads. "Say, how's Lolo doin'?"

Ray massaged his diamond-studded earlobe, thinking about his daughter. "She's good. Hasn't had any problems since going on the anti-radiation rations."

"We've been praying for you guys," Moose said.

Ray turned to scrutinize his brother. He had always been a bit jealous of him. When they were in high school, Moose had started a promising career as an actor. He was also a talented soccer player who could have gone pro. But all those dreams blew up in the apocalypse. And Moose never complained.

"I'll put my foot in my mouth and tell you something I do miss," Moose said.

"Yeah?"

"I miss *this*, man." Moose slapped the bar. "Back in the day when we used to be able to chill, shoot the shit, get tipsy. And all those late nights on the field, kicking ass."

"We grew up," Ray said. "Or *you* did."

Moose laughed and clapped him on the shoulder. "You grew up too. You're doing good shit, man. I heard you took down Tiny."

You have no idea the kind of man I am. "Tiny played with fire too long. Had that bullet coming, for sure."

Moose raised his glass and clinked it against Ray's. What he hadn't told his brother was that he shot Tiny, a dealer with the Bloods, in the back when he threatened to rat him out for not giving him a bigger piece of the pie on a bust.

Ray used to wonder whether his brother or Dominic had ever stolen from a crime scene or taken a bribe. Judging by the slums where they lived, he doubted it. They lived like peasants, and he lived like a prince.

"You up for another round?" Moose asked.

Ray held up his gold watch. "Man, I'd love to, but duty calls."

"Must be important. Never heard you turn down a drink, even for work."

"It is." He reached into his pocket and put a handful of silver coins on the counter—more than enough to pay for their drinks. The older gentleman tending the bar walked over and wiped the scratched wood surface after grabbing the money.

Moose got off his stool, towering a good six inches over Ray.

"Be safe out there, Ray Money," Moose said.

"That's a new one."

"You're a rich man now, apparently."

Ray flashed his dazzling white grin, and they did their special handshake. *Just like old times.*

"Later, bro," Moose said.

Ray walked through the dimly lit bar, avoiding eye contact with the patrons. The Latino kid he had paid to watch his Audi was leaning against the car, arms folded across his chest, like a little boss.

"Gracias, *jefe*," Ray said, tossing the kid a coin.

He caught it and took off.

Ray ran a hand over the hood, where the boy had put his filthy jacket, leaving behind some dust. He wiped the dust with his sleeve, annoyed because he had just washed the car after last night's storm.

He couldn't be too mad, though. Ray liked being generous with the youngsters. It made up for some of his sins and helped him sleep at night.

He checked the wide off-road tires before getting in. The tread helped soften the ride on potholed roads, and he was glad he threw down the extra coin for them. He would need them for traction in the desert a few nights from now. He might even need them tonight.

Ray started the drive across town, feeling a light buzz. Still with two hours to burn, he turned on the strobe. Blue and red flashed in the back window.

Most people knew Detective Ray Clarke and his black Audi A8, and they knew he worked for the Morettis. That meant he was not to be fucked with. But the lights were for anyone who didn't know who he was.

An hour later, he pulled up at the border of Los Alamitos, or what the locals called the Malice Wastes. Shotgunned radiation-warning signs marked the boundary. Radiation and chemical toxins made the former military base one of the most dangerous places in the city.

That was exactly why the government had built a prison here. The concrete fortress known as Casa del Diablo, or House of the Devil, was the one sign of civilization on the demolished former base.

Ten thousand inmates lived within the high razor-wire fences, including one Mariana López, the sicario queen who was once allied with the Vega brothers.

Guard towers looked over the acres of cracked earth. Any prisoner who somehow escaped and made it past the guard towers and the dogs would then have to navigate a minefield. And after that, a radioactive wasteland.

Ray hated this place, not because of the men and women he had sent here to die, but because he was terrified that someday he might call this place home.

Never. I'll die before I go there.

Shaking the thought away, he pulled to the side of the road and killed the engine. By the time the text came, his buzz had worn off and he was starting to feel tired.

Ray hadn't seen his wife or kids in almost three days. But after he finished securing this shipment, he would go home, kiss his kids, make love to his wife, and pass the hell out.

He turned the engine back on and pulled onto Valley Street, heading away from the prison. A few miles later, he spotted the convoy of police cruisers. A Los Angeles Sheriff's Department pickup truck followed the caravan, which was odd to Ray.

This was supposed to be LAPD only.

He followed them into the night, entering an area where the grid was down. His job was simple: make sure the Morettis didn't have any problems out here.

But the sheriff truck was a major problem.

His phone buzzed.

"Yeah?"

"Take care of that sheriff truck, but don't hurt the deputies," said a voice that sounded a lot like Chief Stone.

"Who's this?" Ray asked.

"Just do it, Detective Clarke, or you'll be serving raccoon burgers to junkies, and I doubt that will pay for the RX-Four you need for your kid."

The line severed, and Ray resisted the urge to toss the phone out the window.

No one threatened him, not even the chief of police.

He pushed the pedal down. As he sped to find an intercept point, he tried to think of a way to avoid being spotted by the deputies. He didn't care about the cops, but the deputies, like his brother, lived in a different world. They had little interaction with the corruption of the city. Their main job was to protect the borders and the prison, and he didn't want to hurt them. They were good men like his brother and Dominic.

Ray sped a mile ahead of the convoy and pulled behind an abandoned gas station. The area looked empty, but he hated getting out of his car.

With no other choice, he hopped out and opened his trunk to pull out a ten-gallon gas container and a flare gun. Under the cover of darkness, he lugged it to the side of the road and placed it against the shell of a car.

He ran back to his Audi. The convoy of two cruisers, a van, and the pickup was nearing the ambush point.

Ray aimed the flare gun, waiting for the cars and van to pass.

But then he saw a group of headlights spear the darkness behind the convoy. Then came the rumble of motorcycles. Not crotch rockets, but old-school Harleys and even a couple of British bikes.

"*Shit.*" He was already too late.

Ray jumped back into his car and watched as a group of bikes zoomed down the street in front of four rusted SUVs that had pulled ahead of the riders. The vehicles came up alongside the Sheriff's Department pickup.

These weren't Morettis. From what he could tell, this was a motorcycle gang that worked with the Vegas.

Somehow, they had found out about the transfer.

No. Don't do this.

Muzzle flashes came from the two SUVs, and the pickup truck suddenly braked and swerved into the ditch. Ray watched as the doors opened and deputies piled out, injured and running for cover.

Relieved, he mashed the pedal and squealed out of the parking lot and back onto the road to follow the convoy. But then he saw that several of the bikers had stopped to deal with the deputies.

If these were Vegas, they wouldn't be stupid enough to kill them and start a war with Sheriff Benson.

Heart pounding, he raced to catch up with the convoy, although he had no idea what he would do once he got there. By the time he rounded a corner and saw the caravan again, it had stopped.

A second group of trucks had cut them off.

He slowed and pulled to the side of the road to take in the scene, trying to figure out what he was seeing.

A group of masked men stood guard, weapons aimed in his direction and at the police vehicles. The cops were getting out with their hands up.

Two masked men opened the back door to the van and grabbed a woman in cuffs. Then they pulled out the cops guarding her and shoved them to the ground.

Ray watched in horror—not over the rough treatment of his brothers in blue, but because the Morettis were going to be furious and so was Chief Stone.

His job was to make sure Mariana was picked up by the Morettis. But what could he do now?

An Escalade suddenly swerved away and drove in his direction. He put the car in reverse and started a bootleg turn, but the SUV cut him off.

He kept his hands on the wheel, not making any movements.

The SUV stopped, and the window rolled down. But no muzzle

flashed, and no bullets blew through his brain or even his car door. He slowly took his left hand off the wheel and pushed the button to roll down the window.

The man in the passenger seat of the Escalade pushed up his mask, and Ray saw the face of a Moretti. And not just any Moretti.

"*Hola*, Detective Clarke," Antonio said.

"Uh, sir, I . . ."

"You saw a gang of vigilantes rob this convoy tonight."

Ray didn't reply.

"Right, Detective?"

"Right, sir."

Antonio started to roll up the window, then stopped.

"Oh, and Detective, make sure you get me my guns tomorrow night. I'll be needing those very soon."

"Yes sir."

Ray watched the Escalade drive away.

If it wasn't official before, it was now—Ray Clarke didn't just *work* for the Morettis; he was their go-to guy—their favorite corrupt cop in the City of Angels.

-2-

A magenta sunset bled through the storm clouds hovering over postwar Los Angeles. A brown wall rolled toward the barriers and roadblocks constructed around the four zones of the city. To Dom, it looked like the beginning of the end of the world.

But end-times had already swept through the United States, and the City of Angels was one of the few metropolises still functioning. The Griffith Observatory provided a hilltop view of the damaged city.

Today, it also gave a perfect view of yet another storm threatening those who still called this place home.

Most citizens would be taking shelter, but not Dom and his team. Today, most of them were here to support him. Andre "Moose" Clarke, Callum "Tooth" McCloud, "Chaplain" William Bettis, Camilla Santiago, and the youngest member of the team, Thomas Bartone, known simply as "Rocky" for his muscular build and boxing skills, sat inside the twenty-year-old Ford Explorer.

Namid and a new member of the team, Karl "Pork Chop" Watts, were back at the safe house in City of Industry, fixing a pickup for their next mission.

The Saints were all heroes like Dom's father, in a world where heroes were an endangered breed.

Dom pulled his goggles down off his brown baseball cap and buttoned his jacket up to his chin. It would protect him against the flying grit for now. He grabbed the door handle.

"You guys stay here," he said. "I'll be right back."

With a bundle of flowers in one hand, and his father's SIG Sauer 1911 Nightmare in the other, Dom got out and started down the cracked concrete path.

In the distance, the turbines powering the city spun in the toxic wind. The first gusts stirred dirt up into the sky as the storm slammed through the ruined mansions and estates perched on the bluffs.

The view reminded him how much he had once loved this city. The ball games at Dodger Stadium with his family, and the smell of peanuts and freshly mown grass. The way the sand at Long Beach felt on his bare feet. The open-air concerts. Watching Ferraris rumble down Hollywood Boulevard and trying to glimpse a celebrity behind the wheel. It was all gone now—erased like a memory you could never seem to recall.

The wall of dust rolled over a farm of solar panels next, but city engineers had already battened down the expensive technology. Dom adjusted the breathing apparatus covering his face and velcroed the cuff of his brown uniform down over a sliver of exposed flesh.

Once a tourist hot spot that attracted thousands of visitors a day, the observatory was dark and sealed off by boards and chains. Like most of the city's historical-cultural landmarks, it had been raided years ago for valuables and artwork.

Monica had loved the observatory. Most kids back then asked their parents to go to Disneyland, Universal Studios, or the Santa Monica Pier. But Monica was different from most kids her age. She had always begged their mom and dad to take her to see the science displays here. His sister was set on becoming a scientist, but like most children of her generation, she never got the chance to reach for her dreams.

Storms would eventually bury this place with the bones of the other structures that had already perished. Until that happened, he would keep coming here on her birthday, to ask for her forgiveness in the place she so loved.

"I'm sorry, Monica," he said, gently laying the flowers down.

After all these years, he still had no idea where she was. He had searched every dive and brothel in Las Vegas and Los Angeles. Now all he could do was avenge his father and sister by hunting the Vega narcos and the other crime families that poisoned this city.

He missed them both now more than ever, feeling the loss like a wound that wouldn't scab over. To make it more painful, his mom, Elena, had lost her sanity from the years of grief and now lived in a mental hospital.

An air-raid siren went off in the distance, the sound building from a low whine to a blare—a warning for residents to get inside, and another reminder of the past.

Dom closed his eyes, picturing a squadron of F-35 fighter jets tearing through the skies and dropping payloads on the cities their pilots had sworn to protect, during the first days of the nearly six-month war. The sirens had gone off then, but with hardly enough time for anyone to seek shelter.

When he opened his eyes, he saw the damage from missiles that left the skyscrapers looking like the jagged, crumbling teeth of a meth head. Hundreds of other buildings had collapsed entirely, along with bridges and whole sections of freeway.

A brown wave crested the hills in the distance. There was no reason to put his team at risk. He started back toward the Explorer, which was tucked behind an abandoned RV in the parking lot.

The flowers he had left were whipping wildly under a rock that Tooth had put down to anchor them. Dom nearly broke at the sight. He would never forgive himself for losing Monica. The sadness turned to rage.

He forced his eyes away from the flowers to the dust wall bearing down on the cluster of desalination plants and buildings in the distance. The technology was the main reason Los Angeles had stayed on the map. It provided water to citizens within the borders, and there were plans to build more infrastructure, to deliver the water to refugee camps along the border.

But another war was coming. Whichever crime organization won the battle for the four zones would then make a play for the desal plants.

The Saints couldn't let that happen. For the people out here, water was life. Whoever controlled the flow would control Los Angeles.

Dom lowered his head against the wind as he made his way back to the truck. In the distance, he glimpsed another letter of the Hollywood sign tear away. The second *O* sailed toward the Japanese-owned cell and radio towers before spinning off into the screaming storm.

"Someone's coming!" Moose shouted over the sirens' wail.

Dom spotted a pair of headlights in the distance—a cloud of dust kicking up behind a dark vehicle. He moved quickly back to the Explorer, and Tooth handed him his trusty M1 Scout rifle.

The vehicle raced down the street, heading right for the observatory. Who would be coming out here?

The storm hit him like a sandblaster, but he kept his weapon on the approaching vehicle. The other team members did the same.

There was nowhere to run in a storm that would soon be strong enough to take skin off bone, and the only road out of here was the one the vehicle was coming up.

Visibility worsened by the second, and he lost the target. His heart quickened as the black SUV reappeared. The same type that had taken Monica.

He blinked, following the vehicle in the brown sea of swirling grit. The SUV hurtled up the road, away from the onslaught of dust.

Dom aimed at the windshield.

A dozen thoughts warred for primacy, but he fixed on the one that truly chilled him. Had their enemies finally discovered their identities?

The SUV slowed as it approached the RV and the Explorer. Visibility was down to a hundred feet now, and the storm was screaming so loud Dom couldn't hear the air-raid sirens.

His finger moved inside the trigger guard, ready to fire a 7.62 mm round into the SUV as it slowed to a stop.

A voice called out. It sounded familiar, but he couldn't make it out over the howling storm.

Someone walked away from the driver's door, hands in the air.

Dom squinted and reached up with one glove, wiping his goggles clear.

"Don't shoot!" the man shouted.

"What the hell . . . ?" Dom muttered. He ran out to meet Lieutenant Zed Marks, his father's old friend and brother marine.

Marks pointed to the passenger side of the SUV, and Dom jumped inside while the Saints climbed back into the Explorer.

"What the hell are you doing here, Lieutenant?" Dom asked. He pulled his face mask down and pushed his googles up into his hair.

"I'd ask you the same question, but I know what today is."

Dom reached out and shook Marks's hand. "Good memory."

"I'd never forget Monica's birthday."

"How's your mom?" Marks asked.

Dom shrugged. "Not good."

"Tooth and Bettis doing okay?" Marks asked.

"We're all hanging in there. Want me to grab them?"

"No, that's okay. You can relay what I'm about to tell you."

Dom waited for the news that brought Marks out here. They hadn't spoken in months, and whatever it was had to be important.

"You hear about Saint Louis?" Marks asked.

Dom shook his head.

"The Executive Council has cut off all supplies and aid."

"*What!*"

"Decided to write the city off as another loss, I guess."

"There's a quarter-million people still living there."

"Raleigh's in bad shape too. So is Salem. I'm afraid the flag is going to lose a few more stars soon."

Dom could hear the emotion in Marks's voice. He was a lot like Dom's father—able to show strength even in the darkest situation. This was one of them.

The American flag was down to just nine stars, and they no longer represented states—just the remaining capital cities.

"You didn't come here to talk to me about this, did you?" Dom asked.

Marks reached into his jacket and pulled out a folded piece of paper with a single name.

"Goomah?" Dom asked.

"It's a ship, and it's coming into the port in two nights. Pier nine."

"What's the cargo?"

"A shipment from Mexico," he said. "More of Eduardo Nina's infamous hybrid opiates and some Chinese RX-Four."

"Who else knows?

"Enough people that I don't have to worry about it coming back to me."

Dom tucked the piece of paper into a pocket and looked over at the Explorer. Visibility was so low, he could see only the outline of the RV blocking the vehicle.

"The Saints will take care of this," he said.

"Don't forget there are still laws you have to follow, Dom. That's what sets you and me apart from the gangsters. Do not spill innocent blood, and don't kill cops, even if they're dirty."

"Yeah, got it."

"We are different, and I don't want to see you follow in your father's footsteps. That's what got him killed, and I don't want to lose you too."

Marks looked down as if gripped by a sad memory.

"Ronaldo used to think that to defeat evil we must embrace it. He did that in his search for your sister, and he lost part of what made him a good lawman."

The words stung, but only because they were true.

"Your dad would be proud of you for taking down these evil men as you have. But remember, if you become one of them, you'll lose the battle just like your dad."

Dom nodded.

"Good luck at the port."

"Thanks."

Marks reached out as Dom went to open the car door.

"I forgot to tell you," he said. "Someone kidnapped Mariana López when she was being transferred to a medical facility. They had inside help from the LAPD, which tells me this was the Morettis' work."

"Must have something to do with the Vegas."

"Same thought I had."

"Camilla won't be happy," Dom said, recalling the night she was shot in the stomach at the cemetery where they nabbed Mariana.

"I'm sorry, Lieutenant," Dom said.

He shook his head. "Sometimes I wonder if my bosses are more corrupt than the gangsters."

"I hear that."

Dom hopped out and returned to the Explorer. Camilla put a hand on his shoulder, and Moose gave him a solemn nod before firing up the vehicle.

As they drove away, Dom remembered his sister again.

The flower petals were gone, ripped from the stems, just as Monica was torn from their family that day.

He would be back in a year, but meanwhile, he and his team had some work to do to keep more drugs from flooding the streets.

"Marks has a mission for us," Dom said. "Most important one yet. In two nights, we're headed to the ports to wipe some of the Moretti cancer out of this city."

He looked to Camilla. "And we're going to remove some Vega cancer while we're at it."

* * *

Vinny Moretti took a bite of warm cheese pastry and washed it down with a sip of espresso. The ocean breeze rustled the collar of his expensive black shirt as he enjoyed his breakfast with Daniel "Doberman" Pedretti at the fanciest coffee shop left in Los Angeles. The patio overlooked the gentle breakers off Long Beach.

Less than a decade earlier, the well-to-do would flock here to get caffeinated in the early morning hours.

The coffee shop, though renovated and reopened, still showed signs of the war. The siding had several bullet holes, and in place of the Teslas and expensive sports cars were three black Range Rovers with black rims, and Moretti soldiers standing guard. Their eyes were on the pedestrians on the sidewalks, and the civilians lounging on the beaches.

Potential threats were everywhere. These trained men treated anyone over ten years old as a security risk, just as Don Antonio had taught them. The associates kept a close eye to make sure no one bothered Vinny and Doberman as they enjoyed their food and coffee.

Today was his first day off in months, and Vinny needed a break from the stress of being a Moretti soldier. The war with Esteban Vega and his brother Miguel continued to claim the lives of soldiers on both sides and civilians caught in the cross fire.

Eight long years of fighting had taken its toll on all. Vinny hoped kidnapping Mariana López would help the Morettis win the war, but he wasn't sure what his uncle had in mind.

The deal Don Antonio had with Chief Stone was the only reason the LAPD continued to turn a blind eye to the madness. Eventually, it would bring both organizations down. Hell, it had almost killed Vinny and Doberman. They both had fresh battle wounds from their most recent run-in at a Vega dealing spot a week ago, when Vinny led an attack that killed three sicarios. A bullet had narrowly missed his head.

It wasn't the first time and wouldn't be the last.

Over the years, Vinny had been shot twice, once in the leg and once in the wrist. Both wounds had healed, but Doberman still had painful scars from eight years ago, when Isao Yamazaki slashed his face with a sword.

They both were lucky to be alive. Vinny had made it to his twenty-seventh birthday and was on a fast track to make captain—something his uncle and his father had promised him years ago.

He had already amassed more wealth than he could ever have imagined for his young age, and if he could continue dodging bullets, he might live to enjoy it.

He took in a breath of crisp salt air, trying to relax as he picked up the weekly *Los Angeles Times*. Just ten pages, but it was the only option for news in the city.

"You see this shit?" he asked.

Doberman looked away from his cell phone to check the front page.

"'Mayoral candidate Ryan Colt vows clean water for everyone in the city, including refugees,'" Doberman read.

Vinny scanned the first paragraph and shook his head. "This says he has refrained from commenting on the 'gang violence.'"

"Gang violence?" said Doberman. "Makes us sound like thugs."

A car pulled up out front. Frankie Trentino got out, his long hair blowing in the breeze. Vito Moretti, fatter than ever, shut the driver's door and waddled over. The cocaine-mixing expert was at greater risk of a heart attack than of getting shot.

"Great," Vinny said, closing the paper.

Doberman frowned.

Getting up from his chair, Vinny embraced his second cousin Vito first—a peck on each cheek—then Frankie. Doberman pulled up chairs for the made men as a sign of respect.

"What can I do for you gentlemen this morning?" Vinny asked.

Frankie lit a cigarette while Vito grabbed Vinny's half-eaten pastry.

"You mind, Vin?" he asked.

Vinny narrowed his eyes, then shook his head. The obese slob with greasy hair took a huge bite, raining confectioner's sugar over his open shirt and into his sweat-matted chest hair.

"Did you get the shipment?" Frankie asked.

"Yes," Vinny replied. "My man secured all the guns we requested. He will deliver them before the new food comes in."

Frankie nodded happily, and Vito finished off the pastry in one mouthful. He wiped his hands on his pants.

"*Molto buona*," Vito said through a mouthful of pastry.

Vinny tried to hide his disgust.

"This next shipment from Nina is our biggest yet," said Frankie. "We also got several loads of RX-Four on the boat, and I don't want any problems."

"There won't be," Doberman said.

"No one's talking to you," Frankie replied without looking at Doberman.

"Doberman's right," Vinny said. "There won't be any problems."

"Good." Frankie got up from the chair. "Make sure the guns are delivered by noon tomorrow."

"See ya later, girlies," Vito said. He got up and followed Frankie into the coffee shop to order. As soon as the door shut, Doberman grunted.

"What a fucking pig," Vinny said.

He finished his espresso and watched the ocean lapping the beach. A red kite soared and dipped, a child holding the string as a man coached him.

"Call Ray and tell him we need the guns now," Vinny said.

"You got it." Doberman pulled out a burner phone and stepped away to make the call. Vinny sat there another moment, contemplating their relationship with the detective. Ray was a condescending asshole, but he did good work and always came through.

For the past eight years, Vinny had worked with Ray to make sure the cops held up their end of the bargain at the Four Diamonds slum, in the process making Ray a very wealthy man.

Doberman put the phone away and joined Vinny.

"Well?" Vinny asked.

"He said noon tomorrow will be no problem," Doberman said.

"Better not be, or . . ."

The whine of a crotch rocket cut Vinny off. Frankie and Vito were walking out of the coffee shop toward their vehicles, but both stopped to watch a motorcycle race through traffic. The rider lobbed something through the air, toward the patio.

"Get down! Down!" yelled one of the guards by the vehicles.

Vinny pulled his pistol and aimed at the rider wearing a skull mask—the symbol of the Vegas. The bike swerved, throwing off his aim just as an explosion boomed behind the bike.

Someone slammed into Vinny, knocking him to the patio floor.

Screams sounded in all directions—muffled, terrified voices. A dull ringing pervaded everything. Vinny tried to get up but couldn't move with the body still on top of him.

Smoke burned his nostrils as he took a deep breath. Through the swirling gray, he saw bodies sprawled on the patio. Several lay crumpled, bleeding from shrapnel wounds.

A Moretti soldier wailed on the ground, holding the stump where his right leg had been taken off below the knee. Two men next to him were down and not moving.

Vinny tried to get up, but he was still pinned down by a body. He pushed harder when he heard the crescendoing whine of the motorcycle.

The rider was returning, and this time he had what looked like an Uzi.

"Watch out!" Vinny yelled too late.

The Vega sicario sprayed several Moretti men near the Range Rovers.

One of them took multiple rounds to the body. Another man took one to the kneecap, screaming in agony as he dropped to the concrete.

The pressure on Vinny finally let up, and he rolled over to see Vito stagger to his feet. The big guy gripped his arm, where blood trickled from two holes.

"You good?" he asked Vinny.

Only then did he realize that his cousin had pushed him down to save his life.

"Yeah. Thanks," Vinny said.

He looked for Doberman and found him sitting up, holding his head—dazed but alive. Frankie had his pistol out and ran toward the street.

Vinny got up and bolted after him, both of them firing at the motorcycle. The rider stopped in the distance and turned, coming back in for another run.

Still running, Vinny passed the Range Rovers. Two of their men were dead, and two more were severely wounded. This was, without a doubt, payback for the last attack on the Vegas . . . unless they somehow knew about Mariana.

As far as Vinny knew, word hadn't reached the street yet.

Frankie stopped in the middle of the street, and Vinny halted beside him, both of them aiming their pistols at the biker.

"Take 'im out as soon as he gets close enough," Frankie said.

Vinny nodded back.

But instead of racing toward them, the rider got off his bike and placed something on the concrete median. Then he hopped on and sped away.

Vinny and Frankie sprinted after him, firing as they ran, but within seconds the guy was out of range. The two men slowed, sucking air.

"Careful," Frankie said as they approached the median. "Could be a bomb."

Vinny stopped about two hundred feet away from whatever the Vega soldier had left. He could see something rustling in the wind, under a rock the guy had used to pin it down.

"Looks like a piece of paper," Vinny said. He started off, and Frankie followed. When they got there, Frankie picked up a note.

"Think we should let Don Antonio read it first?" Vinny asked.

Frankie answered by breaking the seal. He read over it quickly, then looked at Vinny.

"What's it say?" Vinny asked.

"Esteban Vega wants to meet," Frankie said. "He wants to discuss peace."

-3-

Ray pulled up to the Los Angeles Police Department's headquarters, a ten-story building on an acre in the heart of the city. The HQ doubled as the mayor's office and chambers for the City Council.

To Ray, it looked like a prison, and sometimes it felt like one inside.

Palm trees grew inside the concertina-wire fence protecting the fortress. Guards patrolled the grounds, and snipers in towers watched for threats.

Tommy ducked to look in the open window. "You're late," he said in his thick Southern drawl.

"I'm always late, man. Better get used to it."

Tommy got in. "So where we goin'?" he asked, fishing out a cigarette and lighter.

"The wastes."

Tommy almost dropped his cigarette, and Ray laughed.

"You fuckin' with me, man?" Tommy reached up and ran a hand through his hair.

"Nah, I'm taking you on your first pickup," Ray said, turning back to the view of the road. "Don't worry, I'll watch your back."

He still hadn't told Tommy what happened to his last partner. Hell, Ray wasn't even sure. Someone had whacked the guy in his sleep.

They drove in silence for the next half hour. Normally, Ray liked the quiet. It was a nice change of pace from the gunshots, screaming, and sirens he was used to. But he could tell that Tommy was nervous.

"You'll be fine," Ray said.

Tommy blew smoke out the window. "Going to be honest. This is my first time."

"You're a wasteland virgin?"

Tommy wiped sweat from his pale forehead. "Before I joined up, I thought about trying my luck and crossing the wastes. Got some cousins my age that live in Arkansas, but haven't seen them since before the war. My mom said they live on a farm that's pretty nice."

The headlights finally hit the steel-and-concrete wall, and Tommy gazed at the junked-out cars stacked across the road. Prefab concrete panels made up other stretches of wall.

Crews were rebuilding a section knocked down in the recent dust storm. For now, the weak points were manned by sheriff's deputies working overtime.

Ray didn't like leaving the border, especially at night, but this wasn't his first run.

Tommy tossed his cigarette out the window as they came up on the first of the concrete barriers. Flatbed semis, concrete trucks, and a crane sat idle along the road.

He turned down the old-school gangster rap as they approached the roadblock. Two deputies waited at the gate.

Ray wore a sleeveless black T-shirt and jeans. Add the black bandanna around his neck, shaved head, and diamond studs in his ears, and someone might mistake him for a wannabee gangster. But unlike the wannabees' bling, his diamonds and gold chain were real.

Ray lowered his window and smiled at the deputy with a submachine gun slung over his armor. A brown duster whipped in the wind as he walked over.

Pulling up his orange goggles, he bent down to look in the car.

"Evenin'," he said, his voice muffled by a breathing apparatus.

Ray showed his badge. "'Sup, Deputy?"

The man shined a flashlight on it, then turned the beam to Ray and Tommy. “You guys must be headed out to the scene of that attack.”

“Yeah,” Ray lied. He prayed that Tommy follow his lead and was relieved when the kid kept quiet.

The deputy looked at the barred gate as if trying to see something beyond the wall and road. On the right side of the car, a second deputy, wearing brown body armor and full face mask, moved to the passenger door.

“Couple of our guys went that way earlier today,” the second guy said. “Raiders hit a group of civvies on their way east. Sheriff Benson sent out a team of scouts to track ’em down.”

“Pyros,” said the man standing next to Ray.

Tommy glanced over with his ginger eyebrows arched.

“Damn, that’s some crazy shit,” Ray said.

“Sure is. You guys be safe out there.”

The deputy tapped the car roof, then moved his finger in a circle. The gate began to open.

Ray and Tommy pulled up their face masks. Even with the windows up, toxic dust could get through the vents.

A whistle sounded from the guard tower, where a sentry waved his hand, indicating they were clear to go.

“Didn’t you just hear what he said about the Pyros?” Tommy asked.

Ray ignored his partner and drove through the gap in the rusted steel doors. He looked in the rearview mirror as the doors shut behind them, blocking their view of the City of Angels. On both sides, signs marked the minefields scattered along the barrier.

A drone zipped overhead. It followed them for a quarter mile before flying off eastward.

“Those pyro freaks aren’t like the other psychos,” Tommy continued, talking faster. “They kill cops and deputies. And they eat—”

“We’re only going fifteen miles outside the city limits, bro. Relax.”

He turned on the brights, illuminating the cracked pavement ahead.

“Just as well turn on the siren too,” Tommy said. “These lights are going to draw those Pyros to us like bugs to a flame.”

“I said relax. I didn’t survive this long by being a fool.”

Tommy didn't look convinced as they sped away from the safety of the walls.

The moon climbed above the dusty hills, spreading its pale glow over the dry terrain and a decaying civilization.

The lights hit the smoldering wreckage that the deputies at the gates had mentioned. Two burned-out pickup trucks had been pushed off to the shoulder. They slowed as he approached just close enough to see the corpses still in their seats, burned to a crisp.

"J*esus*," Tommy said.

Ray gunned it all the way to their turn-off five miles east of the wall. The dirt road led to the compound where he had been picking up Moretti packages for Lieutenant Best over the past two years.

But tonight, no one stood guard at the steel gate.

Ray parked the Audi on the shoulder and popped the trunk. He met Tommy at the back, where they grabbed their ballistic vests and submachine guns. Before he closed the trunk, Ray grabbed the duffel bag.

"Don't get stupid," he reminded Tommy.

They set off down the dirt road, toward the compound. Four buildings with green metal roofs rose above the fenced-off property.

A mounted video camera rotated toward them. Ray held up the duffel bag and smiled. The gate clicked.

Ray pushed open the gate and walked into a yard littered with stacks of tires, junked vehicles, and scrap metal.

Shadows darted away from a tower of tires. A gun hammer clicked. Someone racked a shotgun shell.

Ray saw only one guy, but there had to be four more.

"Easy!" Ray called out. "It's your favorite neighborhood cops, and we come bearing gifts."

A guy wearing a cloak stepped out, and the open sores on his forehead showed in the moonlight.

"'Sup, Snake?" Ray said as if speaking to one of his homies.

"You're late," Snake replied in a crackly voice.

"Got hung up earlier."

Ray tossed the bag into the dirt halfway between himself and Snake.

"Check it, Ian," Snake said.

The guy holding a shotgun moved out from the shadows, and again they could see the open sores on his face.

"Six-months' supply of RX-Four for four people, just like we promised," Ray said.

Ian bent down but kept the shotgun muzzle on Tommy.

"Come on, guys, is this really necessary?" Ray asked.

"You know it is," Snake growled. "Besides, you guys came packin'."

"There was an attack on the highway earlier today," Tommy said. "Some Pyros killed a family heading east."

Snake didn't reply, which made Ray suspicious.

These guys were modern-day lepers, cast out of the city into the wastes, to live out what time they had left. But at least they still had their minds. The Pyros, by contrast, were true psychopaths, prowling the deserts and attacking settlements, sometimes just for the thrill.

"You know, my daughter is on RX-Four now too," Ray said.

Snake grunted. "What's your point?"

"That I can relate to your suffering."

"Trust me, you don't have a clue," Snake said. "With the bacon you bring home, your kid'll never miss a treatment."

Ray was no doctor, but Snake was right. His daughter had never missed a treatment of the genetically engineered virus. It had saved her from the radiation poisoning by scavenging free radicals and preventing her DNA from mutating, or some shit.

All he really knew was that the antiviral agent suppressed the side effects as long as she kept taking it.

But if she did stop, God forbid, she would look like these men, with sores, life-threatening autoimmune disorders, and thickened nerves. And if she stopped taking it altogether, she would go crazy.

"It's all here," Ian said.

"Like I said. Now, where's our shit?" Ray stepped forward, and another gun pointed his way. "It's all good, guys. All good."

Snake gestured to his left, and a third man walked into the moonlight. Wispy hair fluttered in the wind. Not a man.

The woman pushed her mask up, revealing a bulbous nose covered in warty growths. She sniffed the air.

Ah, Snake's lovely wife, Caitlyn.

"Follow me," she said.

They crossed bare dirt to a row of metal sheds. Ray had a feeling some of these sheds housed people, but he didn't see anyone behind the filthy windows.

Snake and his crew had to make a living somehow, and human trafficking was one of the few enterprises available to them.

Caitlyn unlocked the door to the second shed. Ray turned on the tactical flashlight mounted to his submachine gun and shined it inside.

Four open crates held the newest Beretta rifles. Ray held back a grin.

The weapons were a favorite of the Moretti family, and he was going to get one hell of a tip for this.

"Fourteen ARX160s and three GLX160s, plus ten thousand rounds of ammunition," Snake rasped.

"Nice," Ray whispered. "Very fucking nice."

"I got something else you might be interested in too."

Ray caught a waft of rancid breath but didn't turn around. "Oh yeah?"

"I heard there's a big shipment from Eduardo Nina coming into the port a week from tonight. There might be some RX-Four coming in too. I may or may not know the pier and the boat, but it's going to cost you."

This time, Ray did turn. "I'm listening."

"Make me an offer for the info."

Ray thought on it for a moment. "How about three more shipments of RX-Four, on the house?"

"Six."

"Four."

"*Six.*"

Ray shrugged. "A'ight, boss."

"The *Goomah*, midnight, pier nine," Snake said. "Week from tonight."

"Good shit," Ray said. He walked into the shack while Tommy waited outside.

Turning his back to Caitlyn and Snake, he pulled out his cell phone and pretended to take pictures while sending a pretyped text message. After examining the weapons, he slipped the phone away and walked back outside.

"Good stuff, Snake man," Ray said, flashing another grin. He reached out with a gloved hand. Snake always seemed to appreciate a handshake.

"How do you expect to get these back to the city?" Caitlyn asked.

She tilted her head slightly, then turned to sniff the air again. Her bulging lips began to move, but before she could say a word, the top of her skull exploded. A second later, the shot rang out.

Ray brought his submachine gun up and fired a three-round burst into Snake's chest. Then he raked the gun toward Ian, who raised his sawed-off at Tommy.

A deafening boom sounded.

The blast hit Tommy in the side, sending him sprawling across the ground.

Ian fell backward from a burst, sprawling against a stack of tires, dead by the time he slumped to the dirt.

Ray left Tommy moaning on the ground, to hunt the fourth soldier on Snake's payroll. He raked his light over the junkyard, searching for movement.

Come on, ya freak. Where are you?

A shadow moved in his peripheral vision, and he swung the barrel toward a figure running across the dirt. He almost pulled the trigger, then saw that it was just a kid.

The child bent down to Caitlyn's body, sobbing.

Ray moved over to make sure he wasn't armed. The kid looked up, baring his teeth. Tears streaked down the open lesions on his cheeks.

"Ray!" shouted a voice.

The boy took off running, and Ray let him go, whispering, "Sorry, kid."

"Over here!" Ray yelled back.

He moved over to Tommy, still groaning on the ground.

"Let me look," Ray said. "Move your damn hand."

Tommy bled from the vest's side closures, which had let a couple of pellets through. A third cop walked over. He wore black fatigues with a face mask and carried a sniper rifle.

"Nice shootin', Nicky," Ray said.

"It hurts," Tommy said.

"Hold on, bro, we're getting you to a hospital," Ray said. "Nicky, go get your truck and load this shit up, and watch out for a kid. About seven or eight. I'll go grab the car and take Tommy in."

Nicky took off after a nod.

"I can . . . hardly breathe," Tommy gasped.

"Long as you can feel your nuts, you'll be fine," Ray said.

Tommy broke into a coughing fit.

Ray had a morbid thought. This was going to look really bad if they lost Tommy. Hell, even bringing him into a hospital would raise red flags.

But he couldn't leave him here. Ray wasn't a monster.

"I'll be right back," he said.

"Wait," Tommy groaned.

"Chill, bro."

Ray went to grab the bag of RX-4. The shit was nearly worth its weight in gold. On the way back to his car, he called the one man who could help him with the Tommy situation.

"God damn it, Ray," said Lieutenant Best. But his tone changed when he heard about the port.

"You'll see a nice cut from this," Best said.

Ray grinned as he clicked off the phone. He was going to make out well tonight, maybe even bring home enough to buy his wife the ring she wanted.

The grin vanished when a gunshot shattered the silence of the night.

Ray ducked.

A figure staggered through the open gate of the compound, gripping its stomach before dropping to the ground.

"Got the kid!" Nicky yelled, sounding like a hunter who just brought down a buck.

Ray got up and slowly approached the boy in the dirt. Typically, the job didn't get to him. But something felt different. Something had changed.

He had always been a dirty cop, working with the mobsters, narcos, and gangsters. Evil deeds had hardened his heart, but not enough for him to shrug this off.

They had crossed a line out here. And there was no coming back from it.

* * *

Dom stood on the rooftop of the safe house in the City of Industry. He had found this place years ago, and it had been their base ever since. There were other safe houses across the city too, but this place was their headquarters.

Camilla stepped up beside him.

"Want some company?" she asked.

"Was about to go back downstairs."

"Namid and Pork Chop aren't back yet," she said. "We got a few minutes."

"Okay." Dom turned to enjoy the sunset. A magenta streak cleft the orange sky as purple faded to black on the horizon. Bare, skeletal trees dotted the hills.

A section of wall was visible in the distance—shipping containers and crushed auto bodies piled to block entry to the city.

The fading logos of billion-dollar companies from the past marked the derelict warehouses surrounding him. Most were faded and missing letters, but he remembered them from his childhood.

"You okay?" Dom asked Camilla when she didn't say anything.

"Yeah, I just miss Joaquín," she said. "Been thinking about him a lot lately."

"I'm sorry."

"Don't be. I know you understand."

Dom more than understood. The Vegas had killed his dad in the desert and killed her brother years ago by throwing him off the roof of a building. Both men got closed-casket funerals, but they had that much, at least.

That was some closure. Dom still had zero for his sister.

"We'll bury the animals," he said.

"Oh, damn right we will."

Dom looked away from the sunset and faced his friend. He knew her well, and she wasn't here to talk about her brother or his sister. He and Camilla had fought together since the beginning, and he loved her—not in a romantic way, even though he sometimes couldn't help imagining what it would be like. But that could never happen between them.

"Something I need to tell you," he said.

Camilla's brows went up. "Yeah?"

"Someone kidnapped Mariana López."

"*What?*"

Dom braced himself, but Camilla just stared at him. "She was being transferred to a medical facility, and Vegas hit the convoy, or so I'm told."

Camilla shook her head. "I told you we should have killed that bitch."

"You've got to let this go and focus on the mission, okay? All that matters is taking down the Vega brothers and Don Antonio."

She didn't reply.

"Cam," he said.

"Yeah, I heard you. I'm focused."

"Good. Let's head back inside."

They took the rooftop doorway down the stairs to the inside of the safe house. Tooth was sleeping on a couch, and Bettis lay slumped in a chair.

Dom went to the garage where they stored their vehicles. The Chevy Tahoe was on a lift, one of its wheels missing. An old Ford 150 pickup truck and a very old Jeep Cherokee sat nearby.

Moose was lifting free weights, and Rocky was in the boxing ring, practicing his footwork. The youngest member of the team reminded Dom of himself at the beginning of the war.

One of the garage doors opened, and a pickup pulled inside. Namid and Karl "Pork Chop" Watts got out. The two couldn't look more different. Pork Chop sported flaming orange mutton chops on his square jaw. Namid had cut off his long hair and had it styled in a neat, conservative do.

Despite their wildly different appearances, they were the best of friends.

"Good, you're here," Dom said. "Gather round. I've got news."

Camilla went to wake Tooth and Bettis up, and Moose put the massive barbell back on its rack. Rocky climbed down from the ring, catching Dom's thrown towel in midair. Dom tossed another one to Moose.

"Thanks, boss," Rocky said. He wiped off his ripped physique and winked at Camilla when she returned. She gave him a good eye roll.

The kid had the same fighting spirit as Dom but all the maturity of Tooth. He was a younger version of both men combined.

The team gathered around the table where they had planned so many of their guerrilla ambushes over the years. This was going to be their biggest yet.

"Tomorrow night, we hit the biggest shipment of opioids the city has ever seen, as well as a load of RX-Four," Dom said. "When the ship arrives, Moose, Tooth, Bettis, and I will go in and take it out with Russian RPGs while Namid and Pork Chop steal the RX-Four."

"What about me?" Camilla asked.

Dom pulled out a note and an address. "You have another mission."

She took the note and smiled. He was hoping it would make her happy, especially after the info about Mariana's abduction.

"Tomorrow night, we hit the Morettis *and* the Vegas," Dom said. "Tomorrow night, we remind them who the Saints are."

"Hell yeah," Moose said.

The team spent the next few hours around the table, planning out their attacks. At midnight, they called it a wrap, and Dom drove with Moose to their apartment complex not far from the Angel Pyramids.

The already dilapidated concrete buildings rose over thirty stories into the sky and housed over fifty thousand people, crammed in like cattle in a feedlot.

Rumor had it that Miguel Vega still lived in one of the buildings, but no one knew where Esteban was now. Unlike the Morettis, the elusive narco liked to move around.

On the next corner, several drug dealers hung out on park benches, handing out sealed bags of opiates in the darkness.

Half-naked kids, some without shoes, served as lookouts. The highly addictive hybrid opiates they sold were cheap, and half the city was addicted, using it to combat the pain the RX-4 caused. The medicine had its side effects, and half the people who took it were constantly sick from nausea and dizziness.

Dom and Moose walked through a parking lot where people stood around a wood fire burning inside a rusted auto body. They drank from paper sacks and stared blankly at the flames. Coursing through their veins was the real currency of the City of Angels.

Thanks to the dust storms, only a small portion of the metropolis had power tonight. The slums were all on curtailment, which meant no one but the gangsters and the citizens with old money had lights.

Dom and Moose walked with their heads down, trying to avoid attention. He had his SIG Sauer 1911 Nightmare, a microcompact SIG Sauer P365, and a knife strapped to his right ankle. Moose had switched out his submachine guns for a sawed-off shotgun and two M9s under his windbreaker.

There were a lot of threats in the slums, and living there was incredibly dangerous, but it was even more dangerous to live where the city officials, cops, and rich folks lived. That was what made this the best place to hide. Their enemies would never think to look here for a Saint.

Dom walked through the gated entrance and hurried over to the outdoor stairwell that led up to their floor.

"I hope Yolanda didn't wait up for me," Moose said.

Dom watched their back in case anyone had followed them, while Moose pulled out the key to his apartment.

A growl met them as he unlocked the heavy steel door.

"It's okay, girl," Dom said. Cayenne hopped over, wagging her tail. He bent down and massaged the back of the dog's muscular brown neck.

"Long night?" said a female voice inside.

Yolanda stood in the living room, arms folded across her tank top.

"Hey, baby girl," Moose said, going inside to embrace his wife, whose head came only to his chest.

"Thanks for looking after Cayenne," Dom said when they pulled apart.

Yolanda nodded, and pulled a strand of hair behind her ear. She was a good-looking, smart, strong woman, and Moose loved her fiercely.

Two small figures appeared in the dark hallway connecting to the living room.

"Go back to sleep," Yolanda said to Bryon, six, and Tamara, five.

"But we want to say hi to Uncle Dom," Bryon said.

"Hey, guys," Dom said. He gave them each a hug and let them pet Cayenne.

Yolanda cleared her throat, indicating the reunion was over.

"Say good night to Uncle Dom and Cayenne and go back to your rooms."

"See you later, and thanks again," Dom said before leaving the apartment.

"Anytime," Yolanda replied with a smile.

Dom led his dog outside and over to their place, five doors down.

Going in, he reached behind the couch and pulled the drapes across the barred window. This was home. It wasn't much, but he didn't care about supersized TVs, fast cars, designer clothes, or expensive booze. He was hardly ever here, and if he did have free time from the hunt, he took Cayenne on runs or to the park. Even with three legs, she could get around about as well as any other dog.

She wagged her tail and followed him past the small kitchen, where he stopped to give her water. He didn't bother checking the fridge. With the energy curtailments happening nearly every day, there was no point keeping food that could spoil.

The dog stopped to growl at her food bowl.

"You hungry?" he asked, filling it from a bag of kibble—the only thing he kept in the pantry besides some canned food. She never ate when Dom was out.

While Cayenne practically inhaled her food, she watched him and then followed him to the bathroom.

"Eat," he said. "I'm not going anywhere."

She hesitated, then walked back out, stopping in the hall to look back at him.

He turned to look at the cracked mirror. A few grays had sneaked into the sides of his thick brown hair. Even in the dim lighting, he could see the first creases of crow's-feet and the hump on his nose, broken twice as a teenager when he fought mixed martial arts. For a twenty-seven-year-old, he was starting to look pretty rough.

This was what hunting gangsters did to you. It was also the reason his bed had one pillow.

Nights like this reminded him why he didn't have a wife or a girlfriend.

He had been in love once, a long time ago, at least he thought it was love, but maybe he was too young to know. Now love would only be a dangerous distraction. He still didn't know how Moose could function knowing he had Yolanda and his kids waiting for him at home.

Always waiting, and always worrying. *And always at risk.*

He went to his closet-sized bedroom and turned on the lantern. Sitting on the edge of his mattress, he set his guns down. Then he took off his shoes and patted the bed. Cayenne jumped up and curled up next to him, letting out a long sigh.

"Good night," Dom whispered.

He reached over to shut off the lantern but stopped to look at the only framed picture he had in his apartment: a photo of his family at the beach.

The image transported him back to a time when he had known the love of a family. Hard to fathom, but it was all gone now.

And while he still had his mother, not much remained of the mom he remembered. She had numbed her grief over losing Monica and Ronaldo, using the same drugs Dom worked so hard to get off the streets.

He used to feel a deep pain when he saw the picture or when he read the note his dad left him, but now he hardly felt anything. He, too, was numb. He could feel anger and hate, though.

Monica was gone forever; Dom knew that now. He would never find her, never save her. All he could do was avenge her and his dad by removing the evil that was part of this new world—the Vegas, the Morettis, and everyone else who poisoned what good was still left.

Leaning back onto his pillow, he waited for the fatigue to take him.

Tired though he was, after a few minutes, he knew that sleep was out of his reach. His heart pounded hard again, thoughts of revenge filling him with adrenaline.

He trudged back to the sink and splashed water on his face.

It was time to do something he hadn't done in months. As soon as he was done with the port mission, he would go and see his mom.

-4-

Don Antonio Moretti and his brother, Christopher, walked through the iron gate with their two most trusted bodyguards. Christopher's son, Vinny, was also with them tonight. The young soldier had risen through the Moretti ranks quickly, proving himself many times over the years, and Antonio wanted him in this sit-down with Esteban Vega.

Antonio had asked for a truce while he and Christopher flew to Naples to kill the last of the backstabbing Canavaros, and the Vegas had granted it. Now it was Esteban coming with an olive branch, seeking not just a truce, but actual peace.

Antonio smiled. The eight-year war between the two families had taken a toll on both sides, and he had agreed to meet with the narco king—not to hammer out a peace deal, but to probe for whatever weakness would allow him to finish Esteban off for good.

He already had his secret leverage in Mariana, but perhaps he wouldn't need to use her.

Antonio glanced over his shoulder at the small army they had brought with them to this dangerous meeting. Out in front of the dozen soldiers was Captain Carmine Barese, holding one of the new Beretta ARX160 rifles they had recently acquired thanks to Vinny and Detective Ray Clarke.

The rest of the guns and muscle were at the port, where his men were guarding the biggest shipment of drugs he had yet purchased from Eduardo Nina and several loads of the precious RX-4 antirad med that so many people needed to stay alive.

The Vegas now controlled half the drug traffic in Los Angeles. The Norteño Mafia, Zetas, Latin Kings, and MS-13 were no more, and the surviving members had rallied under Esteban's banner, desperate for a piece of what was left, willing to let go of old enmities and blood oaths just to survive in this new world.

The narco brothers also understood how to invest dirty money, using it to build legitimate businesses that the cops and government could never touch.

Every crime family had them, including the Morettis, who were into everything from strip clubs and casinos to prime real estate and expensive clothing.

This evening, Antonio wore something straight off the ship from his birthplace: a three-piece Armani suit. He had shaved his beard and combed his thinning hair.

A sit-down like this was like going on a first date. Everyone had to look their best, even if they wanted to kill each other.

Three Vega men waited at a second pair of iron doors inside the compound. Candles in glass sconces on the adobe walls illuminated tattooed sicarios, their features hidden behind Day of the Dead masks with colorful designs.

The guy on the right wore a white skull with red paint around empty black eye sockets, and white stitches holding the black lips together. Red roses decorated the crest of the skull.

Antonio tightened his white tie, raised his glittering Rolex, and said to the three men, "Don't waste my time."

A guard in a mask with snakes wrapped around the jaw reached out and opened the door while the other two frisked Antonio and then the rest of their group.

"Guns stay here. You can collect them later, Don Antonio," said a soft feminine voice through the open door.

A Latina wearing a strapless, form-fitting crimson dress stood there, arms by her sides. The biggest ruby Antonio had ever seen hung from a gold chain just above her cleavage.

"You must be Elsa Vega," Antonio said. He took her hand and kissed it. "You are even more beautiful than I've heard."

"Gracias, Don Antonio," she said.

Most women would have blushed at a compliment from such a powerful man, but she simply gestured for them to come inside the brightly lit living space with high ceilings. Animal trophies—rhino, polar bear, cape buffalo, sable—were mounted on the walls.

From what Antonio had heard, Esteban and Miguel came from the ghettos of Mexico City, much as he and Christopher had come from the slums in Naples to the ruins of Hollywood. Since those days, both families had built impressive empires—empires they wanted to protect.

Antonio gave Christopher a nod, and they walked into the center of the room furnished with leather couches, Indian rugs, and a long oak table set with china, silver, and gold-rimmed glasses.

A man not much older than Vinny stood in front of the table. He offered a warm dimpled smile, spreading his arms out in a welcoming manner. Antonio recognized him. He was there the night of the Morettis' ambush at the Chevron oil refinery, when Antonio's men had almost killed both Esteban and Miguel. But the two brothers had escaped, and so had their nephew.

"Welcome to Casa Vega," he said. "I'm Pedro Vega, son of Elsa Vega, but you can call me Negro. My uncle Esteban will be with us shortly. Please, have a seat and make yourself comfortable. Can I get you a drink, Don Antonio?"

Antonio folded his arms across his chest, looking at Negro. "I don't drink margaritas."

Yellowtail laughed, and Negro, still smiling, said, "We do have plenty of other offerings, including some of the finest wine in the country."

"Pinot noir," Antonio said.

Elsa walked into a connecting kitchen with blue and red backsplashes and matching, intricately tiled countertops. Antonio turned as three men came down the stairs behind them.

While the Morettis dressed like modern gangsters, the Vegas looked more like rich cowboys. The men wore leather pants or designer jeans, large belt buckles, and Western hats. One of them stopped on the bottom step, directly in the light, and Antonio got his first view of the narco king in over eight years.

A large, drooping nose reflected his indigenous ancestry, and those sharp dark eyes had seen a lot of death.

Esteban reached down and gripped his wide platinum belt buckle. The two men flanking him each had a neck tattoo of a dagger with a ruby in the hilt. It was the mark of a Vega sicario.

"Welcome," Esteban finally said, walking over to Don Antonio. "It's been far too long since we saw each other, and I'm pleased that this time it's under more cordial circumstances."

The last time, Esteban had tried to kill Antonio; but this was business, and in business you had to put transgressions aside, even if you couldn't forgive them.

Like Raff's murder.

Elsa joined Esteban as he crossed the center of the room to stand in front of Antonio. The two men faced each other, two modern kings—and two mortal enemies.

Both men had clawed their way to the top of the food chain in the largest metropolis of the postwar United States.

"Thank you for making the journey," Esteban said. "I know it took a lot of faith."

"If something happens to me, you die too," Antonio said.

Esteban smiled, revealing two gold teeth. "No one's dying tonight, *mi amigo*."

He stretched out a weathered hand.

Antonio wanted to cut it off and stuff it up his *culo*, but he did what any businessman would do.

He shook it like a man here to make a deal. But there couldn't be a deal without Miguel, and Antonio didn't see Esteban's younger brother yet. It had to be because of Mariana.

The brother knew that Antonio was behind the grab. Good. She was their guarantee that they all walk out of here.

"I'm getting older and cherish my time, so let's get on with this," Antonio said.

"You and me both, *cuate*." Esteban's smile widened, showing off more gold.

The Vegas loved their gold and their rubies, but Antonio wasn't one to judge. The Morettis had their vices too: cars, clothes, *women*.

Two housemaids, both beautiful black-haired Latinas, carried plates of meat-filled tamales, a celebratory dish.

It was a reminder of Esteban's roots—a world of dirt and death that he had turned into great wealth.

As the meeting continued, the tamales were replaced with chicken mole, bowls of pozole, chile verde, and carne asada.

"So where's your brother?" Antonio said.

Esteban finished carefully filling a corn tortilla with chunks of meat.

"Miguel prefers to fuck his whores and consume our product more than he cares about *dinero*. I envy you two," he said, raising his steak knife and pointing it at Antonio and then Christopher.

"Bad blood ruins things," Esteban continued. He took a drink of wine. "But we're not here to discuss Miguel. I'm here to discuss a peace treaty so we can form new borders that will ensure a bright future for both our organizations."

His sharp eyes fell on Lino, the captain his man had tried to kill the day the nuke went off in Sacramento.

Lino held his gaze. Antonio had brought him for a reason: to show that bad blood could be forgiven. Every decision he made was careful and deliberate—every word he spoke, every order he gave. That was how you became a king at the end of the world.

And now he knew why Esteban had asked him to come here. The Vega organization was suffering from a rift that threatened to split their drug empire in two. Esteban knew that Antonio would move in at the slightest sign of weakness, and he wanted to make a deal before Miguel went completely off the reservation.

That made Mariana even more important.

Antonio ate in silence, feeling out his enemy while dining at his table. And Esteban seemed to be doing the same.

"I know what you're thinking," Esteban said. "That the reason I called you here is to make peace because of my brother."

He traced his fork back and forth like a symphony conductor. "Not the case."

Esteban took another bite of food, chewed, and swallowed. He was every bit as calculating as Antonio.

"Make no mistake. This does not mean Miguel and I aren't working together," Esteban said. "Nothing changes. We're stronger than ever."

Antonio continued to eat. He wasn't really hungry, but he didn't want to show disrespect right when things were going his way.

"Shall we discuss the borders, then?" Antonio asked.

Esteban set his silverware down and nodded. The staff came around and cleared the plates. Christopher took a map from his suit pocket and spread it on the table.

Negro and Esteban both stood to get a better look.

The map of central Los Angeles was divided into the four zones controlled by the Morettis, Vegas, Nevskys, and everyone else—mostly Bloods, and a few smaller gangs that had managed to avoid extinction.

But there were several disputed areas in Central Los Angeles that Antonio wanted. Streets his soldiers had fought Vega sicarios and bled for over the past five years.

If Esteban wanted peace, Antonio would use it to his advantage.

"I want these areas," Antonio said.

Esteban studied the map. "Then I want these blocks south of the Four Diamonds."

"Hell no," Christopher said out of turn.

Antonio calmly shook his head at Esteban. "You can have the piers at Long Beach."

Esteban laughed. "Nevsky territory."

"Not for long," Antonio said.

Negro spoke in Spanish to his uncle.

Everyone knew that the piers in Long Beach were dying real estate, but Esteban had to know he wasn't going to get any territory around the Four Diamonds.

"It's a deal—if you take care of the Nevskys," Esteban said.

"We will take care of them," Antonio said. He could feel his brother looking at him, but this was part of his plan. Taking care of the Nevskys didn't mean he would *give* Esteban the new territory.

"I will pull my men back from the areas on the map," Esteban said, "and once the Nevskys and the *cucaracha* gangs are gone, we will meet again, perhaps at your table." He stretched out his hand.

Antonio held back. "How can we trust that your brother will respect these new borders?"

Esteban used a spoon to scoop up salsa verde still on the table. "Because if he doesn't, I will put him in a barrel of acid." He tilted the spoon, pouring the green liquid back into the dish. "Perhaps I will do that to Eduardo Nina someday too, like I did to his former *patrón*."

Antonio hadn't forgotten that his supplier and Esteban were enemies, dating back to the cartel wars before the Second Civil War, but he kept tight lipped, not wanting to derail their new deal. Instead, he reached out and again shook the hand of his enemy. Then they sat back down, and one of the lovely housekeepers poured them more wine.

"Make no mistake, we sit here as friends, but once you leave this house and head back to yours, we will again become enemies if the barriers on this map are crossed." Esteban turned his gaze to Lino. "I'm sure our friend here remembers how I deal with my enemies."

Lino didn't take the bait.

"And you should also make no mistake," Antonio said. "If you betray me, I will send you to hell with the rest of the narcos whose coyote I have become by helping them cross to the other side."

Esteban hesitated for a few seconds. Then he folded his hands together. "I'm glad we got that out of the way. Now, who's ready for dessert?"

He snapped his fingers, and a servant opened a door across the room. The click of high heels echoed in the living room as a dozen Latinas in short, tight dresses walked in and stood side by side.

Antonio had seen plenty of sex slaves in his day. His family continued to run its own lucrative operation, but he preferred not to see them.

He rose from his chair, wiping his lips on a napkin. "Thanks, but I have a wife to get home to," he said.

Esteban shrugged. "To each his own." He held up his hands and said, "How about some flan, then? Elsa made a batch that is *glorioso*."

She smiled and started off for the kitchen, but Antonio politely declined.

"I don't like flan, but thank you for a pleasant evening," he said.

Esteban and Negro both nodded.

"Follow me, *por favor*," Elsa said.

She escorted the Morettis toward the door and smiled politely as they left.

Antonio looked over his shoulder halfway down the stone path. Negro winked at him and gave his dimpled grin, but Esteban wasn't smiling anymore.

Something told Antonio this "peace" wasn't going to last very long, and that was exactly the point. He was just biding his time before he could finish off the Vega family once and for all.

* * *

The first thing Vinny Moretti did every morning when he wasn't at home was smoke a cigarette. With one eye open, he fumbled for the pack. Careful not to wake up his girlfriend, he swung his legs over the side of the bed and took the pack to the window.

He didn't believe a damn word Esteban and Negro had said in the meeting, but they probably didn't believe a damn word his uncle or his father had said, either.

Vinny pulled back the ratty drapes. A dark cloud was rolling in from the west, threatening the city with yet another dust storm.

The solar panels on the rooftops across the street were already retracting into their protective cases, and people were rushing to cover their crops with plastic tarps before the toxic dust could kill their plants.

"What the hell, Vin?"

Adriana Napoli, his girlfriend of two years, rolled over to shield her eyes from the glow, exposing her naked back and the dragon tattoo climbing up her spine.

"Sorry," he said, closing the drapes a bit.

He lit a cigarette and enjoyed the view. Blocks of concrete floors rose across the skyline. Metal mezzanines and balconies of the upper floors were already filling with workers wearing masks and goggles to protect their lungs and eyes.

He leaned to the side for a better view.

Being seen in the slums of central Los Angeles was a risk. Several Moretti enemies were in this area, though most were low-level gang-bangers who had survived the violence by keeping a low profile. Guys like Reggie Harper and his cousin, Lil Snipes.

Vinny still couldn't believe Lil Snipes had survived. He was lucky his uncle hadn't finished him off, but sitting in a chair unable to use his cock ever again was enough punishment for any man. Worse than death, some might say.

Taking a drag off the cigarette, Vinny opened the drapes again and blew the smoke outside.

This was the most densely populated area in the entire country. He couldn't see it, but the Goldilocks Zone, formerly Hollywood, was only a few miles away. Because why not build the Las Vegas of LA just outside the ghettos?

The zone was now blocks of clubs, high-end restaurants, and brothels for the city's one-percenters. Places where you could order tender Kobe steak, melt-in-your-mouth toro sashimi shipped from Japan, a fifteen-thousand-dollar bottle of Armand de Brignac Brut Gold champagne, or a woman from any corner of the world. Or a guy, if that was your thing.

The Golden Oyster, a casino his uncle had built eight years ago, was located in the strip of expensive clubs and eateries. Most of its slot machines and card tables had come from the Commerce Hotel.

Now the Oyster was the most famous casino in all California. It was also where he had met Adriana. He loved the all-nighters out there, but with age and advancement came responsibility, and he rarely visited the area now.

"Vin, shut those," she grumbled, flipping back over, so he could now see the flower tattoos just above her breasts.

He turned back to the window for one more glimpse. Gazing out over the real world was something he still loved to do but couldn't at the Moretti compound.

This was real life: the rusted cars, the people up at the ass crack of dawn to make a living, the kids playing soccer in the streets, the smells of ethnic cooking. This was the real world.

The people walking in the streets were slaves to more than the poison running in their veins. They were slaves to the entire corrupt system that ruled Los Angeles—a system that his family helped run.

Last night after the meeting, he had come here instead of going home to his wife, using work as an excuse. He was doing a lot of that lately.

Like a lot of people, he and Carmen had gotten married too young, at a time when he thought more with his dick than his brain. How was he supposed to know that Carmen would break his balls and complain about every damn thing? Nothing he ever did would be good enough for her.

"Vin, come on, shut those!" Adriana said. There was annoyance in her voice, sure, but nothing like the anger and abuse that his wife heaped on him.

He pulled the drapes partly closed and took another drag of his cigarette.

"What time is it?" Adriana moaned, one hand on her head.

"Time to hustle." In his reality, it was always time to hustle. He was always grinding, day in and day out, and would keep doing it until his uncle came through on his promise and made him captain of his own operation.

He was sick of being a grunt and handling shipments. He wanted to be in charge of people and property, not schedules. He had thought that after securing the deal with Eduardo Nina, he was going to be a captain and Doberman would be made. But neither of those things had happened.

Adriana sat up in bed, the silk sheets pulled up just below the flower tattoos. She watched while he dressed.

"When do I get to see you again?" she asked.

He shrugged.

"Vin, when's the last time we had dinner together?"

"I don't know baby, but I'm going to try and arrange that soon." Not exactly a lie, but arranging dinner was not easy. If Carmen found out about Adriana, or if, God forbid, any of his enemies . . .

You can't let that happen. You have to be careful.

She let out a sigh. "You know all I want is you. I don't care about going out. We can eat here, for all I care. As long as I'm with you."

"I know. I'll make it happen soon, I promise." Vinny pulled on the ripped hoodie he used as a disguise when he came here.

"That's sexy," Adriana said.

He tightened his belt and then walked over to kiss her, admiring her light-brown skin in the dim first light. The other reason this could never be anything serious. Adriana was part Italian, but her mother had been black, and being with her would be a serious breach of Moretti tradition—a stupid and racist tradition, but a tradition nonetheless.

But it wasn't her complexion that distinguished Adriana from his wife or any of his other girlfriends in the past. She didn't care about the diamonds or the designer handbags. She loved him for the man he was, even when *he* didn't love the man he was.

He kissed her on the lips, and her long fake nails pressed gently into his neck.

"Stay a bit longer," she said. "We can have round . . ."

"Three," he reminded her. "Sorry, baby, I've got to run."

She gave him a puppy-dog look, and he considered staying. But that would just make him want to leave his wife even more.

"Sorry. Really, I got a long day ahead of me with my cousin." He slipped into his tennis shoes.

"When are you going to make captain? Haven't you earned it?"

"Workin' on it," he said, mumbling with a second cigarette between his lips. He had a plan to find the Saints, and it started with the port.

They had plenty of people there in their pocketbook, and one of them would help lead them to the ghosts terrorizing the Moretti organization.

A loud knock came on the door, and he reached for his pistol.

Adriana jumped out of the bed.

"You expectin' someone?" he whispered.

She shook her head.

Vinny motioned for her to stay back as he crept to the door. Squealing tires on the street outside the window stopped him in mid stride.

Shouts followed.

Not even eight in the morning, and someone was already pissed off.

"Who is it?" he asked.

A rough voice replied. "Open up, Vin."

Vinny checked the peephole to confirm that the voice belonged to his father. He opened the door, but stood in the way to keep Christopher from coming inside. "Whoa, take it easy, please," Vinny said.

"This fucking place smells like piss," Christopher said.

Vinny moved to block his view of Adriana, who was in the other room.

"You really think coming here is smart?" Christopher said, throwing up his hand. He hung back slightly. "What the fuck is wrong with you?"

The anger in his voice surprised Vinny. Something had to be wrong.

"The *Goomah* is coming early," Christopher said.

"Oh shit, how come no one—"

"Check your phone."

Vinny looked at the couch, where he had left it and not looked at it since last night.

"Fucking will get you killed," Christopher said. "You make mistakes when you lust over a woman."

Vinny heard breathing and stepped out to see a tall, muscular man with blacked-out tattoo sleeves and a scar across his face.

Doberman, you son of a bitch.

Doberman was his best friend, but selling Vinny out wasn't cool.

"Sorry, bro," Doberman said as if he could read Vinny's thoughts. "I can't lie to your dad."

"I didn't need him to show me this shithole," Christopher said. "Meet us outside. We've got a new task for you that involves your cousin, after we get the shipment secured."

"What task?" Vinny asked.

"You get to play babysitter." Christopher turned away from the open door and began walking back down the hall, then stopped and turned slightly. "Oh, and tell that sweet piece of ass this is the last time you're going to see her."

Vinny clenched his jaw.

"Dude, I'm sorry," Doberman said after Christopher had rounded the corner.

"I'll be outside in a few," Vinny said.

He closed the door and looked at Adriana.

"Who was that?" she asked.

"No one . . ."

"Vin?"

"Trouble," he admitted. "My family knows where you live now."

"So what?"

Vinny shook his head and grabbed his backpack. "You don't get it, do you?"

He hadn't told Adriana many details about his job, but she had to know his family would never approve of her.

She walked over and wrapped her arms around him from behind, her skin warm on his. He couldn't bring himself to tell her what his father had ordered.

"Be careful out there today." She kissed him on his cheek and then retreated to her closet to look for something to wear to her job at the Golden Oyster.

She pulled out the red dress he had bought for her. "I've been saving this for a night with you."

He forced a smile and grabbed the door handle, his back partially to her.

"Wait," she said.

"Yeah?"

Adriana's cheeks flushed. "I love you, Vin."

Vinny turned to the woman he should have married.

"I love you too."

-5-

Camilla tried to ignore the stares on the bus. She swallowed nervously when the driver stopped outside Staples Center to pick up a group of women and teenagers. Their white uniforms were stained with blood from working in the factory where the city raised and processed hundreds of thousands of chickens.

She wanted to hide in the shadows from the gazes of these hardworking people. Everyone on the bus was poor, judging by their clothes, exhausted faces, and body odor. Some were probably getting off their second shift of the day, still unable to make ends meet.

And here she was, dressed like a narco wife . . . or a *puta*.

Camilla hated getting dressed up. She couldn't think of many things worse than squeezing into a tight sequined dress that required a strapless bra and thong underwear that didn't show through the snug, sheer fabric.

Tonight, she had done both, taking two hours to carefully apply foundation, jet-black liquid eyeliner, fake eyelashes, and merlot-colored lipstick.

She had cursed up a storm as she crammed her feet into three-inch stilettos and clipped in the twelve-inch hair extensions. But God *damn* did she clean up well!

She could feel it in the gazes from men twice her age and from the younger men who turned as she got off the bus and sauntered toward the Catalina rooftop bar.

She wasn't the only good-looking woman navigating the packed dance floor centered between bars on either end of the room. There were a few tens out there. Gringas mostly, in bikinis, with their toes dipped in the pool, backs arched like models, holding cocktails with those little umbrellas. Fake smiles, fake tits. Former Instagram influencers, trying to get by in a dog-eat-dog world.

Judging by their pinpoint pupils, they were high, which would help when the work *really* started.

Camilla used being sober to her advantage. She had already gotten hit on by several low-level narcos. But she wasn't wasting her time on those guys. She was here for someone higher up the food chain.

Flaunting her ass helped. She had more of it than most of the rail-thin *prostitutas*. She worked hard for hers—yoga in the morning, weights at night, and runs when she could manage. It paid off. The Italian gangsters loved her cappuccino skin, and the narcos loved that fine, round ass.

One of the hookers, a bean pole with spiky red hair and a minor case of acne, flung a melancholy glance in her direction, perhaps checking out the competition. The girl, who couldn't be more than eighteen, kept the left side of her face in the shadows, hiding a bruise, probably from a client's fist.

These women—girls, some of them—led a sad life trying to please these sexual freaks. Most of them didn't have a choice. They either were sold into the business or got in to pay the bills.

Camilla never stopped looking for Dom's sister. And she always felt a pang of sadness for girls like the redhead.

Camilla had something in common with this girl, but the scars and bruises from her last run-in with a Vega wannabee were covered with makeup. That was the one good part of getting all dolled up. It didn't cover all the scars, but they weren't visible unless she was naked. And she didn't have to worry about that happening tonight.

Torches hanging off marble pillars lit the rooftop bar, spreading a warm glow over hundreds of patrons standing at the bars, sitting on wicker furniture, or relaxing by the pool.

Keeping to the shadows, she continued the prowl for her next target, sipping her tequila sour and touching the gold cross kept in place by her cleavage. She wasn't very religious anymore, but something about wearing the symbol of the Christian faith calmed her.

The tequila also helped. It was nostalgic. Growing up in a poor Mexican household meant she didn't get to try many delicacies the world had to offer, but there was always tequila and fresh tamales.

The thought of a homemade *tamal* brought back the good memories, and the liquor helped subdue the bad ones. At twenty-seven years old, she had already racked up her fair share of those.

One had occurred right here at the Catalina, a favorite hangout of narcos in LA. She didn't really like calling these assholes Mexicans. Sure, they were from her home country, but they weren't the real deal. Real Mexicans were hardworking, kind, gracious people, who would feed you even if they didn't have much to share.

The narcos blew money on shirts more expensive than what the average Mexican had stashed under the floorboards. These weren't 1980s Pablo Escobar narcos, either. None of these guys gave two shits about helping the poor in their local area.

Heads kept turning as she walked through the crowd toward a bar on the east side of the roof.

She used her fresh looks to her advantage, and so did the leader of her team. Dom had given her a note with this address, promising she would find someone here who had been involved with killing her brother.

While the other Saints were hitting the port, she would strike the Vegas. She would make no arrests tonight. That was supposed to be LAPD's job, but those corrupt pricks wouldn't do anything. They gave good cops—what few were left—a bad name.

The Saints' job was to help eradicate the disease afflicting the city's bones. The crime families had gotten into every niche and recess, into the very marrow. For Camilla, this was personal. Like Dom, she had lost someone to the crime families.

She spent the first hour scoping the area for targets. Mostly low-level narcos at the bar. The big guns were absent. Esteban Vega and his nephew

Negro hadn't made a public appearance in months. She didn't see Esteban's younger brother, Miguel, either, but that didn't surprise her. Word was out they had bad blood.

If Miguel were here, he would already be dead, with one of her stilettos buried in his temple. Even if she died the second after, she would breathe her last knowing she had avenged her brother. She knew deep down that her obsession with this particular revenge wasn't healthy, but she didn't care. It was an internal fire she needed to extinguish, or the angry flames would eventually consume her.

Her heart skipped when she finally got to the bar for a refill. No matter how hard she tried to look away from the eastern fence blocking the view of the city, she couldn't help herself. The owners said they had put it up to block the wind and dust, but the real reason was for safety.

Her brother had died a hundred feet from where she now stood. The sight of it still made her stomach turn.

Thrown over the roof parapet to the ground twelve stories below, over a debt smaller than a modest bar tab.

She was told he survived several minutes—long enough for the paramedics to arrive. The only consolation was that he managed to whisper a few final words.

"Tell Camilla I'm sorry," he had said. "Tell her I love her."

Camilla raised a finger and ordered another tequila sour, double. Then she looked to the west. When her drink came, she took two gulps. The liquor felt good, but it did nothing to suppress the bad memories.

"You thirsty, *mami chula*?" said a voice. "How about another . . . ?" The man to her right leaned over, close enough that she could smell the mezcal on his breath. "That a sour?"

She took another drink and turned toward the railing her brother was tossed over. She saw a narco wearing a cowboy hat. Judging by his outfit, he was low-level, and it was hard to see his face in the dim lighting.

This guy had a scar tracing a line from his dimpled left cheek up to his eye and splitting his eyebrow.

He blinked, and she saw that he was blind in that eye.

Apparently, the other eye liked what it saw.

"Come on, *mami*. Let me buy you another drink."

"I'm good, but thank you," she said politely. She knew how these fuckers ticked, and the last thing she wanted to do was piss off a narco with a big ego and a little dick.

Especially Julio "Blanco" Ocampo.

The gangster with the white eye wasn't low-level after all. One of the Vegas' most powerful dealers in Los Angeles, he spent half his time traveling to El Salvador to oversee shipments of new product. He had also been there the night her brother was killed—along with Miguel Vega. She would kill them all, eventually.

A chill rushed through her, blending with the warmth of the tequila and the satisfying thought of crossing one of these bastards off her list.

"You know who I am?" Blanco said.

She finished off her drink, pivoting slightly so her hips were turned toward his oversized belt buckle.

"No, who are you?" She forced a coy smile and batted her fake eyelashes.

A dead man, she thought as he proudly stated his name. She put her elbow on the bar, leaning down so he could see just enough to know that her breasts were real.

"Oh, you sound important," she said, tapping her fake nails against her glass. Because, shit, that was what girls did, right?

The functional eye narrowed. "Have I seen you before?"

She shook her head—maybe a bit too fast, but she wasn't worried. Every narco, gangster, and banger in the city with half a brain was paranoid. The only way to survive long enough to make any money was by trusting no one.

"You look familiar." He gave her a good once-over, and she turned slightly to get the bartender's attention.

"On second thought, I'll take that drink," she said.

Blanco's milky eye flitted to the bartender, a young white college-age guy trying to do things the right way—through hard work.

"Hey, gringo fuckhead, bring us two tequila sours," Blanco ordered, apparently no longer interested in where he had seen her before.

"On the rocks," she said.

Blanco's grin widened. He liked that.

"You heard the lady, fuckhead. Give us your best tequila, *ese*." He snapped his gold-ringed fingers.

The bartender nodded and went to work on the drinks. Blanco returned his full attention to Camilla, moving closer.

Line . . . sinker.

She could really smell his breath now. He was a smoker, and not just of cigarettes. Whatever cologne he wore wasn't masking the skunky scent of weed on his shiny silver shirt. The top three buttons were undone to show off his chest hair and several gold necklaces. If you didn't have a necklace, a cowboy hat, a belt buckle, and a gun with gold or silver on the barrel, you weren't a narco.

She couldn't see his gun, but she could feel the grip when he got off the stool and brushed up against her.

"I know I've seen you somewhere before," he said, still smiling.

Back to this again, she thought.

"You're not a *prostituta*, are you?"

She recoiled. "Excuse me? If you'd been with me, you'd damn sure remember it."

She maneuvered the small red purse slung over her left shoulder. Inside were several different tools, including her Smith and Wesson Airweight, but she wasn't going to use that on Blanco. She planned something more satisfying for this *pendejo*.

"*Lo siento*," he said. "Didn't mean to offend you, *mami*."

The bartender set two drinks down on the bar, just in time. He smiled as politely as he could manage, but apparently it wasn't enough for Blanco.

"Fuck is this, *ese*?" he snapped.

The bartender scratched his short-cropped hairline.

"Don't scratch your head like an idiot. You think I'm an asshole?"

"No sir, of course not."

"I said bring us your best, and I saw you put Patrón in there."

The man glanced down at the drinks. "Sir, you said 'bring us your best—'"

"Patrón is gringo piss. Bring us Don Julio—that's real Mexican tequila. Fucking asshole." Blanco watched the barman carry the drinks away before turning back to Camilla.

"I'm not a hooker kind of a guy, and since you're here by yourself, I just figured you might be one, baby. Had to ask, you know?"

Not your baby . . .

"I came with my girlfriend, but she already left with some guy. She was my ride." Camilla shrugged.

He cracked a sly grin, and Camilla knew exactly what he was thinking.

Hooked.

Fresh drinks came a few minutes later, and she thanked the bartender politely. He nodded and looked at Blanco. "Sorry for my mistake, sir. Please enjoy these on the house."

Blanco handed Camilla a drink and said, "You still haven't told me your name."

"Nina." Short. Sweet. Mysterious.

"Where you from?"

"Guadalajara." Not a lie this time. "You?"

"Juarez."

She took a drink, feeling his eyes wandering down and stopping on her breasts. Most narcos weren't discreet. When they wanted something, they let it be known.

Blanco was no different, which made the next part easy.

"I'm getting a bit sick of the music here," she said. "Probably head home after this drink."

It was late, and the Saints would be moving into position soon. She wanted to be back to the safe house by the time they finished at the port.

She paced herself for the next thirty minutes, even downed a glass of water. In a few minutes, she was about to score a goal for the team.

And Blanco had no idea. Poor bastard thought he was about to get some first-rate pussy. Not like the girls sitting around the pool, who were now fraternizing with some low-end narcos. Blanco here probably didn't think he would have to wear a condom. Little did he know, he was never getting laid *ever* again.

"What do you do?" Blanco asked her.

"I'll tell you later," she replied.

He seemed to dig this mystery game. He smiled again.

She finished off her drink. "So . . ."

"You ready?" he asked.

She nodded and said, "Meet me on the street. I need to use the powder room."

He tipped his cowboy hat and looked her straight in the eye as he slowly ran his fat tongue over his upper teeth.

She left him at the bar, giving him a great view. Keeping to the shadows, she did her best not to be seen. Half his friends were drunk or well on their way, but they would notice if she left with him.

A few minutes later, they met outside the building's entrance, where a line of patrons was still waiting to get inside. She had already pulled up her face mask to keep out the alkaline dust and hide her features.

"I parked just around the block," he said.

She followed him down the sidewalk, avoiding the gaze of everyone walking in their direction. Around the next corner, he approached a boat of a car, an old Chevy convertible with gold rims and a tan drop-down.

"Want me to put it down?" he asked.

She shook her head. "Dust is bad tonight, and I don't want to mess up my hair."

He opened the passenger door for her, acting like a gentleman for a moment, but she knew the truth. He didn't have a gentlemanly bone in his body.

She ducked into the car and sat, fishing her weapon of choice out of her purse as he came around the other side. The needle was filled with enough concentrated heroin hybrid that he would stop breathing minutes after being jabbed.

Every once in a while, she liked to be ironic, killing them with their own product. It also helped her cover her tracks.

She would love to set him on fire or maybe pluck out his other eye, but too many dead narcos meant more careful narcos, and dressing up like Latina Barbie was already painful enough.

He opened the car door and relaxed onto the camel-brown leather seat that matched the drop-down. When he leaned over with a smile, she prepared to jab him in the throat with the needle, but a voice stopped her.

"Blanco, what the fuck you doing?"

Two Mexican men approached from across the street. Both looked like narco soldiers, but she didn't recognize them.

"Hold tight, *mami*," Blanco said.

Both men leaned down for a look inside. She tried to keep hidden in the shadows, facing forward, but they were directly under a damn streetlight.

"*¿Qué pasa?*" asked one of the men, a short guy with a shaved head and facial ink. He bent down farther, and Camilla saw the crosses and skulls tattooed between his eyes. A former Zeta soldier.

"Who's this *chiquita*?" asked the other. He had even more ink, covering most of his face.

"Nina," Blanco said.

"Thought you were coming back to our place tonight, *jefe*," said the bald guy.

"Later," Blanco said.

"You said you had some stuff for us." The man's eyes narrowed, scrunching the tattoo and making the bones and skull seem to blur.

Blanco looked over. "What do you say, *mami chula*?"

Camilla shrugged. The more the merrier, even though three might be a bit hard to handle with a single needle, especially if these guys were former soldiers. Lots of older Zetas were former Mexican military. But these guys looked too young for that.

She could handle them. One stone, three birds.

"Sure, why not?" she said.

"Get in," Blanco said.

The Zeta twins chuckled and jumped in the back. The engine roared, and Blanco set off through the slums while the Zetas lit a joint.

Camilla took a hit when it was her turn, but she didn't inhale. She watched the road, trying to time this perfectly. But to her surprise, they were heading west.

"Yo, Blanco, where you going?" asked one of the men, apparently thinking the same thing—that they were moving into zone 1, Moretti territory.

She could even see the Four Diamonds slums rising in the distance. Damn, she was going to have to make a move soon.

"For a cruise, amigo," Blanco said. "Chill the fuck out."

In the rearview mirror, Camilla saw that one of the men had pulled a pistol.

"How fast does this bad boy go?" she asked.

Blanco grinned and pushed down on the pedal. "Fast enough we don't have to worry about Moretti bullets."

The Zetas laughed. "*¡Vámonos!*" one shouted.

The tires thumped over a pothole, the tattooed freaks bobbing up in the back seat without their seat belts to hold them in.

Camilla had a feeling this was going to hurt.

The car hit sixty on a bridge. She clicked on her seat belt and gave him a seductive smile.

"You like this, *mami*?" he asked, eyes on the road.

Subtly she reached for the needle, then looked in the rearview mirror. The Zeta had put his pistol away.

"You know how to make a girl wet," Camilla said with a seductive smile.

Blanco turned to focus his remaining eye on her.

"This is for Joaquín," she said, holding up the wrist with her brother's name tattooed on a cross. Her smile turned to a scowl, and before Blanco could react, she thrust the needle into his iris.

"What the fuck!" one of the Zetas yelled.

He reached over the back seat, but the car swerved as Blanco howled in pain, taking his hands off the steering wheel. A tire hit the curb and then the guardrail. Somehow, in the chaos, Blanco managed to pluck the needle out of his eye, right as she unbuckled his belt.

He pushed down on the brakes, but it was already too late.

Camilla braced herself and ducked as they rear-ended a parked car on the side of the road. The twins flew over the seat and hit the windshield as the steering wheel hit Blanco's neck so hard it snapped like a twig. Camilla's belt kept her from hitting the dashboard.

The horn kept blaring as smoke filled the vehicle.

She unlatched the door and forced it open. Stumbling out onto the sidewalk, she tried to orient herself. She was somewhere south of the Four Diamonds, which meant she wouldn't be alone for long.

Headlights shot over the bridge, and several voices rang out. She had to get out of here fast.

"Fucking *puta*," slurred a voice.

The guy with the skull tattoo was still alive. Half his body was through the windshield, and his skin smoked on the hot hood.

"Who are you?" he choked.

She wiped off her lipstick, feeling the fresh cut over her eye. It would leave another scar, but for a good cause.

"I'm Camilla Santiago, but you can call me Saint."

She bent down and took off her shoe. His pinned eyes widened as she swung the stiletto heel into his neck. Twisting the shoe, she tried to yank it out, but it was stuck.

The voices grew louder, and the car, a police cruiser, shot over the bridge. Camilla Santiago left her heel jammed in the man's neck, kicked off the remaining shoe, and ran away barefoot to catch a bus home.

-6-

Dominic Salvatore checked his wristwatch. Thirty minutes to midnight.

Go time.

The workers at the Port of Long Beach changed shifts soon. The window gave the Saints the perfect opportunity to strike at the head of the snake. And not just any snake. Dom and his undercover team were going after the anaconda.

The undeclared king of the concrete jungle, Don Antonio Moretti, head of the most powerful syndicate in the city.

To defeat evil, we must embrace it.

It was a twist on his father's motto, which Marks had warned him about. The Saints followed the law most of the time, but he knew that the time would come. And tonight could very well be that occasion.

"Button up," he said.

"Relax, boss," Moose said, patting his armored vest. "I'm good to go, baby."

"You got our IDs?" Dom asked, twisting around to the back seat.

Rocky pulled the badges out and handed them around. "We're good to go, boss."

Tooth laughed. "Dude, I look high as a kite in this pic, but hey, at least my hair looks good."

"You're a vain son of a bitch, you know that?" said Bettis. Clear tactical glasses covered his brown eyes, which were now focused on the rosary in his gloved hands.

"Got to look good at all times, Chaplain," said Tooth, playing up his Irish lilt. "Never know when I'm going to meet Miss Right."

Rocky broke out in his contagious chuckle. "By 'Miss Right,' do you mean 'lady of the evening'?"

Dom reached for the radio and flipped through the dozen stations broadcasting from the city. "*Good evening, all you sinners and saints,*" said the announcer. "*Got a few classic tracks coming up in a few minutes, but first we have a report from the sexiest meteorologist in the world, our own Regina Díaz.*"

Rocky chuckled in the back seat. "I love that woman."

"*Hi, all you beautiful angels, this is Regina Díaz, bringing you another shitty forecast of alkaline dust with a chance of acid rain . . .*"

Dom changed the station to some old-school rock as they sped toward their target. Nothing like some Led Zeppelin to get the blood flowing.

They passed a gas station with a line of vehicles snaking away almost a quarter mile. Horns blared, and people shouted as they waited hours for the precious fuel to run their aging vehicles.

Moose pulled down another street. A pharmacy on the corner, in the old Walgreens building, specialized in handing out RX-4 rations. A line of over a hundred waited outside, stretching into the adjacent city park.

Teenagers on scooters and motorcycles zipped around the streets, honking their horns and blaring music from rappers long dead and decomposed. In a way, it seemed as if the world had time-traveled back to the early 1990s. But plenty was different out here.

Technology had advanced in some countries, such as Japan and China, which had recovered from the economic collapse. They provided water desalination plants, radio and cell towers, and RX-4, the lifesaving antirad medicine.

"There she is," Rocky said. "The fortress in the wastes."

Dom turned for a view of the Moretti compound. The former Commerce Hotel and Casino. The Saints hadn't been able to get within half a mile of the modern-day castle. Don Antonio took his security seriously. He hired former military forces, spent millions on drones from China, and bought weapons off the black market in Mexico and Europe.

"Watch out!" Tooth yelled.

Moose slammed on the brakes as a shadowy figure darted in front of the vehicle. The man crouched down and bared his teeth. The headlights captured a face covered in open wounds and lesions.

"It's one of the freaks," Rocky said.

The guy took off running down the road, bent down, and climbed through an open storm sewer grate.

Bettis crossed his chest as Moose accelerated down the road.

"I haven't seen someone lookin' that bad for a while," Rocky said. "Amazing that guy is still alive."

"He won't be for long," Moose said. "If he doesn't get a dose of RX-Four soon, the virus will turn him mad."

Moose knew all about it because of Ray's youngest daughter. A tenth of the city now had the virus brought on by the Second Civil War.

They drove through the slums, heading west toward the ocean. An old pickup clunked along ahead, its bed full of migrant workers with masks and scarves wrapped around their faces.

Six men and three women all looked over as the Explorer passed them by. They were covered in dirt and dust from a day spent working construction.

The grit got in everything: hair, eyes, *lungs*.

These were the people Dom was trying to save. They were the honest, hardworking people trying to survive in the postapocalypse.

"Check your gear, check your buddy's gear, and get ready," Dom ordered.

The banter ceased, replaced by the clicks and clacks of preraid preparations. The men were all business now. Dom was extra alert from popping speed, because you didn't take a dull sword to fight a lion.

"All right, listen up," Dom said. "We stop this shipment of drugs, and we're going to sever an artery into the Moretti bank account."

"And we're also going to get more RX-Four to the people who need it the most," Moose added.

"And you're *sure* we can trust Marks?" Rocky asked.

Bettis and Tooth glared at the youngest guy on the team.

"I trust Marks with my life," Dom said.

"Me too," Tooth said. "And I damn sure trust him with *yours*."

Bettis slapped Rocky on the side of his head in an uncharacteristic show of frustration. "Marks would never sell us out, kid."

The SUV headlights slashed through the inky darkness, capturing the cracks in the road and the few other brave souls traveling at this hour.

Moose took the next left and drove toward a cluster of lights in the west. They parked on the side of a gravel road and shut off the lights.

Dom clipped his fake name tag onto his shirt, pulled a baseball cap over his thick hair, and secured his breathing apparatus.

A dozen massive silos rose before them, abandoned like the junkyard next door. The view confirmed that the Saints were on the east side, not far from the oil refinery where he had once fought the Apache.

That night, Marks had lost half his task force in an ambush by the Morettis. Tonight, Dom would get his revenge.

He looked at his watch again. Camilla would be hunting now, and Namid and Pork Chop were moving in to take the shipment of RX-4. Everything was in motion.

"Pray with me," Bettis said. He crossed his chest and whispered the Lord's Prayer. When he finished, Dom added the team motto. "To defeat evil, we must embrace it."

The men bowed their heads.

They got out of the car, and Moose opened the back to pull out two Russian RPG-7 launchers. They each took one, and Bettis grabbed the extra rockets.

Dom tried not to think of Camilla as he flashed the signal to advance toward the scrapyard. He led the Saints into an area of flattened and stacked auto bodies. Shipping containers, three high, blocked the view beyond, but they were close to the water now. The night reeked of dead fish and the sour scent of garbage.

Sneaking into the port wasn't going to be easy. Everything worth a damn in Los Angeles had to pass through the massive port, and everyone knew that it was really controlled by the crime families.

Dom took point, and the team fanned through the metal graveyard toward a block of abandoned warehouses. Graffiti marked the slanted carmine walls.

They walked down an alleyway between the structures. A ten-foot fence topped with razor wire greeted them on the other side. Beyond that, a field of weeds separated them from the Port of Long Beach, where cranes moved containers off ships from countries all around the world.

Just beyond the fences, in the center of the fields, was their first contact. A guard with a shotgun patrolled the area, his flashlight dancing across the ground. He stopped to light a cigarette on the other side of the fences.

Moose joined Dom behind some empty oil drums. This was the place he had scoped out a few nights ago. He pointed at the fence to their right, and Moose pulled back a panel they had already cut open. Dom slipped through and held it open for Moose, who unslung the RPG and passed it through first.

When they were through, they took up position behind a brick wall. Dom crawled over left of the wall and raised his carbine to the back of the man's head.

The Saints weren't in the business of killing people in cold blood, but this guy was going to get one hell of a headache in three . . . two . . .

Moose let out a low whistle, and the guard turned into a right hook that he never saw. He crumpled like a drunk after too many beers.

"Damn, baby," Moose said, rubbing his hand.

"Help me move him," Dom said.

Moose bent down, and together they dragged the unconscious man behind the wall, where they disarmed him, zip-tied his hands, and slapped duct tape over his mouth.

A minute later, the team was moving again.

Another guard stood in front of a shack overlooking rows of stacked shipping containers. He was too far away to sneak up on, so Dom improvised.

He handed Moose his rifle and removed his night-vision goggles.

"Rocky, you know the drill," Dom said. "Moose, cover us."

Moose nodded, readying his weapon.

"Hey, you know where pier ten is?" Dom asked as he walked across the yard, Rocky flanking him in the shadows.

The guard turned. "Who the fuck are you?"

Dom held up his fake badge just as the guard brought up a rifle. He went down from a whack to the back of the head from Rocky's pistol.

They zip-tied and duct-taped the unconscious guard before moving to the edge of the field, where they took cover behind a retaining wall. On the other side, mercury-vapor lamps left few shadows to hide in, and searchlights from the guard towers played over the terrain.

Port authority employees ran the derricks lifting containers off the freighters, and huge forklifts stacked them in place as armed guards hired by the mob stood watch. But the Saints wouldn't need to get up close to complete their mission.

Dom split them into teams.

Moose and Rocky went left; Tooth and Bettis went right with Dom.

Keeping low, they continued toward the docks, using containers and vehicles for cover. The main road accessing the ten piers and nearly seventy berths lay between them and the first of the ships.

Tooth found the target first.

Dom followed his finger toward a ship with a red stern and stripe on the side, docked at pier nine. Holding the spotting scope to his NVGs, he confirmed that it was the *Goomah*.

But something was wrong.

A gangplank had already been extended, and crates were being unloaded on hand forklifts.

"Shit, they're early," Dom muttered.

He clenched his jaw. The Saints were still in the game, but they would have to move fast.

Dom had considered a dozen ways to infiltrate the docks and take out the *Goomah*, from commandeering a small fishing vessel and ramming the ship with C4 to using scuba gear to mine the hull manually. But such heavy-handed methods would sink the ship at its berth, disrupting activity at the port, slowing commerce, and making life worse for the people of Los Angeles, whose lives the Saints had sworn to protect.

Dom had chosen a far easier option: the old-fashioned Russian rocket-propelled grenades that Moose and Tooth carried over their shoulders. They would leave one of the weapons behind to point a finger at the

Nevsky family. If they pulled this off, it would keep the peace treaty between the LAPD and the Morettis while pitting two crime families against each other.

Dom directed the Saints to an abandoned warehouse with a view of the port and the ships. Rocky and Bettis remained outside, guarding their escape route, while everyone else moved to the rooftop.

The groan and clatter of diesel engines muffled their steps as they climbed a ladder to the top. Dom was the first on the flat gypsum roof. He took up position on the north side and peered down at the road, where a convoy of garbage trucks had rounded the corner—ten of them, headed right for the *Goomah*.

"Shit," Tooth whispered. "That's the cavalry, and it's early."

A forklift drove the first stack of crates down a platform to the road as Moose and Tooth moved into position with their RPGs. Dom used his spotting scope to glass the area, focusing on the lead garbage truck, now parked beside the *Goomah*'s berth.

The Morettis were known for hiring muscle to help move their product.

Tonight, they had sent their bulldog, Mexican Mikey, or Mikey the Mutant, as some of his enemies called him.

Dom zoomed in on the psychopathic former MS-13 banger. He was the perfect example of what happened when people stopped taking RX-4 but continued using recreational drugs. Mikey and his men were well known for their barbaric violence. Some were even rumored to be cannibals.

Mikey yawned and hiked his pants up as he watched the crews work. Dom resisted the urge to blow his fat face off.

"Check out nine o'clock," Moose said.

Dom moved to look at a van driving toward pier 9. An hourglass symbol with a twisting strand of DNA inside—the logo of Horizon Bio-Limited, the Chinese company that manufactured RX-4—marked the side panel.

The van, like the garbage trucks, was just a front. The Morettis would move the shipment in the stolen van to a secret location, crush the drugs up, and sell them at a premium.

The van parked alongside the ship, and the Moretti soldiers loaded the back with the stolen crates of RX-4. Two SUVs followed the van out of the port, but they weren't going to make it far. His guys would intercept it before it ever made its destination.

Dom sent Namid a text message: *Package is heading to the party. Two of their friends are tagging along.* The reply flashed across the screen.

"Get ready," Dom said.

Moose and Tooth aimed their RPGs at the superstructure. Several well-placed explosions would destroy the bridge and badly damage the weather deck. They would then unload a few magazines into the other Moretti soldiers, shoot up Mikey and his men, and book it back to their Explorer.

Dom wiped the sweat from his brow with his upper arm, then pressed the scope back to his optics. He moved his finger to the trigger as Moose lowered his RPG.

Lights shot down the road to the east. Dom lowered his rifle and watched a dozen black armored LAPD cruisers race around the corner of the port entrance and onto the main road along the front of the piers.

"What the hell . . ." Tooth whispered.

Mikey and his crew didn't seem concerned at the sight of police. He walked toward the cruisers.

Dom centered his rifle scope on the men Stone had sent to collect, stopping on the pockmarked face of Lieutenant Billy Best, a corrupt cop who had been on the wrong side of the law since the Second Civil War. He limped away from his cruiser, using a cane.

Not shooting Mikey was hard, but resisting the urge to pull the trigger and erase that smug grin from Best's face was even harder.

Dom scanned the other officers, but they all wore masks. He moved the sight back to Mikey, who took a duffel bag from one of his men and then tossed it at the lieutenant's gimp leg.

"Piece of shit," Tooth mumbled.

"What do we do, boss?" Moose asked.

Dom deliberated for several seconds. They could disable the ship from here and make it back to the Explorer without getting gunned down, but the ensuing bloodbath could leave cops dead on the road, and it would break the treaty between the Morettis and Stone.

He didn't care about Best, but there were other men out there who didn't deserve to die. Men who were just looking after their families and trying to make a living in a corrupt system that rewarded evil men.

The Saints could still get the RX-4. Tonight could still be a victory.

"Son of a bitch," Dom said. "Fall back."

"You serious?" Tooth said.

Moose didn't move. "Boss, we can't just leave this shipment."

"Yeah, and that's Mikey the Mutant down there, man," Tooth said. "Please, *please*, let me cap that motherfucker."

Dom cursed under his breath. This was the best opportunity to hit Don Antonio where it mattered most. Aside from his family, his pocketbook was all he cared about.

"Wait until the cops are out of here," Dom said. "Then we open fire and haul ass home."

"Hell yeah," Moose whispered.

Tooth pushed the RPG launcher back up on his shoulder. Dom targeted the trucks with his rifle as the Moretti soldiers pushed crate after crate of the hybrid opiates down the ramp and loaded them into the garbage trucks.

Best took off with the money—his cut for turning a blind eye to one of the biggest drug shipments in the history of postwar Los Angeles.

"You bag of shit," Dom muttered.

The cars sped away, and as soon as they rounded the corner, he gave Tooth and Moose the green-light nod.

The RPGs thumped away, hitting the garbage trucks at the front and back of the convoy. Both vehicles exploded in fiery blasts.

Mexican Mikey, still standing in front of the lead vehicle, cartwheeled away, hitting the water like a fat kid doing a cannonball.

Dom squeezed the trigger of the M1A SOCOM 16, putting three rounds in the side of the middle truck. Then he took down two men who ran for cover. He finished his magazine, ejected it, and slapped in another.

Tooth and Moose fired off two more rockets, lighting the night up with brilliant fireballs. Silhouetted figures darted for cover. Two men burned on the pier, one rolling into the harbor to put out the flames. Another garbage truck exploded.

Dom finished off his second magazine and examined their handiwork in that stolen moment. The metal carcasses of the trucks burned on the road, but more crates remained on the ship.

Flashes of return fire forced Dom down. Both Tooth and Moose fired another rocket at the ship and took cover. The explosions boomed in the distance.

"Time to move," Dom said.

Moose reloaded the launcher. "Just one more, boss."

Rounds peppered the side of the building. Tooth abandoned his launcher and crawled after Dom, toward the exit ladder, while Moose fired his last rocket.

At the bottom, Bettis and Rocky waited with their weapons trained on any shadows that might be hostiles.

"You guys got to have all the fun," Rocky said.

Dom looked up as Moose climbed down the ladder. The moment his boots hit the dirt, the team dashed across the yard, between stacks of containers.

A few errant pot shots zipped past. Dom stopped abruptly as his team hotfooted it back to the Explorer. He took up position behind a forklift and waited to cover his team.

Two Moretti soldiers came running around a corner, and Dom fired a burst, catching one of them in the groin before either of them could bring up his rifle. As the first guy writhed, screaming in agony, Dom took down the other guy with a head shot.

"Let's go, man!" Moose yelled.

Still Dom lingered, firing at more Moretti soldiers advancing in the shadows.

Moose grabbed him and pushed him toward the truck. Breathing heavily, Dom sprinted to the Explorer, where Rocky waited behind the wheel. As soon as they were in, he floored it.

"What the hell was that about?" Moose said. "You could have gotten killed!"

"I knew what I was doing," Dom said. He coughed into his mask in a sudden spasm that he couldn't hold back. By the time it passed, he could taste the metallic hint of blood.

"You okay?" Rocky asked.

"It's nothing."

He turned to look out the back window. Flames from the burning garbage trucks fingered into the night sky.

He couldn't believe their good luck tonight. They had just taken out a huge shipment, killed Mexican Mikey, and, if they were *really* lucky, picked up a van full of RX-4 to redistribute to those who couldn't afford it.

A half smile cracked on his face as he pulled out his cell phone to text Namid and Pork Chop. But when he picked it up, he saw a message from Lieutenant Marks: *Stay in the dugout. Our team is taking the field.*

The lifelong Los Angeles Dodgers fan always used baseball code words, and Dom knew exactly what this meant. It was an order to stay on the sidelines and let the corrupt cops take their cut.

Not anymore, Dom thought as he put the phone away.

"It's all good in the hood," Rocky said, looking over from the wheel. "'Cause the Saints are basically motherfucking Robin Hood."

"Hell yeah, baby!" Moose said, slapping the dashboard.

Bettis kissed his rosary and nodded at Dom, but Dom didn't feel like celebrating yet. He couldn't help but wonder whether he had just dumped fuel on a raging fire.

-7-

"How the fuck did this happen?" Vinny Moretti asked.

Don Antonio Moretti sat behind his mahogany desk, drinking espresso and watching his nephew pace before the bulletproof window of his office. The young man had a lot to learn before becoming a captain.

The debacle at the port showed Vinny's lapse of judgment in an area of their business that Antonio took very seriously: security. But Antonio worried more about his son. The young man didn't know the first thing about the family business. Indeed, he seemed to excel in one subject only: pussy.

Not unusual for a twenty-year-old kid, but in this world, even pussy could kill you.

Antonio enjoyed another luxurious sip of espresso.

"These assholes are dead men," Vinny said. He turned to Doberman. "Tell the handlers to stop feeding the dogs. I want them starving by the time we find the men responsible for tonight."

Doberman hurried out to relay the order.

Antonio checked the clock on the wall behind his desk. It was almost 2:00 a.m. He didn't do well without sleep. Fatigue fueled anger, and when he got angry, things didn't go well. That was why he left most of the nightly work to younger men. Hustling was for the soldiers trying to make a name.

But tonight, he didn't trust the soldiers, the made men, or even his captains. Someone had betrayed him at the port, threatening his operation for the first time in years. It would be weeks, maybe longer, before they could replenish their supply, and meanwhile, their customers would cross over to the competition to buy their drugs.

There were plenty of excuses so far, and his job was to filter through them and figure out what happened and who was responsible. The future of the business depended on his ability to find the truth.

Vinny was nervous, and he should have been. This port was his responsibility.

Christopher was nervous too, sitting in a leather chair in front of Antonio's desk with an unlit cigar in his mouth. He massaged his thick gray goatee while his eyes rested on the gold-framed Italian painting hanging on the wall next to Antonio's desk, depicting the Battle of Salamis.

"Tonight, we were the Persians," Christopher said. "The question is, Who played us? Esteban, you think? Or maybe Miguel, if he found out about Mariana?"

Antonio looked at the painting of Greek ships ramming the Persians in the straits between Piraeus and Salamis. He was a student of history and loved a good underdog, probably because he himself had been an underdog for years.

Easier to fight when you have nothing to lose than when you have everything to lose.

Tonight, someone had gotten the better of them, and his gut told him it was an underdog, and not either of the Vega brothers. This wasn't Esteban's or Miguel's style. They took credit for their attacks.

The mahogany double doors opened, and Marco Moretti walked in. His fancy Italian shoes clicked on the marble floor.

Captain Lino De Caro followed the prince and heir to the Moretti empire into the room. Both men were still in their suits. Marco looked annoyed to be here, probably because it took him away from his favorite pursuit.

You finally give him a chance, and he acts like an asshole, Antonio thought. Perhaps it was a mistake asking his son to come here.

"We're all clear outside," Lino said. "I've doubled our men at every checkpoint within two miles of here, and Doberman deployed the drones to search for heat signatures. No one will get through our net."

Antonio gestured for the men to sit at the chestnut war table. Marco took up position behind the chairs, as usual when he was invited to meetings.

He wanted a seat at the table, but he wasn't ready. Not even close. Billions of dollars had been made around this table over the years, and tonight they were discussing a massive loss. If Marco wanted to learn how things worked, this was a good start.

Antonio slammed his cup down, shattering the fragile china and spilling espresso over the table. He clenched his jaw, took in a breath, and calmly walked over to his seat at the head of the table.

Slowly he pulled the red leather wingback chair out and sat.

"Someone tell me how the *fuck* this happened," Antonio said.

"I really don't know," Frankie said quietly, chewing on the wooden end of a match.

"It could have been Miguel Vega," Yellowtail said. "If he knows it was us who grabbed Mariana."

"They aren't that stupid or that smart," Lino replied.

Yellowtail leaned forward, and the chain holding his lucky cross fell out of his shirtfront.

"Then it had to be that gimp lieutenant," Carmine said. "Fat fucking sack of shit. The attack started as soon as he took the payoff money and left."

Vinny shook his head. "I don't think so. My contact works for Best and is not a stupid cop. Shit, he just sold us the new ARX160s last week. He's never fucked around with us."

"He's still a dirty rat-fucking cop," Lino said.

While the soldiers and captains threw in their opinions, Antonio scrutinized them like a poker player watching his opponents. Studying their features, mannerisms, and posture, looking for a tell that any of them were involved in the betrayal that had cost him the biggest shipment ever.

He couldn't count anything or anyone out right now.

Lino turned his head slightly to play with the hoop in his left earlobe. It was his nervous tic when he felt guilty for letting Antonio down—which told him Lino wasn't responsible for tonight.

Yellowtail was a loyal soldier who would never consider such a thing. The big guy had taken more bullets for the family than everyone else in this room combined. That didn't mean Antonio trusted him fully, though.

Antonio trusted only one man: his brother. And Christopher was suspicious too. He had his gaze on Frankie, who had expressed a desire for more dealing territory over the past few months.

There was also Carmine, who had never liked the deal in place with Chief Stone and the LAPD. He and Frankie both would have preferred just to gun down any cop who got in their way—something Antonio could not allow. Dead cops were bad for business.

But neither man would make a move like this . . . would they? They had been with Antonio all these years, helping him build the empire.

The doors opened again, and Vito waddled in with Doberman. They both carried rocket launchers.

"Fucking Russians," Vito growled in his raspy voice, holding up a launcher. "Bastards left these behind."

Antonio could smell Vito from where he stood—body odor and booze. He had been drinking heavily since taking shrapnel at Long Beach last week.

"So it was Sergei Nevsky," Yellowtail said. "He's got bigger balls than I thought."

Antonio stood, folded his hands together, then put them behind his back as he walked over to the window.

Below, six men and two dogs were standing guard around the fountain in the center of the courtyard. A twelve-foot wall surrounded the two-acre compound, separating the lush gardens and fountains from the brown badlands beyond.

Inside the gates, Antonio had constructed his own paradise, retrofitting the hotel into a lavish fortress.

Spotlights raked over the perfectly kept grass inside the compound, illuminating the mausoleums he had built for those they had lost over the years. Raffaello Tursi was interred inside one, next to his wife. Both victims of the Vega family.

Antonio looked past the crypts and the walls, to the cracked dirt and abandoned buildings beyond, where his drones patrolled the darkness. He wasn't worried about an attack from the Russians, because Sergei Nevsky wasn't responsible for this attack. He had chilled Stoli in his veins, but he wasn't insane. And attacking the Moretti operation was suicide.

"This wasn't Lieutenant Best," Antonio said with his back to his men. "It wasn't Mikey the Mutant or the Vega brothers. It wasn't a betrayal from within, nor was it the work of a gang."

He turned from the window.

"Yeah, it was the Russians," Marco said, pointing toward the weapon.

Antonio smiled at his son. Still so much to learn.

He narrowed his eyes. "You really think Sergei would be that naive or that his soldiers would do something so stupid?"

Marco shrugged, looking back at his father with eyes that still lacked confidence. It was the gaze of a boy, not a man.

"There's only one group out there that could do something like this," Christopher said. It seemed he and Antonio had come to the same conclusion.

"This was the Saints," Antonio said. "*I conigli.*"

He waited for it to sink in.

"But . . . how the hell could they know about one of our shipments?" Vinny stammered. "Of all the ships in the piers, they knew the exact moment when to attack," Vinny said.

"They were tipped off," Antonio said. "But not by Billy Best. That fat idiot knows that doing so would be a death sentence. There's another rat aboard this ship."

The silence in the room was palpable, and again Antonio's gaze swept from face to face.

"How do you know it wasn't the Vegas planting Russian launchers to cover their tracks?" Marco asked.

The hard look from his father made his cheeks flush.

"Right, they wouldn't have destroyed the food," he muttered. "They would have stolen it and sold it."

"Precisely," Antonio said. "Same with our other competitors. But the Saints and their allies, whoever they are, want the food off the streets. They made it look like the Russians because they also want us to go to war. I've done the same thing many times."

He looked to Christopher and nodded. Time to get their special guest.

Marco stepped over to his father, standing right in front of the table. The other men waited for the crown prince to speak.

Was this the moment Antonio had been waiting for? The moment his son stepped up to the plate? He still hadn't spilled the blood of an enemy or been face-to-face with death. He still didn't know what sacrifice was, and that was partly Antonio's fault. He had given Marco everything through the years: fast cars, designer clothes from Europe, cash to throw around. He had even sent him to the best school in Italy, and while Marco had learned all about the world and business, he had no idea how to survive on his own.

He was weak because he had never had to fight for anything.

Sometimes, Antonio wished his son were more like Vinny. But he also remembered a time when Vinny was much like Marco.

"Let me end the Saints once and for all," Marco said. "It's time to hang them from the overpasses so the city can see who's really in charge: Don Antonio Moretti."

Antonio felt the grin forming, but he didn't let it out.

"I *can* do this," Marco said. "The Saints are just a few vigilantes hiding behind masks. But there are allies out there—people helping them who know their identities. People who don't want us to take over the most precious resource in this city: water."

The other men all seemed to scrutinize Marco at the same time. Antonio knew what they were thinking: that his son was right, but he would never be able to bring these seasoned guerrilla fighters out of the woodwork.

They were as elusive as cockroaches, and as hard to kill.

The Saints were more dangerous than any other threat. Antonio had met his other enemies face-to-face at one time or another. He knew where they slept at night. The Saints, on the other hand, were cowards who attacked in the dark. And the people protecting them were also cowards.

Chief Stone, the City Council, and the mayor benefited from millions of Moretti dollars. They claimed even they didn't know the identities of these rats, and so did all the other cops on his payroll.

But someone knew. Someone *had* to know.

Lino pulled out his cell phone and stepped away.

"You got to be fucking kidding me," he said.

Antonio's gaze went from his son to his trusted bodyguard, who put the phone away and cursed.

"You're not going to believe this, but our shipment of RX-Four was also hit," Lino said. "Our van was destroyed, and the RX-Four is missing."

Antonio wanted to pull out his gun and fire it at the bulletproof window. Instead, he said softly, "Put a million dollars in silver on each of their heads. No . . ."

He hadn't built this empire by being cheap. He had built it by spending money to make money, and the Saints were costing him a shitload of it.

"Two million a head," Antonio said. "Talk to your contacts on the streets, and the cops on your routes. Get the word out any way you can."

Christopher opened the door and stepped inside with two associates who held a woman by the arms. Her mouth was gagged.

The narco queen didn't look so regal without makeup. Her matted hair and the bruises on her arms and legs didn't help.

"Who's that?" Marco asked.

Mariana squirmed in the grip of the men.

"A feisty bitch, is who," Christopher replied. He pinched her cheek. "Or *puta*, as your people say, right?"

She struggled harder, eyes wide with rage, veins popping out on her forehead.

"This is Mariana López," Antonio said. "And she is going to help us win the war against the Vegas. Aren't you?"

She glared at him, growling incoherently through the gag.

"Oh yes, you are," Antonio said, "like it or not."

He looked around at his men.

"You fucked up tonight—all of you. But fortunately, I took matters into my own hands the other night to grab Mariana." He shook his head wearily. "Get out of my sight," he growled.

The group got up from their chairs and left the room, and the guards took Mariana away. But he stopped his son with a snap of his fingers. Marco walked over, and Antonio placed a hand on his shoulder.

"You want to help the family?" Antonio asked.

Marco nodded.

"Lucia and I never wanted this for you, but if this is what you want, I'll give you a chance. You help my men find the Saints, and you'll earn your spot at this table."

Marco grinned proudly, but Antonio slapped the grin off his face.

Reaching up, Marco put a hand on his cheek, his eyes as wide with rage as Mariana's had been.

"Do not underestimate these men," Antonio said. "They are not sheep like the other cops in this city. These men are *wolves*."

-8-

The moon broke through the clouds over Central Los Angeles, then quickly hid again.

Dom rolled down the window of their burner vehicle, a black pickup sporting a brush guard and oversized tires. They had parked on South Vermont Avenue, on the left side of the street next to Machado Lake and the cracked dirt of an old park. A junkie staggered and jerked through the shadows like some kind of zombie. He found a park bench and curled up to sleep. Dom filled his lungs with sultry air carrying a bouquet of jasmine and rotting garbage.

Sweet and putrid—that was the scent of Los Angeles.

It was going on three in the morning, but Dom wasn't tired. After the successful raid on the port, he was still riding high on adrenaline. Or maybe it was the last of the Dexedrine pills.

He didn't need more to stay awake. Knowing that the Morettis had woken their leader in the middle of the night with the disastrous news of the attack was enough to keep Dom going.

But the text from Lieutenant Marks kept resurfacing in his mind. He had disobeyed a direct order from his commanding officer, a man he respected like a second father.

He checked his phone again and found a text message from Camilla.

Back home. Got three good tips tonight.

He smiled. She had taken out three Vega sicarios. The Saints were having a monster night.

Nice, he texted back.

Moose looked over at the cell phone. "That Cam?"

"Yeah, and she did good. Real good."

"Yeah, baby, that's what I'm talkin' about." Moose rubbed his hands together. "We're on fire."

"The night isn't over yet."

While most of the team was already back at the safe house, Dom and Moose were out here, making sure the stolen RX-4 got to those who needed it most.

"Namid and Pork Chop should be here any minute," Dom said, glancing down at his watch.

He checked the road again when he heard the slow hum of a Mosquito. The city-operated truck with the Horizon Bio-Limited logo slowly rounded the corner, bristles sweeping the street under the belly of the vehicle. Oscillating sprinklers on the bed sprayed chemical mist from a blue tank into the air to neutralize toxic chemicals.

Rumor had it that Antonio Moretti was fueling a significant portion of the operation, which helped him look like a philanthropist to those who didn't know him. It seemed he was trying to be the Pablo Escobar of Los Angeles since the Vega family clearly wasn't interested in the role.

And you'll die like Pablo, Dom thought.

He checked the west side of the street. Harbor College, now a housing project, had been turned into a campground. Tents were scattered over the dry lawn where the overflow of refugees slept. All across the city, the processing centers, where some people waited months to find placement, were bulging at the seams.

"Poor bastards," Moose said.

Dom checked his cell phone. A message buzzed from Namid. They were on their way. The Mosquito hummed by, cleaning the streets and the air.

He rolled up his window and tightened the filtration mask on his face. He didn't know how the chemical shit worked, and he didn't like breathing it in on some city official's blithe assurances that it was safe.

An engine rumbled in the distance.

"Here we go," Dom said.

He ducked at the sound of a second car, this one with a supercharged engine.

"That ain't Namid," Moose said, leaning out of view.

Two black Mercedes sedans raced down the road. They zipped past the pickup and swerved around the next corner.

"Morettis," Dom said.

"They're all over the place."

They sat up, and Dom put the pickup in gear.

Another pair of headlights hit the road a few minutes later. He recognized the brown truck instantly. It was one of several they had stolen from an old warehouse. The UPS label was still visible on the side.

Namid and Pork Chop sat in the front seats, looking ahead as they passed the pickup. Pulling onto the road, Dom followed them.

Several cars drove toward them. One swerved into the center lane, then back, and Moose readied his Beretta PMX submachine gun just in case they stopped.

The first car passed, and someone leaned out the window, screaming.

Dom reached over to Moose as he raised his weapon.

"Just some teenagers," he said.

"Dangerous place to be at three a.m.," Moose said, relaxing in his seat.

"We all did stupid shit back in the day. Remember that time your bro and I about got into it on the basketball courts at one in the morning after sharing a case of beer?"

"Which time?" Moose laughed. "I remember a bunch of late nights I had to stop you from beating each other's asses."

They chuckled as Dom followed the delivery truck down another street toward their destination: the former Kaiser Permanente South Bay Medical Center complex, now a city-operated hospital the locals called Hope Hotel.

It was one of the most overcrowded and understaffed hospitals left in the city. Most of its patients suffered from radiation poisoning, so Dom made sure they were supplied with RX-4 as often as possible.

He had already made a call on his burner phone to let his doctor friend, Abdul, know that the shipment was coming, but Namid and Pork Chop knew better than to drive right up and park outside.

Two hospital employees smoking on the corner outside paid no attention to the brown truck pulling up on the street outside the entrance bay to the ER.

Dom drove the pickup to a parking lot, secluded from view. He looked at the hospital for a moment, wondering how his mom was doing inside. This was home for her now.

He tried not to think about her—how the grief had finally driven her crazy, sending her outside to search for Monica. All those days outside without a mask. Now she was here, kept alive by the very drug they were now delivering.

"Stay with the truck," he said to Moose. "And watch our back."

Moose kept the truck running as Dom hopped out and crossed the parking lot.

A guy in scrubs walked out of the ER. "You can't park there!" he yelled.

A security guard followed the doctor outside.

Headlights hit the road, stopping Dom before he could cross. He fiddled with his dust mask and pulled the bill of his baseball cap down.

Another doctor wearing a mask and scrubs showed up at the entrance to the ER. Dom recognized the caramel skin of his old friend Abdul. He jogged out and waved to a drop-off zone.

The doc looked down the street in both directions before stepping back into the shadows. Pork Chop and Namid drove the truck back into the open bay, and Dom crossed over to the parking lot, nodding at the two Saints. He couldn't see their features, and they couldn't see his, but they wore the same gear and recognized him by that alone.

"You got somewhere safe to store this?" Pork Chop asked the doctor.

Abdul stepped into the light, eyes flitting from mask to mask. Then he ran a hand through his graying hair. He was one of the best docs in the city, practically living in the hospital. He had patched Dom up after a bullet a year ago, and they had been friends ever since.

Dom trusted the guy with his life—and with his secret, which meant basically the same thing.

Pork Chop and Namid opened the back doors, exposing the interior of the delivery van, stacked with the RX-4 boxes.

"Make sure this gets to the people that need it most," Pork Chop said.

Abdul smiled warmly. "Thank you. I'll make sure."

The other doctor, some twenty years younger, looked away. "I don't want any part of this."

"We're doctors, Javier," Abdul said. "We're here to save lives, and this will save a lot. Now, get back inside and keep quiet."

Javier looked at them all in turn and folded his arms across his chest.

"Better keep this between us," Namid said.

"Yeah," Pork Chop replied, taking a step toward the doctor.

Javier dropped his arms to his side and started walking back to the parking lot. He was halfway there when screeching tires sounded.

The five of them turned to look down the street, where the two Moretti Mercedeses came squealing around the corner.

Dom reached for the sidearm tucked under his shirt.

Only ten minutes had passed, and someone had already sold them out from inside the hospital. But the Saints knew what to do.

"Namid, grab our weapons," Pork Chop said.

The Mojave warrior jumped inside the back of the delivery truck and pulled out two automatic rifles. He tossed one to Pork Chop before moving for cover.

"Get out of here!" Dom shouted to Abdul, waving. "We'll deal with these guys."

Namid shouldered his rifle and fired. Rounds spiderwebbed the windshield of the first car. The driver threw on the brakes, screeching to a stop.

The doors swung open, and shooters jumped out using them as cover.

Namid held his fire until one of the men popped up to return fire. A head shot knocked him right back down. Pork Chop fired a burst into the other door, dropping the hidden soldier.

The second car stopped and disgorged four more Moretti men.

Automatic gunfire chattered in the night. Rounds punched through metal and shattered glass.

Dom squeezed off calculated shots and then dived for cover behind a parked car. A flurry of bullets chased him, deflating both rear tires.

He looked back at the loading bay where Abdul had taken refuge. He hit the door and leaned down, waving at Javier.

"Javier, get in here!" he yelled.

The other doctor, Javier, was trapped in the parking lot a few cars ahead of Dom.

"I'll cover you!" Dom shouted.

The young doc hesitated, then nodded.

"Go!" Dom yelled. He stood and fired off several rounds, giving the guy a chance to get into the bay. He rolled under just as the door closed.

"Changing!" Namid yelled.

Pork Chop and Dom laid down suppressive fire as they dashed across the parking lot. Car windows shattered all around them, and alarms blared.

The four Moretti soldiers were tactically trained, taking turns to fire and keeping the Saints pinned down. And Dom knew that it was just a matter of time before reinforcements joined them.

He cursed as he punched in a new magazine. It wasn't supposed to go down this way. It was supposed to be an easy in-and-out, but someone in the hospital was a fucking rat.

The Morettis had moles everywhere. Dom prayed that none of them had seen Abdul or Javier.

He looked over at Namid, who bolted for the vehicle Dom was hiding behind. A flanking Moretti soldier made a run for their position with a rifle.

"Down!" Dom yelled. He grabbed Namid, pulling him to cover as bullets ripped through the tire and chipped the pavement.

Dom got up and fired several rounds. A few cars down, Pork Chop stood and fired at the approaching Moretti soldier, hitting him in the neck and face, but not before he got off a shot. It hit Dom square in the chest, knocking him on his butt.

He felt as if a mule had kicked him in the ribs. He could hear Namid yelling over the din of gunfire, but he couldn't answer. Dom had been shot before, but he didn't remember it hurting this bad.

A good sign, he realized. The last time, he was in shock and hardly felt anything. This time, his vest had taken all the impact.

Namid helped him sit up, and Dom opened his eyes to the same postapocalyptic cityscape—the jagged edges of bombed high-rises in the distance, torched vehicles and crumbling streets, and gunfire.

He blinked away the stars, still trying to catch his breath.

Namid fired off several bursts. "They're closing in," he said in the respite.

He looked down at Dom, fear in his eyes. But Dom knew that the Mojave tracker wasn't afraid for himself—he feared leaving his four-year-old kid and his pregnant wife.

Dom forced himself up, fighting the pain. He glanced around the bumper to see a Moretti soldier striding toward them, shoulder-firing a rifle. Two more remained at the car, using the doors as cover.

A bullet zipped past Dom's head, and he pulled back.

Motion flashed in the parking lot across the road. He sneaked another look as the high beams from a pickup dazzled the Moretti shooters. The guy on the driver's side of the Mercedes turned to fire, but too late. The truck's brush guard crushed him against the car.

Moose leaned out the window, his hat catching on the side and falling onto the street. He angled a sawed-off shotgun at the other two men and fired a blast into each, knocking them off their feet.

Namid bent down and helped Dom up and across the parking lot, where Pork Chop met them, sweeping with his rifle for contacts.

They hurried to the street, where Moose backed the truck up.

"Get in!" he yelled.

With Namid's help, Dom climbed in on the passenger side. Then he jumped into the back with Pork Chop.

Moose hit it, and the tires squealed. He sped away from the hospital, leaving the lifesaving RX-4 drugs and a pile of dead Morettis behind.

"Hell yeah, baby!" Moose yelled, pounding the wheel.

Dom cracked a pained smile.

Tonight was a good night, a much-needed win for the Saints. But it would take more than a few dead Moretti soldiers to reclaim the city from evil.

* * *

Vinny sat at a blackjack table at the Golden Oyster, looking out at the degenerates around him. Quite a few for this early hour.

It was almost four, and he had decided to come here after the disaster at the port, and the meeting that followed back at the compound. Across town, Moretti soldiers were looking for the missing RX-4 shipment, and he was monitoring the situation from the blackjack table.

Vinny looked over at the Moretti associates standing guard nearby, then at the other tables—guys in business suits at one, hoodies and sweats at the others. Businessmen and gangsters, all trying to squeeze in a gambling win and a bit more alcohol before the sun came up on another day.

But Vinny wasn't here for either of those things. He had come for the one thing that gave him comfort: Adriana. She was working the night shift, serving cocktails to men and a few women who were partying with the associates and rich businessmen.

Some came from other countries; others were contractors who had survived the war and had come to rebuild housing complexes that weren't much better than slums.

Vinny tried not to watch Adriana as she brought more drinks to a group of Chinese men who owned construction companies that had built the Four Diamonds. They were here for a new project, looking to cash in on a massive complex that would help with the refugee crisis—something the Chinese knew a lot about.

"Mr. Moretti, it's your turn," said the dealer. He tapped the felt, then smiled politely, his mustache curling around his lips.

"When you're ready, sir," he said.

Vinny looked down at a jack and a deuce in front of him. The dealer had a queen next to a card facedown.

"Hit me," Vinny said.

The dealer peeled an ace off the deck. Vinny cursed under his breath and checked the three hundred dollars in chips he had wagered on the hand.

"Hit m—"

A voice boomed behind him. "Vin!"

He turned in his chair to see Doberman running over.

"What?" Vinny said.

Doberman panted, bending over slightly. The dealer and the three other blackjack players looked over.

"What, dude?" Vinny asked.

Doberman glanced around at the onlookers, then jerked his chin for Vinny to follow. He looked back at the table one last time to see a six, giving him nineteen.

"Stay," Vinny said.

The dealer flipped over his facedown card to reveal another queen. "Sorry, Mr. Moretti," he said.

Vinny cursed again as the dealer scooped his chips away. He took his remaining chips and followed Doberman toward the lobby, sneaking one last look at Adriana as she bent down to place a cocktail on the table.

That got his attention, and he halted.

"Vin!" Doberman shouted.

She looked over at him but didn't raise a hand, which could attract some unwanted attention.

"God damn it," Doberman said. "We got a major fucking problem, man!"

Vinny followed him into the lobby and then outside.

"What is so important?"

Doberman shook his head. "I just got word about that missing RX-Four shipment. It was dropped off at Hope Hotel."

"Dropped off?"

"One of our guys at the hospital called it in to Joey's crew. When he showed up, they were ambushed. Six of our guys are dead, and the RX-Four is inside the hospital now, out of our reach."

"Wait, back up," Vinny said. "Joey's dead?"

Doberman nodded.

"Let's go," Vinny said.

He led them into the parking lot. Just when the violence was supposed to end with the new Vega peace treaty, another enemy had wiped out an entire crew.

Doberman drove them away from the Golden Oyster and down the brightly lit strip of the Goldilocks Zone. Intoxicated rich customers walked down the sidewalks, leaving the clubs with their bodyguards.

Vinny ignored them, his heart pounding.

For eight years, he had achieved success after success: infiltrating the LAPD without getting killed; kidnapping Carly Sarcone and killing her father, Enzo. Traveling to Mexico, where he almost died at the hands of pirates first and then the Mexican military, only to secure their current deal with Eduardo Nina, mortal enemy of Esteban Vega.

And he had done evil things that still haunted him. From killing Isao Yamazaki after guaranteeing his safety, to pouring acid down Chuy's throat—a man who had been Vinny's friend.

All those sacrifices, crimes, and close calls would count for nil if the Saints got their way. Making captain was fading away before his eyes, and at this rate Doberman would never get made. The elusive vigilantes had destroyed a huge shipment of drugs, stolen the RX-4, and killed Joey and his crew.

Doberman drove out of the protected zone and entered the slums that began two blocks away. It was hard for Vinny to feel too angry over his situation when he saw people sleeping on benches or in ratty tents, their bellies empty.

His life was paradise compared to this. When he had first met Adriana, she, too, was sleeping in a tent but was too embarrassed to tell him. They used to screw in his car or in one of several hotels in the Goldilocks Zone.

It wasn't until he followed her home after one of those all-night sessions that he saw where she really lived, not far from the park they were passing now.

Doberman gunned it as they entered light traffic. He weaved around slower vehicles, speeding toward the hospital.

Vinny felt his phone buzz. He pulled it out and saw that it was his father.

Flashing lights in the distance distracted him—blue and red strobes from dozens of police cruisers. The cops had already locked down the area.

Doberman kept a respectful distance, pulling to the side of the road. Vinny spotted the two Mercedeses that Joey and his men had driven here. Even from this distance, he could see the bullet holes speckling the sides. Bodies covered with white sheets lay in the street.

Vinny's cell phone buzzed again, and he brought it to his ear.

"Hello?"

"Get the fuck back to the compound," said his father.

"On my way."

Vinny hung up and told Doberman to pull up closer. He drove toward the taped-off area that gave them a view of the street. For a moment, they sat there, staring at the shrouded corpses of men they had fought beside for years.

Joey, only a few years older than Vinny, was a personal friend. A made guy who had helped run a dealer spot outside the Four Diamonds. Now he was dead, slaughtered by the Saints.

Vinny clenched his jaw in rage. He wondered who these men were who could be so stupid and so brave.

Were they his age? Or were they older men like his uncle and his father, men who had experience fighting wars?

Whoever it was, they were well trained and understood what it took for an underdog to win a battle. Their guerrilla tactics continued to take gangsters off the streets, and Vinny began to fear that he was next.

"My uncle was right when he said these men are wolves, but I'll be damned if Marco gets them first," Vinny said.

Doberman glanced over.

"The Saints might have won this battle, but we will crush them in the war," Vinny said. "This is how I make captain, and how you get made."

-9-

Ray Clarke nursed a coffee on his way to the hospital. He drove his Audi alone this morning. Tommy was still inside the intensive care unit, but Ray wasn't here to check on his new partner.

He was here to see the handiwork of what could only be the Saints, and to figure out who their inside source was. After the port attack and the hijacking of the RX-4 shipment, the Morettis were going to be knocking on doors, and he wanted to have something for them when they came knocking on his. Any pragmatic man would do the same.

If he wants to stay alive.

He parked in a blocked-off area with several other city vehicles. The sun hid behind clouds and a thick layer of haze over the city, but he could clearly see the crime scene ahead. The Saints had left behind their calling card: dead Morettis.

Bloody white sheets still covered eight corpses, and the forensic units were busy working the scene. He walked past them, nodding at one of his buddies in uniform.

Dressed in jeans and a black sleeveless T-shirt that showed off the tattoos on his dark skin, Ray didn't look much like a cop this morning, but that was the point. He didn't want to draw attention to his unofficial business.

He took a drag off a cigarette, filling his lungs with chemicals on top of those already in the air. A bandanna hung loosely around his neck, but he didn't bother using it this morning.

Everyone was going to die, and he had the feeling that a bullet would bring him down before lung cancer ever did.

He flipped his shades down over his eyes as the sun peeked through the clouds. Keeping his distance, he examined the scene. The road and parking lot looked like a war zone: empty bullet casings littering the asphalt, broken windows, bullet holes, and dried or drying blood.

The Saints had had one hell of a night.

They thought they were some sort of superheroes, or Robin Hood and his merry men, or some such shit. But the team was engaging in outlawry with its tactics. Whoever they were, they didn't seek warrants or ask questions. Not that Ray did either, but still . . .

Cops had one all-important law to follow: not to fuck with the crime families. And certainly not to kill any of their men.

The Saints thought they were helping. But in fact, they were making things worse for this city and the cops, especially now. They had broken the deal between Chief Stone and Don Antonio Moretti.

That was what the assholes didn't seem to understand. They were running through a minefield that had no end.

But why? What would drive them on this suicide mission? Ray had a feeling it was some sort of vendetta against the Moretti and Vega families. Maybe they all were just batshit crazy.

Anyone else might have said the same thing about Ray. After all, he was playing both sides, having just sold the ARX160s and GLX160s to Vinny Moretti. But playing with fire was always his thing. It made him feel alive.

He finished off his coffee and tossed the empty cup onto an overfilled trash barrel as he walked through the parking lot. The RX-4 would be long gone by now, already getting to those who needed it most. Ray couldn't blame the Saints for that. Stealing it and giving it to the impoverished did help save lives in the short term. But it would mean more dead locals when, and not *if*, the Morettis retaliated.

There was a pact between good and evil in the City of Angels, and Ray was only trying to keep that contract in place. Maybe, just maybe, the Morettis would see these as the actions of a vigilante group that wasn't connected to the LAPD, but he had his doubts. And Don Antonio didn't forgive.

Ray glanced up at the side of the hospital as he walked to the entrance, checking which windows had a view of the road and the parking lot paved with empty brass.

It looked as though a real firefight had gone down here. And once again the Saints had made it out apparently unscathed. But even superheroes died eventually.

He walked inside the packed emergency room. People with radiation poisoning, people with injuries from domestic assaults or casual street violence—the sights were all pretty typical.

He showed his badge to a hospital guard wearing baggy pants and dirty glasses. The guy looked like a washout from the police academy.

"Go ahead," the man said.

Medical personnel hustled past as Ray approached a checkpoint. He kept his cool, trying to blend in with the hospital staff and people visiting their families. Signs led him to the administration office, where he stopped and knocked.

A heavyset woman with very short hair studied a stack of papers on her metal desk. "What?" she asked, hardly looking up.

Ray flashed his million-dollar smile.

"Detective Ray Clarke"—he leaned in to look at her name tag—"Ms. Kingsley."

"I already talked to the cops," she said. "I have no idea where the RX-Four is."

"Of course you don't, and I'm not here to ask you about that. I'm here to see who was on duty last night."

She glanced up, clearly annoyed.

"I already handed that over too." Raising a brow and tilting her head slightly, she said, "You got a badge, Detective . . ."

"Clarke." He gave her a quick look at his badge and snapped the leather case shut.

"Dr. Jennifer Collins, Dr. Abdul Hogan, and Dr. Amelia Garcia were on duty last night, but they all went home," she said. "For a full roster of staff, I suggest you check with Sergeant Smith."

He nodded. "Thanks for the info, darlin'."

She rolled her eyes, and Ray went to the third floor, pausing when he saw that it was the radiation ward. He hated visiting places like this. Most of these people were in bad shape—covered in lesions, bald, with failing organs. Chances were, some of that RX-4 was already up here.

He opened the door and walked past a room where a family huddled around the bed of a kid no older than his youngest boy, Jamal.

"Can I help you?" a nurse asked.

Ray looked down, obscuring his face from a direct view.

"Yeah, I need to ask your patients some questions," he said, flashing his badge again.

The young girl looked at it and said, "About the shooting?"

"Yeah. I want to know if anyone saw anything."

She hesitated, as if unsure whether she should talk.

"Go ahead, sweetie. You can trust me." He smiled. Not the sly grin he used on girls, but the smile he would use on their parents.

Apparently, she wasn't buying it.

"No one saw anything up here," she said.

Ray shrugged it off and continued down the hallway. The next two nurses had amazingly not seen anything, either. Nor had the guy covered in lesions whose room had a front-row seat over the parking lot.

No one wanted to talk to him. Not that he blamed them. People were terrified of the cops and even more terrified of the gangsters. But someone had seen something. Nothing happened in this city without *someone* seeing it. He just had to figure out who would talk to him about it.

On his way back out, he stopped at the first room. The window didn't look over the parking lot, but it did have a view of the road.

Ray knocked. The dad opened the door, and the boy looked over as Ray walked inside.

He showed his badge to the family and said, "I'd like to ask your son a few questions, if that's okay?"

The father and mother exchanged a glance, and he gave a nod. Before they could change their minds, Ray moved to the side of the bed and knelt.

“Hey there, buddy, I’m a police officer. I’m one of the good guys, like that guy,” he said, gesturing toward the stuffed toy reindeer the boy clutched under his arm.

“What’s your friend’s name?”

The boy looked down at the reindeer. It was missing a patch of hair between its antlers.

“Bingo,” he said. “This is Bingo.”

“Nice to meet you, Bingo. I’m Detective Clarke, but you can call me Ray.”

“Hi, Ray,” the boy said. “Are you really one of the good guys?’

The question took Ray off guard, and for a fleeting moment he wasn’t sure how to answer. Lying was part of his job, but he wasn’t sure anymore which he was: good guy or bad.

“Yeah,” he replied after a pause. “And I was hoping you could tell me what you saw last night, so I can catch the bad guys.”

The kid crinkled his freckled nose and looked at his dad.

“Go ahead, Jackie,” the man said.

“I saw people in the parking lot shooting, and I saw . . .”

He looked at his dad again.

“It’s okay, Jackie,” Ray said with a smile. “Maybe you can just tell me what Bingo saw.”

The little cracked lips smiled. Before replying, Jackie gave a deep cough that rattled in his lungs.

“Sometimes, I can’t sleep at night,” he said. “And I like to watch the city. I was at the window before the shooting, and I saw my doctor out there talking to guys with black masks and baseball caps on.”

“What’s your doctor’s name?” Ray asked.

“Abdul,” the dad said. “Dr. Abdul Hogan.”

Ray smiled at the boy. “That’s good, but what did you see *after* the shooting started?”

Again Jackie looked to his father.

Reaching out, Ray patted Bingo on the head. “It’s okay, you can tell me.”

The mother pulled on the father's sleeve, as if she didn't want them to say anything. But the father shook his head.

"Go ahead and tell Detective Clarke," he said.

Jackie met Ray's gaze. "I saw the driver of the pickup truck that killed those guys in the street. He lost his baseball cap, and he had hair that reminded me of Bingo."

Antlers.

"What else did you notice about this guy?"

Jackie shrugged. "He was big and had dark skin. Kind of like yours."

Ray forced a smile, his gut in knots. He stood and patted the kid on the arm. "You'd make a good cop, kid. Thanks for the info."

"Did I help you catch the bad guys?" Jackie called out after him.

Ray nodded, then looked back at the parents.

"Who else knows what Jackie saw?"

"Nobody," the mother said.

"Just you," replied the father.

Ray walked over to the closed door. "Best to keep that to yourselves. We don't want the Morettis finding out what little Jackie Boy saw."

* * *

Dom flipped burgers on the rusted grill. Each balcony of the shoddy postwar government housing units had one, and tonight they also had power.

He carefully turned each hunk of meat in the glow, just as he had seen his father do during their last barbecue, over ten years ago.

Moose pointed at a burger. "That one needs a little bit more."

A side-eye from Dom shut him up.

"I asked if you'd rather do it yourself," Dom said.

Moose grinned and turned to look through his apartment door, hanging ajar. The other Saints were inside drinking beer and laughing, celebrating their recent victory at the port.

His kids, Bryon and Tamara, played with Cayenne on the stained carpet. The dog's tail whipped back and forth. Namid's son, Isaac, giggled as he stroked the dog's sleek brownish-red coat.

In the kitchen, Yolanda chopped up freshly picked vegetables with Namid's wife, Victoria, who was three months pregnant and starting to show.

Dom worried about her and Namid living so far away with their Isaac, but Victoria had declined when Dom offered to find them a place in his building.

"Too dangerous here," she had said.

Too dangerous everywhere, Dom thought. He turned back to the grill and flipped a sizzling burger.

"I'm gonna inhale these, baby," Moose said, patting his belly. "I'm so hungry, I could eat a freaking dinosaur."

Dom chuckled, prompting a cough that turned into a wheezing fit. He pulled up his face mask and coughed into his sleeve.

"That don't sound good," Moose said.

"It's just the smoke from the grill." Dom took a swig of warm beer and fought the urge to cough again. He pulled his face mask back up over his mouth and nose, but Moose kept looking at him, clearly worried.

"I'm fine, bro," Dom said. "I'm going inside. You got this?"

"Yeah, no problem, man."

A voice called out from the balcony. Three units down the long open space, Dom saw Lieutenant Marks in civilian clothes, walking toward them, holding two cases of Mexican beer.

"Gentlemen," Marks said.

"Hey there, sir," Moose replied.

Dom swallowed the coppery taste of blood and pulled his face mask down again. He had a feeling Marks would be mad over what happened at the port, and hadn't expected to see him here.

"Thought I might find you all here," Marks said. He looked over his shoulder in case anyone was listening. Then he joined Dom at the railing while Moose started lifting off the cooked burgers.

"We need to talk," Marks said.

Dom tilted his head, and they walked away from the party, over to Dom's apartment a few doors down.

"What the hell were you thinking?" Marks said as soon as Dom shut the door.

"Take it easy," Dom said. "We left behind Russian RPG launchers and didn't kill any civilians."

Marks shook his head wearily. "You took a major fucking risk, and you disobeyed a direct order to stand down. You put every cop on that pier in jeopardy."

"All due respect, but they all made their choices, and they're all still alive."

Marks bit the inside of his lip, clearly trying to manage his anger. It had been a long time since Dom saw him this mad.

"Look, no one wanted that garbage off the street more than I did, but you have to play by the rules, Dominic. I've told you this. If you don't, I'm not going to be able to protect you anymore. Even Councilman Castle is pissed."

"I'm sorry," Dom said, going for his most rueful voice. "I swear I did not see your text until after we attacked."

Marks let out a sigh, then reached into his pocket. "I want you guys to find my CI and watch him. He's the kid that told me about the shipment, and I'm afraid the Morettis are going to cap him."

"What's his name?"

"Sammy Reynolds. Here's his address." Marks handed him a piece of paper.

"No problem," Dom said.

"There's something else." Marks looked agitated, his eyes flitting away before roving back to Dom.

"Yeah?" Dom asked.

"I might have a lead on Monica."

Dom felt his heart quicken. After eight years, they actually had a lead?

"One of the guards at the Casa de los Diablos heard a former Moretti associate, one Max Sammartino, bragging about a girl he took eight years ago from the same school where Monica was taken. Max hasn't made a peep since, and when questioned, he denied the entire thing."

Dom stared as the realization sank in. He had always blamed the Vegas, not just for killing his dad but also for taking his sister and selling her into their network known as the Shepherds. But it had been the Morettis all along who stole Monica . . .

"I figured you'd want to ask him a few questions yourself," Marks said.

You got that right, boss.

"I can get you into the prison, Dominic, but you've got to promise me you aren't going to do anything crazy."

"Define 'crazy.'"

"If I really need to spell it out, then forget about it."

"I won't get caught, whatever I do."

Marks sighed again and looked at his watch. "I've got to get back to the office, but I'll be in touch as soon as I can get you in."

"Please, as soon as possible."

"You have my word," Marks said.

They hugged, and Marks left Dom standing in his little apartment. A few minutes later, he joined his team back at Moose's. He felt numb as he opened the door.

Rocky and Bryon were arm-wrestling on the floor, while Isaac laughed and cheered.

"That's all you got, kid?" Rocky said.

Moose's son grunted. He was no match for Rocky, but Rocky was putting on a good act. Face red, muscles bulging, panting, he appeared to be putting up a good fight.

Bryon looked just as serious.

"Oh no, oh no, oh no," Rocky panted, lowering his arm slowly toward the carpet. He grunted louder before letting his hand touch. Bryon threw his arms up in victory.

"Damn," Rocky said, massaging his biceps. "You're stronger than you look, kid."

"Uncle Dom, I got him!" Bryon crowed. "I got Rocky!"

"Nice work, buddy," Dom said, trying not to think about what Marks had just told him.

"Rocky's weak," Tooth said with a playful grin. "I beat him every time we get in the ring."

From the couch, Bettis laughed for the first time in days.

"That's not true, and I look forward to beating your . . . your butt next time we get in the ring, brother."

"Bring it," Tooth replied, taking a swig of beer.

"Do you guys ever stop with the dick-measuring?" Camilla said, apparently less delicate than Rocky with her word choices.

She rolled her eyes, got up, and returned from the kitchen with two beers. Taking a swig from one, she sat on the floor with Cayenne and Tamara, who was rubbing the pit bull's belly. She handed Dom one of the beers.

"You okay?" she asked. "You don't look so good."

"Got a cough, probably from taking that bullet to my vest," he said, rubbing his sore ribs. "You're the one that looks rough, though."

A bandage covered her forehead above her right eyebrow, and a nasty bruise crossed her chest diagonally, like a macabre beauty-pageant sash.

She smiled. "Oh, this was *so* worth it," she said with a cute smile.

"Dom, got a second?"

Yolanda beckoned him from the hallway. He followed her into the shadows, out of view of the other Saints and the kids. She checked the front door to make sure it was closed.

Seeing Moose still outside, she said, "I'm going to be frank, Dom. I'm really worried. I haven't seen Andre much lately, and he's been more irritable. Won't tell me what's going on."

"Things are getting better," Dom said. "I'm looking after him, don't worry."

She looked at the floor, thinking, then looked back up. "Andre promised me he won't make me a widow, but I need you to make me a promise too."

Dom nodded.

"Promise me you won't sacrifice yourself or my husband—even if it means killing Antonio Moretti."

"I promise I won't ever sacrifice Andre," Dom said.

She put a hand on his arm, a gentle touch, and left him in the hallway. Camilla moved into view, brows arched.

Dom took a swig of his beer as the front door opened and Moose brought in the meat, kicking the door shut behind him. "Dinner is served, baby."

"I'm fucking starving," Tooth said, nearly jumping off the couch.

Yolanda shot Tooth a glare. "Callum! Language!"

"Sorry. I'm *freaking* starving," he said, grinning.

"Better," Yolanda replied.

Camilla helped her set the table.

The lights suddenly flickered, and the oscillating fan clanked off.

"Well, that's shit," Rocky said.

Tooth wagged his head. "Grid must be down again."

"We have candles and lanterns in the corner," Yolanda said, treating it as no big deal.

The kids took seats as Camilla and Dom worked on lighting candles and turning on the lanterns. When they finished, the adults and kids clustered around the small wooden table set in the kitchen. Victoria helped four-year-old Isaac, the youngest of the kids, into a chair.

Moose placed the burgers in the center of the table, and Yolanda passed a plate of veggies around. She smiled at Bryon and Tamara, both grinning like kids on Christmas morning.

Dinner rarely involved fresh meat, especially beef, but Yolanda had managed to grab some at the market and invited everyone over.

Bettis held out his hands. "I'd like to say a prayer."

"Man, always with the prayers," Rocky said. He glanced up at Bettis. "No offense."

"Go ahead," Yolanda said to the kids, who bowed their heads.

Dom squeezed Camilla's hand, and she squeezed back. He held Tamara's soft little hand in his other.

"Dear God, thank you for this bountiful food," Bettis said. "Thank you for our friends and for the family that we all have become. We ask you to bless this food and bless us. In the Lord's name, we pray." He crossed himself and leaned back in his chair. "I also want to thank our leader, Dominic."

Everyone looked over at Dom, who reared back slightly, his napkin like a white flag in his hand. He didn't like the attention and normally wasn't much for speeches.

"Thank you for putting together our team and making us a family, in a place where family is all we have," Bettis said. "Without you, we would all be lost."

"Thanks, boss," Tooth said. "Tonight, we celebrate our most recent victory."

"Thanks for looking after my dad, Uncle Dom," Bryon said quietly. "He's lucky to have such a good best friend."

"Oh, I'm the lucky one," Dom said. He tore off a piece of meat and handed it down to the only team member who couldn't talk.

Cayenne greedily accepted the bite.

"Shit is dope," Pork Chop said. He wiped the ketchup from his beard with his sleeve.

Namid shook his head. "You don't have *any* manners, do you?"

They ate in the glow of candles, and despite the heat and the noise outside, Dom relaxed in his chair, enjoying this moment with the people he would do anything for.

This was his family now.

But as he looked around at the smiling faces, he couldn't help feeling that it was all temporary, like a can of soup with an expiration date. The Saints had been lucky thus far, but their luck wouldn't last forever.

One thing was certain, though: Max Sammartino had run out of lives.

Soon, Dom would pay the man a visit at the House of the Devil and find out whether he had been behind Monica's kidnapping.

Maybe she was still out there. Maybe he *would* find her.

A small flicker of hope emerged in his hardened heart, and he embraced it. Halfway through the meal, a knock came on the door. Namid got up from the table and looked through the peephole.

"It's your brother, Ray," he said to Moose.

Moose looked at Dom, who shrugged. As far as Ray knew, they all were sheriff's deputies who worked at Refugee Processing Center 4, nothing more.

"Let him in," Moose said.

Namid opened the door, and Ray walked in wearing a leather jacket and holding a six-pack. He smiled. "Well, hell, no one told me you guys were having a party. How come no one invited me to this shindig?"

-10-

"I don't want this life for Marco," said Lucia. "We both agreed that he would not join the family business. That's why we sent him to school in—"

Antonio raised a hand to cut her off. His wife shied away from him. Not because she was afraid he would hit her—he had never laid a hand on her—but because she knew when she had said something disrespectful.

"I *will* protect him, and so will Vin," Antonio growled.

Vinny stood in the living room, hands cupped behind his back, looking as nervous as his father. They had good reason. Lucia was not happy with the decision to introduce Marco to the family business.

"That expensive school taught Marco nothing about real life," Antonio said. "All he does is party. Vinny will teach him how to be a man."

"It was your idea to send him to Italy," Lucia replied. "I listened to you then because you convinced me it was best, but this . . ."

"I know, and I'm still glad we sent him away for those years, because he learned legit business. Now he must learn *our* business."

"So you're going to give him a seat at the table?"

"If he earns it, yes. And I promise you, if that happens, he will do something safe. Something with numbers, in an office, not out on the streets."

"I don't like this at all," she said. "We have one child—"

"He's *not* a child anymore. Chrissy, Vin, meet me downstairs," Antonio said.

He walked over to the window while his brother and nephew left, the door clicking shut behind them. Antonio knew that Lucia would follow him to the bulletproof picture window, and he wanted her to see what he was looking at.

The view of the pool wasn't good from this angle, but it was easy to make out Marco down there with his friends. Girls in bikinis sunbathed on this unusually clear and hot day while his guy friends drank beers, smoked joints, and listened to music that Antonio could hear faintly.

He saw one of the kids snorting off a table. The sight made him clench his jaw, but it was the thumping bass line that infuriated him.

Antonio hated noise. He hated seeing his son waste his life even more.

"You know what?" Antonio said. "Let's go downstairs and settle this the old-fashioned way."

"He won't like being embarrassed in front of his friends," Lucia said.

Antonio turned to his wife. "What he *likes* is not part of the conversation."

She bit the side of her lip.

"Lucia, this has been a long time coming," Antonio said. "Let's go."

They left their apartment and stepped into the elevator. His heart pounded, not just because of his disagreement with his wife, but because of everything else going on. Maybe he should just tell her. Maybe that would help her realize just how much he had on his plate.

Or it could make things worse.

They had lost a crew and an entire shipment of product and medicine in an ambush. And while the peace treaty with Esteban was still intact, it could easily shatter if the Vegas saw any weakness.

Antonio couldn't let that happen. Now more than ever, he had to show strength.

Christopher and Vinny were waiting in the lobby downstairs. They both stood, and Antonio waved them over.

He led them through the back exit, to the pool. Two guards watching over the party stiffened and gave nods as the four approached.

Antonio put on his sunglasses and pushed open the door, holding it for Lucia.

She stepped out into the sunshine, basking for a moment. This was the nicest day in months, although the midmorning temperature was already tipping ninety degrees—a bit high for his liking.

He loosened his tie as he walked to the pool.

Four girls and four boys hung out with Marco. Antonio knew his guy friends. There was Nick, a well-built southern boy with a mane of blond hair and striking blue eyes. Giovanni, a handsome kid with movie-star good looks second only to Marco's. And, of course, the identical twin brothers Alex and Pietro. Antonio still couldn't tell the entitled pricks apart.

Several of the girls sat up, sweat dripping down their perfectly sculpted bodies.

"Mr. Moretti," Giovanni said, giving them a million-dollar grin.

"Don Antonio," Vinny said.

"Ah, yes, my apologies, Don Antonio," Giovanni replied.

Marco, who had just jumped in the water, surfaced and swam over.

"Dad, Mom," he said. "What are you guys doing down here? I thought I was . . ."

Antonio crouched at the edge of the pool. "Playtime's over," he said.

Marco looked to Lucia, and Antonio was relieved to see her backing him. She gestured for their son to get out of the water.

"But we're—"

"Finished here," Antonio said.

The other youngsters groaned but quickly grabbed their clothes and left. Marco watched them go, his face red with anger.

"Later, Marco," said one of the girls.

Marco sucked in a deep, angry breath. "This is *bullshit*," he said. "How dare you come and embarrass me like that in front of my friends!"

Antonio resisted the urge to push his son back into the pool.

"You said you wanted a seat at the table," he said. "This is not how you earn it. Now, get some clothes on and meet your cousin in thirty minutes."

Marco looked to Vinny. He hung back with Christopher. Still in their dark suits, they had begun to sweat.

"I already got something in motion," Marco said. "You'd be proud, Dad, but I guess you'd rather just come down here and embarrass me than *trust* that I know what I'm doing."

Antonio almost laughed, but the rage building in him suffocated any jocularity. He looked at his brother and nephew and then jerked his chin at the door. They both took off without saying a word.

"Wait, Vin," Antonio called out.

Vinny stopped.

Marco wrapped a towel around his waist. Like his friends, he spent hours in the gym almost every day. Antonio wished his son would focus as hard on doing something with his life as he did on his body and chasing girls.

Lucia walked inside with Marco, and Antonio remained out in the sun with his nephew. He had no idea what his son had in motion, but he was curious.

"You know what Marco was talking about?" Antonio asked Vinny.

"Not a clue."

Antonio watched his son open the door and go inside. He pulled out a handkerchief and dabbed at his forehead.

"Thank you for agreeing to look after your cousin," Antonio said.

"Sure."

Antonio was surprised by the short answers, which he saw as a sign of disrespect. He knew that Vinny didn't like the idea of taking Marco under his wing, but normally he was a lot more diplomatic about orders he didn't like.

That made Antonio even angrier.

He stepped closer, leaning in.

"What happened at the port was your fault, Vin. You got caught with your pants down."

"I'm—"

"Don't talk," Antonio said. "Just remember, what happened there can happen *at any time*. I didn't think I would need to explain this to you like I did to Marco, but the Saints are our most dangerous enemy yet."

"I won't underestimate them again."

"I know, because next time I won't be so forgiving."

Antonio drew in a breath and looked at the ruined skyline. "I need you to show Marco how to survive out there—to teach him how things work, and most of all, to keep him alive."

* * *

The crackle of static filled the Jeep as Camilla twisted through the channels. She stopped on the weather channel for another predictable forecast.

"Hot, hot, and really fucking hot," she muttered as she took a swig of water. The type of heat that made people irritable—and sometimes got them killed.

Only two in the afternoon, and it was already a hundred degrees. In the past hour, she had listened over the encrypted police-band radio to reports of three murders, confirming her theory.

A sweat necklace rimmed the white tank top under her brown long-sleeved T-shirt. She sat in the Jeep with Namid and Pork Chop, waiting for their new CI to make a move.

"*It's going to be blazing hot this afternoon, my friends,*" said meteorologist Regina Díaz. "*But I've got good news. We're looking at clear skies for the next twenty-four hours. No dust storms or acid rain in sight.*"

Camilla turned the radio off and went back to fiddling with the air-conditioning controls.

"Great time for it to go out," Pork Chop said. He dragged a bandanna across his forehead.

"Could be worse," Namid said, shrugging. "At least, there aren't any dust storms today."

"How's Victoria doing?" Camilla asked, trying to make small talk.

Namid smiled. "She's fine. Isaac has been helping out. He's going to make a good big brother."

Camilla smiled as she fiddled with the air vents, but the hot air just made things worse. She finally gave up and rolled down the window. Dust billowed up from a passing car, trash swirling in the wake.

The city smelled like a dumpster.

It didn't deter the hoopsters in Lincoln Heights. Several games were going on the courts, between guys wearing nothing but shorts and sneakers.

She glanced back over her filtered mask at Pork Chop, then over at Namid. They all were operating on a few hours' sleep, but you couldn't really tell by looking at Namid—surprising since he also had his pregnant wife and young son to look after.

The handsome Mojave Indian had perfect tan skin and a hard part in his black hair. In his early thirties, he always spoke in a calm and sophisticated tone.

Pork Chop, on the other hand, looked like a junkie. The white kid from rural Nebraska had a mottled complexion, and bags rimming his bloodshot blue eyes. A trucker hat turned backward covered his bald head.

Camilla stole a glance in the mirror. Cuts and bruises from her night at the Catalina still marked her freckled face.

But instead of time off, Dom had sent them right back into the field. He was always the guy with a plan, the smartest guy she knew. Sometimes, she wondered what he would be if the United States hadn't collapsed. He had killer instincts to go with his smarts, so maybe an entrepreneur or CEO. Perhaps even a fancy-pants politician.

Nah, politics isn't for Dom.

She never thought about what she would be doing if not this. The streets around her were her reality, and she scanned them for the target. The CI was the one who had tipped Marks off about the port shipment. Now they had to bring him in.

"I figured he'd be lying low after what happened," Camilla said.

Namid nodded. "Kid has balls, I'll give him that. But apparently he forgot to tell Marks the cops were going to show up."

"Sounds like an idiot to me," Pork Chop said.

"We're going to find out." Namid unbuckled his seat belt. "Pork Chop, let's go wait for him outside the courts."

"Don't spook him," Camilla said.

"We ain't gonna spook him," Pork Chop said, rolling his eyes. "Just going to watch him."

Namid tied a bandanna over his perfectly combed hair. He was the OCD type—everything always had to be perfect. It made him a good cop, but it also annoyed the hell out of Camilla.

The two Saints took off toward the park, blending in with the civilians who were about. A bead of sweat trickled down her forehead, burning through a cut. She took off her shades and dripped some water on her sleeve, then dabbed her forehead.

She had patched herself up and would have the scars to show for it.

A car raced by, distracting her, and she looked away from the mirror. The city was busier than normal. People were enjoying the heat and the absence of blowing dust.

She sometimes wondered what it was like across the world, in places where life had continued to progress. Where people raised their families in peace and had normal nine-to-five jobs.

She never wanted that life. Some of the guys, like Namid and Pork Chop, were fighting for just that. But she wasn't.

Camilla had joined the Saints for revenge—something Dom promised. By the time it was over, she would have a lot more scars or she would be six feet under.

"Hey, baby," said a deep voice.

She looked to the right of the car, where a Latino man had seen her sitting in the Jeep.

"You all alone?" he asked.

She gave him the bird.

The guy just stared at her, as if unsure what to do. Then he frowned. "You got too many scars, anyways."

He walked away, and Camilla almost got out and yelled at him, but something about the way he said that made her feel . . . *broken.*

She leaned back for a view of the park. *Forget that asshole.*

Hundreds of people were out, surrounding the courts or chilling in the dry grass. Most of them wore face masks and bandannas, which helped Namid and Pork Chop blend in. They took a seat on a park bench and watched a pickup game.

After a few minutes, the teams took a break, and Sammy moved over to a row of backpacks lying near the fence. He was in his early twenties, but with his acne, he could pass for a teenager. His tender age didn't deceive Camilla. The "kid" was smart enough to land a job at the port at sixteen and work his way up to supervising shipments by the time he was twenty.

Apparently, Marks had brought him in on a burglary charge a year ago and offered him a way to avoid a stint in Casa de los Diablos: help them take down the Moretti organization by telling them when the big shipments were coming in.

Last night, the kid had finally come through.

Sammy tipped back a bottle of water and handed it to another tall, skinny guy who had joined him. They laughed and then walked over to the gate.

Namid and Pork Chop stood and followed them away from the courts. Camilla had to turn to get a look, but they appeared to be heading to the bathroom.

She wasn't sure exactly what Namid and Pork Chop had planned. They normally didn't try to talk to the kid during the day.

His friend went into the single-hole bathroom while Sammy stayed outside. Namid and Pork Chop walked across the lawn, under some trees.

"What the hell are you doing . . . ?" Camilla whispered.

The other guy finished in the bathroom and closed the door. Sammy handed him a joint, and they set off back toward the courts. Namid and Pork Chop followed alongside the path.

Five kids on skateboards flew down the sidewalk. Sammy and his friend jumped out of the way. They both turned and yelled at the punks just as gunfire sounded.

Camilla twisted for a better view, reaching for her weapon at the same time.

The kids on skateboards took off running with their boards under their arms, and she didn't see any of them firing. Sammy had fallen to the ground, but his friend stood on the side of the path, looking at the trees.

Not the trees, Camilla realized. The kid was looking at a man with a gun, which he pointed and fired. Sammy scrambled away as his friend jerked from the bullets ripping into him.

He dropped to the ground, trying to crawl.

The shooter walked over and fired two more shots point-blank into his skull. Before Namid and Pork Chop could get a shot, the assassin took off running, sprinting like a track star toward the crowd of fleeing civilians.

"Shit, shit, shit," Camilla said. She put the Jeep into reverse and backed up, one tire going up on the curb. Then she put it in drive and did a bootleg turn across the road.

Namid and Pork Chop had decided not to pursue the shooter and were running after Sammy. She pulled into the parking lot choked with cars and civilians trying to escape. A car tried to back up, but she cut in front of it, laying down the horn.

On the other side of the lot, Namid had almost caught up to Sammy. Pork Chop was busy flanking them.

She found a gap between the cars pulling out and weaved in and out all the way to the other side of the parking lot, where she reached over and opened the door just in time to see Namid tackle Sammy.

"Get in!" she shouted.

Pork Chop helped Namid pick Sammy up and haul him over to the Jeep. In the chaos, no one seemed to notice the gun Namid put in Sammy's back.

They tossed him into the back seat, and Pork Chop slid in. Namid got in the front passenger seat. Before he had even closed the door, she hit the gas and squealed away.

"Let me go!" Sammy shouted.

"We're not going to hurt you, man," Pork Chop said, "so calm the fuck down."

But Sammy didn't listen. He grabbed the door handle and tried to open it. Pork Chop grabbed for him, and Sammy threw an elbow, hitting him in the nose.

A hammer clicked, and Sammy froze.

"Don't fucking do that again," Namid said, training his revolver between Sammy's eyes.

Camilla looked in the rearview mirror to check on Pork Chop. He held his head back to keep the blood from pouring out of his nose. Sammy held up his hands.

"All right, all right," he said.

"Try anything else, and I'll give you a three-fifty-seven Magnum ear piercing," Namid said.

-11-

"*This* is what you told your dad you had in motion?" Vinny said. He shook his head. "I wanted to *interrogate* Jason first!"

Marco sat slumped in the back seat.

"Jesus, man! How'd you screw this up so bad?"

"My guy wasn't supposed to kill him," Marco said. "I paid him to grab him and bring him to us. But, dude, what does it matter? Jason's *dead*. He isn't going to be leaking any more port shipments to anyone."

Vinny wanted to slap him. His cousin couldn't really be that stupid. But apparently, he was.

How the fuck did I end up on Marco duty? Vinny wondered. *Oh right, because of the damn port.*

Now Vinny knew how Raff had felt looking after Marco all those years. Or maybe not, since Marco was just a boy back then.

Thinking of Raff made Vinny miss the quiet old soldier. He drew in a deep breath as his mind shifted back to their new problem.

"You might have just whacked the only guy that knows the true identities of the Saints," Vinny said. "This is why we use our own people, not some shit-for-brains gangbangers. If you want to catch the Saints, you're going to have to start listening. Got it?"

"Yeah, I got it."

A moment of silence passed between the two of them. Doberman, who had driven them out of the compound this afternoon, kept his eyes on the road. He knew his place. This was the second day Vinny had taken Marco under his wing, and so far, it was like teaching a deaf old dog new tricks.

"Where are we going?" Marco asked.

"My contact at the hospital. He called in the stolen RX-Four to Joey's crew last night and gave me the name of the doctor that was with the Saints. If anyone knows where that RX-Four is or who the Saints are, it's going to be him."

Marco brightened. "Don't worry," he said. "I won't screw this up."

"I know you won't, because you're staying in the car."

Doberman parked outside an apartment complex.

"Watch my ride," Doberman said to Marco.

"Fuck that, I ain't no babysitter," Marco said. "And you're not my boss, Vin."

"I know. I'm *your babysitter.*"

Doberman chuckled, and Marco fumed.

Vinny scratched at the back of his neck and looked down at his cousin's clenched fist.

"Seriously, dude?" he said. "After the stunt your hired dog pulled in Lincoln Heights, you might want to lighten up."

"Or what? You going to rat me out?"

"I'm no rat, Marco, and hitting me isn't your best option."

Marco opened the car door and got out.

"What you wanna do?" Doberman asked, looking over at Vinny.

After a few choice Italian expletives, Vinny pulled his black mask over his face and opened the door. He met Doberman at the trunk, where they fished out a stolen police vest. Vinny handed it to Marco.

"Put this on," he said.

After cinching up their vests, they walked through the parking lot toward a building much nicer than the government projects in the slums. The people who lived here were the 1 percent, mostly doctors and business owners.

Solar panels covered the roofs, and vegetable gardens grew outside the three brick buildings. Several people were weeding and watering. They paid no attention as the three men went in the back door.

Unlike most apartment buildings in Los Angeles, this one didn't smell like piss. But they kept their masks up as they climbed the stairwell to the third floor.

"Number three fourteen," he said.

A woman was locking her door around the next corner.

"Police, ma'am, please watch out," Doberman said.

When they were clear, Vinny pulled the slide back on his suppressed pistol. He hated wearing the stolen vests, not because they were hot but because they represented something that seemed fake to him.

At least the gangsters didn't pretend to be the good guys. And at least his family gave back to the community. Most of the cops just took their cut and sat on their asses.

At apartment 314, Vinny took up position on the left side of the door, and Marco on the right.

Doberman knocked. "Police. Open up, Dr. Hogan."

Another rap, and still no answer.

Vinny gave Doberman a nod. These doors weren't made of steel like the ones in the slums, because security usually prevented anyone undesirable from getting inside. But the police vests had solved that problem.

Doberman twisted the knob, and surprisingly, it opened.

What kind of idiot keeps his door unlocked?

They swept the small kitchen, the living room, and then the two bedrooms.

"In here," Doberman said.

Vinny and Marco hovered behind Doberman, staring into the small bathroom. Dr. Abdul Hogan—what was left of him—lay in the bathtub.

"What the fuck, man?" Marco said, turning away.

Doberman moved aside to let Vinny into the room. He knelt next to the bathtub. The right arm, no longer connected to the torso, was still handcuffed to a metal handrail inside the tub.

Whoever killed him had tortured him first, and from the looks of it, they took their time. The brutality of the wounds, and the severed limb, had the markings of a Vega job. But not quite.

Vinny bent down to examine the corpse.

"We better get out of here," Marco said.

"Hold up," Vinny replied. He grabbed the severed arm and turned the wrist to look at the handcuffs. Sure enough, they were standard LAPD issue.

This wasn't the Vegas, the Russians, or some gangbanger junkie. A cop, or someone who knew how cops worked, had done this. Were the Saints trying to cover their tracks? Vinny shook his head. It made no sense.

"We're really screwed now," he muttered. "The only two guys that might have known who the Saints are have already been whacked."

* * *

Dom stood in the safe house's office, studying pictures of the crime families they were trying to bring down. Cayenne slept on the floor, looking up every few minutes to make sure he was still there.

"It's okay, girl," Dom said.

Camilla, Pork Chop, and Namid would soon return from Lincoln Heights with their CI. They were just supposed to follow him and see what he was up to, not kidnap him and bring him back here. But maybe this was better. Sammy was important, and they had to keep him safe now that the Morettis were clearly after him.

Dom checked the video equipment in the corner. Rocky had designed the security system, and it had worked thus far. Junkies would sometimes stumble into the area, triggering an alarm, but no one had come close to discovering the safe house.

He looked at the don's picture. If Max Sammartino had kidnapped Monica, then it was under Antonio Moretti's orders.

"I'll get you soon, shithead," Dom said.

He gestured to Cayenne, who was camped out on the floor. She hopped after him to the stairwell.

Tooth stood guard on the rooftop, smoking a cigarette. The alkaline dust was starting to fly in the rising wind. Dom pulled up his face mask and looked around.

Tooth sucked on his cigarette and pointed to the west. "Here they come."

"Let me see those," Dom said, taking the binoculars from around Tooth's neck.

He zoomed in on the Jeep racing down the street, then checked to make sure they didn't have a tail. The road looked clear—nothing but scorched vehicles and blowing trash. That was exactly why he had chosen this place for their safe house.

"You really think bringing the kid here is a good idea?" Tooth asked. He used his thumbnail to pick between his impressive front teeth.

"After what happened in Lincoln Heights? Yeah, I do," Dom replied. "The kid's too valuable to us. We can't let him get killed."

"Do you think the shooter whacked the wrong guy, and Sammy was the real target?"

"I don't know, but we're going to find out."

Cayenne wagged her tail and sank down on her belly, resting her red muzzle on one paw.

Tooth pointed at the horizon, where the distant shapes of the Moretti empire could be seen. Then he made a gun of his hand, using his thumb as the hammer.

"Boom, motherfuckers," he said, drawing a look from Cayenne.

"Keep watch," Dom said. "I'm going back in to meet them."

He opened the door, and Cayenne followed him inside.

This wasn't just a hideout. It was a barracks, armory, and garage, and Dom had created several more, just in case they needed to escape or lie low for a few days. Today was one of those days.

His team thought him paranoid, but that paranoia had kept them all alive. So far.

They passed the living space, where Rocky was snoring on a cot. Bettis was on his knees in the corner, praying.

"Need to talk when you're done, Chaplain," Dom said.

Cayenne hopped after him into the open garage. Camilla stood in front of her locker, behind the boxing ring and weight benches.

"Where's Sammy?" he asked.

"Pork Chop and Namid took him to the cell."

"Were you followed here?" Dom asked her.

She shook her bandaged head.

Bettis stepped into the garage. "You need to see me?"

"In a sec," Dom said.

Pork Chop and Namid returned.

"Got to say, I'm ready for a beer," Pork Chop said.

Rocky joined them in the garage, rubbing his eyes like a kid waking up from a nap—which, Dom realized, he was.

"Everyone, grab a beer," Dom said. "You deserve it. Bettis and I will talk to Sammy first, then we'll join you guys."

Dom stopped on his way out of the garage.

"You sure you're okay?" he asked Camilla.

She gave him a playful punch. "You worry too much, Dom."

"You still haven't explained exactly what happened at the Catalina."

"I will when we have time" she said. "Just focus on the kid. He's our most valuable asset."

He knew she could take care of herself, but it was his nature to want to protect her, especially after failing to protect his kid sister.

They both wanted justice for their siblings. It bound them, in some ways even more tightly than Dom was to the other members of the team.

"See you in a bit," he said to Camilla. He looked down at Cayenne. "Stay here, girl."

Dom and Bettis went to the single jail cell, an old bathroom they had repurposed with bars and a door dividing the space in half. A narrow window high in the wall let in a sliver of light. Sammy sat with his knees pulled up to his chest, back to the wall. Bettis closed the door behind them.

"You guys gotta let me go," Sammy said. "I didn't do nothin' wrong, and my old lady's gonna have my ass if I don't come home soon."

"You aren't going anywhere for a while," Dom said.

"Who the fuck are you guys?" Sammy said, standing up and coming to the bars.

"Friends. And you're here for your own good," Dom said. "After what happened at Lincoln Heights, you're lucky to be alive."

"Who was your friend?" Bettis asked.

Sammy's eyes lowered to the ground. "Jason. He was one of the port guys in charge of last night's shipment."

"The Morettis killed him," Bettis said. "Same guys you've been helping at the port."

"If they got to him, it's just a matter of time before they get to you. We have enough on you to take you in," Dom lied. "Might be a better option, going to jail. Then again, the Morettis have guys on the inside too. I know from experience."

Sammy looked up. "Experience?"

Dom didn't reply.

"This fucking bullshit is so unfair!" Sammy said.

"Tell that to all the people suffering in this city because dirtbags like you help the Morettis," Bettis said. "They will kill anyone that gets in their way."

"I only help with the shit from Europe," Sammy said. "Got nothing to do with the drugs from Mexico. Why do you think I'm still alive? If they thought I'd helped Jason, I woulda got capped too."

Dom looked at Bettis. The kid had a point, but it was also possible *he* was the target and the assassins had failed.

"I blame the cops for what happened to Jason," the kid said. "I told Lieutenant Marks about the shipment, and look what fucking happened. Cops show up at the port, guns blazing."

Dom and Bettis stayed silent.

"I bet it was the Saints," Sammy said. "No one else is crazy enough to fuck with a Moretti shipment."

The kid had balls. But that came with youth. Dom remembered how invincible he had felt when he was younger. It wasn't until Abdul had patched him up in the ER for a second time that Dom had been reminded that he was mortal.

Sammy backed away from the bars to sit on the bench.

"You guys think I'm some kinda animal, but I'm just trying to survive.

I've been taking care of my mom four years now. Wanted to go to school, but she got sick and I got a job."

Dom listened. He wanted to hear what Sammy had to say.

"My mom hates this city. Always wanted to get out, but then my pops died. My older brother got gunned down, so we're stranded here."

Bettis looked over at Dom, who kept listening.

"I shoulda never helped the cops," Sammy said. "The Morettis will come for me, and before they kill me, they'll torture me. Probably my mom too."

"That's why you're here," Dom reminded him. "For your own good."

Sammy got up from the bench. "Who the fuck are—" He reared back. "Wait a damn second."

"We're the only ones fighting evil in this city," Dom said. "And we're the only ones who can help you."

"Wow," Sammy said, raising a hand. "Holy shit. You guys are *Saints*? Whoa! I'd be better off selling *you* to the Morettis. You guys are seriously whacked, you realize that?"

"Back up," Bettis said. "First off, you don't know who we are, and you don't know *where you* are right now. So enough threats."

"We want to help you, kid," Dom said.

Sammy rolled his eyes. "Yeah, right. Why would you want to help me?"

"Because you're a good kid," Dom said. "Because your mom raised you right. That's why you work at the port to look after her and you're not off with the other kids your age doing H or running with some gang."

"The alternative is to get locked away in Casa de los Diablos," Bettis said. "You've seen it, right?"

Of course you have. Everyone knew that shithole that swallowed people whole. It was a society within a society, controlled more by the inmates than by the guards, much as LA was controlled by the gangsters, not the cops.

"We can put you in isolation there so no one gets to you," Dom lied.

Sammy seemed to consider his options. Dom and Bettis waited for him to finish scratching his ear.

"How can I help you guys?"

"By helping us take down the Morettis," Dom said. "If you do, I'll make sure you and your mom get out of LA, to one of the communes out east."

Sammy gave Dom a cockeyed look, then went back to scratching his ear.

"Did you hear me?" Dom asked.

Sammy stepped up to the bars. "If I'm going to trust you, I need to see your face. My dad always said you gotta see a man's face before you can decide whether to trust him."

Bettis shook his head. "No way, kid."

Normally, Dom wouldn't have considered pulling down his mask, but there was something about Sammy that he liked. It was like looking into a mirror from ten years ago.

He reached up to his mask.

"What are you doing, boss?" Bettis protested, holding up his hand.

"Not you," Sammy said. He pointed to Bettis. "I want to see *his* face. My dad also said you can't trust a man that isn't willing to take a risk."

Bettis said nothing, waiting for a decision.

Dom thought on it, then gave the nod that would expose him to a kid they couldn't trust but needed more than ever.

"All right," Dom said as Bettis lowered his mask. "Happy?"

"Yeah," Sammy replied.

"Hungry?" Dom asked.

Sammy nodded.

"I'll be back in a bit with some food," Dom said.

He walked down the hallway with Bettis, who actually cursed.

"Relax," Dom said. "The kid isn't going anywhere."

In the garage, Tooth and Rocky were sparring.

"Told you I'd beat your ass," Tooth said.

Rocky answered with a punch to the jaw.

"Damn," Dom said, impressed.

Tooth put his glove up to his cheek in shock. "Oh, it's on, little man," he said, heavy on the Irish accent. He swung, and Rocky ducked.

Namid and Camilla sat at the card table, playing poker and laughing. Across the space, Pork Chop worked on the Chevy Tahoe, showering sparks on the floor as he welded on a panel.

Moose was in their gym as usual, bench-pressing. He pushed the weights up, the bar bowing slightly in the middle. Gangster rap played over the speakers: Rocky's custom mix track of old-school 50 Cent, Tupac, Lil Wayne, and Ice Cube.

"Guys," Namid said, standing up from the table.

The Saints all stopped what they were doing and stood. Namid handed Dom a beer.

"What's this about?" Dom asked.

"We couldn't toast the other night," Camilla said. "Thought we should take a few minutes today, before you send us back out there."

Dom popped his beer and raised it.

"Congratulations, boss!" Moose said.

Pork Chop turned up the bass.

"Check it," Tooth said, pointing at Rocky.

The kid was starting his infamous robot dance.

"Yeah, baby!" Moose yelled.

"Get it, Rock!" Camilla shouted.

Cayenne whipped her tail and ran over to the ring, wanting in on the action. Rocky dropped to the mat and started break dancing.

As the team celebrated, Dom made the rounds, thanking each member before walking over and turning the music off.

"The port was a huge victory for us," Dom said. "I've got some planning to do, so everybody gets the rest of the day and night off."

"Woot, woot!" Camilla said.

"I'm gonna sleep the *entire* time," Tooth said.

"Not before our rematch," Rocky said.

They went back to boxing, and Pork Chop and Bettis joined Namid and Camilla at their card game. Moose watched the boxing for a few minutes, then walked over to Dom.

"You got something you need help with?" he asked.

Dom shook his head. He still hadn't told Moose about the lead on Monica, and he wouldn't until Marks called with access to the prison.

"You sure?" Moose asked, pulling out his phone.

"Sure," Dom said.

"Gotta take this." Moose stepped away.

Dom finished his beer and refilled Cayenne's bowls with fresh water and kibble. Her tail whipped against the cabinet as she wolfed down the chow. He crouched and stroked the dog as she ate.

A shadow loomed over them, and he looked up at Moose. The big man wiped the sweat from his face with a towel.

Dom stood waited for bad news. "What?"

"My brother," Moose said. "Ray just got word there's a two-million-dollar bounty on the head of every Saint in the city. Asked me if I knew anything about it."

Dom nodded at Pork Chop to turn the music down.

"Hey, turn that back on," Rocky said. He and Tooth came over to the ropes of the boxing ring.

"What's going on?" Camilla asked, looking up from her cards.

For a moment, Dom thought about keeping this from the team for now. They all desperately needed to rest and have some fun without worrying about torture and death.

But this was something he couldn't keep from them. Mindful of Sammy in the cell, Dom gathered the team around him and spoke in a whisper.

"Don Antonio didn't bite on the RPGs," Dom said. "The son of a bitch has a bounty on all our heads."

"How much?" Tooth asked.

"Two million in silver."

"Two fucking *million*?" Rocky said. "Who knew I was worth that much!"

Camilla tossed her cards on the table. "It was just a matter of time."

Bettis made a cross over his tattooed chest.

"Changes nothing," Pork Chop said.

"Nothing?" Namid leaned back in his chair. "This changes *everything*."

"Yup, we're pretty well fucked," Rocky said. "Everyone in the freaking city's going to be looking for us."

"Maybe it's time to go see my uncle," Camilla said. "Just in case we have to get the hell out of Dodge."

"Who said anything about leaving?" Dom said. "This is when we double down."

"We could hide out at the rez if we need," Namid said. "They would take us all in."

Camilla shrugged. "It's good to have a backup plan, you know. Just in case shit goes south."

Dom looked around him. "If anybody wants out, that's fine. But I'm just getting started, and I'll stop when Don Antonio and Esteban Vega are in the ground."

-12-

Ray sat on the tattered leather couch of his three-bedroom apartment, swigging from a forty. The bland lager was one of the cheap imports from China, like almost everything else you could buy in what passed for a grocery store in postwar Los Angeles.

He used to get Mexican stuff, but Mexico wasn't in much better shape than the United States. So it was Japanese beer. Tonight, he didn't care that it tasted like carbonated piss. He was just happy to be at home with his family.

His six- and seven-year-old boys, Jamal and Will, were outside playing basketball, and the two youngest were on the floor in front of him, arguing over a doll's wardrobe.

"Lolo, Maddie, knock that shit off," Ray said.

His wife, Alicia, walked inside from the balcony, where she was pulling dry laundry off a line.

"What I tell you about language, Ray?" she said.

"Sorry, babe, been a long day."

He gulped down a quarter of the beer, set it on the table, and sat down on the floor with Maddie and Lolo. Both girls glanced up, curious.

"Wanna play with us?" Maddie asked.

"Maybe later," Ray replied.

Maddie went back to braiding the doll's hair while her little sister looked on.

"See, just like this," Maddie said.

Lolo leaned down, exposing the thinning hair on the back of her scalp.

"Sweetie, did you take your medicine today?" Ray asked.

"Do I have to?" she whined.

Leaning in, Ray kissed her on the forehead, just above the scar from the first and only open sore she ever got.

He kissed Maddie on the head next, then got up and went to the safe in the bedroom. He brought back the RX-4 syringe.

Lolo knew the drill. She stood and lifted up her shirt to let Ray inject the needle into her tummy fat. She winced, then smiled at Ray.

"All done, sweetheart," he said. "Why don't you and Maddie go play video games."

Lolo perked up. "Really?"

Maddie grinned.

"Yeah," Ray said. They scrambled over to the TV, and he walked out to the balcony with his beer in hand.

"You okay?" Alicia asked.

He took another swig. "Yeah, baby. I'm good."

They never talked about his work. It was better that way. She wouldn't understand, anyway, and she had enough to worry about with four kids living in the slums.

He looked out over their complex, and she went back into the kitchen. The courtyard below was packed full of people. Most of them were probably discussing the attack on the port. Everyone had heard about it, and most people suspected it was probably the Saints. But with rumors flying about the Russians, law enforcement didn't seem so sure.

But Ray was. He knew about the RX-4 delivered to Hope Hotel. It had to be the Saints. No one but those vigilantes would give away the precious medicine.

He cursed under his breath as he thought back to what little Jackie had told him at the radiation ward of the hospital. The boy had described seeing a Saint with hair like antlers. The dude was big and black, like Ray.

Plenty of other guys in the city wore their hair like Moose, but how many cops?

His gut sank at the prospect of his brother being one of the Saints. Not because he hated them for their vigilante quest to bring down the Morettis, Vegas, and all the other corrupt crime families, but because he knew what would happen to Moose if he was a Saint and he ever got caught.

But he couldn't see his brother doing something so stupid, not with a family to think about. He had worked as a deputy with Dom for years—ever since Dom's dad got killed outside the border.

Nah, Ray didn't believe his bro and his bro's friend were the men behind the masks. But someone on the LAPD had to be helping the Saints, and he was going to find out who.

"Alicia, I'll be back later," he said.

"Where do you think you're going?" she said. "Dinner's almost ready."

He walked into the kitchen, where she had a dinner of champions cooking: government-issue macaroni noodles with hunks of Spam.

"Looks delicious," he lied. "Save a plate for me. I'll be back later."

"When?" She put her hands on her hips and narrowed her brown eyes at him.

Damn, you still look sexy when you're mad.

He had fallen in love with those exotic eyes. They married eight years ago and started making their beautiful babies a year later. But life in Los Angeles, and his job, had driven a wedge between them.

"Soon as I can, babe," he said.

She shrugged. "Be safe," she said, almost as if she meant it.

He had expected an argument, but this was a welcome surprise. Hurrying out of the kitchen before she changed her mind, he didn't stop except to kiss his daughters again.

"Bye, Daddy," Maddie said. "I hope you catch some bad guys."

Lolo smiled, revealing two missing baby teeth. His girls were adorable, just like their mom. Everything he did out there was for his family.

Ray drove across the city, still working on the forty, his mind racing. The Mosquitos were out tonight, spraying the air with chemicals. So were the kids on their scooters and mopeds, and the biker gangs.

Engines rumbled as old-school motorcycles vroomed by. They were bounty hunters and guns for hire. Most of the time, they left the cops alone, but tonight they were probably out looking for the Saints, salivating over that $2-million-a-head bounty.

Ray drove for over an hour—past the Port of Long Beach and all the way to Anaheim, where Angel Stadium was now a refugee camp. Thousands of people lived in the tent city set up inside, where the Angels once played, and in the parking lots outside.

Ray had trouble believing that this was one of the most civilized places left in the country. The other cities still standing were in far worse shape. At least the crime families gave some sort of organization to the madness.

Of all the sights, though, it was always the concrete fortress in the Malice Wastes that hit him the hardest. Maybe it was because he had sent hundreds of men to die there over the years.

Or maybe it was because the idea of being imprisoned there terrified him.

The House of the Devil.

Ray knew a few cops serving time in the massive facility. Most of them would never see daylight again. Some had already been murdered by the same scum they had put away.

He couldn't think of a much worse fate than going inside those walls. The place was a den of living, breathing evil, from raiders captured attacking the walls, to the gangsters and thugs who pressed their luck one too many times—or failed to pay off the cops.

Finishing off the last of the forty, he tossed it out the window and drove away. The alcohol warmed his gut, and he pushed the pedal, racing down the highway at a hundred miles an hour.

The beams bounced up and down over several potholes, but he kept his foot down, going faster. The Audi raced by a rusted sedan going half its speed.

Maybe the job had finally cracked him—maybe the last spark of good in his heart had gone out, and maybe his family would be better off if he was dead.

The next car in the right lane was a police cruiser. They turned on their lights, then turned them off.

He felt a little flutter inside, not because he was worried about getting pulled over, but because he realized he had a freaking death wish.

He took his foot off the pedal at the thought of leaving his family behind. All his side deals, all the hustling, all the bodies left in excavations and landfills—all of it was to provide for them. They had food on the table, clothes to wear, RX-4 for Lolo, a video game system they played on a television that had cost him a week's pay.

But life wasn't like the video games his kids played. He got only one life, which meant he had to keep being smart and never give up. He had to keep fighting for Alicia, Jamal, Will, Lolo, and Maddie.

He took the next exit and pulled out his cell phone. A missed call from his CO. Ignoring it, he dialed his brother instead.

"'Sup?" Moose answered.

"Wanna grab a beer?"

"Already had a few. Heading back to my crib soon. You good, man?"

"Yeah, I'm good."

"'Cause you don't usually call me twice in a day, bro," Moose said.

"Yeah, just thinking about old times."

There was a pause on the other end. "Maybe in a few days, man—been busy at work."

"Yeah, me too. Talk later, brother."

Ray ran a hand over his neatly trimmed beard. His brother was hiding something. He could hear it in his voice, and he had seen it at the barbecue a few days ago. But that didn't mean he was a Saint.

Soon. I'll talk to him about this soon.

First he had some more business to take care of. He dialed his CO back. The lieutenant sounded nervous when he answered.

"Hey, Ray, we need to meet up. Where you at?"

"Just leaving Anaheim."

"What the fuck'd you go there for?"

"Sightseeing."

"Dangerous place to be tonight. Meet me at the usual spot in thirty minutes."

His CO hung up, and Ray tucked the cell phone back into his pocket.

He got on the interstate and headed north. The ride gave him plenty of time to think about everything that had happened over the past week. First, his partner getting shot, then the attack on the port and the Saints hitting the RX-4 shipment.

Normally, he had control over shit. He didn't let people get the drop on him. Ray Clarke got the drop on *them*.

But things were spiraling out of control. The Saints were screwing everything up. They had to go, and if his brother was one of them, Ray was going to face a choice.

The headlights hit the dirt industrial area surrounding the abandoned Inglewood oil field. He turned onto the frontage road. His off-road tires handled well on the bumpy path, and he sped down the winding trails.

Seeing the warehouse, he slowed down to make sure his P320 was full, with one in the pipe. The area looked clear, but he wasn't taking any chances. The edge Ray had heard in the lieutenant's voice made him uneasy, even though it wasn't unusual to meet out here late at night.

He pulled up next to the black Cadillac and rolled his window down. Lieutenant Best sat in the driver's seat, smoking a cigar. He took a puff, making his fat cheeks seem to shrink.

"What's up, Lieutenant?" Ray asked.

Best blew out the smoke and reached over to the passenger seat. Ray pointed his P320 at the door, ready to fire if this turned out to be an ambush. He didn't trust the guy for shit.

"Here's your cut from the port last night," Best said. He grabbed an envelope and handed it out through the window. Keeping the pistol in his right hand, Ray grabbed it with his left.

"Thanks."

"So, what you been hearing out there today? Anything from our Italian friends?" Best asked.

"I heard about the two million price tag on each Saint's head, but I haven't talked to Vinny. Figured I'd let shit die down after the port."

"Better them than us . . ." Best took another drag before looking over, fear in his gaze. "I heard there were Russian RPGs used in the attack."

"I heard that too," Ray said. "I don't think Don Antonio is going to think you're stupid enough to have been involved. Chances are, he'll go after the Russians *and* the Saints."

Best grinned and tossed the cigar on the ground. "The Morettis aren't the only ones looking for Robin Hood and his merry band of assholes. Chief Stone has ordered the boys and girls of the LAPD to find and bring them in."

* * *

At 7:00 p.m., Dom pulled out his buzzing phone to find a text message from Lieutenant Marks.

Got tickets for you and one other person. Tomorrow morning.

Marks had found a way to get Dom and Moose into the secure prison, the House of the Devil. Putting the phone away, he took a breath and walked into the hospital to see his mom.

Camilla had offered to join him, but he felt her time was better spent visiting her uncle. She was right—the Saints needed a backup plan. Namid could always go home to the Mojave reservation, but the rest of them would never be safe there.

The huge bounty was a game changer, but Dom was trying not to worry about it too much. The money didn't matter to the people who knew their identities, and that was only a handful besides Lieutenant Marks and Councilman Castle.

And Sammy. The new CI had seen Bettis's face. But he was locked away at their safe house and wasn't going anywhere.

Dom took in a deeper breath when he got to the mental health ward. He hated this place—the smell of disinfectants, the same white walls, the too-bright fluorescent lights. Mostly, he hated that his mom lived here, that he couldn't take care of her anymore.

The nurse—a new one he didn't recognize—buzzed him in. She had curly red hair and big black-rimmed glasses.

"Dominic Salvatore here to see Elena Salvatore," he said.

"Go on in."

He made his way through the halls with the night guard, Blake. He wore white scrubs like the rest of the staff but carried a black nightstick, like the one Dom had been issued when he joined the LAPD.

"How's she been?" Dom asked.

Blake frowned. "She's displaying more psychotic behavior since your last visit."

"And she's been taking all her RX-Four doses?"

"Yup, we supervise each one."

A doctor Dom hadn't seen before walked down the hallway, and Blake waved him over.

"Dr. Watts, you got a moment to talk to Mr. Salvatore?"

"Sure," Watts said.

"How you doin', Doc?" Dom said.

"Good. You're here to see Elena?"

Dom nodded. "Blake said she's been displaying some concerning behaviors."

The doctor brought up her file on his tablet. "The antiviral agent is preventing the genetically modified virus from further damaging her immune system, and she has no symptoms of thickened nerves or lesions, which leads me to believe the behavior is caused mostly by mental illness."

"In other words, she's just crazy," Dom replied.

Watts pursed his lips, then nodded. "She has extreme mental health issues, and we're focusing on helping her with coping mechanisms."

"Thank you, Doctor."

He nodded and continued his rounds as Blake pulled out a pair of keys to unlock the door.

"Don't get her all worked up," he said. "We just got her to sleep about an hour ago."

"Okay."

Blake opened the door. "Take as much time as you want."

The door clicked shut behind Dom, and he walked over to his mom's bedside. She was curled up in a fetal position, clutching something to her chest. He stopped a few feet from the bed, watching her in the glow of moonlight coming in the window.

She looked so . . . *small.* Like a child.

He didn't want to wake her when she looked so peaceful, so he sat in the chair by her bed and watched her for a few minutes. He could see her face clearly: the scars from the lesions, the wrinkles from endless hours of crying, and her thin gray hair.

And he could also see the tattered stuffed elephant she clutched to her chest like a pillow. Seeing Mumbo, Monica's favorite stuffed animal, nearly brought Dom to tears.

The past eight years had been hell for him and his mom, literally driving her insane from the grief. The drugs didn't help, especially the opioids that she used to numb the pain. But she was being weaned off them, and she was still alive thanks to the miraculous RX-4.

Most weren't so lucky. Of all the people in the city with mental health problems, only a fraction had medical support like this. He paid a lot for her care here, but it was the only thing he could do for her. There was no way he could care for her back at his apartment.

The fact that she hated him didn't help matters. Every time he came here, he hoped she would forgive him for losing Monica and failing to find her since that day, but she never changed.

She would never forgive him or his dad.

He watched her torso's even rise and fall, her vertebrae protruding against her white gown like the spines of some ancient reptile. Seeing her sleep made him tired, and he closed his eyes for a moment.

A low voice woke him.

"Dominic, is that you?"

He looked over at the bed, where his mom had sat up, still gripping Mumbo against her chest like a baby.

"Hey, Mom," he said, forcing a smile. "How are you doing?"

Her eyes narrowed, forming a mask of wrinkles.

"Did you find her?"

Dom resisted the urge to sigh. He almost told her about Max, but that would only upset her further and result in endless questions. Besides, he couldn't trust that she wouldn't repeat it to anyone.

"Did you find Monica?" she asked again.

"No, Mom, I'm sorry."

"I told you not to come back until you bring Monica. I miss my baby." Elena rolled away, turning her back to him. "Now, go. Go and get your sister."

"Mom . . ." Dom said. He got up and moved over to the other side of the bed. "Mom, don't you miss me, too? I sure miss you, and I thought I'd come see how you're doing. I might not be able to come back for a while."

She looked up, glaring at him, rage and confusion in her eyes.

"I don't want to see you until you bring Monica home."

Dom sighed. "Okay, Mom." He leaned down and kissed her on the forehead. She let him do that, and for a moment her eyes seemed to brighten.

"I love you, Mom."

She blinked, as if trying to focus. Then she reached out a bony hand, brushing Dom's arm ever so slightly. "I love you, Dominic," she whispered.

Sighing, she looked away, hugging the stuffed animal tightly. Her words and the change of demeanor nearly broke Dom. He remained there for a moment, watching her as she drifted off to sleep.

Part of his mom was still in there, and he would do whatever it took to keep her from drifting into the darkness, even if it meant that he himself had to slip deeper into it.

"I'm going to kill the men who took Monica," he whispered. "I promise you that."

Elena stirred but didn't turn, either not hearing him or not wanting to say anything further.

"Bye, Mom," he said.

Dom left the mental ward as fast as he could walk, but he didn't leave the hospital right away. He wanted to talk to Abdul about his mom's treatment, maybe even grab a spot and talk about the RX-4.

He stopped at the ER desk on the ground floor.

"Excuse me," he said.

The receptionist looked up from a pile of papers. "May I help you?" she asked.

"Is Dr. Hogan in?"

The receptionist shook her head. "No, I'm sorry."

"If he's busy, I can wait," Dom said.

A nurse standing behind the desk came over. "I'm sorry, but Dr. Hogan didn't show up for his shift today. We sent someone to check on him, and they found him . . ."

"Found him?" Dom said.

The nurse nodded ruefully. "I'm sorry, but Dr. Hogan was murdered yesterday."

-13-

“Be careful,” said Bettis. “I’ll be right here if you need anything.”

“Thanks,” Camilla said. She pulled up her face mask and her hood and set off toward the Los Angeles River.

Chatsworth had looked a lot different when she first came with her family from Guadalajara. It was before the war and before the droughts turned the landscape into a desert.

Back then, while many people were fleeing violence in South America, her uncle, Álvaro Santiago, had convinced her father to come to “*el cielo*,” as he had called it—to heaven. Her uncle had built a business of helping people flee postwar violence to safe zones and communes out east—places where fallout hadn’t poisoned the soil, and gangs hadn’t poisoned everything else.

But it was one of those expeditions that ended up killing her mother and father—the same expedition that cost Álvaro an eye and a leg.

Painful memories welled up in her as she walked up a street winding through the hills. The remains of mansions rose above her, their shattered windows reminding her of broken teeth.

Gusting wind stirred up the dust on the short walk to the river. She couldn’t remember the last time it rained. Two weeks? Three? The entire city was reliant on the desalination plants.

While the landscape and living conditions had changed vastly since the war, one thing hadn't. Her uncle was still a smuggler. She hadn't seen him in over six months and wasn't sure he even still lived in the city. Business had never been better for his crew, with locals who had money paying him a small fortune to take them east.

There were plenty of people to hire for the job. Biker gangs, veterans turned contractors, and even cops. But no one had Álvaro's track record. He was one of the only men to survive the journey across the wastes more than fifty times. He had also helped Dom and Moose get safely through the deserts to Vegas. But his expertise hadn't saved her parents.

This evening, she pushed the feelings aside and focused on the reason she was here to see him. At the first sign of civilization, Camilla reached behind her, making sure her hooded sweatshirt covered the Smith and Wesson .45 holstered inside her waistband.

Tents were scattered across a dead park at the bottom of the hill. Several cars drove past.

She walked downhill along a shaded lane, to a gated-off area. A guard wearing camouflage fatigues, goggles, and a breathing apparatus stood at the barred entrance. He held a shotgun across his broad chest.

"I'm here to see Álvaro," she said.

"And who are you?"

"His niece, Camilla."

The guard looked at her ID as she pulled down her mask. After a long look, he handed the card back and unlocked the gate.

"There's someone at the bottom that will take you to him," the man said.

"Thanks."

He opened the gate, and she walked in and took the ladder down to the bottom. Her boots hit the concrete bed of a "river" that she could step across.

The area had been put to good use, thanks to her uncle. His fleet of trucks had brought in the dirt for the gardens. Farmers tended the produce with the utmost care, composting and cultivating.

Several guards patrolled the area. One walked over to her holding an AK-47 with a stock wrapped in duct tape. They were simple people, but they protected their way of life.

"I'm here to see Álvaro," she said.

"Follow me."

She followed him along the edges of the gardens. Graffiti covered the concrete slopes above them.

Ahead, the riverbed broke off into two parts. On the right, the gardens continued, but on the left a massive steel door blocked off the mouth of a tunnel. A crooked sign hung above a pedestrian door hinged inside the larger door.

A bell chimed as she followed the guard. Farmers looked up from their work. Several people moved over to the pulley system they had developed to cover the crops during dust storms or acid rain.

Tarps were drawn overhead, so that by the time she got to the door of the tunnel, the improvised roof was complete, cloaking the riverbed in darkness.

The lights built into the concrete bank flickered on, powered by solar panels she had seen on the walk in. This was one impressive place—a true testament to the ingenuity and hard work of people like her uncle. They had saved the city from ending up a true wasteland like so many others.

"Wait here," said the guard.

She stopped outside the door. The farmers were back to work, pruning plants by lamplight. Several of them carried burlap bags of potatoes.

"Cam," said a voice.

She turned back to the open doorway, where her uncle stood holding a cane.

"*Hola, tío, ¿qué tal?*" she said, pulling down her face mask.

The thick silver mustache lifted in a smile. The prosthetic right leg creaked as he limped forward. He reached out, but she backed away from his embrace.

Álvaro's mustache drooped, and his shoulders slumped a little.

"Been a while," he said. "Come on in."

She followed him inside the open door, into a warehouse. The door clanked shut behind them.

"How you been, Cam?" he asked with his thick accent. "The border treating you okay?"

She shrugged. "Being a deputy is kind of like being a firefighter. Most days, you sit around waiting for a fire. How about you?"

He turned to look at the tunnel, which he had made into a long garage. Two semis were parked inside. Sparks flew off the brush guard of the truck on the right, where two men welded on a new spike.

"Took a real beating on the last run," he said. "But got another one going out tomorrow. Need to be ready."

"Where to?"

"This one is going to a commune in Iowa. Place called Decorah, where a former college town has fortified a small slice of paradise. It's a hidden gem in a sea of radioactive farmland."

"Sounds nice."

He motioned for her to move aside and pointed his cane at a shack they had built inside the tunnel. She joined him in the small office, stepping over to a desk with pictures of her family.

He closed the door and sat at his desk.

"I miss them every day," he said.

Camilla picked up a frame with her mother, father, and brother. The picture was taken on a secluded beach, when she was just seven or eight. They used to go there one Saturday a month to lie in the sun, play in the water, and eat freshly baked donuts, street tacos, and macaroons.

"Joaquín was a little over two in that picture," Álvaro said. "Fabiola sure did have a hard time with him when he was younger. Your brother was a real pistol."

His eyes flitted to the table.

Camilla wasn't the only one who had lost her family. Her uncle shared her pain. She laid the picture down. It was time to get to the point.

"I might need one of your crews in the near future," she said. "Got a kid and his mom that might need to get out of the city. And some . . . friends."

Álvaro leaned forward, making a pyramid of his wrinkled fingers.

"Who are these friends?" he asked.

"Can you help me, or not?" she asked.

"Depends on how many people, and when. Like I said, both my crews are going out tomorrow, and I'm going with them."

"That's okay, I'll figure something else out. Sorry to bother you." She turned to leave, but he reached out.

"Camilla, wait."

She held the door handle but didn't open it. Álvaro stood behind her and she turned to face him. Her heart sank at the sadness in his gaze and his posture. Seeing him standing there on a carbon-fiber leg, leaning on a cane, nearly broke her.

It also reminded her of her father and all she had lost.

"I didn't say, no," Álvaro said. "But I think it's time to tell me what's going on."

She wanted to tell him, but it would put his life at risk. She couldn't do that to her last surviving family member.

"I'll be in touch." She left the room without saying goodbye, too afraid that he would see the tears in her eyes.

* * *

Two days after the attack on the port, Vinny sat in the back of a Range Rover, nearly spilling his cup as they jolted over a pothole. Behind the wheel was Lino De Caro, wearing a gold pair of Gucci aviators.

"Watch it," said Christopher from the passenger seat.

"When is some of the money we give to the City Council members going toward roads?" Marco said. "Or does it all go to the wall?"

Vinny laughed. He cinched a strap on his ballistic vest and grabbed his new Beretta ARX160, the charcoal-gray gas-operated fully automatic assault rifle used by the Italian Army.

"Where the hell'd we get these?" Marco asked.

Vinny wasn't going to tell his cousin shit.

"Pretty nice, yeah?" Christopher said.

"Where's mine?" Marco asked, admiring the weapons.

"Your dad wants you out of the action," Christopher said. "You're here to watch and learn."

"So why this?" Marco asked. He patted his vest.

Vinny knew why. It was to protect the heir to the empire, and it also backed up his suspicions. Something big was about to go down, and odds were good it had to do with the Saints.

But why bring Marco along? Especially when Lucia was so adamant about not involving him in any violence?

It wasn't often that the prince of the Moretti family left the safety of his castle. If he did leave, it was usually for the Goldilocks Zone, with a posse of heavily armed soldiers.

Christopher opened a tactical bag in the front seat. For the first time in weeks, he wore black fatigues instead of one of his many Armani suits.

Lino wore a vest over his T-shirt, his inked, muscular arms flexing as he gripped the wheel and tried to keep the rig steady on the fragmented street. He cursed under his breath and wiped sweat from his forehead.

The sweat wasn't from the heat but from nerves, and Lino was usually the last man to get nervous—something else that told Vinny they were going after the Saints. The elusive cops were going to become *real* ghosts today.

Christopher pulled out magazines loaded with hollow-point rounds. Perhaps a lot of people were going to die.

"Come on," Marco said. "I should have one."

"No." Christopher's response earned him a scowl from Marco.

"Did you guys find out who the Saints are?" Marco asked.

Christopher had already turned back around to the front.

"Come on, let me in on this," Marco said. "I don't want to sit and watch. How'm I supposed to learn by doing that?"

Lino chuckled. "You got plenty of time to prove you got a big *cazzo*, kid, but today you best listen to orders."

Vinny palmed a magazine into his gun. He chambered a round and looked back out the window. They were moving into the outskirts of an old residential area. Most of the houses had burned down in the wildfires and droughts that followed the war.

He fingered his rifle's safety catch as a car came up on their left. It backed off when the driver saw the three Range Rovers.

Wise man, Vinny thought.

Several other cars passed on the other side of the highway. Most were rust buckets carrying migrant workers. An ancient Honda van with mattresses lashed to the top puttered down the road. Two kids were in the back seat, the parents in front. Two motorcyclists in body armor escorted the family.

They were trying to escape the darkness of LA, but for most people there was no escaping the misery. And there were far worse things than gangsters and junkies where the van was headed—raiders and cannibals prowled the deserts they must cross to reach the Midwest.

A cell phone chimed. Christopher pulled his out and brought it to his ear. "Okay, we're on our way," he said.

He put the phone away and muttered something to Lino, who accelerated to catch up to the other two Range Rovers. One of them had taken some damage in the attack at the coffee shop days earlier. The broken windows had been replaced, but shrapnel holes and dents peppered the passenger side.

All the pointless suspense was making Vinny mad. Why the hell keep *him* in the dark? He was a made man!

Lino took the freeway into the city, heading for the western slums in zone 2, Vega territory. Government housing complexes, stacked like gray concrete Legos, rose across the skyline.

"All right, go time in five minutes," Christopher said as they approached the dreary pyramidal structures. He looked to Marco. "Remember what I said. You're just here to watch. You got it?"

"Yeah, yeah." Marco stared out the window as the convoy moved into heavier traffic, standing out in stark contrast to the rusty heaps surrounding them. He suddenly looked away. "I don't like this," he said. "We shouldn't be on this strip."

"Your dad spent a small fortune on these ballistic door panels and bulletproof windows," Christopher said without turning. "We'll be fine."

"Yeah, but won't the cops recognize us?"

"Nope." Christopher pulled out ballistic helmets from the bag on the floor and handed them out.

Vinny grabbed one and stared at it. He was a Moretti. They didn't hide their faces when attacking. They weren't cowards like the Saints, or the Vegas with their colorful metal face masks.

"Just wear it," Christopher said when he saw Vinny glaring at the mask.

The convoy passed through an open marketplace, where thousands of people were out bartering goods. The Rovers attracted plenty of attention, and some people stopped what they were doing to watch. Others saw it as an opportunity to panhandle and loitered right in the middle of traffic.

Horns from the other cars honked. The front Range Rover halted, and one of the soldiers inside tossed a handful of coins onto the sidewalk. The onlookers bolted for a chance at a silver dime, clearing the roadway. And just like that, they were moving again.

Christopher took another call.

"Yeah?" he said. "We're almost there. ETA two minutes."

Vinny felt the first trickle of adrenaline.

The convoy took a right on the next street, entering a zone of halfway decent houses and apartment buildings. This was West Hollywood, where city officials and some of the wealthier businesspeople lived.

Cars, motorcycles, and trucks zipped by as traffic increased. A police cruiser turned on its lights and chased two men on a scooter.

The convoy took another right, onto a road framed with businesses, coffee shops, bars, and restaurants. The lead Range Rover peeled off, taking a left down an alleyway, but Lino kept following the one with the shrapnel damage.

"There," Christopher said, pointing at two armored black sedans parked in front of a coffee shop. Pedestrians crossed the street ahead, and civilians bustled along the sidewalks.

The Range Rover in front of them made a U-turn, and Lino gunned the engine, pulling into the opposite lane of traffic and slamming on the brakes a hundred feet from the armored sedans.

"That's them," Christopher said, pulling his mask up over his face. Lino followed suit, and they both jumped out.

The second Range Rover emptied, disgorging Moretti soldiers in tactical gear and ballistic masks. Weapons shouldered, they strode toward a group of people sitting at tables outside the coffee shop.

Three police officers drinking coffee stood up and went for their pistols. The one on the right, a young guy with a porn-star mustache, fell dead before he cleared the holster.

Bullets ripped into the chest of the other man, sending him sprawling back on the table.

"Holy fuck!" Marco said. "Are those the Saints?"

Vinny squinted for a better look, but these cops didn't look like anyone special. They looked like straight beat cops.

The third cop managed to pull his revolver, but a volley of hollow-points hit him in the skull, blowing brains, bone, and hair outward.

The front door to the coffee shop opened, and a fourth officer stumbled out. He managed to aim his handgun and get off the luckiest shot in the world. The round punched through the eye socket of a Moretti soldier's ballistic mask. He dropped to his knees and onto his side.

Vinny resisted the urge to break orders and jump out of the vehicle.

Christopher and Lino both looked over at their fallen comrade, limp as a doll, blood trickling out of his helmet.

"Stay here!" Christopher yelled.

He and Lino joined the fight.

The other seven Moretti associates and soldiers fired at the building, shattering storefront windows and hitting the cop with a dozen bullets. He crashed backward through the shards of the glass door.

Innocent people were cut down in the spray, falling to the pavement and screeching in agony. A shotgun blast rose over the noise. The fire came from the left of the parked Range Rover, somewhere on the sidewalk.

Marco pulled a pistol from his coat and opened the door before Vinny could grab him.

"Wait!" he yelled.

Vinny jumped out on his side. He hugged the vehicle and looked for contacts in the street, but all he saw were frightened people and cars racing away from the violence.

Gunfire continued as he crept around to the front of the Rover. Marco was crouching and aiming his pistol. The boom of a shotgun came again, and the blast slammed into the side of the Range Rover.

And Marco.

Vinny watched in horror as Marco slumped, his hand on his vest. He caught a blur of motion on the sidewalk as he moved for his cousin. The cop with the shotgun crouched behind a concrete park bench chipped by bullets—all misses from Marco.

The cop loaded fresh shells into his shotgun, eyes locking on Vinny. They widened as Vinny swung up his ARX160.

Three rounds obliterated the man's forehead, blowing out one eye.

"MOVE!" Lino shouted. He ran over and reached down to help Marco to his feet. The other Range Rover was already pulling away, but Christopher was standing in the seating area, over one of the cops.

Vinny ran over. The guy was still alive, trying to crawl away.

"You thought you could rob the Morettis?" Christopher yelled. "Turn over, dipshit."

The cop struggled for air, lungs crackling. Several gold chains hung over his heaving chest.

"I'm sorry . . . It wasn't supposed to go down like that," he said, gasping. "Please, please don't kill me."

This man was no Saint, Vinny realized. He was one of the cops who showed up with Lieutenant Best at the port before the attack.

"The Morettis are done dicking around with you rat fucks," Christopher said. "The deal with Captain Stone ends now."

The man put his hand out in front of his face. "Please, no . . . NO!"

Two rounds punched through his hand and face. Christopher spat on the corpse and jerked his chin at their ride.

"Let's go, Vin," he said calmly.

They hustled back to the vehicle and peeled away. Marco was moaning in the back seat, and Vinny quickly helped him out of his vest.

There was no blood, but he could see right away that his cousin was going to have a nasty bruise.

"You're fine," Vinny said. He patted Marco on the shoulder.

"What the fuck'd I tell you?" Christopher asked, turning around as he reloaded his rifle.

"I'm sorry," Marco said, breathing heavily. "That cop came out of nowhere."

"And he almost dirtied up the car door with your educated brains," Christopher said.

Lino chuckled. "How do your balls feel?"

Christopher looked to Vinny. "Nice shooting, but you didn't follow orders, either. Your job is to watch your cousin."

He normally didn't question his father, but he couldn't hold back.

"Since when did we kill cops? The Saints are one thing, but those guys were nobodies."

Christopher snorted. "Those were some of the 'nobodies' from the port the other night."

Lino turned down another street, tires screeching. They gunned it for three more blocks, but they weren't heading back to the freeway yet.

The mission wasn't over.

Houses with barred windows and doors lined the street. It was quiet here, the earlier violence over.

"There," Christopher said.

Lino nodded and followed the other Range Rover to the right side of the street, where the third Rover was parked. His brother, John, was standing on the street, holding sentry with his rifle.

"Marco, you good to move?" Christopher asked.

"Yeah, I'm fine."

"Come with me, then," Christopher said. "You too, Vin."

As soon as the vehicle parked, Vinny and Marco jumped out. Marco winced from the bruised ribs, but he moved well enough.

They jogged toward an open front gate and up a curving path to a house. The front door was broken open, and Christopher walked right through. He moved through a living room with decent furniture and a large-screen TV, down a hallway and into a kitchen, where a shirtless man sat at his kitchen table.

"Fucking guineas," the man grumbled.

Vinny recognized him by the acne scars.

"Sorry to disturb your breakfast," Christopher said, pulling up a chair. "So where is it?"

Lieutenant Best looked up from his plate of cold eggs and bacon but didn't reply.

Christopher grabbed the plate and whacked him in the side of the head. Then he grabbed the back of his neck and slammed his head onto the table.

Best fell out of his chair and onto the tile floor, grunting and spitting blood.

"I'm not here to play games," Christopher said, leaning down. He picked a piece of bacon off the floor, sniffed it, and jammed it in the lieutenant's open mouth.

"Tell me where the money from the other night is, or you're going to die on your kitchen floor—a fat pig choking on bacon."

Best spat the meat out and looked up, a grin on his chubby face. Blood dripped from his nose and the cuts on his forehead. "You wouldn't kill a cop. We have a deal—I was there the night Stone made it with Don Antonio."

Christopher stood up and pointed his rifle muzzle at Best's head.

"Deal's over," he said. "We just killed six of you corrupt, worthless fucks, and now it's your turn unless you tell me who the Saints are."

The blue eyes narrowed, scrutinizing Christopher for a lie. Marco watched his uncle, who, like his father, had years of experience dealing with men like Best.

The lieutenant pushed against the floor and labored to his feet, his belly sagging over his blue uniform pants. "I don't know who the Saints are, I swear," he said. "But I do have the money from the port. I'll give it to you. Just please . . . please don't shoot."

"Got a lot of heat incoming," said a voice. "Better move, Chrissy."

Lino stood in the hallway with his rifle cradled.

Christopher grabbed Best by the arm. "Guess you're coming with us."

Vinny pushed the muzzle of his gun into the man's back as they led him from the house.

"You can't do this to me," Best said, looking over his shoulder. "You can't do this to a cop. Don Antonio and I are partners."

"The fuck we can't," Vinny said. "We're the Morettis. We don't have partners. We own you, and we own this city."

-14-

Antonio walked over to the bulletproof office window with a steaming cup of espresso in hand. He was a cautious man who understood that expensive security was worth the price. Twelve floors below his fine Italian shoes, he had an end-of-the-world bunker just in case the US government decided to go nuclear again.

When his family fled the violence in Naples, he had promised Christopher they would build an empire out of the ashes. Like his other promises, it had come true.

Long ago, he had promised his wife that he would never let Marco become part of this world. He also told her he would always protect their son, no matter what.

But to fulfill the second promise, he had to break the first. Their son needed experience to survive in this cutthroat world that, Antonio now realized, he could never escape from.

Lucia stood next to him at the window, watching for the first sign of their son. The wait wasn't long. A convoy of Range Rovers blazed down the road, kicking up a plume of dust. The guards manning the gate were already opening the thick steel doors.

Antonio gestured for Lucia to take a seat. Her arms were folded across her chest, and she had that look—the kind that told him she was in no mood for bullshit.

"When are you going to tell me what's going on?" she asked.

Antonio sipped his espresso, savoring the bitter taste.

"The motions put in place today will come to light soon," he said. "This is just the first of several moves I'm making to ensure our survival."

"I don't want to *survive*, Antonio. That's not why I married you. I married you because—"

He raised a hand. "Because I promised you we would *thrive*. And we are."

"Thriving means nothing if Marco is dead. So tell me why you sent our son out there to kill cops. You said he was going to have a desk job or something, where he wasn't at risk."

"Marco was instructed to remain in his vehicle—"

"He shouldn't even have been out there," she said, talking faster. "He's not ready for this world, Tony."

Antonio braced for the coming storm. She called him Tony only when she was mad or he was about to get lucky, and the latter hadn't happened for almost a month.

"He's not ready," she repeated. "And what about the deal you had with Chief Stone?"

"His men broke that contract."

"You're not worried he will ask the military for support?"

Antonio laughed. "What military? The Executive Council will never send troops out here again. The people will turn on them. There will be riots, violence."

"But if they do, they could ruin us, like they almost did the last time the military was in Los Angeles."

Antonio put a hand under her chin, lifting it so she would meet his gaze.

"No one will ruin us again, my love," he said.

Lucia let her arms down, exposing the three gold chains around her neck. The gold accentuated her olive skin. She loved gold—and diamonds too: the two-carat studs in her ears, the three-carat stone on her finger.

Thriving indeed.

Antonio pulled out one of two guest chairs in front of his desk. "Have a seat, Lu." Turning her own tactic back on her and using her shortened name seemed only to infuriate her more.

"No. I don't want to sit. You're being an asshole."

"Suit yourself."

Most of his soldiers' wives would have gotten a slap for talking to them this way. But Antonio wasn't like most men in this line of work. He saw the woman in front of him as his equal.

"Marco will never be ready if he stays locked away here or out all night at one of his clubs," Antonio said.

"I'd rather see him drink too much and make poor decisions with girls than see him gunned down in the street," Lucia replied. "The Saints will kill him the first chance they get. You know this, Antonio."

He got up and moved to her as her fierce eyes met his.

"I heard you agreed to let him hunt the Saints so he could earn a place at the table. So clearly, your deal about a desk job was a lie."

Deals, so many deals.

Don Antonio was a man of deals. Even now in middle age, when most men of his stature were content to sit back, he was still hustling. He had a fresh deal with Esteban Vega, deals with the cops, deals with the Russians, deals with the gangbangers, deals with the City Council, and soon a new deal with Mayor Buren.

But the deal that mattered most was the one he had made with his wife many years ago, when Marco was born.

"I'm taking care of the Saints," he said. "Don't worry, my love. Marco is safe. You will see."

She shook her head. "I did *not* want this life for him."

"Neither did I, but Marco must choose his own way. And this is what he wants. It's also the only way to keep him safe. I realize that now, more than ever. There is no escaping the empire we have created. We own it, but it also owns us."

"I'd rather he spent his days at the pool getting drunk than see him murdered."

"He has a lot better odds of not being killed if we teach him how to survive . . . Besides, someday I will be gone, and he must be the man of the house."

Lucia seemed to soften at that assertion.

Antonio brushed the side of her face with his ring. Its gold *M* glided over her olive skin. She held his gaze, then reluctantly took the offered chair.

Perhaps she didn't like the idea of her husband dying, or perhaps she knew he was right about their son needing to cut his teeth out there in the slums.

"Marco isn't street smart like Vinny, or strong like you," she said. "I don't know what's happened to him."

"You coddled him. He will never learn if you continue enabling him."

"We both did." The fierce brown eyes settled on his. They seemed to lighten a bit as she relaxed in the plush seat.

"No more enabling," Antonio said.

"Okay," she said, her voice softening further with resignation. "Marco's failures are my own. I'm just worried we're going to lose him to the same world we have tried to protect him from—the world we did not want him to know."

Antonio sat down in the chair beside her. He put his hand over hers.

"Christopher and Vinny are looking after Marco, and so am I. I won't let anything happen to him. I almost lost you both in Naples, and I will never let that happen again."

Lucia bit the inside of her lip. "Promise me. Promise me on your soul."

"On my soul. I will protect you both, no matter the cost."

A rap on the door interrupted their conversation, but he held her gaze for several beats. Then he picked up her hand, brought it to his lips, and gave a gentle kiss, pausing for a moment to look at the diamond he had given her when he promised to be with her for life.

That promise wasn't part of a deal like the others.

"Don Antonio," said a voice out in the hallway. The double mahogany doors opened. Lino was first into the room, tucking his shades up into his hair. Marco rushed inside, a smile on his face.

"Marco!" Lucia exclaimed. She hurried over to give the boy a hug, but Antonio simply stood and watched. Judging by Marco's grin, he was just fine.

It was time the kid learned to be a man.

Marco groaned as Lucia embraced him.

"Mom, come on," he grumbled.

The other captains and soldiers laughed but were silenced by her icy glare. The reaction made Antonio crack a smile. Sometimes, his wife was a thorn in his side, but her aggressiveness was part of the reason he had fallen in love with her.

She was a great mother and a great wife. And Antonio would do everything he could to honor his promise to her, even if it meant breaking others.

He walked over to the window.

"It's done," Lino said. He joined him at the glass overlooking the compound. "We're ready for phase two of the plan."

Antonio nodded.

Below, the front gates parted and began to swing inward. Two Toyota pickup trucks were lined up behind a white maintenance van. Men in tactical gear, wearing ballistic masks and carrying automatic rifles, piled into the vehicles.

Vinny and Christopher approached the second pickup, and Christopher stopped and looked up at the window.

"Dad, there's something I need to tell you," Marco said.

Antonio remained at the window.

"I had the contact from the port killed at Lincoln Heights. I thought . . ." Marco stiffened. "I messed up, Dad. I was just trying to make you proud, but we should have talked to him first to see if he had leaked the shipment to the Saints."

Antonio stared at his son.

"We had another lead on a doctor that was at the hospital with the Saints," Marco said, "but someone got to him before us."

Antonio already knew both these things, but he didn't tell his son. He needed to keep some decisions secret. Things were in motion that his son and his wife couldn't know about.

He looked down at his soldiers below, and Marco stepped up beside him at the window.

It felt good to have his boy here.

"Where are Uncle Chrissy and Vinny going?" Marco asked.

Antonio watched the convoy leave the compound. Soon he would teach his son about how to build, broker, and break a deal.

But not yet. Marco first needed to see how it was done.

Today, Antonio was the dealmaker, but by tonight, he would also be a deal breaker.

* * *

Max Sammartino. Dom repeated the name to himself.

"You ready, boss?" Moose asked.

"Only for the last eight years."

They both wore shades and filtration masks as Moose drove the Jeep in the bright morning sun. Their destination wasn't far, and he slowed as they approached the first of several roadblocks surrounding the Southland's most infamous prison.

From the outside, the House of the Devil looked a lot like the other government buildings constructed after the war. Built almost completely of concrete, with barred windows, and solar panels jutting off the rooftop. But unlike the housing projects in the slums, the grounds were surrounded by concentric razor-wire-topped fences, minefields, and radioactive dirt.

Moose pulled up to the first roadblock. Both he and Dom wore their Sheriff's Department uniforms and got waved through without any issues.

The guards here were mostly young men or women without experience working the border, or men too old to work that more hazardous job. For all they knew, Dom and Moose were deputies here to see a prisoner. No one would dream they were Saints.

Moose parked the Jeep by an open warehouse-sized garage sheltering a motor pool of MRAPs and flatbed trucks. The former military vehicles were painted brown and marked with LASD logos.

Guarding the secure steel entrance were two deputies wearing layered coats, helmets, and orange goggles. Not an inch of skin was exposed to the elements.

They stepped aside as Dom and Moose approached.

"Morning," Dom said.

"Yup," replied one of the men, his voice muffled by the mask. He used a key card to unlock the door. A third guard waited inside. Moose and Dom followed him down a passage to a desk.

"We're here to see Prisoner Four One Five Oh," Dom said, holding out the paperwork Marks had given him.

The woman at the desk looked up from a book, clearly annoyed at having to check their paperwork and identification. After glancing at each, she lazily hit a button.

The next door buzzed and opened.

"Have fun," she said, looking back down at her book. "Oh, and you might want to keep your masks on—sewage line's backed up again."

Dom and Moose walked into a hallway with vaulted ceilings and two floors of cells. Prisoners got up from their bunks to look out through the bars.

Flies buzzed thick around buckets of feces inside the multiperson cells. Most of the inmates were thin as scarecrows, their bones protruding against the faded gray shirts and tattered pants. Sweat dripped down their filthy bodies, radiating a stench Dom could smell through his breathing apparatus.

The prisoners let out a blue streak of profanities at the passing deputies. Some even spat through the bars.

A guard hit the iron bars with his baton, forcing the inmates back.

"Quiet, maggots!" another guard yelled. "Or I'm collecting some fingernails tonight."

In a few minutes, Dom was going to do far worse to Max.

They walked through the minimum-security wing and came up on the maximum zone. Only a few light bulbs worked, casting shadows over a hallway that reeked of feces, old sweat, and rot.

A guard took Dom and Moose to a steel door. Unlocking it, he gestured toward a man inside, sitting on a bench that must have also been his bunk. His feet and hands were shackled to a chain anchored to the wall.

Dom scrutinized the gaunt man under a light that flickered on. What remained of him still looked Italian: the slicked-back hair, the dark eyes, the cross tattooed on his neck.

"Max Sammartino," Moose said.

The prisoner blinked in the light, holding a shackled hand up to shield his eyes. They widened when they flitted from Moose to Dom.

"What do you pigs want?" His chains rattled as he got off the bunk. "I've already answered your dumb-ass questions."

"We're here to ask you a few more," Dom said calmly.

Moose nodded at the bench. "Sit."

Reluctantly Max sat, blinking rapidly. It was more of a twitch, really. He was a jittery son of a bitch, his right leg bouncing like a sewing machine needle. Dom wondered whether the guy would recall anything from so long ago, but he was prepared to beat the memory out of him if necessary.

"We heard you picked up a girl at the Downey High School eight years ago," Dom said. "I want to know where you took her."

Max looked away.

"You're going—" Moose started to say.

Dom took a step closer and hunched slightly. "What my friend was about to say is that you're going to answer our questions, or this is going to be very unpleasant."

Moose bent down too. "We're not like the other guys you've talked to."

A cackle broke from Max's cracked lips. "You can't do shit to me that I haven't already endured."

"Is that so?" Moose said, with a grin that even Dom found a little unnerving.

Max's sullen glare didn't change.

"Now for the questions," Dom said. He asked Max if he remembered going to the high school the day his sister was kidnapped. The date didn't ring a bell, but mention of the school did seem to evoke some memory that flashed in the prisoner's eyes.

A crooked black grin crossed his face. He closed his lips over the rot and looked away. He was going to need some encouragement to talk.

Dom took out the needle-nose pliers from his duty belt, letting Max watch him as he paced in front of his bench.

"You ever had a fingernail peeled off?" Dom asked. "The guards say it can sometimes happen around here."

Max laughed, and Dom decided it was time to prove he was serious. Instead of taking a fingernail, he grabbed Max's ear in the pliers, squeezed, and twisted. He held up the hunk of cartilage admiringly.

Max yowled, and Moose stuffed a bandanna into his mouth.

Bulging eyes roved from Dom to Moose as Max kept up his muffled screaming into the cloth.

Dom wiped the chunk of ear off onto Max's shirt. "I'm going to ask you again," he said.

Moose reached over to take the bandanna. "You scream, and he'll have your eye looking back at you. You understand?"

Max looked at the pliers and then nodded. Moose slapped him on the side of the head, then yanked the bandanna out.

Moose and Dom waited for Max to catch his breath. Then he said, "I went to that school, yeah. I went to a lot of schools. They were part of our stops back then."

"You took kids from the schools during the war?" Moose asked. "Girls?"

"And a few boys."

Dom and Moose exchanged a glance.

"Sold 'em for great prices too. Even got me a little taste when the boss wasn't lookin'."

Dom felt his blood turn to ice water.

"You remember this girl?" he managed to say through a clenched jaw. He held up a picture of Monica.

Max squinted.

"She don't look familiar, but who knows? I seen a thousand that age."

Dom swallowed. *A thousand girls.* He could feel Moose's eyes on him, evaluating when the ice would turn to lava and blow.

"Look, guys, I don't got the best memory no more."

Dom held the picture out again. "Think real hard."

Max leaned closer. "Yeah, I think I remember her. But I don't know where they took her after we dropped her off."

"We?" Dom asked.

Moose stepped closer, and Dom clacked the bloody pliers together. "The guys you worked with are the last thing you should be worried about right now. Mobsters can't kill you in here. We, on the other hand, are right here in your cell."

Max swallowed hard but didn't reply.

Dom clicked the pliers again. "Not playing, Maxie. If you don't start talking right now, the next divot comes out of your itty-bitty pecker."

Moose gave him a worried glance, but Dom didn't care.

"Vito," Max finally said. "It was almost always me and Vito."

"Vito got a last name?" Moose asked.

Max looked at him as if he were stupid.

Dom already knew who he was talking about. Vito was a cousin of Don Antonio. The fat bastard was rumored to be the kingpin behind their drug operation.

"Vito Moretti. Yeah, we've heard of him," Dom said. "Back to what you were saying about the girl. Where'd you drop her off?"

Sweat beaded on Max's brow as his eyes shifted back and forth, from Dom to Moose and back again. Then he relaxed, as if realizing that this was it for him. He had nothing waiting for him outside, even if he did get released someday.

Max suddenly swatted at his ear like someone trying to get rid of an annoying mosquito.

"You jonesing, Max?" Dom said. "If you tell me what I need to know, I'll give you something to relieve your pain. All you gotta do is tell me where they would have taken her after you dropped her off."

Max looked up, the fear gone, replaced by the prospect of a fix. "I . . . I might be able to recall."

"*Mite* lives on a stray dog's ass," Moose said, shaking his head. "Not really what we're looking for."

Dom was losing his patience again. The scattered thoughts, his thumping heart, and his sweaty hands were all signs the volcano was about to blow. He needed to hold it together a little longer.

"Tell me where they would have taken this girl, and I'll give you something for your pain," Dom said, speaking slowly.

"Why is she so important?" Max asked, tilting his head curiously.

"Answer the question," Moose said. He took off his coat and draped it on the side of the sink. Max looked at the bulging biceps and watched him crack his knuckles.

"Probably got taken to Vegas," Max said.

Dom and Moose exchanged another look. They had already searched Sin City for Monica. Hearing that it was likely the place confirmed what Dom already assumed: his sister was gone forever.

"That's where most of the calves went."

The comparison of his sister to livestock was the final straw. Dom grabbed Max by the cheeks, pressing in so hard, he felt a rotted tooth break off. He squeezed harder.

Then he let go and punched Max in the nose, popping his head backward.

Moose walked over to the door and peered through the window, then nodded back at Dom. He pulled a knife out of his pocket, flipped it open, and brought it over.

Max choked, sobbing into his hands. "No," he stammered. "I answered your questions. Please . . . You said you'd get me a fix."

Moose forced the wadded-up bandanna back in his mouth, then put him in a full Nelson hold.

Lieutenant Marks's words surfaced in his mind. *That's what separates us from them.*

Then he remembered his dad's words.

Sometimes, you have to use evil to fight evil.

Dom had followed the law for years—conflicted but never wavering too far from his promise to Marks that he wouldn't become like his dad or the gangsters.

But over the past few nights, he had deviated further and further from his promise.

Tonight, for the first time in eight years, he knew who was responsible for taking his sister. And his next stop was to find Vito Moretti. When he was done with Vito, he would go after the king of the entire operation. The man who, Dom had always known deep down, was responsible for the destruction of his family.

Don Antonio Moretti.

"Here's your fix," Dom said. He went to work, stabbing Max over and over with the tip of the pliers until he let out a last evil breath and went limp.

-15-

"Morning," Camilla said.

She hopped into the back seat of the Jeep, next to Rocky, who was sleeping off a hangover.

"Morning," Moose said.

Dom just nodded.

Rocky moaned and looked up. He had a nice shiner from a blow Tooth had landed in the boxing ring last night.

"Where you guys been?" Camilla asked.

"We had an errand to run this morning," Dom said.

Moose pulled away from her apartment building, and Dom looked in the back seat. "Did you talk to your uncle?"

"Yeah. He has a caravan going out, but he's down to help us if needed."

Dom nodded again and turned back to the front seat.

Something was on his mind. Something was on his uniform too.

"Is that blood?" she asked.

Dom looked down but didn't reply.

"Did I miss something?" Rocky asked.

"No," Dom and Moose said in unison.

"Okay, I'm going back to sleep," Rocky said, resting his head against the window.

"Did you get any sleep at all?" she asked Dom.

"Not really."

"How's your mom doing?" Camilla asked, almost afraid to do so. That was probably what preoccupied him, she realized.

Dom fished a loose pill out of his pocket and swallowed it with a chug of water.

Camilla didn't ask. For all she knew, it was just ibuprofen.

Or speed . . .

"Dom, did you hear me?" she asked.

He looked over, his tired eyes focusing on her. "Hear what?"

"Your mom—how is she?"

Dom shrugged. "Same. She's never going to forgive me, and she's never getting better."

She turned back to the view of the factories on the right side of the street. They passed a Mosquito spraying the air and cleaning the roads. Several of them were out in the agricultural zone this morning.

Camilla always enjoyed driving through the zone of warehouses retrofitted as greenhouses for corn, potatoes, tomatoes, and spinach. Most of the food that didn't come from China through the Port of Long Beach or from government-run farms in the Midwest was grown and distributed right here in the ag zone. Seeing it always gave her a little surge of hope.

They cut through the area on their way to pick up Cayenne.

"I'll grab her after I talk to Yolanda and the kids," Moose said. He hopped out and jogged toward the courtyard of his building.

Sometimes, she envied Moose for having someone to go home to. But then again, having someone to love meant having someone to lose. After Joaquín and her parents were killed, she had decided to focus on work—just work.

"Abdul was killed yesterday," Dom said quietly.

"*What!*" Camilla gasped.

"Someone killed him in his apartment."

Rocky stirred in the back seat. "What's going on?"

First Jason and now Abdul. Camilla had a feeling she knew who was next.

"Do you think Abdul told whoever killed him who we are?" she asked.

"He doesn't know who any of you guys are," Dom replied. "Just me."

Moose returned a few minutes later with Cayenne in tow. She hopped over to the Jeep and jumped into the front passenger seat with Dom.

"Hey, girl," he said.

Cayenne licked his smiling face.

Moose pulled the Jeep back out into traffic, away from the Angel Pyramids, on the long ride to their safe house in the City of Industry. Camilla tried not to think about all the things suddenly stacked against them. But how could they go so quickly from victorious to on the run?

That's what happens when you kill Morettis and Vegas.

She gave a low sigh and focused on the drive. The sidewalks framing the road were already busy with traffic this morning. Kids, adults—even old folks—were out and about. Several cyclists pedaled on the right side of the road.

"Watch out!" Dom yelled.

Moose yanked the wheel to the right just as a car shot by, horn blaring.

"What the hell," Rocky said.

Dom leaned forward to see. It wasn't some random driver, but an armored black LAPD cruiser.

"Jesus," Dom said. "Could turn his lights on."

Camilla watched two more cruisers fly past them. Their lights were also off.

"A bit early in the morning for this shit," Rocky said. He rested his head back on the window, but a second later, two more cruisers tore across the intersection ahead.

"Something big is going down," Dom said.

Rocky pawed at his eyes like a little kid stirring from a nap and tried to get the police scanner on. In the minutes that followed, another four police cars raced by, with several fire trucks and ambulances giving chase.

"Last time I saw this many cops was during the riots last summer," Dom said.

Rocky shrugged. "Let's hope the mayor doesn't shut off the power to the slums again, or I'm rioting too."

Camilla recalled the busy weeks last summer. Hundreds of people had died from the heat, and even more from the violence that followed. She saw no sign of smoke on the skyline and heard no gunfire—both good signs that whatever was happening wasn't too terrible.

"Pull off," Dom said. "You guys stay here and try and get the radio to work. I'm going to see if I can figure out what's shakin'."

Moose parked on the side of the road, in the shade of a silk-floss tree. He killed the engine, while Rocky searched for fresh batteries in their supply duffel in the back seat.

Dom pulled his face mask down and got out with Cayenne, who hopped after him on the sidewalk. Several teenagers skateboarded in front of the reinforced entryway to an apartment building.

Cayenne barked at one that came too close, and Dom snapped his fingers for her to follow him.

"You got any water up there?" Rocky asked.

Camilla handed him a bottle.

He slugged down half and went back to work on the radio. It came to life a moment later.

"*Six officers down . . . Ten civilian casualties . . . Suspects seen in black Range Rovers . . .*"

Camilla covered her mouth in shock as reports of violence rolled in from West Hollywood, where men wearing ballistic masks and armor had used automatic weapons on a group of police officers getting coffee.

"Christ, this is jacked up," Rocky said. "Six dead cops."

Dom came back to the Jeep.

"Listen to this," Rocky said. He turned the police-band radio up.

"Six dead cops and multiple casualties in West Hollywood," Camilla said.

"When?" Dom asked.

"A few hours ago," Rocky replied.

Dom recoiled as if he had just been punched in the face. He massaged his thick brown stubble.

"Those sons of bitches finally did it," he said quietly. "Holy shit, they finally crossed the red line. They didn't just put a price tag on *our* heads; they went after the cops who were at the port the other night."

"Oh shit, this is . . . this is because of *us*?" Rocky said.

No one spoke.

"No," Moose said. "Don't say that."

"The Morettis did this," Dom said. "We all know who's behind those masks."

It was hard for Camilla to believe that the gangsters had committed such unprecedented violence against the police. The last time a bunch of cops were killed was eight years ago at the Chevron oil refinery, when the task force under Marks had been caught in an ambush. Since then, an unwritten contract was in force. Cops were untouchable, especially the crooked ones.

But the contract had just been ripped up. Unless Stone had approved this one, just as some people believed he had approved the slaughter of the task force that night at the oil refinery.

"They'll go after the Russians next," Moose said.

Dom avoided the eyes of the other Saints. Even Cayenne must have sensed the tension. She licked his hand. He hammered the dashboard.

Cayenne hunkered down. Her handler was starting to lose his cool.

"It's going to be okay, Dom," Camilla said soothingly.

He needed some sleep, and to come off that damn speed. But at least he hadn't been drinking lately—that she knew of . . .

She reached forward and put a hand on his shoulder.

"Drive us to the safe house," Dom told Moose.

Camilla could feel her heartbeat ramping up. Cops were lying dead in the streets out there, and when it came down to it, this was partly the Saints' fault. She had always believed in karma, and Lieutenant Best probably deserved what he got, but what about the other officers?

They were still cops. Even if they pocketed money from time to time, they had all sworn the same oath. Most of them were just trying to make the city safer for the people scraping by.

When they finally got back to the safe house, all the Saints were there. And no one seemed to have heard the news from West Hollywood.

Namid and Tooth were cleaning their weapons in the garage while Bettis worked with Pork Chop on the Tahoe.

"Circle up," Dom said.

Bettis wiped his greasy hands on his pants, and Pork Chop slid out from under the truck's chassis, grabbed his trucker hat off the hood, and stuck it on his bald head.

They met at the long metal war table. Poker chips, playing cards, and empty beer bottles littered the surface.

"Abdul was found dead yesterday," Dom said. "And a few hours ago, six cops from Lieutenant Best's crew were gunned down in West Hollywood. Cops are all over the city looking for the assassins."

The Saints who hadn't heard the news broke out in chatter.

"Quiet," Dom said.

Camilla hated seeing him this way. After recent events and seeing his mom in the mental health ward, the leader of the Saints was near his breaking point. But there was still strength in him.

"My dad once told me you have to make your enemies fear you," Dom said. "We did that the other night. Our enemy responded with force, and now we have to hit them back, harder."

"*Now?*" Rocky asked. "Isn't now when we should be lying low?"

Dom shook his head. "This is the beginning of a battle that will determine the fate of everyone living in the City of Angels."

He let the team chew on that and then added, "But we're prepared for this. We trained for this. All the safe houses, all the hoarded weapons and vehicles. And we have Sammy."

Dom walked around the table, looking at them all in turn. Cayenne watched him, her saggy lips curved into what looked a lot like a smile.

"Maybe we should try to find more allies," Rocky suggested.

"I agree," Tooth added. "Maybe it's time to recruit more Saints."

"What we really need is an army," Pork Chop chimed in.

Namid just sat taking it all in.

Dom put his hands on Rocky's shoulders, and the youngest member of the Saints glanced up at him.

"We have everything we need right here," Dom said. "We protect Sammy at all costs and let him lead us to Don Antonio. When we topple the king, all this ends. The Moretti organization will crumble, and we will pick off the scraps."

Bettis made the sign of the cross over his chest.

"I'm with you, brother," Moose said. He stood up from his chair and thumped his left pec. "Ride and die, baby."

"I fought with your father, and I'll fight with you," Namid said.

"Us too," Tooth said, glancing at Bettis, who nodded.

They were almost all in agreement—they wouldn't sit back and hide, and they wouldn't leave the city. But Camilla hesitated.

"You with me?" Dom asked.

She nodded, though she wasn't sure they were prepared for this battle. If it turned into a war, they could lose everything—not only their lives, but the lives of everyone they were fighting to save.

* * *

Ray had blood on his hands. And this time it wasn't the blood of criminals.

He grabbed his ARX160. It was from the batch he had sold to the Morettis—the same guns they had used to gun down his brothers in West Hollywood. The rifle wasn't going to do him any good if the gangsters found him.

For the first time in his life, he was being hunted by the mobsters he was in bed with. He should have seen this coming. He should have known, after the Saints attacked the port and stole the RX-4 shipment, that the Morettis would retaliate.

But slaughter a bunch of cops? With the same guns he had sold them?

Ray wanted to puke. He had never expected his actions to cause the deaths of so many of his brothers. Neither had Lieutenant Best and the other officers. They were enjoying a morning coffee when the Morettis rolled up in their fancy Range Rovers and gunned them down like dogs.

Ray was lucky he was in his car when he heard the calls come in over the radio. Hearing them, he knew exactly what was going down. First off, he called Alicia and told her to go to her aunt's house and not to argue.

The second thing he did was hightail it to his cache of weapons and coin. He loaded up his car with half the weapons and money, buried the rest, and drove to his safe house in Harvard Park to consider his options.

There weren't many. He could go into the station and ask Chief Stone for protection. He could go underground and wait this out. Or he could call up Vinny and try to make a deal with the info he had collected over the past few days.

After ten hours of sitting, drinking, and thinking, the only option he had written off was going to Chief Stone. In some ways, the fucker was worse than the Morettis.

Ray finished off his cigarillo and stubbed out the glowing tip in the glass bowl on the table. The smoke filled the room with a cherry scent. He sat in the cracked leather chair, his muscular body flinching at the rap on a door down the hall. He grabbed his ARX160 and leveled it at the door.

The building was noisy tonight. Opening and slamming doors. Crying babies. People yelling or fucking, or both.

The paper-thin walls gave him an audio track to the events around him. He didn't come here for the peace and quiet, that was for sure. He had rented this place just in case he ever needed somewhere to hide.

Although he hadn't seen the violence in West Hollywood coming, he had planned for it. The one thing his degenerate gambler dad had taught him was always to leave himself outs. And that was exactly what he had done.

Ray Clarke had something the gangsters wanted. It was also why he was still alive after all these years dealing with monsters and scumbags.

Maybe it's also because it takes one to know one.

The things he had done over the past few weeks had him thinking a lot about the blood on his hands. Like a tattoo, it wasn't coming off.

Pulling back the drapes, he stood and checked the parking lot. Several wannabee gangbangers sat on the hoods of their cars, smoking and listening to old-school rap.

He knew one of them, a huge guy with linebacker shoulders and a silver nose ring that made Ray think of a bull. He had fought hard when Ray brought him in a few years ago on a domestic.

He laughed at the memory of ripping the guy's nose ring out. He could turn a blind eye to the small stuff like drugs, or even dealing. But a man who beat on a woman? Nah, Ray Clarke couldn't let that slide.

Two cars drag-raced out of the parking lot and onto the road, their headlights zooming past a crater the size of a college football stadium. It was all that remained of a shopping mall across the street. The aerial blast had leveled the area and killed thousands of people sheltering there.

Ray had grown up just a few miles away, in a house with two of the best parents in the world. They, too, were killed in the violence—burned alive in a fire set by gangbangers trying to kill him or Moose.

A tear blurred his eye at that memory, and he pushed it away for better ones. He missed hot summer days when he and Moose would stay outside until the streetlights came on, playing ball, chasing girls, and doing the usual dumb shit that teenagers did.

He had always looked up to Moose, even though Ray was the older brother. And that was why he had to help Moose.

Ray took the ARX160 over to the bed. A SIG Sauer P320 rested under one of the pillows, and his shotgun was propped against the wall.

He sat on the mattress and pointed the ARX160 at the door again. Then he pulled out his cell phone and saw a missed call from Alicia.

Letting the rifle rest on his chest, he dialed her number.

"Ray, are you okay?" Alicia answered.

"Yeah, babe. Are you at your aunt's house?"

"Just got here. When are you coming home?"

"Good."

A pause, and voices in the background. Lolo was crying.

"When are you coming home?" Alicia repeated.

"I don't know, babe."

"What's wrong, Ray? What aren't you telling me? Does this have anything to do with what happened in West Hollywood?"

"Don't you worry about that now. I'll call you when I can. Just stay at your aunt's place. Okay?"

A pause.

"Okay, Ray. I love you."

"I . . ." His words trailed off as the door to the apartment exploded off its hinges. He dropped the phone, but before he could grab his rifle, a bullet hit him in the chest.

His body convulsed, his muscles locking up. A group of men stormed into the room as his back arched up off the floor. Then he saw the two electrical nodes sticking out of his chest, just above his ballistic vest.

These guys, whoever they were, hadn't shot him, which meant they wanted him alive.

Or it may just mean he had a *long* evening of torture ahead.

He tried to get up, but someone grabbed him by the legs, and someone else grabbed him by the shoulders. He blinked away the stars and focused on a husky figure standing in front of the bed.

A voice screamed in the distance. It sounded familiar.

He almost didn't recognize the guy with the bandages on one side of his face. The hair on the right side of his scalp was singed off.

"Detective Ray Clarke, it's been a long time since I saw your mug."

Ray blinked again and focused on the features of Mexican Mikey, Mikey the Mutant, or whatever the fat fuck wanted to be called. He really did look like a mutant now.

"I . . . I heard you were dead," Ray said.

Mikey lifted his chin proudly. "The Lord still has work for me to do. And it starts with cutting you up and feeding you to the pigs."

He reached out, and one of his men handed him a machete.

Ray heard the familiar voice again. That's when he realized it was coming from his phone. Alicia was still on the line and could hear everything.

"No," Ray said, squirming in the grip of the two soldiers. "No, please."

The guy holding his chest down laughed. "He's crying like a little girl."

Mikey chuckled, then nodded. The soldier walked over with a roll of duct tape.

"Wait," Ray said. "I can help you. I have something the Morettis will pay millions for."

The guy ripped off a strip of tape and went to put it over Ray's mouth, but Mikey held up a bandaged hand.

"You saying what I think you're saying?" he asked.

Ray nodded slowly.

Mikey raised half a burned eyebrow. "Bring him with. This little *puto* might be useful to us after all."

-16-

There was no way in hell to make it home for dinner, but the wrath of his wife was the least of Vinny's concerns tonight. He was starting to worry that he might not be coming home at all.

This mission was far more dangerous than taking out some rookie cops carrying Glocks and shotguns. Tonight, they were facing heavily armed, battle-hardened soldiers.

He finished his final gear check in the warehouse, where they had spent the past eight hours lying low and waiting for the green light from Don Antonio. All across town, their soldiers and contacts were hunting the Saints and killing the cops from the port raid.

But this mission was for something very different.

Reaching into a bag, he grabbed his spiffy new night-vision goggles and the new Ronin tactical ballistic helmets that he and Doberman had personally acquired in a shipment from Japan.

"Pretty cool, right?" Doberman said, holding up one of the helmets.

Vinny nodded as his father gave a whistle.

"Gather around and listen up," Christopher said. He unslung his ARX160 and waited for the other ten men to form up. Some of these guys were former soldiers and cops, who had switched sides, abandoning the shattered government to work for the Morettis.

They paid better, especially to guys with skills.

Most of these men had mad skills. Nicholas Dietz was a former Force Recon marine, and Rush was a sergeant with the AMP. Former enemies, now allies.

They weren't blood, which meant they could never be made, but they were still Moretti soldiers, and Vinny was glad to have them by his side.

"Our target is Sergei Nevsky and his cousin Ivan," Christopher said. "This is payback for the port."

Vinny almost shook his head. His uncle was a wily son of a bitch, suggesting that the Nevsky crew was behind the attack at the port, to rile up the Moretti army and whet their thirst for revenge. Christopher and the other captains knew the truth, and so did Vinny, but it was brilliant to leave the other men wondering.

For all they knew, the Russians had fired those RPGs that had killed Moretti soldiers on the docks. And for all they knew, the cops in West Hollywood had been in on it.

But Vinny knew, the Saints were behind everything.

"They will have women and children with them," Christopher said, "and I don't want any of them harmed."

Vinny knew that his father had a soft spot for women and kids ever since his wife, Vinny's mom, was gunned down in the church in Naples.

"Fuck all of 'em," said Frankie.

Christopher shot him a glare. "Kids and women are not to be harmed. You got that, Frankie?"

"Yeah," Frankie said after a pause. One of Antonio's longest-serving soldiers, he had served him well over the past decade, with a list of greatest hits that included killing Chief Diamond.

Vinny had never liked Frankie or Carmine much. Like Vito, who had helped kidnap and imprison thousands of teenagers over the years, they had no soul.

But not all his uncle's men were assholes like those three from the old country. Raffaello Tursi would never have harmed a woman or a child. Indeed, he had spent most of the Second Civil War protecting Marco and

Lucia from those who would. And, like too many of the good men, he was gone now.

"Memorize your route through the sewers," Christopher said. "It's going to be dark and cramped down there. Once we get out, we wait for Doberman to take out the power with an EMP from the van he's going to park a few blocks away."

"EMP?" Yellowtail asked.

Doberman looked up from the glow of his tablet and explained how the weapon worked, in language that the men could understand.

There were a few side conversations, but Christopher ended them with a snap of his fingers.

"You got something to say, Carmine?" Christopher asked.

Carmine ran a hand through his slicked-back hair and then spat a wad of tobacco on the ground. "This plan is no good, Chrissy. Sergei is no idiot. He's going to be ready for an attack, and these helmets won't stop what he's packing."

"I got to agree with Carmine," said Frankie. "This plan is going to get some of us killed tonight, and personally, I want to come home. Thursday is steak night with my *goomah*."

Christopher gave Frankie a side glance. "Steak night with your broad can wait. These orders come from Don Antonio. So pull your dicks out from between your legs and get set."

Carmine laughed, but Frankie glared at Christopher like a high school jock with hurt feelings in the locker room. He'd been taken down a peg in front of his peers, and Vinny thought for a second he might do something about it.

Frankie went back to chewing on a matchstick—his surrogate cigarette—and Christopher knocked it out of his mouth.

"What the hell, Chrissy!" Frankie said.

"You're lucky I didn't light it in your mouth," Christopher said. He turned back to the other men. "Does anyone have a question that *doesn't* make them look like a damn pussy?"

Rush spoke up. "How many soldiers does Sergei have at this location?"

"Twenty, maybe a few more, but tonight we have the element of surprise."

Frankie took another match from his vest pocket and stuck it in his mouth. "Christ, brother, that's double our numbers," he said.

Yellowtail ran a hand through his bleach-blond Mohawk. "Frankie's got a point."

"So what?" Vinny said. "We're Morettis, and we got Doberman and his tech."

The older men looked in his direction, but this time he didn't get the usual judgmental gazes. He had saved Marco's life today, proving yet again why he had earned his button eight years ago.

"These are *Don* Antonio's orders," Yellowtail reminded the men. His gaze lingered on Carmine and Frankie.

"Let's move out," Christopher said.

Carmine and Frankie exchanged a glance but moved to the two Toyota pickup trucks with the other men. Before Vinny could walk to his ride, he felt a hand on his shoulder.

"You good to go?" Christopher asked him.

"Yeah, I'm good." He paused to make sure no one was around to hear. "I don't get why we're going after Sergei if the Saints are who planted the RPGs. Even though the other guys don't know the truth, it feels weird."

"Because it's time to take him out, and since the men don't know it *wasn't* him at the port, now we have an excuse."

His father confirmed his suspicions. God *damn*, his uncle was a genius.

Two soldiers lifted the garage door to a crescent moon hanging over the city. Vinny took shotgun in the pickup, and Christopher jumped behind the wheel.

"You mind?" Vinny asked, reaching for the radio.

Christopher shook his head. "Long as you don't play any of that girly shit."

Vinny flipped through the few radio channels while they drove away from the garage.

"*Good evening, you sinners and saints,*" said the radio host. "*Tonight, we have more tragic news coming in from West Hollywood, where several Los Angeles police officers were gunned down by masked assailants. So far, the police aren't releasing any names of suspects or those deceased.*"

Christopher eyed the radio and then jerked his chin. "Pig fuckers got what they deserved, and soon the rest will get theirs."

Vinny had a feeling his father was talking about Billy Best. The lieutenant had been taken to an undisclosed location, where he was probably being tortured for information on the Saints.

"So much for letting Marco take care of it," Vinny said.

Christopher pulled a cigar out of his vest and let out a rough chuckle. "Marco can't even whack a pig from twenty feet away. What makes you think he can take out the Saints?"

"He wants his spot at the table."

"And you want to be captain."

Vinny nodded.

"You find the Saints, and I bet Don Antonio will give you the Nevsky territory," Christopher said.

Vinny held back a smile. He couldn't wait to tell Adriana. The fact that he didn't even care to tell his wife was another indication that their marriage was circling the toilet bowl. The thought chilled his pounding heart. He felt trapped, like a caged rat.

Vinny twisted the dial to electronic music.

"I can't stand this shit," Christopher said.

"Give it a chance. It'll help get you in the mood for killing."

Mood for killing.

The words were something he really had never thought he would say. But this was his life now. He was a Moretti, and killing was part of his job.

The music filled the cab, his heart beating in sync with the amplified bass. He smiled at his father—a rare moment of bonding between two men who normally didn't speak much.

As far as Vinny was concerned, his father was a god. Christopher had fought in the Middle East with Don Antonio, in the Fourth Alpini Paratroopers Regiment. The brothers had survived war in Naples, and the Second Civil War in the United States, to build a dynasty literally from dust.

Blood, tears, and hard work had molded his father into an immortal figure in Vinny's eyes—a figure that no bullet could cut down.

Vinny turned down the music and said, "How come you never talk about what you did in the military?"

Christopher shrugged. "I ain't proud of what we did out there. The evil is something I'd rather forget."

Vinny wasn't sure what evils his father was referring to, but he had a feeling it had come with him to Los Angeles. That was how his father and uncle had risen to the top—by being the most brutal bastards on the streets.

The pickups' headlights cut through the night as they made their way down the nearly empty highway toward the Russians' shrinking piece of territory on the south side of the city.

"Be sharp," Christopher said.

They were already coming up on a section of highway destroyed during the war. Twisted overpasses hung sixty feet in the air, rebar jutting out of the ends like the twisted veins of a mangled limb. Swimming-pool-sized craters marked the ditches and rights-of-way where bombs had missed their targets.

Vinny could almost hear the fighter planes rumbling in overhead and dumping their payloads on the fleeing civilians. He had been in the Morettis' old warehouse, hiding in a basement, when the worst of it happened. He shook the memories away.

Fifteen minutes later, they were out of the wastelands and back into civilization, crossing over into the southern territory still controlled by Sergei Nevsky and his crew.

"Here we go," Christopher said, pulling out his walkie-talkie. "Radio silence here on out. Lights off."

One by one, the vehicles went dark. Vinny flipped his expensive NVGs over his eyes.

The lead truck took a right, speeding down a frontage road toward an old marsh long since dried up. They passed an abandoned school, once used as a fortified billet for AMP fighters in the war. Now it was home to the junkies who shot competing Russian H into their veins. Soon, these people would migrate to western or eastern LA to feed their habit.

Vinny didn't normally think of the lives ruined by his family's product, but sometimes, when he was out here, he did pause to wonder whether he had a spot in hell waiting for him.

But as with most young men, death seemed far away.

He felt invincible, like his old man.

The convoy finally stopped in a residential neighborhood outside a derelict water treatment plant. Frankie hopped out of the truck ahead and ran over to the gate with a pair of wire cutters. Doberman continued driving the van to the second location, where he would fire the EMP launcher.

Good luck, brother, Vinny thought.

"Stay with me once we get inside," Christopher said. The rough tone of his voice carried a rare hint of nerves.

Frankie opened the barred gate, allowing the pickups through. Once they were all safely inside the vehicle bay, the gates closed and the men piled out.

Christopher flashed the signal to advance toward a pair of doors across the garage, but Vinny whirled at the sound of footsteps outside the gate. He raised his rifle barrel at a figure standing on the sidewalk on the other side of the bars.

Carmine raised his rifle too, but Vinny quickly waved him off.

"Just a kid," he whispered.

The boy stood there, looking at both men.

Christopher walked over. "Go home, kid," he said.

In the drip of moonlight, the boy's brown eyes seemed to focus. "Are you robots?"

Vinny flipped his night-vision goggles up and pulled off his mask, revealing his eyes. He bent down in front of the gate.

"We're engineers, here to fix the water," he said. "And you never saw us. Because if you *did* see us, then we won't be able to fix the water. Got it?"

The boy tilted his head, curious. "You don't look like an engineer."

"Can't let him go," Carmine said. "Got to tie him up or take him out."

Christopher shook his head. "I said no kids, God damn it."

"You're the boss," Carmine said, backing off.

"Go home and don't say anything," Vinny said.

Please, listen.

The boy stepped up to the bars to give the garage a closer look. Christopher reached out.

"Come here, bud, we're not going to hurt you," he said.

Yellowtail pulled some rope from his bag.

The kid must have seen that and suddenly backed away, stumbling. He lost his balance and fell on his butt. "Ouch," he said, raising his scratched palm to see blood in the moonlight.

He pushed himself up and took off running. "Mom—" he started to yell when something cut him off.

Two pops followed the sound of his little feet hitting the pavement.

Vinny and Christopher both whirled about, to see Frankie holding a suppressed pistol. He lowered the gun and shrugged.

Glancing back at the kid, Vinny tried to make sense of the limp body on the sidewalk, blood pooling from the two .45 rounds that had blown out his heart and shattered Vinny's.

"You son of a bitch," Christopher growled.

Frankie lowered the gun, keeping his voice low. "Kid was going to make us, man. Kill the mission before it got started."

"Help me with 'im," Carmine whispered to Vinny.

But Vinny couldn't move. He could hardly breathe. He had seen a lot of death in his young life and had killed his fair share of men, but never had he seen a child gunned down right in front of him.

"Come on, Vin," Carmine said.

Vinny finally snapped out of the trance and moved over to the gate. They opened it, and Carmine grabbed the boy by his feet while Vinny took his hands. Blood leaked from the hole through his chest as they carried him into the garage and set him down.

This was someone's child. Just a kid, maybe seven years old.

Vinny set the boy down gently and looked up at Christopher, who stood face-to-face with Frankie, their masks nearly touching.

Back off, Dad. This isn't the time or the place.

He could tell that Christopher was doing everything he could to hold back the rage inside him.

"I'm sorry," Frankie said. "Really, man, but it was him or us. What's more important, taking down Sergei or letting some kid live and blow the mission?"

Christopher didn't reply.

The other men watched uneasily.

Carmine moved back to the gate to keep an eye on the street.

"Let's go, Chrissy," he said. "Nothing we can do for the kid now."

"You could have tied him up," Vinny said. "You didn't have to blow him away."

Frankie turned to Vinny. "Kid was running and—"

In the blink of an eye, Christopher whipped out his holstered pistol and fired two shots directly into Frankie' chest, then a third into his neck. The fully jacketed rounds punched through his armored vest and made a neat hole through his Adam's apple. He staggered backward, hands on his neck, blood already gushing out.

Christopher kicked Frankie's pistol toward Vinny, and Vinny picked it up off the ground.

"Kill a kid, and you end up like Frankie," Christopher said quietly but loudly enough for everyone in the garage to hear. "You all got that?"

Vinny watched Carmine's hands, making sure he wasn't about to do anything stupid to avenge his friend. But not even the street-hardened captain was dumb enough to take on the second in command of the family.

"Let's go," Christopher said. He flashed another hand signal toward the door, and the men quickly began moving out.

Vinny walked around the mixing rivulets of blood from the boy and Frankie, who was rattling out his last few breaths.

The asshole had been right—not all the Moretti soldiers were coming home tonight. But neither was a seven-year-old boy.

-17-

Don Antonio relaxed in the back seat of a BMW M7 as Lino drove away from the Moretti compound. Vito loosened his tie in the passenger seat, grunting. All three men wore Armani suits—even Antonio.

It felt good to dress like a king again. It also felt good to leave the compound. Aside from his sit-down with Esteban Vega, it had been months since Antonio traveled outside the secure walls.

He checked his watch for the third time in the past hour. His brother's crew would soon be entering the storm sewers outside the Nevsky compound. The Russians took their security just as seriously as Antonio, but they were about to get something their security wasn't designed to repel.

He wished he were there to see the look on Sergei's face.

But Antonio's days of night raids were over. He would always miss the rush that came with fighting in the darkness.

Back when he was an Alpino fighting in Afghanistan, he had earned a nickname from a night mission that lagged into the dawn. Low on ammo, injured, and exhausted, he threw on the black clothes of a dead insurgent and stormed the enemy stronghold, disguised as one of them. He killed most of them with his rifle. When the magazine ran out, he used his knife and, finally, his bare hands.

From that night on, his men called him "*il folletto nero*," the Black Jinni.

By the time the sun rose, he would have a new nickname: King Killer. As soon as Sergei Nevsky drew his last breath, Antonio would control most of the city, with only the warring Vega brothers, a few old-school gangs like the Bloods, and the underdog Saints to stand in his way.

He was glad the Saints had left behind those RPGs. It helped sell the urgency of destroying the Nevsky family to anyone who might question his orders.

If all went to plan, the Vega brothers and the Bloods would move on the Nevskys' zone 3, and he would sit back and let them duke it out.

Four black Suburbans, which his soldiers had found in the underground garage of some former rap star, closed in around the BMW, like soldiers surrounding their general. Antonio wasn't taking any chances tonight.

He had been thinking more about his mortality lately, and what would happen when he was gone. It was another reason he had broken his promise to keep Marco out of this life. Selfishly, he wanted his boy to take the reins when he was capable.

Christopher was the natural successor, but despite their fraternal bond and his love for his nephew, something wouldn't let Antonio see the family banner passed into Vinny's hands instead of Marco's if something should happen to both Antonio and his brother.

Lights flashed on the horizon, distracting him from his thoughts. The spotlights raked over the dark sky above a newly opened club.

This was the only section left of the old Hollywood. And this was exactly where he knew he would find his only son, and the heir to the Moretti fortunes.

"Which club is Marco at?" Antonio asked.

"He's with his friends at the Dragon," Lino replied.

"That shithole?" Vito asked.

"What's wrong with the Dragon?" Lino asked, taking his eyes off the road to look at Vito. "I thought you loved Asian girls."

Vito laughed. "I don't discriminate."

"This we know—and so does your wife," Antonio said.

All the men laughed, just like old times, but the laughter faded as headlights hit the back of the BMW.

Antonio checked the side mirror as a black Mercedes came up on their right. In front was a mounted brush guard. The SUVs moved over to keep the car away from the BMW.

Vito raised his submachine gun as the Mercedes passed. Metal plates over the doors, and shutters over the windows disguised the driver. These vehicles were a common sight out here, where people took their security seriously.

Vito lowered his weapon.

A few minutes later, they pulled off the Hollywood Freeway and rolled past Sunset's restaurants and strip clubs.

The new addition had gone up since he last saw the Golden Oyster. Business was good. Most of its clients were Moretti soldiers, city officials, cops, and businessmen.

He still found the casino's dazzling gold top arresting. From being a barefoot urchin on the streets of Naples to owning half the largest remaining city in the United States had been a long journey. And this was just the beginning.

In an effort to expand into legitimate businesses, he had already bought two nightclubs and a half-dozen restaurants, and he owned dozens of apartment buildings in Los Angeles besides the Four Diamonds. Business was booming, and even with the loss of the drugs at the port, he was having the best year ever, distributing 5 percent of profits to new green spaces, playgrounds, and apartment buildings for the impoverished. He did it not so he might sleep better at night but to keep the mayor and the cops from intervening.

Eventually, when he was strong enough, he would expand his empire to Sin City, where he had yet to tap the huge drug market. The Vega family had tried, but they were forced out by a former AMP lieutenant who had slaughtered his rivals and taken over the city.

"Vito, Lino, get the word to Mayor Buren. We're increasing our donations to the city by ten million dollars this year."

Vito twisted to look in the back seat. "That's a lot of cheddar," he said.

"To keep everyone happy," Antonio replied. "After West Hollywood, we might have some new enemies. We don't want the Saints to get any more allies."

A few blocks from the casino, Lino parked the BMW next to a pair of Honda sedans with souped-up engines. Their owners, two muscular African American men wearing large silver chains over Hawaiian shirts, stood on the sidewalk.

Bangers didn't dress as they had in the old days.

Lino opened the back door, letting Antonio out. He stepped onto the street, straightening his collar. One of the bangers took a hit off a joint. It smelled like good stuff, Antonio would give them that.

"Ah shit, is that . . ." said the man with the joint.

The other guy stepped out of the way, opening a path between the vehicles to the sidewalk as a sign of respect—or perhaps fear.

Lino, chewing on a toothpick, winked at the two men as he passed.

"You sure you don't want to take a back entrance?" Vito asked.

"No," Antonio said. He wanted to be seen tonight, especially after gunning down the cops. Everyone here had heard about it by now, and everyone knew that the Morettis were likely behind it. But no one could touch him. Even the cops patrolling the area wouldn't dare, lest they end up like the crooked fucks from the port.

What worried Antonio more was some underdog with nothing to lose, like the Saints, taking a shot at him. But they would have to get through a lot of muscle to do so.

His guards quickly formed a phalanx, some walking along the sidewalk, others fanning out into the street. He wouldn't make the same mistake his enemies had made when he came to Los Angeles. They should have killed him on day one, when he was nobody.

"Move it," Vito growled at some punks ahead. The kids, all sporting colorful Mohawks, laughed. One of them, who had a nose ring, stepped forward, a bottle of beer in his hand.

"Who the fuck's this guy supposed to be?" He glanced back at his friends. "Fucking wannabe gangster pricks think they—"

When the kid turned, Vito's pistol caught him in the face, breaking his nose with a satisfying crack. Vito pointed it at the other kids.

"We're the Morettis, jerk-off. Now, trot the fuck out of here."

They scattered like rats from fire.

Antonio followed his men around the crowds and toward a flashing sign with a dragon's head and a curled tail. Lino kept looking across the street, and Antonio finally saw why. Two police officers stood next to their motorcycles, arms folded across their uniforms, eyes following the Morettis. And they couldn't do a damn thing but watch.

He almost smiled, but remembered his cardinal rule: never get drunk on power. Instead, he took in a breath of warm air. It felt like freedom filling his lungs.

Ahead, a line of thirty teenage girls in skintight dresses and a few boys in designer suits were hanging outside a roped-off entrance where five armed bouncers in black suits held security.

It was odd to see so much wealth gathered in a single place. Most of these kids had rich parents. They were the 1 percent of the 1 percent. Wealthy citizens who were in Don Antonio's pocket.

"Get back," shouted a husky Asian man guarding the rope. He shooed away the girls at the front of the line. Two of them protested as they were brushed aside.

Several of the Moretti soldiers went inside, then came back to give the green light. Vito, Antonio, and Lino strode right through the opening, and the rope clicked behind them as the bouncers re-formed their wall of muscle. Half the Moretti men remained out on the street to stand guard.

A short Asian woman in a black dress with pink cherry blossoms stood inside the glass doors. She smiled warmly and stepped in front of a waterfall emptying into a koi pond.

"Welcome to the Dragon, Mr. Moretti. If you would please follow me to the VIP lounge . . ."

He could hardly hear her over the thumping bass as they walked past palm trees growing toward skylights overhead.

Vito glanced over his shoulder as they followed the hostess. "Want a drink, Don Antonio?"

"Vodka. Bring me a bottle."

"*Vodka?*" Vito asked.

It was an unorthodox choice, and especially ironic on this evening. Antonio nodded.

With one hand inside his coat, Lino scanned the room from the dance floor to the packed couches in the sitting area.

Several Moretti men were already walking through the masses, looking for any signs of potential trouble. They were experts at spotting that certain mix of cockiness and stupidity.

"I fucking hate clubs," Lino grumbled.

As they entered the packed area outside the dance floor, the throng parted like the Red Sea for Moses.

Now he remembered what he once liked about these places: the stares, the whispers, the seductive smiles from beautiful women.

It was still a rush.

Most of the movie and music stars were gone, but there were still celebrities in the City of Angels, like Regina Díaz. Antonio saw former Dodger catcher Mike Hendricks, a regular craps player at the Golden Oyster.

Jango Thomas, a former Lakers forward, was sitting at a table with several hard-looking men who fought in the diamond cage at Memorial Stadium.

But Don Antonio Moretti was the only A-list star left.

The Black Jinni.

He walked across the dance floor, toward the stairway. At the top of the stairs, Vito took a right toward the VIP lounge, a blocked-off area of sectional couches. They navigated the packed area toward the farthest corner, where Antonio got a first glimpse of his son.

Marco sat on a leather couch, with his arms around two girls.

Four soldiers guarded the roped-off area. They both stepped away, and Lino unclicked the rope, allowing Antonio into the section.

As soon as he walked through, Marco threw up his arms as if to say, *What the hell are you doing here?* Whatever his son did say, Antonio couldn't hear him. He put the bottle of vodka on the glass table centered between the three couches and Marco's friends. He didn't know the girls, but he recognized the boys: Nick, Giovanni, and the twins Alex and Pietro.

At least the boys were smart enough to pay their respect by rising to their feet. Nick even raised a glass and said, "To Don Antonio!"

Glasses clinked together, but Marco turned his head slightly, wiping his nose.

Antonio knew what he was trying to wipe away, but it was a moot point. Cocaine lines were still in plain sight on the glass table.

"Dad, we're just here celebrating . . ." Marco tried his million-dollar smile, but it fell flat.

Antonio resisted the urge to slap his son into the couch. Instead, he gestured for the scantily dressed girls to move out of his way. Then he walked to the rail overlooking the club below and waited for his son to join him.

"Dad, I'm . . ." Marco's slurred words trailed off again.

That wasn't good. He would need to sober up for what came next.

"Lino, bring us water," Antonio said.

Lino snapped his fingers at a waitress.

Returning his gaze to the crowd below, Antonio watched sweaty young people mushed together on the dance floor. Men kissing women. Women kissing women.

It was time for Marco to put this scene behind him, as Antonio had at the same age—around the same time he met Lucia.

Red and blue lights flashed outside the club. Through the windows, Antonio saw several squad cars and a half-dozen officers.

Lino walked over and leaned close. "Don Antonio, we got company."

"I can see that." He remained at the railing with his son, both of them watching the police enter the club. A dark-skinned man suddenly bolted from the dance floor and ran up the stairs, two cops on his heels.

The men guarding Antonio formed a fence around the entrance to the VIP lounge, and most of the officers moved past. Only one stopped to look at the Moretti crew.

Lino waved and flashed a shit-eating grin.

The officer, panting, ran after their suspect.

You can't touch me, Antonio thought. *I own you, your boss, and his boss.*

He pointed at the bottle on the table. "Grab the vodka and follow me."

Marco was intoxicated, but he was with it enough to know that look from his father. He scooped the bottle off the table.

"Where we going?" he asked.

"To do something I should have done a long time ago," Antonio replied. "Tonight, you will see what being a Moretti means."

* * *

Dom had snagged a few hours of sleep on the couch in the garage safe house. When he woke up, Rocky and Tooth were back at it in the boxing ring. Cayenne stretched and yawned.

Dreams about his family had Dom on edge. He wiped away the sweat that always came with the nightmares, and blinked away the grogginess as the two boxers pounded away at each other.

"You got to work on the right hook," Moose said, miming one. "Want me to come in there and show you boys how it's done?"

Rocky walked over to the ropes, panting.

"I'm good, bro, but I will take some water."

"Me too," Tooth said.

Dom got up off the couch and walked over with a bottle, tossing it to Rocky. The garage was lit with battery-operated lanterns, and he didn't see any other Saints in the glow.

"Where is everyone?" he asked.

"Bettis just left to take Camilla back to her crib," Moose said. "Namid and Pork Chop went home."

"Feel free to head home too, man," Dom said. "You got a family to look after."

Moose pulled out his cell phone. "I better take this," he said.

Dom cracked his neck from side to side and stretched. He hated splitting the team up, but they couldn't stay here forever. Some of them had families waiting, and until their cover was truly blown, he wasn't going to keep everyone against their will.

The dust would settle soon, and in the meantime, he would plan their next move.

Moose lowered his phone and gave Dom the look that said something major was going down.

"What?" Dom asked.

"That was my buddy working the Goldilocks Zone."

"And?"

"Fucking Antonio Moretti," Moose said. "He's at the Dragon with a small crew."

Dom was moving before Moose finished his sentence. Tooth and Rocky jumped over the ropes of the improvised boxing ring.

Five minutes later, all but one of them had piled into the Jeep Cherokee, vests strapped, weapons loaded, masks on.

Only Tooth remained behind with Cayenne to watch Sammy.

"Put a bullet in the motherfucker's dome for me," Tooth said with a grin. Cayenne wagged her tail and hopped over to the Jeep as Tooth opened the garage door.

"It's okay, girl," Dom said. "I'll be back soon."

Moose eased out of the garage, careful not to hit Cayenne.

"I know I've been hard on you in the past about your shitty driving," Dom said, "but tonight you drive as fast as you want, as long as you get us to the Dragon before the bastard leaves."

Moose chuckled behind his mask and floored it.

"Even if we do get there before he leaves, Don Antonio is going to have a lot of firepower with him," Rocky said. "Don't you think we should call Camilla and Bettis for backup?"

"No time, and I don't want us all out there at the same time. But I am calling Namid. He lives just a few minutes away."

"'Sup, boss?" Namid answered.

"You at home?"

"Yes, why?"

"The king is at the Dragon. We're on our way. See if you can get eyes on him. Don't let him out of your sight. We'll take him once he leaves."

"Hell yeah. You got it."

Dom reached in his pocket for his last speed pill, drawing a glance from Moose.

"I'm done with this shit after tonight," Dom said. "I promise, but I need this to focus."

"Nah, you don't, bro." Moose looked away.

The drive to the Goldilocks Zone was agonizing. Everything they had fought for could come about tonight—with a single bullet, if they got really lucky.

The engine protested as Moose stomped the pedal: 90, 100, 105 miles an hour.

"That's her top," Moose said. "Don't want to push it beyond that."

"This is it, I can feel it," Dom said. "We haven't had this kind of opportunity in a year."

They pulled off the Hollywood Freeway thirty minutes later and took the next right toward the neons and the spotlights raking back and forth over Sunset Boulevard.

Dom palmed a magazine into his M1A SOCOM 16 and then checked his .45. He closed his eyes as adrenaline and Dexedrine warmed his veins. When he opened them, Moose was slowing the Jeep toward a roadblock at the end of the exit ramp.

Two black SUVs were blocking the route into what was once Hollywood. The Goldilocks Zone flashed in the distance.

Dom leaned forward to see guards behind the vehicles, armed with submachine guns and wearing some sort of armored helmets.

"What the hell is this?" Moose asked.

"Security," Dom said. He motioned for Moose to turn around.

He should have known that Don Antonio wouldn't leave the compound without a small army. The guys at the roadblock were checking vehicles and keeping the roads clear to give their boss an escape route.

And, of course, Dom didn't see any cops patrolling. Chief Stone still hadn't responded to West Hollywood, and Dom didn't trust him to send out any cars.

Any justice was up to the Saints.

To defeat evil, we must embrace it.

Dom drew in a deep breath. He had gunned down a lot of Morettis over the past few days and didn't regret a damn one. But he had to be careful no civilians got caught in the cross fire.

That was a line he wasn't prepared to cross, even if it meant nabbing Don Antonio. If they were lucky, maybe Vito would be with him tonight, and he could kill both the bastards.

"Take the back way," Dom ordered. "Drive in the fucking dirt if you have to."

Moose turned and then drove across the shoulder back to the freeway.

"If those guys are still here, it means Don Antonio is too," Rocky said.

Dom pulled out his buzzing cell phone.

"Whattya got?" Dom asked.

Namid whispered, as if he didn't want to be heard, and Dom couldn't make out much of it, but he did catch two words.

"*Heading out.*"

"Can't hear you, man," Dom said.

"The king is on his way out of there with the prince. They are in a black BMW and surrounded by a convoy of black Suburbans, westbound. I'm on foot and about to lose them."

"All right, we got this," Dom said. "Now, get somewhere safe."

He pocketed the cell phone and scanned the road and overpasses.

"They're heading for the freeway in a black BMW," Dom said.

Moose looked over. "Have you considered that this might be a trap?" he asked. "To draw us out?"

"Yeah, but I don't think so. This is Don Antonio, flexing his muscles and saying he can do whatever the fuck he wants after West Hollywood. And not to fuck with him."

Moose didn't respond, but he did push down on the pedal, speeding toward the next exit to get ahead of the Moretti convoy.

They had to hit him here, on the road, before he could escape. But they couldn't just pull up alongside and empty their magazines. That was suicide.

"Up there," Dom said, pointing at a bridge that spanned the freeway.

Moose veered off onto the shoulder and then took the exit. He sped down the ramp and slowed as they approached the intersection. Several cars passed through.

"I don't see any roadblocks," Dom said.

They pulled up to the stop sign and took a left. Seeing a cluster of headlights on the road below, he felt his pulse quicken.

"Hurry!" Dom yelled.

He jumped out of the Jeep and ran over to the railing. Rocky and Moose joined him a moment later.

"Watch our six, Rocky," Dom said. He raised his rifle and angled it at the road. Headlights shot down the westbound lanes.

Rocky checked the right and left of the road to make sure they weren't being flanked. "We're clear," he said.

Dom looked down the scope of his M1A SOCOM 16 and searched the convoy for the BMW. The car was right in the middle, protected by two black Suburbans. He moved his finger to the trigger.

He had waited a long time for this.

"Paint that motherfucker!" Dom yelled.

Gunfire cracked on his flanks as the three Saints opened fire. Bullets shattered the BMW's windshield and punched through the roof. The tires went next, and the car swerved out of control, slamming into one of the Suburbans before sliding onto the shoulder, where it stopped in a cloud of dust.

Dom leaned over and fired single rounds into the vehicle until the bolt clicked back. He ejected the spent magazine, grabbed another from his vest, and slapped it in.

"Changing!" Moose said. He and Rocky slapped in their second magazines and rained more lead down on the BMW. The Suburbans had pulled off, and soldiers jumped out.

Moose and Rocky fired their fresh magazines, cutting them down before they could fire back.

Dom aimed for the gas tank of the BMW.

"Burn in hell, Antonio," he said.

A memory of Monica flashed through his mind as he pulled the trigger.

Rounds peppered the metal. An explosion burst from the back end, flames poofing into the night, forcing Dom to step back from the bridge railing.

"Let's go!" Moose shouted.

Rocky ran back to the Jeep, but Dom stayed, feeling the heat from the fireball just below the overpass. He stood watching the BMW and the men inside burn, until Moose pulled him away.

-18-

Camilla splashed cold water on her face, making the cut sting. She used a towel to blot it dry, then leaned in to check the stitches. The swelling had gone down, but her brown eyes looked sunken, and several small cuts hid the freckles on her nose.

Dom was right—she was lucky. And he didn't even know the half of it.

Better to spare him the details.

She took off her shirt, and she saw the other scars that tattooed her flesh: the snaking line from below her right breast to her naval, where a knife had traced her flesh; the raised scar on her left biceps, where a 9 mm bullet had punched into her muscle.

Each scar had a story, and she didn't like dwelling on them.

She threw on a tank top. The rough cotton fabric felt good on her skin. It reminded her of her childhood, when things were simple and the biggest concern was when her *papi* drank too much tequila and lost his temper with her *mamá*, Fabiola.

Now *she* was the one who drank too much and had a bad temper.

She checked her cell phone, saw that it was dead, and put it on the charger. Grabbing a pair of boots, she shoved them on and carefully slipped her .380 subcompact revolver inside the right boot, and her knife in the left. With the weapons concealed, she headed out for dinner.

Fires burned in barrels in the courtyard behind her building, where dozens of people watched a game of basketball and drank moonshine or cheap beer.

She walked toward a place that served more of the cheap stuff: a corner bar called the Pig's Ear. They had halfway decent food there.

Hookers shouted their pitches to drivers and pedestrians from the curb outside the old public library. One of them hooked a fish, and they walked inside the library turned brothel that sported a sign: Silver & Gold.

The sight reminded Camilla that life could be a great deal worse.

She set off toward a black police cruiser parked in a lot across from the library. Tires squealed at the next intersection. Two cars shot across, their engines rumbling as they raced down the road.

But the officer seemed too preoccupied to follow.

Camilla walked past the car and spotted a mop of hair moving over the cop's lap. Neither of his hands gripped the wheel. He glanced over and caught Camilla's gaze, grinning wide.

"Wow," she murmured. "That's what we're up against."

Two junkies hung out on the benches around the corner. She recognized both as locals.

"Ma'am," said a dark-skinned guy missing most of his front teeth. He rose to his feet, his muscular frame and biceps captured in the streetlight.

"Hey there, Mr. Mayweather," she said with a smile.

Mayweather, whose real name was Joe, returned the gesture, showing off his missing teeth. The man was an anomaly. About as ripped as Rocky, he had once been a Golden Gloves champ, hence the nickname.

"You got any money I can borrow?" he asked.

Borrow . . .

"You can fight me for it," she said, putting up her fists.

"I don't hit ladies, ma'am, but damn! Someone else sure must have." His pinned eyes squinted at her face.

"I fell," she lied.

Reaching into her pocket, she took out a couple of silver dimes.

"Get yourself something to eat," Camilla said. "Maybe something for your buddy to eat too."

She handed the coins to Joe.

"Much obliged, ma'am," he said.

Camilla jogged the rest of the way to the Pig's Ear. Over twenty people packed the small, narrow space furnished with a long bar and ten red tables.

She took a seat at the bar and ordered a basket of tacos al carbón and a side of salsa verde. It was some of the best in the entire city—and fresh too. And the hogs were raised not far away.

The barmaid, a woman in her fifties named Sandy, popped the top off a sweating bottle of Carta Blanca and set it down in front of Camilla.

"Long day?" Sandy asked.

"Is it that obvious?" Camilla grabbed the cold beer and brought it to her lips, enjoying the first gulp more than sex—not *great* sex, but decent sex. That was what she really wanted, but the man she wanted it with was off limits.

She and Dom could never be together. It would tarnish their working relationship. But, damn, sometimes she couldn't help but think of him in that way. Intelligent, kind, generous, with a strong moral compass, not to mention handsome—he was the antithesis of the men she hunted.

Although she worried that he was starting to change. Popping the speed and taking bigger risks had her worried. She kept telling herself he was doing it to help him fight a war and that he would stop. But the pills were addictive, and he already had a drinking problem.

You're one to talk, she thought as she finished off the beer.

Sandy popped another and slid it to her with a warm smile.

Camilla sighed in the breeze of an old ceiling fan. She downed the second beer and a shot of tequila, her anxiety-ridden body welcoming the chill and then the burn.

She could already feel eyes on her. Two forty-something white guys in jeans, T-shirts, and ball caps sat off to her left, a fort of empty beer bottles on the bar in front of them. The woman on her right got off the barstool, opening up a spot.

Oh, great.

The tacos came out, and she mowed them down, chasing each bite with a swig. Maybe her eating like a pig would deter the assholes to her left from bothering her.

She was wrong.

They walked over, sitting on the two empty barstools to either side.

"Hey, lady," the guy on the left said. "You alone?"

"What's it look like, prick?" She wiped her fingers on her shirt and grabbed the fresh beer the barmaid had set down.

"Well, damn, maybe there's a reason for that," the guy said. "You got a mouth on ya, don't you?"

She tipped back the beer, giving the guy a quick side glance. He had a handsome face, with dimples and a five o'clock shadow. But she didn't like his eyes. She knew eyes, and his seemed empty, dead—the gaze of a man harboring bad secrets.

"I'm alone for a reason," she said. "Now, fuck off and let me enjoy my cerveza."

Sandy smiled, a cigarette bobbing in her mouth, and went back to wringing out a filthy mop into a bucket.

The guys weren't amused or deterred.

"You really should be more polite," said the one on her right. "Maybe you would avoid all them scars and cuts if you were. I mean, you ain't *that* good lookin', lady."

She still hadn't bothered to look at his face but decided to give him a glance. Unlike his friend, he had a beak of a nose and barely a chin.

"Maybe you shouldn't sit down uninvited," she replied.

She threw down a few coins to pay her tab, grabbed her beer, and said, "Thanks Sandy."

Sandy nodded, then glared at the two men.

Camilla walked out of the Pig's Ear, figuring it was over. Again she was wrong.

She kept walking, listening to the footfalls behind her. When she rounded the corner of the building, she stopped, looking out over an abandoned parking lot.

Walking away wasn't her style.

She turned around, pissed. When they came around the corner, they just kept coming, even when she shouted for them to stop.

Before she could react, a fist hit her in the nose. Stars burst in her vision, and heat flared in her brain.

She stumbled back and tripped on a hunk of broken concrete. A cold wave of fear rushed through her as she fell.

She hit the ground hard, the bottle in her hand shattering.

The ugly guy went to grab her leg, but she kicked him in the face. The other guy reached down to grab her arm, and she slashed him across the wrist with the broken bottle.

"Crazy bitch!" he screeched.

She got back up, holding the broken bottle and swiping the air. The two guys stumbled away, holding their wounds and cursing.

"You're lucky we don't kill you!"

"She broke my nose. Holy shit, I think she broke my nose!"

Around the corner came Sandy, with a guy wearing an apron and carrying a meat cleaver.

"Get out of here, you punks!" he yelled.

Sandy walked over to Camilla, who was still holding the broken bottle in a shaky hand.

The two lowlifes moved around the corner, still screaming profanities.

"Miss?" Sandy asked.

"You okay?" asked the cook.

"I'm fine," Camilla said.

"Better let me look at that nose," Sandy said.

Camilla wiped the blood away on her arm.

"I'll be okay. But thanks. Those tacos are amazing!" she said as if nothing had happened.

The cook and Sandy exchanged a glance as Camilla walked past them.

For the next half hour, she walked the streets, mind racing and heart pounding. She stopped at a corner grocery store to pick up some gauze, then continued to the Santa Monica Pier, or what was left of it.

Chain-link fences blocked off the coastline. The boardwalk and shops were gone, burned to the ground during the war. No Trespassing signs were posted every quarter mile or so.

Waves beat the shoreline behind the fences, eating at the ledge of dirt and sand. The beautiful beaches that once attracted tourists from all over the world were gone, eroded and washed away.

She walked over to the fence and found a section partly cut away. Ducking under the flap, she walked to the high-tide shelf and sat dangling her feet over the side. There, she did something she hadn't done in years. Camilla Santiago sobbed and sobbed, her salty tears falling into the saltwater that lapped at her feet.

* * *

Sweat dripped down Vinny's forehead behind the night-vision goggles and his mask.

The Moretti fire team, bottlenecked in the narrow concrete passage, had come across several obstructions, some of which required careful checking for booby traps.

But for Vinny, it was the image of the dead boy that slowed him down tonight. He couldn't get it out of his mind.

Focus, Vin. You got to keep focused on the mission.

In a few minutes, they would be out of the sewers and on Nevksy territory. And with one man already down, he continued to feel the pinch of fear that came with waiting. Waiting gave the idle brain too much time to worry.

But there was an upside to Frankie biting the dust. It opened up a dealing spot at the Four Diamonds, and Don Antonio would need another captain to run the operation.

Vinny almost smiled, but the night was young, and plenty of risks lay ahead. The Nevskys weren't the only threat. The storm sewers were often home to the crazies, cast away from society on the surface.

Vinny had seen only a few face-to-face. Most were rounded up by the cops and cast into the wastelands, but a few escaped to dark places like this.

He wasn't surprised when he smelled, then saw, bodies ahead.

Judging by their condition—mostly reduced to bones, hair, and clothing—they were probably refugees after the Second Civil War.

A random drip of water hit his helmet as he passed under a grate. There were about a hundred other places he would rather be than down here, and he suddenly envied his cousin. While Vinny was down here risking his ass, Marco was probably drinking champagne, and doing lines off some hooker's tits.

Vinny focused on the mission and also on Carmine. He didn't like that the man was walking behind his father, but he also didn't think Carmine was going to do anything right now to avenge his friend Frankie.

The asshole made a big mistake. Even Carmine had to know that. All the men knew the rules. Similar to the old ways of La Costa Nostra in Naples, but with the rigid chain of command that Antonio and Christopher brought with them from the Italian Army.

If you directly disobeyed an order, you were punished accordingly. In Frankie's case, that meant a bullet—three, actually.

Carmine raised a fist, and Vinny halted.

A rat skittered past, vanishing into a crack in the wall, reminding him of the biggest threat to the Moretti family.

Human-sized rats. *The Saints.* They were next on the hit list.

Carmine lowered his hand, and the team continued into a large room with tunnels jutting off in four directions. Christopher split the fire team, with Yellowtail leading four men on the left while Vinny, Carmine, and Rush followed Christopher on the right. They walked up concrete steps and ducked into a tunnel with a low ceiling. Halfway down the passage, a steel ladder rose through a shaft to the surface.

"Carmine, check it out," Christopher ordered.

Carmine grumbled as he climbed. A few tense minutes later, he climbed back down.

"The lid is welded shut," he whispered. "Microcam shows a motion detector topside."

"Not for long," Christopher said. He brought a finger to his earpiece, breaking radio silence for the first time to send Doberman a message.

"In position," Christopher said over the comms.

Doberman's voice came through. "Activating Christmas lights in three, two, one . . ."

Somewhere five blocks away, Vinny's best friend fired the EMP device into the roof of the Nevsky compound, killing the power in a single invisible blast and disabling their security system.

"On me," Christopher said. He stepped onto the ladder, his rifle hanging over his back.

Vinny went next.

At the top, Christopher put a shoulder into the lid, and the weld broke free. The superacid gel Carmine applied around the lid had already worked, eating through the steel. He pushed the lid up with ease, took a look, then shoved the lid aside.

Seconds later, the team was fanning out in a field of weeds. Only a few scraggly pandanus trees dotted the landscape, providing almost zero concealment. A half-moon glowed over the dusty terrain.

The team moved toward a ten-foot concrete wall around the Russian compound. The roofs of several buildings rose toward the clouds. Two towers overlooked the eastern and western walls.

Shouts sounded on the other side of the wall. Then a voice, in English.

"What the fuck happened to the lights?"

Christopher pointed to the east tower and gave the order.

Two suppressed shots took the guards out, and both bodies slumped, one toppling over the edge and into the field. Two more suppressed shots to the west tower took out the guards posted there. Yellowtail and his men ran toward the wall.

When the two teams were in position, Carmine pulled a grappling hook and coiled line off his pack and threw it over the side of the wall. Yellowtail followed suit. They gave the lines a yank, pulling the razor wire down in both places.

Two rope ladders were thrown over, and both teams scrambled up them and down the other side.

By the time they were inside, only two minutes had passed since the EMP blast, and they hadn't been spotted.

Vinny's boots hit the grass on enemy territory, and he crouched down to orient himself.

Four houses made up the compound. A long driveway through the center ended in a circle outside the main structure. Several vehicles were parked there. Trees and gardens provided cover or concealment in the green spaces between the houses.

A guard patrolling a stone path walked around the corner of the house to the right and stopped to listen. Christopher slit his throat and pulled him backward into the holly bushes. Seeing his dad kill with such ease made Vinny wonder how many men he had executed in that fashion when he was in Afghanistan.

Yellowtail took out two more guards with bursts from his rifle as he advanced. Vinny followed his father to the right, around the side of the smaller building. They stopped at a corner and signaled Carmine and Rush to take up position on the other side of the driveway.

They darted across in the darkness, leaving Vinny alone with his dad. Hand signals from Carmine confirmed three targets outside the entrance of the main house, a two-story Victorian with a dozen wide windows.

If Sergei was anything like his uncle, the windows were bulletproof.

Vinny spotted three soldiers on the stairwell. He spotted a fourth walking near a group of vehicles in the circular drive.

Christopher pulled Vinny back, and Vinny knelt beside his father, moving his finger from guard to trigger. They waited a few more seconds for Yellowtail to get into position.

A shout rang out to the right, and before Vinny could react, automatic gunfire cracked across the driveway.

Their cover was blown.

Rush and Carmine turned into a hail of gunfire. Car windows shattered as bullets punched into the vehicles. Rush suddenly cried out and went skidding. Carmine pulled him to safety while the shooter moved behind a cypress tree to reload.

"God damn it," Christopher grumbled. He strode away from the corner and fired across the driveway. The 7.62 mm NATO rounds punched through the tree, clipping the soldier and spinning him about.

Carmine's next shot caught the wounded Russian in the face, and he fell still.

"On me!" Christopher yelled.

Carmine had a hand on Rush, who wasn't moving.

"He's gone," he said.

Vinny looked away from the former AMP soldier's crumpled body.

He had served them well over the years. Losing him was a major hit to the family.

"Vin, come on," Christopher said.

He followed his dad to the left side of the drive. The guards on the stairwell yelled in Russian and fired into the darkness.

Vinny slowed his pace, aimed, and pulled the trigger. Two of the guards went down right away, tumbling onto the circular drive. The third took up position behind a large stoneware planter full of flowers.

Rounds lanced into the position, shattering clay pots and cracking stone.

Yellowtail led his team into the battle, firing on full auto. Windows above shattered as Russians began firing from the second story.

Christopher bolted for cover behind a Mercedes SUV, and Vinny crouched beside him. Next came Carmine.

"You hit?" Christopher asked Carmine.

He shook his head.

Gunfire cut through the darkness all around them. Muzzle flashes blinking like fireflies in the night. Rounds blew out car windows and plinked through body metal. Vinny heard a bullet whiz overhead. The tire to his right hissed out its air.

Three more guards streamed into the circular drive, using cars as cover.

"Covering fire!" Christopher yelled.

The adrenaline rushed through Vinny. He had never felt anything like this before—not even being high on coke and drunk at the same time.

This was the ultimate rush, and he couldn't be more terrified.

And yet he still rose up, found a target, and pulled the trigger. A three-round burst took down one of the Russkies taking aim at his dad.

Christopher bolted for another car, stopped with his back against the rear bumper, and nodded at Vinny. They both stood up, firing at the same time. The gunfire took down another guard, and Vinny aimed at the windows above, firing at the muzzle flashes.

In his peripheral vision, he saw Carmine moving his rifle left, toward his father. His shot blew past Christopher and hit another Nevsky soldier on the stairs. Vinny ducked back down and looked over at Carmine.

"Nice shot," Vinny said. He waited for a lull and then picked out another window, unloading a dozen rounds at the target. Gunfire peppered the hood of the car, forcing him back down.

Yellowtail led his team into the circular drive, firing at the windows.

Vinny rose again to help lay down covering fire and saw his dad running toward the stairs.

"Dad!" he yelled.

Yellowtail and Christopher made it to the stairs at the same time. They loped up the steps, hurdling dead bodies.

"No kids, no women," Christopher said over the comms.

"Let's move," Carmine said to Vinny. He got up and ran across the circular drive, but Vinny hesitated, seeing motion on the right. Four figures darted out of a garden down the driveway and ran for a garage.

"Contacts on east side of main building," he said into his comm.

"Hold position," Christopher replied.

Vinny caught a glimpse of an older man in the center of the group of four, making a run for the garage.

Sergei Nevsky, you old bastard.

"Eyes on target, engaging," Vinny said.

"Hold position, Vinny," Christopher ordered. "I repeat, hold . . ."

But Vinny didn't listen. This was his chance to make up for the port and finally make captain. He would bring down the Russian boss while his cousin snorted another line of coke off some hooker's tits.

Vinny took off running with his rifle cradled. He wanted to wait until the last second before surprising the targets.

He knelt beside a car and searched for targets. He found several, one of them female. The orders about women sounded in the back of his mind as he waited for a shot.

He followed one of the men in his sights, then pulled the trigger.

Return fire cracked as two more soldiers fired from across the road. The rounds hit a car a hundred feet away. The assholes couldn't see him, but they could get lucky.

Breathing heavily, Vinny took cover behind a big eucalyptus tree. He glanced around. Sergei's little group were inside the garage now. He wasn't sure whether the EMP would kill the vehicles too, but he wasn't taking any chances.

Leaving the tree, he ran across the driveway toward the entrance to the garage, passing the man he had just killed.

Heart thumping in his ears, he approached the side door to the garage. The main door suddenly swung up, opened manually.

Gunfire continued at the main house, and Vinny used the noise to sneak closer.

A mid-1960s Mustang rumbled in the garage. He aimed at the driver's door and squeezed the trigger, shattering the glass as the car lurched out of the garage and coasted to a stop.

A woman fell out the back door, screaming in horror.

Vinny strode over, yelling and waving with one hand for her to get back while he aimed his rifle with the other hand.

She backed away, and Vinny leveled the gun at the car door. He walked up and opened it, stepping back as a body slumped out.

Not Sergei.

"Fucking dago," growled a deep voice from the darkness of the garage.

Vinny spun toward the Russian-accented voice and pulled the trigger just as something slammed into his helmet. He went down hard on the concrete, feeling as if an elephant had sat on him.

He tried to move but couldn't. Was his spine broken?

The muffled pop of gunfire rang out over the dull ringing in both his ears. He finally opened his eyes and saw movement on the ground inside the garage.

Sergei lay on the concrete, one hand gripping his shoulder, the other holding the pistol he had shot Vinny with. The old man aimed it at him again.

Vinny kept his eyes open, staring down the barrel. He had tried to imagine what it would be like to die. Would he be brave, or would he piss himself like most people?

Oddly, he didn't feel brave or scared. In this defining moment, all he could think about was Adriana.

A flash of motion broke across his vision, and two men darted into the garage. Sergei turned and fired one shot before the Morettis were on him, kicking him over and over.

Vinny squirmed on the ground, finally able to move again. He felt a hand on his back—a good sign he didn't have a broken neck.

"Vin! Vin!" said a voice. "Can you hear me?"

It was his dad, but Vinny couldn't respond. The numbness turned to pain. He fought the darkness closing in.

"Did we get him?" Vinny finally managed to say.

Christopher pulled his mask up and grinned. "Yeah, kid, *you* got him."

-19-

Ray smelled trash. His eyes opened to stacks of tires and mountains of stinking garbage.

But everything was strangely upside down.

No. You *are upside down.*

Blinking, he focused on the vehicle directly beneath him. Not just any vehicle, but a garbage truck, its back open and its metal belly half full of refuse.

Mumbling came from his left, and he glanced over.

"Tommy?" he muttered.

His partner hung from a crane.

Ray didn't need to look up to see that he, too, was hanging from a rope tied around his ankles. Looking past his feet, he was rewarded with a clear sky bejeweled with stars. The last sky he would ever see.

"You boys ready for a bath?"

He knew that voice. Sure enough, Mikey the Mutant walked into view.

"Please!" Tommy wailed. He was still in a hospital gown. The brazen bastards had kidnapped him from the hospital and brought him out here with Ray.

"I'm going to give you both a nice dip in this trash," Mikey said. "Get you real slimy and shit before I crush you into quesadillas."

The ugly bastard waddled out from between the two trucks. He pulled his pants up and gave Ray a shit-eating grin of rotten teeth.

A dozen of his comrades had circled around the trucks, all wearing filthy black jumpsuits. They smelled like their surroundings, maybe even worse.

Standing next to Mikey was his right-hand man, Richard Ontiveros, also known as "El Chef." He wore a rubber butcher's apron and held a machete. He swatted a fly away from his dreadlocks and went back to smoking his cigarette.

It amazed Ray that the Morettis dealt with these psychos. But they did run the biggest garbage operation in the county, which made their trucks very useful for distributing product and disposing of corpses.

"You're going to taste *real* good, *güero*," Mikey said, licking his lips and looking at Tommy. "You too, Detective."

Ray had heard the rumors but always figured it was just part of their mystique—one of those stories the gangsters used to get people to pay up or speak up.

Now Ray knew better—it wasn't a front at all. The mutant freak was a cannibal, and El Chef was an actual fucking chef who served up humans.

"Before you start crying again like little bitches, I'm going to be honest with you," Mikey said. "Don Antonio knows you two were involved with the port."

"What the hell are you talking about, man? We weren't even there!" Ray said, squirming in the air over the garbage truck.

"Maybe, maybe not, but I'm going to find out one way or the other. Only reason you *putos* are still alive is because I think you know who did *this* to me . . ."

He peeled back the yellowed bandage on the right side of his face, exposing flesh as bright and red as ahi tuna.

"The Saints should have made sure I was dead," Mikey said. "'Cause I'm going to spend the rest of my life hunting them down and picking them apart fingernail by fingernail, hair by hair, bone by bone."

He craned his neck to look up at Ray.

"You're wrong, Mikey," Ray said.

"Save your breath, Detective, 'cause I already know you were working with Lieutenant Best at the port."

Best, that son of a bitch . . .

It made sense that the lieutenant had sold him out to save his own skin. But Tommy? The guy was in the hospital during the attack.

"You're right, I knew," Ray said. "But we weren't there, I swear. And Tommy had *nothing* to do with this, man."

Mikey grinned. "You know what I *do* think?"

"Please," Tommy wailed. "I can't breathe . . ."

"I think you two are Saints," Mikey said, pointing at each of them. "I think you two were the guys that used the Morettis and my people as target practice."

"What!" Tommy blurted. "No way, man. I'm not a Saint. I was in the hospital during the attack, and I would never join those assholes!"

"Maybe, maybe not," Mikey said again. He smiled and turned to the crane booth, where one of his men sat at the controls holding Tommy aloft.

Mikey gave the operator a nod.

The machinery clanked, and Tommy descended toward the garbage truck. The compactor unit rumbled to life.

"NO!" Tommy shouted.

"Don't do this, Mikey," Ray said. "We're not Saints, and we can help you."

"That's what you said back in your rent-a-shack, but I still haven't heard anything that wets my broken beak," Mikey said. "Only way Tommy here doesn't turn into provolone and tomato sauce is if you give me the Saints."

Tommy struggled violently, swinging back and forth. A thin stream of liquid trickled off his body, into the crunching garbage below.

"He pissed himself!" one of Mikey's men yelled.

The other guys broke out laughing.

Tommy sobbed harder. "Ray, help me," he choked. "Help me, please!"

"A guy named Snake told us about the port," Ray said, "and Lieutenant Best went to get his cut, just like usual. I swear on my kids. We didn't know the Saints were going to show up. It was just a routine collection."

Mikey shook his head wearily and looked back to the crane operator, nodding. Tommy's head was nearing the opening of the garbage truck. The young cop fought harder, squirming back and forth.

"We're not Saints!" Ray yelled.

"Then tell me who is!" Mikey yelled back.

A scream rang out as the rope around Tommy's ankles slid off and he nose-dived into the open compactor. An inhuman screech filled the night, cut off abruptly by a meaty *thunk* and then crunching. It was over so fast, Ray hadn't even blinked.

The other men seemed equally surprised and were silent for a few seconds.

And then they started laughing.

Mikey bent over, hands on his knees. "That was fucking awesome!" he bellowed.

Ray wanted to puke.

"*Lo siento*," Mikey said, raising a hand but still chuckling. "That wasn't supposed to happen."

He wiped his nose and walked over until he was almost directly below Ray.

"Only one way you don't end up like that redhead *puto*, and that's by giving me the Saints," he said. "If you don't, then I might continue on this little spree once I'm done with you. Might go look up your family. I remember you having a fine-ass wife. Am I right, boys?"

The other men all hollered and grunted.

You touch her, and I will cut your balls off and feed them to the pigs. Ray scrutinized the burned face of the man he was going to kill.

"I'm not a Saint, but I know the identity of one," Ray said. "You let me go, and I'll bring 'im to you. You got my word."

Mikey tilted his head slightly and smirked. "Why should I trust the word of a *rata*?"

"What other choice you got? You guys have killed off all the other cops that were at the port, and if you're asking *me* for info, then my guess is, no one else knew."

Mikey thought on it a moment, then pressed the bandage back on his cheek. When it popped right back off, he tore the entire thing away and threw it to the dirt.

"Tell me who this person is," Mikey said. "Then if the dude ends up being a Saint, we can talk about you doing more work for me."

In your sick dreams, asshole.

Mikey must have seen the reaction on Ray's face, because he snorted and said, "Don't act like you're better than me, *pendejo*. You're a dirty *rata* cop. I ain't no *rata*."

He thumped his hairy chest, rattling the chains that hung over it. "That's why the Morettis work with me. They trust me to get shit done."

"I was wonderin' why they work with you, actually," Ray said. "Now I know."

Mikey raised his chin proudly. Then he looked over at the second crane and started to raise his hand.

Ray knew that what he said next would determine whether he lived or died.

"Only way I'm helping you is if you let me take care of this on my terms," Ray said.

Mikey snorted again and gestured to the operator to proceed. The crane cable lowered, dropping Ray toward the back of the garbage truck.

"Two million bucks," Ray said. "That's how much you get if I'm right!"

The compactor groaned. The trash below stank terribly.

"In gold!" Ray shouted.

Mikey held up his hand, and Ray's body jerked to a stop. He swayed slightly, holding his breath.

"You fuck me, and I will find your family and have my fun. Then I will eat their pretty faces."

* * *

"I think we lost them," Moose said.

He took a right down another street and sped down the empty road while Dom tried to calm his heart rate. It was thumping fast, and sweat dripped off his forehead.

Watching Don Antonio's BMW burn was one of the greatest feelings of his life. So why did he feel so much anxiety?

Maybe it was because he had wanted to do this with his bare hands, or maybe it was because they were in the middle of a lawless zone. Or it could be because he hadn't slept more than three hours at a time for a week straight.

His body was going to crash; it was just a matter of time.

Dom downed half a bottle of water, hoping it would help.

"You okay there, boss?" Moose asked.

"Hell yeah, baby," Dom said, forcing a smile.

"I will be if we get out of here alive," Rocky added.

After the attack on the Hollywood Freeway, Moretti soldiers had deployed all across the city to hunt the Saints.

They really needed to ditch the Jeep, but he wasn't about to start walking in this part of town.

"Where the fuck are we?" Rocky asked, gripping his rifle and keeping low in the back seat.

"You don't want to know," Dom said. "Keep an eye out for tails—and freaks."

Rocky pointed his rifle at the back window, shattered from several Moretti bullets. Dom didn't blame him for being nervous. They were in the second-worst part of LA—almost as bad as the Malice Wastes. It was the state of nature, like most of the United States.

Tonight, the world seemed a shade darker. A foreshadowing of what was to come, perhaps, or maybe it just seemed that way to Dom, who saw the world for what it was now: decayed and dying.

The police didn't even come here. Ruled by members of old gangs and cliques that survived the war with the LAPD eight years ago, it had no laws. No code. No rules.

Worse, the grid was down, making the Jeep lights a target in the dark city blocks.

"Shut off the lights," Dom said.

Moose glanced over again. "You serious?"

"Do it."

Moose clicked off the beams and pulled over to the shoulder. Dom walked to the rear and shattered the brake lights with his rifle butt. He scanned the shadows as he walked back.

Several gang-run communities were clustered in this former industrial zone, occupying the graffiti-covered buildings with broken windows.

He got back in, and they drove to a former residential area where the houses had burned down to the aluminum wall studs. The apocalyptic sight sent a chill through his body. Or maybe he was just coming down from the speed.

Dom knew he had to stop with the Dexedrine, but without it, he feared he wouldn't be able to keep up his pace. Besides that, his biggest fear was of turning into the same men he hunted.

You will never *be like them.*

Suddenly light-headed, he blinked away the stars before his eyes to study the oblique shapes. Metal fences formed a periphery around several brick apartment buildings. He didn't see a soul outside.

"Get us out of here," Rocky said. "This place gives me the creeps."

A black cat darted across the road, stopping to hiss at the Jeep.

"See? Place is cursed," Rocky said.

Moose snorted. "It ain't cursed, kid."

"Whatever, man. This is where people come to get skinned alive. Just as well be outside the wall."

"Shut it," Moose said. "You're giving me a headache."

Dom looked right, then left. "I'm not exactly sure where we are," he said.

"Well, ain't that fucking great," Rocky murmured.

The Jeep slowed.

"You see that?" Moose said, leaning to the side for a better look.

Dom squinted at the intersection ahead. Several rusted vehicles blocked the route. Figures perched on the roofs like gargoyles. But these weren't statues.

"Back up," Dom whispered.

"I don't think they see us," Moose said.

Dom aimed his rifle at the windshield and zoomed in to see male faces covered in lesions.

"Oh shit," Dom whispered.

"What?" Rocky said.

Moose put the Jeep in reverse and swung a bootleg turn, tires squealing as he turned.

Two men jumped off the vehicles and took off running toward the Jeep. Their deranged screams pierced the night.

Dom leaned out the window and fired high, trying to scare them off without killing them. That did the trick. The crazy pricks knew they weren't invincible. Both pursuers dropped to the concrete as Moose raced away down another street.

"Go, go, go!" Rocky shouted.

They passed another abandoned apartment complex and several streets of fire-gutted houses before finally finding a street that wasn't blocked off.

Dom lowered his rifle and pulled out the magazine to check the rounds. It was almost empty, and he swapped it out for a full one just in case they ran into more trouble before they got back to the safe house.

They made it out of the gang-controlled territory a few minutes later, and Rocky slumped in the back seat, letting out a sigh.

"Don't relax," Dom said. "We're back in Moretti territory."

"Shit," Rocky mumbled.

Moose flipped the headlights back on. Tents littered an open park at the end of the street. Thin people shuffled along a sidewalk toward a city-run soup kitchen set up on the next corner.

Ironically, it was one of the stations Moretti funded.

Two scooters zipped down the street, passing the Jeep, no doubt carrying Moretti product to sell to the people in the lines. The riders yelled at the crowd.

Moose took a left through an intersection to avoid the cars waiting at a stop sign. The road ahead appeared mostly clear—only a few cars out on its two lanes. Palm trees and weeds shifted in the sultry breeze.

It seemed almost peaceful.

Dom pulled out the police-band radio and turned it on, eager to hear anything about Don Antonio now they were out of the lawless zone and had ditched their tails.

"How we doin' on gas?" Dom asked.

Moose checked the fuel gauge. "Not much left, but we should be good."

Dom bent down, listening to multiple reports of violent crimes across the city. For the LAPD, business was brisk. He strained to hear over the rush of wind coming in the broken windows. A 10-10. Two 10-16s.

Fights, especially domestic assaults, spiked around midnight when the booze ran out. So did murders. On a good night, only a few people were killed in the city. On a bad one, the morgues were packed.

Tonight was going to be one of the latter. Especially after Dom heard the report about deputies needing backup on the wall. He had already heard the low whine in the distance. As they got closer, it rose into the full wail of an air-raid siren. The city was being attacked.

"Raiders," Moose said.

"Jesus Christ," Dom said.

Rocky's eyes widened in the back seat. "This isn't happening . . . Holy shit!"

They listened for several minutes as reports came in of multiple vehicles attacking one of the main gates. It wasn't often Chief of Police Stone authorized officers to help Sheriff Benson.

Dom massaged his temples. News of violence across the city made celebrating their assassination of the king of Los Angeles difficult. It still hadn't quite sunk in.

They had killed Don Antonio.

The Jeep slowed as they came upon a line of cars curving around the next corner. Beat cops were searching the vehicles.

"Another fucking roadblock," Moose said.

Lights flashed in the distance, heading toward the wall where the raider attack had occurred. The distant air-raid sirens wailed on, the threat still present.

The cops ahead were looking either for raiders who had made it in, or Saints, or both.

"We're about to get boxed in," Rocky said.

"Pull a U-ey," Dom said.

Moose backed up, then whipped into the oncoming lane. One of the cops, bent over, looked up from the passenger window of a stopped vehicle.

They were clearly looking for a vehicle, and the Saints couldn't take the chance it was theirs—not with a two-million-dollar bounty on each of their heads. These cops didn't know that the king was dead and the bounty thus gone.

Moose waited for his moment to cut across, but several teenagers on scooters were speeding away from the cops, shouting.

"Come on, let's go," Dom said.

"What? And run over one of these punks?"

The officer checking the vehicle ahead raised a hand as the beams from another car hit him in the face. Dom didn't recognize this man in the glow, but he was young, probably just a rookie.

"Stop!" he called out.

The second officer ran toward their vehicle, drawing his pistol as he moved.

"Shit, shit, shit!" Moose said.

"Get us out of here!" Rocky yelled.

Moose squealed out into the other lane, narrowly missing one of the mopeds. Dom watched the two officers running after them.

"Get down!" he yelled.

Two flashes, then the crack of gunfire. One round shattered the passenger side mirror. The other hit the door. Dom ducked instead of returning the fire. He had killed enough people tonight.

The Jeep rounded a corner, fleeing the gunfire.

"You okay?" Moose asked.

Dom nodded and looked to the back seat.

"I'm really getting sick of everyone trying to kill me!" Rocky said. "Morettis, bangers, and now cops!"

"Better get used to it, kid," Moose said.

The old clunker picked up speed, racing around slower vehicles. City of Industry wasn't far now. Just another few minutes.

"We're going to have to ditch this vehicle," Dom said.

They tore down another road, away from civilization. Radiation signs marked the side of the road, but the threat was minimal out here.

"Keep heading east and take a right on Canyon Road," Dom said.

They were taking the back way to City of Industry and were coming up on the city limits. Traffic was almost nonexistent until they turned down Canyon Road. Now he saw why.

Smoke rose from glowing fires on the southern border.

"Those raiders must have been Pyros," Dom said.

"Got some contacts ahead," Moose said.

Dom readied his rifle.

They moved to the shoulder as four former military trucks sped down the opposite side of the road, packed full of deputies wearing brown armor, orange goggles, and breathing apparatuses.

"Must be heading to the border," Moose said.

"Or outside the gates to hunt down the raiders," Rocky said.

They sat there for a few moments until the trucks were out of sight.

Dom pulled down his face mask and wiped the sweat off his face. The adrenaline had subsided.

Before he could crack a grin, another report came over the police band: an attack on the Nevsky compound.

Dom turned up the volume.

"Two bosses, baby," Moose said. "That's one hell of a night for the Saints!"

"Oh yeah!" Rocky yelled. He did his robot dance in the back seat. Moose laughed, but Dom suddenly didn't feel like smiling. Something felt off, as if they were in the path of a storm he couldn't see.

"Time to crack some beers," Rocky said. He moved forward between the two front seats. "Can't wait to tell Tooth the news."

Dom felt a buzz in his vest and pulled out his burner cell phone. He didn't recognize the number, but only one person had this one.

"Who's that?" Moose asked.

Dom brought the phone to his ear to talk to Lieutenant Zed Marks.

"This line secure?"

"Yeah," Dom replied.

"You hear about Sergei Nevsky?"

"Yeah, you hear about Antonio Moretti?"

There was a short pause on the other line.

"I've had my hands full tonight with Sergei and a coordinated attack by Pyros in zone one, but I did hear about an attack at Cahuenga Pass. So that was you, huh?"

"We finally got the king," Dom said proudly.

"No," Marks replied dryly. "You didn't, but you did just start a war."

Dom almost dropped the phone.

"It was a decoy convoy. Antonio wasn't there."

Marks let the words sink in just long enough for Dom to realize that wasn't the reason he called.

"You're playing with fire now and putting everything we've worked so carefully for at risk," Marks continued. "In three days, Mayor Buren is going to announce a new project to help save what's left of this city, and Councilman Castle is going to speak. Until then, sit tight, and don't do shit—or I'm shutting you down for good."

The line severed, leaving Dom holding the phone in a shaky hand. He had screwed up, and bad. And this time he hadn't just poked the hornet's nest.

The Saints had knocked it out of the tree.

-20-

Tonight was shaping up to be even better than Antonio had thought, with the Nevsky family all but wiped out and his son about to learn a life lesson. But first, they had some unfinished business.

"Be quiet," Antonio said to Marco, who sat in the back seat of the Escalade. They waited in a line between two Toyota pickups, stopped at a roadblock on the city border.

"But . . ."

Antonio's iron glare silenced his intoxicated son. It was better than a backhand with his gold Moretti ring.

A sheriff's deputy walked away from the pickup ahead. He lowered his orange goggles at the open window.

"Not a great night to be leaving the walls," he said. "Don't you hear the sirens?"

Vito nodded.

"Then you know there was a raider attack in zone one tonight. Had to call the LAPD for backup. A few of those freaks got into the city, but we're huntin' 'em down."

Don Antonio kept his head down in the back seat while Vito handed a bag of coins out the window.

"Good luck finding them," Vito said. "But we'll be fine out here."

The deputy tried to look in, but Vito moved to block his view.

"I've got business to take care of," he said, "so unless you want to give that silver back, I suggest you get the fuck out of our way."

The deputy stood and circled his fingers through the air, the conversation over.

On the shoulder, a crane rumbled, and the operator used an electromagnet to pick up the shipping container blocking the road. It lifted the red box into the air, exposing another set of roadblocks ahead.

"Almost cheaper than the cops," Vito said. He answered his cell phone as the deputies moved concrete barriers out of the way.

"Have they found them yet?" Antonio asked.

Vito shook his head. "We're still looking, sir, but don't worry. They won't escape this time."

Antonio clenched and unclenched his fist, in and out, trying to manage his temper. As he had suspected, the Saints seized the opportunity to attack the decoy BMW he had sent out with the Suburbans after he left through the Dragon's back door.

It was all part of his plan, but he wouldn't know whether the trap had netted the Saints until he got back to the city. In a few minutes, they would lose cell phone coverage.

Vito looked back at Antonio.

"You sure about this, sir? The raiders are still out there."

In answer, Antonio lifted the ARX160 resting against the door.

"Raiders?" Marco slurred.

The convoy moved around the concrete barriers and passed through the gate, leaving the city limits under a dazzling star-filled sky.

Marco looked at the minefield warning signs posted along the road. "Where the hell are we going?" he asked.

Antonio handed him a bottle of water. "Drink this."

Marco took the bottle, and Antonio looked at his watch. Almost 1:00 a.m. He expected to feel tired, but instead he felt energized.

Marco screwed the cap off the water and gulped it down. "This better be worth it," he said. "I was about to close on Jenny—been working on that for a month."

"Is pussy *all* you think about, man?" Vito asked.

Not a man yet . . . Antonio went back to checking the horizon for the star-blotting movement of a dust storm. They frightened him more than any raiders.

Marco muttered a response under his breath, and Antonio almost slapped him. A little tough love might help the kid. But that would come soon.

For now, he just needed Marco to sober up.

A sliver of moon hung over the desert, casting a glow on the cracked brown dirt and dried-up foliage. The temperature continued to drop in the early-morning hour. Antonio spotted a coyote darting away from the road.

Tonight, it wasn't the only hunter in these parts.

The Morettis had spent the past twenty-four hours hunting down their enemies, and they weren't finished yet. He still had a few more things to do before he could claim his throne and move on the utilities in Los Angeles—something he'd had his eyes on for eight years now. Once he controlled those, no one could stop him.

If his men hadn't captured the Saints by that point, he had a very simple backup plan: turn off the lights and water until the city handed them over.

He grabbed the ARX160 propped up against the Escalade's door. It felt good to hold a rifle again. The weapon, like the bulletproof windows and the trucks ahead, was a precaution. So were the breathing masks and the gallons of drinking water.

Everything he did, he did with security in mind.

The threat of running into raiders was higher than normal tonight, but his soldiers could take them easily if confronted—the nomadic psychos weren't skilled fighters, although they were crazy, which made them harder to kill.

They were now twenty miles from the nearest settlement of people cast out from Los Angeles. Most of the people who came here voluntarily just wanted to be left alone—people like Snake and his crew.

It was a damn shame what happened to him, Antonio thought, recalling the story Carmine relayed after talking to Detective Ray Clarke. It was also a shame that Ray had been involved with the port. He was one of the cops on their payroll that Antonio had actually liked. Smart and aggressive.

If only Marco could be more like that. Perhaps a week or two out in the wastes, living on one of the homesteads with the sick outcasts like Snake, would stiffen his spine. Antonio should have sent his son out here instead of that expensive school in Italy.

Vito followed the trucks out onto a frontage road away from the interstate. Familiar shapes of rocks broke through the darkness. Antonio hadn't been here in over a year, but he recognized the terrain.

Faces of a dozen enemies surfaced in his mind. Enzo, don of the Sarcone family, was nothing but bones by now. Some of the Yamazakis were also buried here—the ones that Antonio had decided not to throw in the landfill. The Boai, mostly former triads, who had risen to power five years earlier, were also in shallow graves.

Soon, the dirt would be filled with other neutralized threats to the Moretti operation. And in time, there would be unmarked graves for Esteban Vega and his brother Miguel.

But not the Saints. Antonio had other plans for them. Much bigger plans.

"Where the hell are we?" Marco asked.

Antonio finally looked back at his son, slumped in his rumpled white Armani suit.

"Devil's graveyard," Antonio said.

Marco sat up straight. "We're in the desert?"

"You just realized that?" Vito said, laughing.

"Why . . ." Marco's voice cracked.

"You'll find out soon. Now, drink that fucking water," Antonio snapped.

After driving another forty minutes, the small convoy finally stopped. Vito pulled over behind the trucks. Several men piled out of the vehicles and opened the lift gates.

The Escalade's headlights captured two bodies tied up in the back of the truck on the right and one in the truck on the left.

"Who are they?" Marco asked.

"Get out," Antonio said.

They followed Vito across the dirt to the pickups.

The wind wasn't bad tonight, and there was no sign of any dust storms brewing.

Six men moved out with their rifles to form a perimeter, while Yellowtail, Carmine, Christopher, Doberman, and Vinny stood watch. Several other soldiers jumped into the backs of the pickups and pulled out the prisoners, tossing them to the dirt.

Antonio looked for Sergei's bearded face, but the man was facedown.

"What the hell happened to your head, Vin?" Marco asked, apparently more interested in his cousin than the prisoners.

Vinny touched the bandage wrapped around his forehead. Then he gave Marco the once-over. "Enjoy your night on the town?"

Marco brushed his hair back into place. "I was until I got yanked from my party. I was celebrating West Hollywood, bro."

"Celebrating the street bench you shot up before I saved your ass?"

The other men all laughed, and Marco clenched his jaw.

Vinny waved his hand when Marco didn't reply. "Don't mention it. I know you would have saved my ass too, if the roles were reversed."

"He also helped capture our Russian friend," Yellowtail said, eyes on the prisoner.

Christopher nodded proudly. "He took a risk, but it paid off. Sergei would have escaped if it weren't for Vinny."

"I got lucky, I guess." Vinny turned to Antonio. "Those Ronin helmets were well worth the price tag. Thank you, Don Antonio."

"Didn't save Rush," Christopher said.

Antonio froze. "Rush?"

The death stung, especially after losing Joey and his entire crew earlier in the week. But this was war, and in war, soldiers died.

Antonio had to remain positive and focus on the endgame.

"Frankie's also gone," Carmine said. "But we have Christopher to thank for that."

"What!" Antonio snapped.

His younger brother stroked the gray tip of his beard. "Piece of shit shot a kid."

"What do you mean, he 'shot a kid'?" Antonio asked. They didn't have many rules, but you didn't kill children.

"Kid saw us before we went into the tunnels," Christopher said. "I told everyone no kids and no women—except for that one."

He pointed at Natalia Nevsky, lying facedown in the dirt beside her husband.

Antonio wasn't entirely surprised to hear that Frankie had offed a kid. The old soldier had always been a loose cannon. Maybe it was for the best.

No, you're losing too many men.

The losses more than stung. They *hurt.* Frankie was one of his best earners, and Rush had been a loyal associate ever since deserting AMP to work for the Moretti family.

He managed his rage and turned his attention back to Sergei and his wife. The duct tape covering Natalia's mouth came undone as she struggled.

"Don't kill us, please!" she wailed. "We will give you everything!"

Antonio pulled out a shovel from the bed of a pickup. "I already have everything." He casually walked over to her, spat on Sergei, and then smacked Natalia over the head with the flat of the blade.

The crack echoed in the night, silencing the woman and everyone else but Sergei. He flopped on the ground like a landed fish, but Antonio didn't ease his suffering with a good whack.

He tossed the shovel to his son instead.

The kid caught it, holding it up in the air as if it were some sort of alien object.

"You've got to be kidding me," Marco said.

Antonio folded his arms across his chest.

"Start digging," he said. "You too, Carmine."

Carmine muttered and grabbed another shovel. Antonio didn't like his attitude, and he didn't like the way he had looked at Christopher, but he understood why. Carmine and Frankie had been close for decades.

Could he still trust the captain, or should he deal with him while they were here at the Devil's Graveyard?

Give him one last chance. You need him.

Carmine and Marco moved in front of the pickup trucks, where the headlights provided plenty of light to dig by.

"Yellowtail, send a few more lookouts just in case some hillbillies try and sneak up on us," Christopher said. Three associates followed the soldier out into the dark.

Antonio made his way over to their other prisoner, on his knees, gut hanging over blue pants soaked with piss. Lieutenant Billy Best tried to straighten up as best he could with his hands behind his back.

"I'm disappointed," Antonio said. He squatted down to look the crooked cop in the eye. "Very disappointed."

Best whined and mumbled, trying to talk through the duct tape. He stopped and swallowed when Christopher walked over with his pistol aimed at the man's head.

"Not yet," Antonio said. He turned back to Best and ripped the tape off the officer's battered face.

Best sucked in a deep breath and started pleading for his life.

"You thought you could steal from me?" Antonio asked.

"I swear I had nothin' to do with the port, Don Antonio. Swear on my daughter's life."

"This isn't for the port. This is for skimming off the top, you disgusting pile of *merda*."

Best sobbed. "I'm sorry, Don Antonio, please forgive me. I'll repay you every dime."

Antonio rose to his feet and walked away, the dirt crunching under his boots as Best whimpered behind him.

"Shut him up," Antonio ordered.

Vinny pulled off a new swatch of tape and slapped it over Best's mouth while Christopher pulled out a cigar and handed one to Antonio. Vinny joined them, smoking a cigarette.

The three of them watched the two prisoners squirm and cry in the dirt beside their designated final resting places.

It was a sight Antonio had witnessed more times than he could count.

He lit his cigar and blew the smoke skyward, studying the sparkling sky. The tradition was one of many he had developed with his brother over the years, and each time, it strengthened their bond.

They were gods in this life. Giants. And even though Antonio knew he was destined for hell in the next, he didn't fear his fate.

All that mattered was taking everything he could *now*, during this moment. He would do the same thing in hell.

"Almost done," Carmine shouted. He stood in one hole while Marco dug away inside the other.

"Got another one to dig when you're done," Vinny said.

Marco muttered something under his breath. Not surprising. Like many men their age, the two were constantly vying to show who had bigger balls.

He climbed out of the shallow grave. "I can't believe you brought me out here to dig a fucking hole in the middle of the night after I almost got killed."

"I brought you out here to turn you into a man," Antonio said.

Marco looked at Christopher, who walked over with a pistol.

"No," Antonio said. "Too easy."

Christopher halted and looked over his shoulder.

"You're going to use that shovel to kill the pig first, then Sergei, and then his wife," Antonio said.

Marco stared in shock at his father. "But . . ."

Antonio put a hand on his son's shoulder in a rare display of affection. He met the gaze of his flesh and blood, but Marco glanced away.

"Look at me, Marco," he said, grabbing the back of his neck. "You want to fill these shoes? You want a spot at the table, and to take over this family when I'm gone?"

Antonio could feel his son's heart thumping. Marco used the time to look over at the three captives. Then he looked back at Antonio and nodded.

"Prove it and show me," Antonio said, releasing his grip.

Christopher and Vinny dragged Sergei and his wife by their feet over to the freshly dug graves. Best took off running.

The men laughed as he stumbled and hit the dirt, nearly rolling into one of the graves.

"Kill him," Antonio said to his son. "Now."

Marco walked over, brandishing the shovel over his head and hesitated. Best tried to push himself up, then fell. He rolled to his back, hands still tied behind him. He scooted backward, shaking his head at Marco.

Do it, goddamn it.

Best let out a muffled scream as Marco finally brought the shovel down. The swipe missed his head, whooshing through the air and hitting him between the legs.

The cop's eyes bulged, and Marco stumbled backward, still a bit drunk.

The other soldiers laughed as Best groaned in pain.

"Kill the pig!" Carmine shouted.

"Beat his face in," yelled another soldier.

Antonio remained silent with Christopher and Vinny, watching Marco hold the shovel like a baseball bat. He staggered, steadied his feet, and then brought the tool down at a forty-five degree angle on Best's head, almost severing his ear. The crack of metal on bone sounded like a home run.

But somehow, the whack didn't do the trick.

Best fell onto his back, snorting and grunting like a real pig. The duct tape came off as he rolled to his side.

"Please, please . . ." Tears mixed with the blood on his face. "Please, let me go." He coughed. "Please, Don Antonio, I beg you. I'll do anything. Anything . . ."

Marco's eyes locked on Antonio's as if to say, *Dad, please don't make me do this.*

Antonio gave him a simple nod.

Heaving a sigh, Marco brought the shovel up.

"No . . ." Best whimpered.

This time, Marco swung the edge of the shovel down into Best's neck, slicing deep into muscle and sinew. He fell to the side, blood flowing down his neck. And yet, somehow, Best managed to get on his stomach and started crawling.

Marco followed and brought the sharp edge down on his back. The officer arched like an obese wolf howling at the moon.

Marco hit him again, then again, blood peppering his face and the white Armani suit.

Best managed to wiggle his chubby body a few more feet, leaving a dark trail in the dirt.

"What a mess," Christopher muttered. "Let me end this. I'm getting tired." He pulled his pistol out again, but Antonio held up his hand.

Exhausted and still tipsy, Marco dropped the shovel in the dirt, leaned over, and vomited into the grave.

On the ground next to Sergei, Natalia jerked. Her eyes widened, and she started screaming again. Even with her mouth taped shut, the noise grated on Antonio's nerves.

A part of him considered ending this quickly, as Christopher wanted, but Marco abruptly straightened up, took off his white coat, which now looked like the smock of a crazed butcher, and draped it neatly over his arm. He brought it over to Carmine.

"Hold this," he said.

The twenty-one-year-old prince of the Moretti family rolled up his sleeves and wiped the vomit off his lips. For a fleeting instant, Antonio thought he was witnessing the moment he had waited years for.

Every man standing watch had gone deathly quiet, leaving only Natalia's muffled pleas.

When he looked back again, Marco had pulled out a concealed handgun from a holster on his ankle. He pulled the slide back and walked over to Best.

Pop! Pop! Pop!

The first shot hit the dirt, the second punched through his back, and the third clipped his leg. Best continued to jerk as Marco unloaded the magazine. The last shot hit him in the back of the head, and he finally went limp.

Sergei and his wife watched him with frightened eyes.

"You're not done," Antonio said. He gestured toward the couple. "And this time, use the damn shovel like I told you."

Marco hesitated. He wiped the blood off his face with his shirtsleeve, then looked over at Vinny.

"You want that button someday, right?" Antonio said. He took a puff of his cigar while his son picked up the shovel. Both Sergei and Natalia struggled to get away, but there was nowhere to crawl—only the hole where they would rot and turn to dust.

Marco beat the couple to death with fewer strokes than Antonio had thought it would take. The crack and thump of the shovel on bone and flesh filled him with grim satisfaction and something else . . .

Pride.

He remembered the moment he became a man. It wasn't so different from now. Then, as tonight, he was in a desert with his brother, executing enemies.

Tonight, they were executing enemies of a different flag—not Italy's but their own: the Moretti flag.

-21-

Three days had passed since the Morettis extinguished the Nevsky family and slaughtered the officers from the port. No one had seen Don Antonio since he left the Dragon.

"Lieutenant Best is still missing," Moose said from the open doorway of the office.

Dom stared at the images of Don Antonio plastered to the wall. The anaconda of the City of Angels had tried to trap Dom, and Dom had fallen right into it, putting his team at risk.

"Dom," Moose said quietly. "I said Lieutenant Best—"

"God *damn* it!" Dom yelled. He slammed his fist through the picture, punching a hole in the drywall. Cayenne hopped up from her nap, tail down between her legs.

Moose took a step into the room. "Dom, man . . ."

"We'll never find Best, and we won't get a shot at Don Antonio again like we had the other night." Dom held up his hand to look at his bleeding knuckles.

"All due respect, boss, but you need some rest," Moose said. "And some food."

"I'm fine."

Moose came into the room and stopped directly in front of Dom. His crooked nose sniffled.

"You're not fine," Moose said. "You've been high on that shit for the past week, trying to stay awake."

"I'll sleep when this is over." He started to move, but Moose blocked his way.

"You're going to end up making poor decisions if you don't get some rest, Dominic. Might even get some of us killed. You don't want that, do you?"

Dom raised his chin slightly.

"I mean no disrespect, boss."

"I'm doing my best, Andre," Dom replied.

Dom never used Moose's name unless he was mad at him, which rarely happened.

"I'm just worried about you, that's all." Moose put a hand on his shoulder, but Dom shook it off and turned back to the wall of photos. His body ached from exhaustion, but his mind could focus only on one thing.

"We were so close to killing him," Dom said.

"And we will get another chance." Moose backed away. "Everyone's in the garage waiting. Except Namid—he's at home taking care of his wife."

"I'll be there in a few minutes."

Moose lingered but then nodded and left. Cayenne nudged up against Dom's leg, sensing his anguish. He bent down and accepted a warm lick on his face.

"I love you too, girl," he said. "Sorry if I scared you."

She licked him again.

He walked back to the garage. Everyone but Namid and Tooth was sitting around the metal table, talking.

"Tell Tooth to come down from the roof," Dom said.

Moose ran up to get him from guard duty. Then they all sat and waited for Dom to throw out a compelling strategy to stop the flames from spreading across the city.

The port had started a chain reaction, and with every hour that passed, tensions between the Saints intensified.

The question now was how to move the team forward—or perhaps, whether to call it quits before they were all killed.

"The turf war is down to the Morettis and the Vegas," Dom said. "I called you all here to talk about the coming battles. Whoever wins this war is going after the water supply and energy grid. Our job is to keep that from happening—at all costs."

"There are six thousand cops in this city, and three thousand deputies guarding the borders," Camilla said. "They can't all be okay with the Morettis gunning down Best's men. Or taking over the utilities."

"Chief Stone doesn't give a shit as long as he keeps getting paid," Pork Chop said.

Bettis concurred. "And we all know Cowboy Dale Benson. Guy is all about the walls, not what's *within* the walls."

"Never did like that guy," Tooth said. "Your father wasn't a fan, either."

Dom thought of his father. What would he think now? Would he encourage Dom to keep fighting? Even double down?

"There are some good cops out there," Moose said, "but right now isn't the time to try and find them. "We can't trust anyone. Sorry to say it, but I think we're on our own."

"We've always been on our own, in case nobody noticed," Rocky said.

"Truth," said Tooth.

"There's no one we can go to?" Camilla asked.

Dom wasn't sure which of their contacts he could still trust, and he didn't want to put anyone at risk, especially after Abdul was killed.

Moose was right. They couldn't trust anyone.

Dom decided that the best thing to do was just to tell his team about the call with Lieutenant Marks. Then take them to an event downtown that was supposed to remind everyone what they were fighting to save.

"There's something else I need to tell you guys," Dom said.

The Saints all looked at him, waiting—even Cayenne, who let out a low whine.

"Lieutenant Marks threatened to cut off our support," Dom said.

"What?" Tooth said, running a hand over his slicked-back ginger hair.

Camilla stopped chewing on her bubble gum.

Moose took his palms off the table. "He wants to shut us down?"

"Cops are dead," Dom said coldly. "Marks told us to stand down at the port for a reason, and I disobeyed a direct order. This is my fault. I take full responsibility."

"Fuck that noise," Rocky said. "We took out a huge shipment of drugs and stole an entire shipment of RX-Four. Too bad about Best and his boys, but if you ask me, he got what he deserved."

Judging by looks, not everyone seemed to agree. Bettis mumbled something about Abdul as he pulled back his ponytail, and Tooth grunted in agreement.

"Not all those cops deserved what the Morettis did to 'em," Moose said. "I have a few friends still on the force that skim off the top, but only to feed their families."

"Like your bro?" Tooth said.

Moose sat up straighter in his chair and glared at Tooth. "Ray ain't like that."

"Yeah?" Tooth asked, also sitting up. "That's funny, because—"

"*Enough*," Dom said in a voice just shy of a shout. He had to break the tension before it exploded out of control.

Camilla blew a bubble, the pop drawing attention.

"If we start to fall apart now, we lose everything we've fought for," Dom said. "And that's not going to happen, right, Andre?"

Moose finally looked away from Tooth and relaxed in his chair. "Right, boss," he said.

"Good, because we have some good news." Dom looked at each Saint in turn. "The Morettis don't know who we are or where we are, and they haven't made any moves since West Hollywood and the Nevsky attack."

"Whatever drugs and RX-Four they were selling on the streets has got to be drying up, which means there will be another one coming into the port soon," Camilla said.

"And that's exactly why Sammy is so important, and why we need to get him back to work," Dom said.

"The fate of the Saints rests in the hands of a young punk with acne," Tooth said, leaning back in his chair.

"He's our golden ticket," Dom said.

"You got to be kiddin' me," Rocky said. "We can't let him go back to the port. What's stopping him from selling us out, or the Morettis from killing him?"

Dom knew that the only way his team would understand was by talking to the kid, just as he had multiple times.

"Put on your masks," Dom said. "I'm bringing him out."

When he entered the garage, the other Saints all scrutinized the kid as they would a murder suspect.

"Go ahead," Dom said. "Tell 'em what you told me."

His Adam's apple bobbed as he looked at the team.

"Believe it or not, I want what you all want," Sammy finally said. "I want to see the Morettis burned out of this city."

"Sure you do," Rocky said. "That's why you work for 'em, right?"

Dom held up his hand and nodded at Sammy. "Tell them how it works at the port."

"There's just five of us that work on shipments for the Morettis. I do most of the foreign stuff like cars and those fancy suits they like. Before you guys blew the shit out of the *Goomah*, I was working on a new shipment with Vinny Moretti."

"What the hell?" Tooth said, leaning forward over the table. "How come we didn't know this?"

"How the fuck are you still alive?" Camilla asked.

Sammy shrugged. "Like I said, there are a few of us that work with the Morettis. Jason and his supervisor, Lenny, worked on the drugs. They specialized in that shit, and this isn't the first time one of the shipments was hit."

"What's stopping Vinny from whacking Sammy?" Moose asked.

"The other guys Sammy told me about are still alive," Dom said. "His story checks out. They only went after Jason and Lenny."

Tooth scowled. "I don't like it, man."

"You got any other ideas on how to bring down Antonio Moretti?" Dom asked.

The room went silent.

Camilla looked at her nails. Moose twisted one of his antler dreads. No one said a word—not even Rocky, who normally wouldn't shut his trap.

"Yeah, that's what I thought," Dom said.

Sammy cleared his throat. "Look, I know you guys don't trust me, and I'm not just saying this to get out of here, but I really do want to help."

"Why should we believe you?" Rocky asked.

"Because of what happened to my brother," Sammy said. His eyes flitted to his tattered tennis shoes. "My older brother was a cop. He helped raise me when my dad died. The Morettis gunned him down."

Dom nodded. "It's true."

"Let me get this straight," Camilla said. "You have been working with Vinny Moretti even though his family shot your brother dead?"

"What else am I supposed to do? I'm all my mom has left, and I pay the bills."

Over the past few days, Dom had spent some time talking to their CI and getting to know him more. He was basically a good kid wrapped up in some bad shit, like many of LA's youth. The fact that he worked his ass off to take care of his mom told Dom they could trust him. He just hoped he could protect Sammy—not only because they needed him, but because he was the type of person they were fighting to keep alive.

"All right," Dom said, "I've made my decision. We're taking Sammy back to the city so he can go back to work at the port. We'll take turns watching him. Get a blindfold on him."

"*Watching* me?" Sammy asked.

Tooth pulled out his Glock and set it on the table. "That's right," he said. "*Everywhere* you go."

"Step out for a minute," Dom said.

The kid opened the door, then stopped. "You swear on your team you got my back if the Morettis do come after me?"

Dom put a hand on his shoulder. "We've got your back, I swear, but don't fuck us." He squeezed his shoulder harder. "And don't mistake me for a cop. I'm not like the others."

Sammy returned to his cell, and Dom turned back to his team. "I know you don't like this, and it's not an ideal plan. But like I said, we don't have many options."

"If this is what you think we should do, then I'm with you," Bettis said.

"Me too," Moose said.

Tooth, Pork Chop, Rocky, and Camilla all nodded. But he could easily read their uneasy looks—they were staring down a gun barrel, unsure whether it had a round chambered.

Dom remembered the call with Marks, and his threat to shut the Saints down for good. As much as Dom didn't want to admit it, he knew they couldn't go around blowing stuff up and killing Morettis in the street. They had to be surgical, as in the past.

He had been playing Russian roulette, and sooner or later a round would come hurtling down that barrel. Another reason they all needed a break from the violence, and a reminder of what they were fighting to save.

Going downtown might be dangerous, but it was necessary.

"All right, people, let's get going," he said. "There's an event I want you to attend. And not just any event—this is about the very future of Los Angeles."

* * *

The Saints walked down the concrete path in MacArthur Park. Palm trees swayed in the wind around the edges of the dried-up lake bed. Westlake Theatre and the skyscrapers beyond huddled under a sky the color of lava.

"Never thought I would see so many people here again," Dom said.

"I remember playing here as a kid," Rocky said. "My mom got pissed when I swam out to the middle."

"Not surprising, with all the No Swimming signs," Camilla said.

Rocky shrugged a muscular shoulder. "You know how I roll." He raised his fists like a boxer preparing to fight.

"Someday, you and Dom should spar," Camilla said.

"I've been waiting for an invitation, boss," Rocky replied. "Rumor has it you were quite the MMA fighter in high school."

Dom was a humble guy and never bragged about his skills, so Camilla thought it only fair to brag for him.

"He was ten and oh in the cage, with three KOs," she said. "I saw one of them, but it was his days fighting at the Vega matches that he really showed his skills."

"Vega matches?" Rocky asked. He lowered his shades. "Damn, bo-oy-y-y."

Camilla smiled. "Did you know we were also Spanish partners in high school?"

"She tried her best to teach me," Dom said. "But back then I kept getting distracted by those dimples."

"Ha! 'Back then,'" Moose laughed.

Camilla pulled the baseball cap down to hide her blushing cheeks and moved ahead on the path, leading the team.

Coming out here today was perhaps the best thing for the team. Dom was right. They needed to feel like normal people for once.

They were dressed like everyday civilians—even Bettis, who wore a Hawaiian shirt and black shades. But it was Moose who had gotten the most jokes for his black button-down shirt with pink flamingos, and his red sunglasses.

Tooth continued to poke fun at Bettis and Moose.

"You look like a fat, gay reindeer," Tooth said. "And, Bettis, dude, chaplains and priests really shouldn't wear shades around kids—no one knows what you're looking at."

Bettis sighed. "What did I say about those types of jokes?"

Dom didn't laugh at the second joke, either. He had grown up Catholic, like Camilla, and neither of them liked to hear jesting about the Church's dark past.

"Have you no honor?" Bettis asked Tooth.

Tooth shrugged, and Rocky poked him in his gel-spiked hair, laughing.

"It's Tooth—what do you expect?" Rocky said.

Tooth swiped Rocky's hand away "Don't touch the hair, kid."

"Hey, there's Namid," Pork Chop said.

Namid ran to catch up. "Sorry I'm late," he said. "My wife wasn't feeling so good."

Pork Chop pulled his trucker hat up and wiped his forehead. "She okay, man?"

"Yeah, she's good," Namid said. He nodded at Dom, and Dom took Camilla's place at the head of the group.

Tonight, he didn't appear to be as jittery or on edge as usual. Camilla was feeling good herself, despite all the violent chaos.

The crew was all together, and if she put aside the past week of violence, it almost seemed as if they were just out to enjoy a night in the park.

Across the empty lake, hundreds had gathered. Many of these people had benefited from the Saints' work and the resources they had delivered over the years.

But today they were here for the most important resource.

People clustered around a podium set up along the edge of the lake bed. From under the podium, two six-inch-diameter pipes extended over the dry concrete bowl.

"Here we go," Dom said as they approached.

Councilman Tom Castle wheeled his chair out onto the platform, next to the podium where Mayor Buren stood in the center of the Los Angeles City Council.

Camilla had met Castle only once, but she knew how much Dom respected him. She had heard the story of the day the AMP soldiers ambushed his father's platoon outside Phoenix, leaving Castle paralyzed for the rest of his life. Now he was running for mayor against Buren, and she prayed Castle won.

He had proved himself to be a valuable ally over the years, helping the Saints arrange safe houses, arming them with better weapons, and supporting them in their under-the-radar fight against the crime families.

"Good evening, everyone," Buren boomed. "Welcome to MacArthur Park. I've had the great honor of overseeing a new program that will benefit everyone living in the City of Angeles, including the refugees waiting for permanent housing."

Dom pulled his hands out of his pocket but didn't clap. "This is bullshit," he said. "Councilman Castle has been the one overseeing the programs."

Buren waited for the applause to die down. "With the addition of two more desalination plants, we finally have enough water to provide for everyone in the city, including our refugee friends," he said. "No more rationing. You can have as much as you want."

The crowd cheered. Parents lifted their children onto their shoulders to see the councilman. Everyone wanted a look at one of the only people trying to save Los Angeles. A man who everyone knew wasn't in bed with the crime families.

"We are also working on adding more solar panels to our power grid," Buren said. "If all goes to plan, in the near future we will be able to power all four zones of the city with renewable energy, regardless of dust storms."

More cheers and shouts.

"These have been dark times for our country and for our city, but the future is looking brighter every day," the mayor continued. "I'd like to thank the council members with me for helping me achieve some of these goals."

Camilla clapped along with the rest of the Saints. What happened next caught her off guard. The mayor reached into his suit jacket and pulled out a handgun. Then he pointed it into the air and pulled the trigger.

The report didn't seem to bother anyone. They all were used to gunfire in this city.

As the shot echoed, a gurgling sounded.

Then came the water, gushing out of the pipes under the platform and pooling in the dry lake bed. The crowd of civilians roared.

Police officers standing guard at the edges moved to stop people from running down the sides, but Buren put a stop to that.

"Let the kids play," he said into the mike.

The officers backed away, and children ran down the sides of the lake. Parents followed the smaller kids and carried them over to the spreading clear water.

Most people were smiling ear to ear, but not Dom.

"He just won the next election," he said. "Castle won't stand a chance now, even though he's done way more than Buren."

Shouts and laughter came from the lake that was now filling for the first time in years. Children stomped in the water and splashed one another, squealing with joy.

Something about the sight filled Camilla with hope that they could still turn things around here, that they *could* save the City of Angels. But she wasn't sure how anymore.

Castle wheeled to the side to make way for Chief Stone, in his dress blues. And they weren't the only ones who had come dressed up tonight. Across the lake bed, standing outside black Range Rovers, a group of men wearing suits and shades had gathered. The passenger window rolled down, and Camilla squinted to make out who was sitting in the back seat, wearing sunglasses.

Her guts tightened when she realized it was Antonio Moretti.

The bastard had helped finance these projects, and Buren and Stone had worked with him, ignoring the poison he put on the streets, the people he tortured and killed, and the families he ruined.

Families like Dom's.

She squeezed his hand and jerked her chin.

"Look," she said.

Dom started to move, but Moose held him back. "Not here," he said.

Dom clenched his jaw, his eyes pinned on the man responsible for selling his sister and countless other people to the Shepherds in Vegas.

Normally, they would all be carrying heavy weapons, but tonight they were dressed like tourists and weren't even wearing their masks. The only guns they had were concealed pistols.

There wasn't time to shoot the bastards anyway. The Range Rovers sped off toward the safety of the Moretti compound.

"They're getting away," Rocky said.

"What do you want to do, boss?" Moose asked.

Chief Stone stepped up to give a speech. He tapped the mike.

"Let's get back out there," Dom said.

"I thought we were going to chill a bit," Tooth said.

"You all can chill," Dom said. "I'm getting back to the hunt."

-22-

Vinny spent the day physically with his wife, though his mind was with Adriana.

He couldn't stop thinking about her: what she was doing, where she was, who she was with. He hated the thought of her out there in the slums, working in the casino where men went to gamble and party with the strippers and hookers.

He also hated to think what would happen if someone besides his father found out about her. If his wife, the Vega family, or any other of his enemies saw her with him, she would be as good as dead.

The scent of gravy cooking on the stove brought him out of his office.

Carmen stood at the stove, dressed in a Gucci shirt and black slacks. Her choker and all four gold chains sparkled in the light of the crystal chandelier above the marble island. She looked ready to go to the Goldilocks Zone, where Vinny had met her on the dance floor. She didn't look all that different now, seven years later.

His shoes clicked on the white herringbone marble mosaic tile. Sconce lamps with bronze stems lit the hallway, spreading a glow over original paintings. They even had a Picasso Vinny had bought after it was salvaged from some abandoned celebrity mansion.

But Vinny didn't give two shits about the expensive art that looked like squiggles from a toddler, the scratchy Indian rugs, the uncomfortable Italian furniture that Carmen bitched at him for sitting on, the china dishes they never used, and closets full of designer clothing.

All Vinny cared about was seeing Adriana. She had become his escape while he continued the grind toward his goal of becoming a captain.

He looked in the bathroom mirror, checking the welt just above his right eyebrow. An inch lower, and the round would have broken through the helmet's eye shield and killed him.

Back in the kitchen, Carmen had set out two plates of linguine carbonara with chopped-up bacon.

"It's your favorite," she said softly. Almost ruefully.

He glanced at his Rolex. "I can't, I'm sorry. Leave it in the fridge for me or wait until my meeting is done."

"What!" She put her hands on her hips. "You fucking kidding me?"

"I told you I had an important meeting with Don Antonio."

"And you have to leave *now*? I worked hard on dinner."

"I'm sorry."

"You're never home anymore," she grumped. "You're either out with the guys or sleeping with your whores."

Vinny bit the inside of his lip.

She clicked her tongue the way his mom used to when he was in trouble. One of the things he would never forget about her.

"Don't tell me you're not fucking around, 'cause I know you are, Vin, and when I find the broad, I'm going to kill her."

Yup, Adriana had a target on her back, just like the Saints.

"I'm not screwing around," he said, loosening his tie. "I'm not like the other guys. You know that. I love you, babe."

"You're a liar. You're *just* like the other guys. Probably even worse. The only one that's different is your uncle. Don Antonio knows how to treat a woman, but apparently he didn't teach you that—just how to kill people."

Vinny wasn't going to argue with her there. His uncle seemed the only one who could keep it in his pants outside his marriage. But Carmen knew damn well what she had signed up for, and so did the other wives. They got to live in luxury in the postwar hell world—a fair trade-off with the men risking their lives to bring home the bacon.

And he continued to bring home a hell of a lot of bacon.

He looked her in the eye and saw the hate there, and maybe a bit of something else. Was it possible to both love and hate someone?

It wasn't supposed to be like that. His dad had loved his mom fiercely before she died. His uncle loved his aunt. But Carmen had no love for him right now.

Deep down, Vinny knew that the rage in her eyes was all his fault. He did feel guilty for it, but God *damn* he was sick of her ball-breaking attitude. No amount of money or gifts would ever be good enough.

"Okay, just be silent and walk away," she said, sitting down on a chair and turning so he couldn't see her cry. He hesitated, and she waved at the air like shooing a pesky fly.

"Just go!" she yelled.

As he walked toward the door, she yelled after him, "If we weren't Catholic, I would divorce you, Vincent J. Moretti."

The words stung more than he expected.

"You're not a good man. I deserve better, and I wish the church would let me out of this"—she let out an exasperated sigh—"this prison we call home."

"Good luck living out in the slums without me. I rescued you. The least you could do is not yell at me one fucking day of your life."

He walked away, flinching when a plate hit the wall by the door, but not daring to turn. The anger flowing through his veins might tempt him to do something he would regret.

Down the hallway, Doberman opened a door to see what the yelling was about.

"Don't say anything," Vinny said to him.

"I got some news, though," Doberman said as they started walking. "That shipment of cars your uncle ordered—they'll be on the boat tomorrow."

Vinny nodded.

"I've got a dozen guys assigned to this one. No one's taking us by surprise this time. Now that Lenny and Jason are dead, we gotta work with some new guys, but I made sure everyone's fully vetted."

"Good work," Vinny said. "Go get the Beemer ready. We're leaving after this meeting."

"You got it, bro." Doberman paused. "Look, man, I'm sorry for selling you out to your dad about you-know-who."

"Thought you had my back, man."

"I do. I'd take a fucking *bullet* for you, Vin."

Vinny scrutinized the friend who had done so much for him over the years. Soon, Vinny would pay him back in kind by getting him made. It was long overdue.

He patted Doberman on the arm and left without uttering another word. Once inside the stairwell, he let the door click shut, then exhaled a long breath.

Everything's good, man. You got this.

A few moments of peace in the enclosed space let him calm down and focus on his meeting. He had no idea what his uncle wanted to talk to him about, but he held out hope it was good.

The news he had been waiting years to hear: that taking down Sergei had earned him a seat at the table as a captain.

Vinny climbed the tiled stairs to the tenth floor instead of using the elevator. At the top, he regretted his decision. The sweat might make him look nervous and weak.

Two guards waited in the oak-trimmed carpeted hallway. He nodded and marched past them to the oak double doors, where he rapped twice.

They opened a moment later, and he stood ramrod straight, like a soldier.

To his surprise, his aunt Lucia greeted him inside the office. She gave him a warm smile.

"Good evening, Vinny."

"Good evening, Aunt Lucia." He gave her a kiss on both cheeks and followed her inside.

Don Antonio stood with his hands behind his back, looking out the big window, at the terrace and courtyard below.

"Can I get you something to drink?" Lucia asked. "Coffee? Wine? Water?"

"Coffee would be great."

Antonio turned from the window, wearing a pair of glasses with metal frames. It was the first time Vinny had seen him wearing them.

Damn, he is getting old.

Antonio sat behind his desk, then pointed at the two chairs in front of the desk.

"How's your head?"

"Could have been much worse," Vinny replied.

"It wasn't your time."

"No, Don Antonio, I was lucky."

"Luck is one way to stay alive in this world. But skill is another. Skill and strength." Antonio leaned back in his chair. "Unfortunately, as you already know, your cousin Marco lacks both those virtues."

Vinny didn't take the bait. The last thing he would ever do was bad-mouth his cousin to the kid's father. Don Antonio already knew the truth, anyway.

Antonio cracked a half smile—something he rarely did.

"You can speak freely here, Vinny. Go ahead, tell me what you think of how Marco performed in West Hollywood and at the Devil's Graveyard."

Vinny straightened his tie. "In West Hollywood, Marco didn't follow orders and almost got himself killed, but he rose to the occasion at the Devil's Graveyard."

Antonio pulled off his glasses and put them on his desk. Sometimes his slow, methodical actions surprised Vinny. But they were just part of his makeup—always thinking deeply, down to the smallest things, before implementing a plan.

"Tell me what you and Marco have done to catch the Saints so far," Antonio said.

Vinny explained tracking down the doctor and finding him dead. Then he explained the port worker Marco had ordered some thugs to kill.

"I see," Antonio said. "At this point, I believe the information about the port came from someone other than Lieutenant Best."

"You think someone on the LAPD is still helping the Saints?"

Antonio nodded.

"That's where we'll focus our hunt, then," Vinny said.

"Good." He folded his hands together calmly. "These men are like cockroaches. Every time I try to stomp them, they skitter away."

Lucia returned with two cups of coffee on a silver tray. She handed one to Antonio and the other to Vinny, who stood and accepted it graciously.

She smiled, but instead of leaving the room, she placed the tray on the desk and sat beside him in the other chair.

Vinny looked at his aunt and uncle in turn, confusion setting in.

"We wanted to talk to you together today," Antonio said.

"About Marco." Lucia placed her hands in the lap of her tight white dress. Her lips were drawn tight. "We know that you love your cousin and want the best for him. You saved his life the other day, Vinny, and I can't thank you enough for that."

"And I'm fully aware you want to become a captain," Antonio said. "You've more than earned it, especially after saving Marco and keeping Sergei from escaping the other night."

"But it would look bad if we made you captain before Marco even becomes a soldier," Lucia said. She took in a deep breath. "I didn't want this life for my boy, but if he's going to sit at the table, the other men need to respect him first."

Antonio took a sip of coffee and set the cup down. "You heard me make a deal with Marco about catching the Saints, and promise him a seat at the table if he does."

Lucia shot Antonio a look. Maybe this was something his uncle hadn't told his aunt.

The door opened.

"Ah, just in time," Antonio said.

Christopher walked over and stood by his brother's side, behind the desk.

"You have exceeded your father's expectations, Vinny. Mine too. Actually, you remind me of Christopher when he was your age."

"Thank you," Vinny said.

Christopher bowed his head.

"We called you here today to thank you and congratulate you, but also to make you an offer," Antonio said.

He looked up at Christopher—not a request for approval, but a nod of respect.

"Show Marco all the ropes of the business," Antonio said. "Help him catch the Saints without catching a bullet. You do that, and I'll give you Frankie's territory at the Four Diamonds. You'll be captain, and Doberman will join our ranks with Marco."

* * *

Ray was still alive but on borrowed time, and he knew it. In his mind, there were only two ways out for him, and sucking on his pistol was the one he hoped to avoid. Besides, Mikey the Mutant had already threatened to kill his wife and kids if he took the easy route.

Escaping the city wasn't an option, either. That would just be killing his family in a different way. They couldn't survive without him. Besides, where the hell would he go? To the wastes?

He didn't trust some one-legged wetback or a bunch of bikers to get his family somewhere safe. Especially with Lolo needing her daily doses.

If he was whacked or lost his job, she would have to go on rations. Most of the people on rations ended up with side effects or worse.

He pounded the steering wheel of his Audi. Over and over, pretending it was the Mexican Mikey's ugly face.

It had been several days since Ray found himself hanging from a crane hook over a garbage truck at the landfill. He still didn't know whether that homicidal freak really knew where Alicia had taken the kids, but he wasn't taking any chances.

So yeah, he really had only one out: deliver one or more of the Saints to Mikey the Mutant and Don Antonio Moretti, or lose everything he held dear.

Ray took a swig of tequila from the flask and sighed. He sat in the dark parking lot, listening to the sirens and the chatter of the radio.

"*Good eeeevenin', City of Angels,*" said the announcer. "*Breaking news tonight to help you sleep a tad better. Sheriff's deputies tracked down and killed the rest of the Pyros who penetrated the border two nights ago.*"

Ray shut off the radio. He didn't much care about the raiders' attack, although hearing about the twenty deputies they'd killed had him worried about his brother's safety.

Assuming his brother was even a deputy . . .

He took another slug of tequila and let it warm his insides, wondering how it all had come to this.

You know how it came to this.

The Saints had fucked this all up. They had gotten greedy by hitting the Morettis too hard. They had detonated a nuclear warhead and let everyone else get hit by the fallout.

Ray had seen a lot of death in his life, more than most cops and even some soldiers. And his gut told him this was just the beginning.

But could he really turn a Saint over to the Morettis if his brother turned out to be one? Could he do that to save his wife and kids?

The thought made him revisit the idea of blowing his own brains out.

If he did turn over a Saint, the gangsters would torture that Saint until they knew everyone's identity, including his brother's if he was indeed one of them.

You're going to find out really soon . . .

Ray pulled out of the parking lot on the eastern edge of the Four Diamonds, watching another vehicle's headlights flick on as soon as he hit the street. The tail was one of Mikey's guys, driving a green Subaru Outback with tinted windows and blacked-out rims. The twenty-year-old vehicle, built to survive, was common on the streets in Los Angeles. But it couldn't keep up with his Audi.

He gunned the engine on the next street and made a run for the foothills, where crumbling mansions littered the sepia terrain like bones in the desert. Traffic was light tonight, especially out here on the border between death and life. Most people had been avoiding the roads just in case some Pyros were still out here.

But his tail wasn't giving up.

Ray passed a motorcycle and a pickup truck. Several pedestrians were out walking on the sidewalks and hanging outside the local food establishments.

The city was already returning to normal after the violence that had raged for the past week. This section of town was also safer for being Moretti-controlled territory. The gangsters did a good job cleansing it of gangbangers and the psychos. He wouldn't be surprised if the gangsters had actually hunted the Pyros who attacked the border three days ago.

Ray looked in his rearview mirror at the guy on his tail.

"See ya later, motherfucker," he said.

He steered around a curve and floored it. Seeing no other traffic, he flipped off his lights and sped down another street. About halfway down, he took a hard right into an alleyway, whipping up a trail of dust between the decaying buildings.

He pulled into a parking lot and maneuvered his car under a eucalyptus tree. By the time the Subaru shot by, the dust had settled.

Ray sat there several minutes. When he was sure he had blown his tail, he pulled back onto the street and backtracked to the highway.

The drive across the city gave him plenty of time to think about his family. There was no way they could survive without him in this world. Lolo needed her medicine. Alicia needed the money for food and rent. His boys needed him to teach them how to be tough and smart on the mean streets. Without Ray, they were as good as dead.

Something wet rolled down his cheek, and he wiped it away, not realizing what it was until it happened again.

Don't do that, Ray. Don't fucking do that!

Now was not the time to be weak. He had to keep his head in the game.

Ray finished off the tequila. The burn helped relieve the sorrow. He slipped the flask back in his jacket and drove to the city's eastern border. Junked cars, shipping containers, and rubble blocked the intersections. No inch was left unprotected or unguarded.

High fences blocked off the terrain between the roads. Red signs marked minefields. Spotlights raked over the terrain beyond the walls, and he glimpsed guard towers where deputies spent the hot, lonely nights looking over the wastes.

Ray never did understand why Andre had transferred from the LAPD to the Sheriff's Department. Most of the time, the job was boring as hell.

Until the raiders attacked.

The damage from the attack was still evident from the shipping containers scattered across a road. Their metal sides were blown open among hunks of soot-covered concrete.

The area was cordoned off, and several deputies patrolled, their capes whipping in the dusty wind along the border. He spotted a drone flying overhead, its red light blinking as it zipped through the sky.

He took a left and headed for Refugee Processing Center 4. The warehouse-style housing units were surrounded by razor-wire fences and patrolled by deputies with German shepherds.

Everyone who came into the city came here first, where they were vetted to make sure they weren't sick, or raiders in disguise.

Usually, Ray didn't talk much about work with his brother, but this was the place Moose was stationed when not on patrol.

Ray drove up to the gate, where a guard manned a booth. The deputy stepped out and looked at his badge.

"Here to see Sergeant Andre Clarke," Ray said.

"Not familiar with that name." The guard looked at his clipboard, flipped a page, and said, "Got nothing, man. I'm new here, though, and he might have been moved. You know the turnover and shit out here."

"Sorry to hear about the deputies killed in the attack," Ray said.

The man nodded, and Ray backed out.

He fished out his cell phone from his leather jacket and considered calling his brother, then decided just to head for the apartment complex where Moose lived with Yolanda and his kids.

He sped there, his mind racing with implications he tried to bury. It wasn't long before he saw the Angel Pyramids.

The parking lot where his brother lived with his family was packed full of junker cars. He hated leaving his Audi with them. The vehicle was a target, and so was a black cop in Vega territory.

Seeing no other choice, he parked and tucked his pistol in his back pocket. Three kids no older than eight or nine were hanging out on a bench at the other end of the parking lot.

Ray waved them over. They were hesitant at first, so he fished a few coins out of his pocket.

"Got one for each of you if you watch my car. Anyone comes close, you scream, okay?"

Three nods.

Ray took off for the apartment building. When he got to his brother's door, he took in a deep breath, then knocked. Several clicks sounded—chains being unlocked.

The door creaked open, and Yolanda peeked out, looking left and right before settling back on him.

"What are you doin' here, Ray?"

"How ya' doin', Yolanda?"

She shrugged. Tamara and Bryon walked into the living room behind her, and she blocked the kids from view.

"Is my bro here?" Ray asked.

"No."

"Do you know where he is?"

"At work."

"So, he's okay?"

"Yes."

Her short answers were starting to tick Ray off. His sister-in-law had always kept him at arm's length, and they were never close, but tonight she was acting more standoffish than ever.

"Did you try calling him?" she asked. "He's probably busy from the attack the other night."

"Yeah, he didn't pick up."

"They found those Pyros, right?"

Ray nodded and reached into his coat. Yolanda backed up a bit as he pulled out a sealed letter.

"Give this to him when you see him, but don't open it. This is for his eyes only, okay?"

She hesitated, then nodded and took the note.

"You in trouble again, Ray?" she asked.

He had to laugh. "I'm always in trouble, sweetie."

-23-

Several days had passed since Dom talked to Sammy, and this was the first meet-up with the CI since they let him return home. Pork Chop and Bettis had kept a close eye on him, and so far, he seemed to be going to work and coming home without any tails other than the Saints.

For the meeting, Dom had picked the basketball courts at Franklin Classical Middle School for their proximity to the ports and because the courts were always busy. He was early, but he didn't mind; he enjoyed watching the kids shoot hoops, especially the kids who were with their fathers.

God, he missed his dad. They had spent countless blissful hours of his childhood playing catch or basketball.

A gust of wind pulled him back from the memories. The dust was bad tonight, and civilians stood around the mesh fences wearing surgical masks, bandannas, and the more expensive face masks with built-in filters.

Despite the weather, people were out enjoying the lights. It was the first time in a week this zone had power after storms knocked out part of the solar farm.

The soccer field was also teeming with players.

A group of kids on skateboards rolled by. He backed away to let them pass, when a girl hit a crack in the sidewalk and went down. The other kids all laughed, but Dom jogged over to help her up.

The girl, no older than eleven, had a freckled nose and curly black hair hanging out from under a stocking cap. The resemblance to his sister was remarkable. And like his sister, she rejected any help when Dom reached down.

"I'm good, man," she said.

Dom lowered his hand.

The other kids all went back to boarding, leaving her alone with Dom.

"Thanks, though," she said.

Dom watched her go, his heart aching at memories of Monica. For a moment he forgot why he was here and remembered why he was fighting. The refugee camps and places like this were part of the reason he had formed the Saints: to protect innocent kids like the skater girl from the evil forces trying to corrupt their minds and bodies.

Tonight, there weren't any dealers trying to sell product, or any lookouts watching for the cops, who probably wouldn't do anything in zone 3 anyway. Until very recently, this was Nevsky territory.

But the dealers had already moved in like sharks on blood. Gangbangers hung out in the shadows. They weren't here to sell—they were here to scout. The wolves were already eyeing the prey on these courts, and soon all the major parties would battle for the real estate.

Dom studied the men from afar. These weren't simple gangbangers. He spotted several Bloods, even Lil Snipes in his wheelchair, his skin shiny and scarred from burns, and his back broken in an ambush on the Morettis that went bad.

Rumor had it that Antonio Moretti himself had burned Lil Snipes and let him live out his days in the chair as a warning to others. But Dom wasn't sure that was true, or that it was even a good idea.

The leader of the Bloods had gained ground in the past eight years, and he clearly had his eye on the Nevskys' fallen domain.

Dom looked at his watch as the horizon swallowed the sun. Sammy was late.

Where the hell are you, kid?

All sorts of crazy thoughts ran through Dom's mind about the reason for Sammy's absence. Had he flipped? Was he being tortured right now for information on the Saints?

Feeling the paranoia set in, Dom scanned the abandoned apartment buildings on the east side of the basketball courts. Every broken window was a potential hiding spot for Moretti spies or soldiers.

That was why he had brought Moose along. He was out there, watching from a distance. They had already discussed their exit route and what to do if this was a trap. But if the worst-case scenario about Sammy selling them out was true, it didn't really matter.

That was why Dom hadn't risked bringing the other Saints. And anyway, they were all on their own assigned tasks.

Nothing they could do would save him if the Morettis were waiting. Dom stood as still as the statue of the Virgin Mary, looking for Sammy while the wind blew trash across the cracked dirt around the courts.

A few young couples walked past, laughing, smoking a joint, and having a good time, oblivious that they were so close to the leader of the Saints, something that could translate into millions in bounty money.

Dom turned to look in the other direction for Sammy. He wasn't a spiritual man, not anymore. But tonight, he had said a prayer. They needed all the help they could get.

Come on, kid. Please don't do this to me.

Just as he pulled out his phone, the industrial light poles clicked off, one by one. It didn't take long for shouting to ring out in all directions.

"Turn them back on!" someone yelled.

But angry rants and profanity weren't going to bring the power back on tonight. The temperature had probably dropped enough that city officials decided to kill the power.

Most of the area emptied over the next ten minutes, only a few of the kids remaining behind to play in the moonlight.

Dom finally decided to head back to the Jeep. He walked east toward the abandoned apartment buildings. Graffiti decorated the structures that had once housed aspiring actresses, dancers, and musicians who came to Los Angeles to chase pipe dreams.

But those dreams were as dead as the gangly headless stalks of palm trees that had finally succumbed to the drought.

The sidewalk twisted onto another dark block. Dom could feel his heart rate ramping up. Several wheelless cars sat on cinder blocks in a parking lot. He took cover behind one when he heard a whistling.

This wasn't the wind.

Another whistle answered the first. The war cry of the Vegas—an ancient call to battle. It wasn't the Morettis out there after all.

But the sounds made no sense—unless Sammy had sold him out to the Vegas instead.

He moved into the shadows of a cypress tree growing behind a half-collapsed brick wall. The sound of footfalls across the street echoed through the quiet night. More skittered in the opposite direction.

He readied his SIG Sauer, a round already chambered.

The next whistle gave him an idea where the Vegas were coming from. He caught a glimpse of a shadowy figure darting across the street, wearing one of the ceremonial masks the Vega sicarios used in battle. That didn't make sense, either.

Dom flinched at a gunshot.

The pop of handguns followed, then the staccato chatter of an automatic rifle.

He braced himself, but no rounds ripped his flesh or slammed into the tree trunk. He sneaked a cautious glance. Muzzle flashes lit up the other end of the street.

The bullets weren't meant for him.

Sicarios ran down the sidewalk in the opposite direction, firing at dark figures wearing bright red hats and bandannas.

Dom used the opportunity to run, keeping as low as he could, trying to process the events unfolding around him. The Vegas were making a move on Lil Snipes and the Bloods.

The battle for this turf exploded, gunfire ringing out in all directions. Dom had walked right into the middle of it. He should have known better—after the Nevsky raid, the area wasn't safe.

But this was a brazen move even by Vega standards.

He sprinted around a corner, where he slammed into someone, knocking them both to the ground with such force that air burst from his lungs. His pistol skidded away, and before Dom could get up, someone kicked him in the gut, rolling him onto his side.

He tried to move, but his limbs wouldn't work. Then, in a moment of clarity, he saw his attacker: a Vega sicario in a mask representing some Mayan deity. Sinewy arms covered in tattoos flexed as the man raised a submachine gun in one hand and a machete in the other.

The soldier Dom had collided with pushed himself off the ground and joined his friend. He wiped blood off his face and reached for his friend's machete.

"You ran the wrong way when we shut off those lights, you dumb fuck," he growled. He twirled the machete and pointed the blade downward at Dom.

The Vegas may have cut the lights to spare civilians, but they would show him no mercy—not after he had spilled their blood, even if it was just a tiny cut. And he wasn't about to apologize or beg for his life to these fucks. It wouldn't matter anyway. He was as good as dead.

The guy with the machete raised it above his head. A boom sounded, and the Mayan mask vanished in a spray of bone and blood.

The second shotgun blast hit the other Vega man in the side, sending him crashing into the wall of the building and painting the bricks with blood.

Moose came lumbering across the street, pumping out an empty shell and chambering the next round. Dom grabbed his pistol and aimed it at a figure that emerged from the shadows behind Moose. Moose stepped in front of the barrel before Dom could shoot.

"Hold up!"

When Dom saw the lanky shape in the faint light, he realized that his luck wasn't as bad as he thought.

"You idiots just about walked into a turf war," Sammy said. "Come on now, before you get me killed. I got some good news for ya dummies."

* * *

Marco was unusually quiet tonight. This didn't exactly surprise Vinny. His cousin had killed three people in the desert and hadn't been the same since.

"You'll feel better in time," Vinny said.

Marco took a shot of whiskey and chased it with a slug of beer. Vinny knew from experience that trying to kill memories with alcohol was not a winning strategy.

"I should be at the club," Marco said. "Jenny's probably at the Bling Factory tonight."

Vinny also knew that acting tough didn't make you tough. His cousin always tried a little too hard to put on a front.

"You need to relax, man, take it easy," Vinny said. "Hang with us; forget about pussy for a while."

Marco gave a weak shrug and took another long gulp of beer.

Doberman finished his cigarette and walked away from the balcony to sit by Vinny.

"You ever killed anybody?" Marco asked.

Doberman pulled another cigarette out and tucked it behind his ear.

"Yo, did you hear me?" Marco asked.

"Yeah, man," Doberman replied, "but I don't really like to talk about that shit."

Marco leaned forward in his chair, and Doberman sighed. He could ignore the prince of the family for only so long.

"Killed four men, and Vinny's right," Doberman said. "It gets easier, but you will no doubt have a few of the ghosts visit you at night."

Marco seemed to ponder their words in the cool evening breeze. They sat on a balcony on the twelfth floor of the tower, surrounded by small trees and bushes the hired help somehow kept alive in the harsh climate.

All the captains and highest-ranked soldiers were here.

Yellowtail, Carmine, Christopher, and Lino all sat around a poker table in the shade, tipping back beers and booze. But three seats were empty tonight.

One belonged to Vito, who was at the Diamond Arena watching the gladiator fights, where his son was taking part. The other two had belonged to Rush and Frankie.

A funeral would be held for Rush in a few days, but Frankie wouldn't be getting the same send-off.

The bodies were quickly stacking up in the City of Angels. And everyone on the rooftop knew that this was just the beginning of Don Antonio's plans for a wider war that would allow him to move on his final objective. Only then would he be the true king of Los Angeles.

After a few days holed up in the compound, it was starting to feel like being locked in a vault. The walls were closing in.

"I'll kill the Saints next," Marco said, a strange confidence in his voice. Almost as if he were talking to himself in a mirror. "No one thinks I can do it, but I'll find them. I'll show everyone."

Vinny didn't respond. The bullshit his cousin spewed made him nervous. But he must deal with it if he wanted to be a captain.

"Long as the LAPD doesn't give us any trouble," Marco added. "You don't think they will, do you?"

"Why the hell do you think we're cooped up here?" Yellowtail said, looking over his shoulder from the card table.

"The cops can't touch us, right?" Marco asked, looking up. "They wouldn't dare start another war."

"I don't know about you, but they can't touch me," Yellowtail said. He kissed the clunky gold cross hanging from his neck and tucked it inside his shirt.

The other men all laughed. Everyone except Marco.

He downed his beer and walked over to the poker table. "Deal me in."

The others scooted over.

"Come on, Vin," Marco said.

Vinny wasn't in the mood, but he also didn't feel like going back to his apartment. Carmen would be three glasses of vino into her night, and if he came back now, she would bust his balls until morning.

Vinny and Doberman moved to the table and grabbed an extra chair.

"Finally, a fucking game," Christopher said.

Carmine opened a box of chips. "How much you guys buying in for?"

Vinny eyed the other stacks. Everyone had around ten thousand in front of them.

"I'll take a stack of high society," Vinny said.

Marco nodded. "Make that two."

"I'm good with the min," Doberman said.

The other men laughed.

"Cheap fuck," Yellowtail said.

They played for an hour, cracking jokes and talking smack. Most of the pots were small, but Marco nabbed a decent-sized one against Carmine with a flush over a straight.

"That's right," Marco said, scooping the chips over to his pile.

Carmine muttered and chugged the rest of his beer. The sliding glass doors opened behind them, and Don Antonio walked out, holding a beer.

The men all stood.

"Relax," Antonio said. He looked to Vinny, then Marco.

"You both performed well under pressure during the attacks and in the aftermath," Antonio said. "Two seats at this table have recently become vacant. One soldier, and one captain. They will soon be filled with fresh blood. My blood."

Doberman glared at Vinny. One of those spots was supposed to be for him.

But Doberman wasn't the only one glaring at Vinny. Carmine, still mourning Frankie's death, stared at the man who was getting his spot.

"*Salute*," Christopher said, raising his glass.

Carmine directed his hateful eyes at Christopher, then raised his glass. The crew clinked their glasses with Don Antonio.

Yellowtail looked out over the city. "Don Antonio, when are we going to get back out there?"

Antonio followed his gaze.

"When I tell you," he said.

Yellowtail, usually a smartass with anyone else, simply nodded.

"Why not go take out Esteban and Miguel?" Marco asked. "They're next up, right?"

Antonio regarded his son. "It's not time yet."

"But why let either of them move into the Nevsky territory?" Marco asked. "Why not—"

Antonio cut him off. "Lil Snipes has his eye on zone three and wants to expand into some of it."

"I still don't get why you didn't finish off that bastard all those years ago," Marco said.

Antonio managed his anger by drawing in a deep breath—something Vinny had seen him do a lot around Marco lately.

"That half-cremated lump of shit is a warning wherever he goes," Antonio said. "And now his time has come." He looked at his watch, then cracked a half smile. "You were too young to remember when the Vegas first came here, so let me tell you a story."

Still in diapers, Vinny wanted to say.

"The two brothers were like orcas when they first came to this city. They hunted and killed together. But now they have bad blood. Now they will kill *each other* for territory. Why do you think I made a deal with Esteban?"

Marco still didn't reply.

"It's just a matter of time before they go to war," Antonio said, "and we get to sit by and watch them cannibalize each other. As we speak, the Vegas are wiping out the Bloods across the city."

"*What!*" Carmine gasped.

"Esteban sent his sicarios to finish off another of our enemies," Antonio said. "When it's over, they'll be weakened, and I'll use Mariana to draw Miguel out and finish him off."

Vinny marveled at his uncle. Their leader hadn't risen to power through brutality alone. He had done it by being smarter than everyone else.

"For now, we sit and we wait," Antonio said. "Play cards. Get drunk. Fuck your girlfriends or wives. Do whatever you want, because soon I will need you all."

No one said much after Antonio left. Distant sirens suggested he was right about the Vegas and the Bloods.

The men all looked up from their cards, listening. A battle was being waged, but the only one the Morettis were fighting tonight was at the poker table.

Vinny checked his two cards: two kings, his best hand of the evening.

First to act, he threw out triple the big blind, making the bet three hundred to go. The other players folded, around to Yellowtail and Marco, who both called the bet.

"Careful there, cuz," Marco said. His perfect teeth seemed to glow in the lights. He popped the top off his fifth beer, chasing three shots of whiskey. By the time the first three community cards were down in the middle, he had guzzled a third of the beer.

Vinny glanced at the cards in the center of the table. Queen, *king*, ten.

All hearts.

The beautiful sight made his heart kick. He kept calm, careful not to show any emotion.

He tapped the felt. "Check."

Yellowtail picked up chips, paused to count, then pushed ten black hundreds into the pot.

Marco flicked a yellow thousand chip into the middle, then went back to his beer.

Vinny made his decision fast, following his cousin's quick reaction to make it look as if he were on a draw. He hated the three hearts and the straight draw, but if another queen, or ten came in the community cards, he would have a full house, beating any straight or flush that Marco or Yellowtail might have.

The fourth community card came down, but the turn was no help to Vinny. The six of diamonds. He checked again with a tap of his finger. So did Yellowtail.

Marco looked down at the board, then tossed three yellow thousand chips out. He finished his beer and banged the bottle down.

"Come on, guys, one of you has to call me," he said, grinning. "I can't win two hands in a row, right?"

Vinny, still convinced he probably had the best hand, tossed in three yellow chips.

After a quick thought, Yellowtail did as well. He was drawing to a straight or a flush, maybe even both. No way he already had it, unless he was better than Vinny thought.

The next card came. The queen of diamonds.

Bingo.

Vinny had the fourth-best hand possible now. Only four queens, a straight flush, or a royal flush could beat him. But all were highly unlikely.

Vinny reached for chips, and Marco seemed suddenly more alert.

"Make it twelve thousand to go," Vinny said.

Yellowtail cursed and tossed his cards down, but Marco just smiled.

"Bad move, cuz." He held Vinny's gaze for a quick second, then said, "All in."

Vinny checked the board again. Was it possible his cousin really had a straight or royal flush or four queens?

Can't fold here. You can't. Chances of him having either hand are next to nothing.

Vinny pushed the rest of his chips in.

He flipped over the kings the same moment Marco showed his cards. A king, the last one in the deck, and a queen.

"Full house," Marco gloated.

"Me too," Vinny said. "And mine wins."

The other men laughed—even Christopher, who shouted, "Oh shit!"

"That's rough, Marco," Yellowtail added.

Doberman reached over and threw Vinny a high five.

Marco didn't seem to notice. He was still looking down at his cards as if he couldn't comprehend not having the best hand.

"Guess you were right," Vinny said. "You can't win two hands in a row. Not against your cuz." He smiled for the first time tonight and reached forward to grab the chips. The thirty-six-thousand-dollar pot was a nice win.

Marco's empty bottle shattered against the wall behind the table.

"You son of a bitch, Vinny!" he shouted. "Why you always got to show me up? Why you always got to embarrass me?"

Vinny held up his hands over the pile of chips. "Jesus Christ, man, it's a *game*. Settle down!"

"Chill out, Marco," Christopher said.

"Shut the fuck up," Marco replied, still glaring at Vinny.

Christopher stood, his hard eyes getting harder.

"You're out of line," he growled.

"You're not my boss," Marco snarled, finally glancing over. "None of you fuckers are. I'll catch those fucking Saints on my own. You'll see."

And before anyone could react, he stormed off.

"Marco, get the fuck back here!" Carmine called after him. "We want more of your money."

Yellowtail chuckled uneasily while Vinny and his dad shared a glance. Neither of them joined in the merriment.

Christopher settled back into his seat and picked up the deck of cards.

"Kid's just fucked up from the other night," Yellowtail said. "I still remember my first kill. It was private, unlike that shit show."

Carmine ran a hand through his hair. "Yeah, maybe Don Antonio should have eased the kid into it a bit."

Christopher put a chewed-up cigar back in his mouth. "Maybe you shouldn't tell us what the *don* should've done, yeah?" he said.

"You're right, Chrissy, my apologies."

They went back to playing cards in uneasy silence as sirens cried in the distance. The same tension seemed to have the whole city on edge.

Vinny switched from beer to water. Maybe he should just go home. Maybe Carmen wouldn't be in a ball-breaking mood.

A motorcycle rumbled in the courtyard below, followed by shouting and the squeal of tires.

Vinny sprang up and hurried over to the railing with Doberman.

"You stupid son of a . . ." Vinny whispered.

Doberman announced, "It's Marco, on his crotch rocket!"

The others joined them at the railing. Marco rode his bike toward the opening gates.

"Stop him!" Christopher shouted.

The guards, realizing their mistake, tried to close the gate, but Marco gunned the engine through the gap.

"Fuck. I'll go get him," Vinny said.

"It's not safe out there," Christopher said. "You heard your uncle—the Vegas are fighting for zone three."

"This is my fault," Vinny said. "I'll bring him back."

As he walked past, Christopher grabbed his arm. For a second, he thought his dad was going to hold him back, but he just said, "Be careful, Vin. Bring that dumb kid home in one piece."

"I will," Vinny said. "I have a feeling I know where he's going."

-24-

A small black dot crossed the sky, growing in size until it became a helicopter. Ray watched it from the driver's seat of his car. It wasn't just any helicopter.

An Iron Eagle with a contrarotating main rotor roared over the city, drawing the eyes of everyone on the ground.

And that, of course, was the point. The military wanted everyone, including the crime families, the gangs, and the cops, to see them coming.

"What the hell are they doing here?" he muttered.

You know exactly what they are doing.

The Morettis had wiped out the Nevskys and killed a bunch of cops, and the Vegas had gone to war with the Bloods, racking up dozens of civilian deaths.

Add in all the other violence in the past few days, and Ray figured the empty-suit politicians out east had decided it was time to send in someone to check on their investment.

"Bad move," Ray muttered. The last time the military set foot in the city was eight years ago, when they were on their way out after helping the LAPD take back the streets from the gangs.

If they were back, then things were worse than Ray had thought. It also meant he might have some more outs.

He watched the Chinese-built chopper cross the skyline and finally descend over central Los Angeles, which told him it was headed for LAPD headquarters.

He went over his plan. Mikey the Mutant was running out of patience, and Ray had only a few more days to make good on his promise.

But he didn't need days. His work was almost done.

Pulling out his phone, he dialed Alicia. His wife and kids were still at their aunt's place across town.

"Ray?" she said. "Ray, are you okay?"

"I'm fine, baby. I'm taking care of everything. I promise, everything is going to be fine."

His wife's voice cracked on the other line. "I'm really worried, Ray. When are you coming home?"

"Soon, baby. Just got some stuff to take care of. I love you."

"I love you too. *Please* come home to us soon. The kids are worried."

"Give the kids a kiss for me and tell them not to worry."

He hung up the phone and got out of his Audi to do what he had come here to do.

You got to do this. For them. Ray pulled the black leather jacket over his black tank top, concealing his pistol. The parking lot was full of cars but almost empty of people.

His heart felt heavy in his chest. The detective part of his mind kept telling him what he didn't want to admit: that his brother was a Saint. He had pretty much known since the kid at the hospital described a guy with antlers driving a pickup, but when the guard at Processing Center 4 didn't know Andre or Dominic, that clinched it.

Still, Ray needed to hear the truth. And that was exactly what he had come here to do.

He covered his face with his breathing mask and wrapped a bandanna over his freshly shaved head. Then he got out of his car and set off across the parking lot toward the courtyard of a three-story apartment building with an empty concrete pool. The streetlights actually worked here, and he avoided the glow by keeping to the shadows.

He jumped the fence when he got to the entrance of the building.

Two stairwells led up to the apartments overlooking the pool. According to the info he had looked up at the station earlier today, the guy he was searching for lived on the second floor.

Reaching into his coat, he grabbed his P320.

Two guys were smoking on the balcony across the complex.

He walked slowly, hoping they would finish their cigarettes soon. While they gabbed, he climbed a stairwell and waited until they went back inside.

Then he hurried over to the apartment he was looking for. One of the lights was on inside, and several candles burned on an entertainment center.

Remember who you're doing this for . . . Images of his family popped into his mind, fueling him with the courage he needed to shoot the lock and kick the door in.

A scream sounded as he raked the barrel of his pistol over the living room. He nearly pulled the trigger when he saw a woman. She held her belly with one hand and held a boy no older than four behind her with the other.

The man he was looking for came bolting around the corner, and Ray aimed the gun at the woman's head.

"No one says a fucking word, or I'll do 'em both right here," he said. It was a lie, of course. He wasn't here to kill the wife and kid, but he couldn't quite bring himself to shoot this man in front of them, either.

Son of a bitch. What are you doing, Ray?

The bronze-skinned man raised his hands. "You can take whatever you want," he said. "We don't have—"

Ray cut him off.

"I want *you*, Namid," he said.

A flash of realization passed over the Mojave Indian's eyes. He licked his lips and seemed to consider his options. Then he slowly walked over, hands still up.

"I'll go with you. Just please don't hurt my family, I beg you."

Ray waved him to the doorway.

"Where are you taking him?" the woman cried.

"Shut up," Ray said. His heart pounded, not from fear but from anxiety. This was wrong. All so wrong. This family could have been his own, held at gunpoint by someone like Mikey.

But that was the problem.

You're doing this for Alicia and the kids.

"Put these on," Ray said, giving him handcuffs. Again Namid seemed to consider fighting back, but the moment of hesitation passed, and he followed the order.

"Don't do anything stupid," Ray said.

"Easy, man," Namid replied.

Ray led him out of the apartment with the gun pointed at his head. He had come here to interrogate and kill this man, but something had stopped him. Now he wasn't sure what he was doing.

Stepping onto the balcony, Ray turned slightly to look at the woman and her child.

"I'm sorry," he said.

* * *

Antonio had told his men not to disturb him while he was in the basement of the compound. It was good they were playing cards and drinking. They needed a break from what came next.

But there was no break for Antonio. He was ready to implement the final part of his plan.

Turning on the lights, he entered the dark abandoned kitchen. No one came down here anymore who wasn't a soldier or an associate. And tonight, the only guards were the two at the door behind him.

They had insisted on joining him, but he wanted to be alone.

"We'll be right here if you need us," one had said.

Antonio pulled a cleaver from its magnetic wall mount and went to the decommissioned freezer where he had once kept some captured Vega soldiers. It hadn't gone well for those men.

Right here, before letting Lino have revenge, he had waterboarded a man with gasoline.

War required evil actions, and Antonio knew evil well. It was a required part of his business, just as putting out flames was required of a firefighter.

Grabbing the latch, he opened the freezer to look in on a woman also known for evil acts. The barbaric and brutal narco queen was so evil Antonio had a hard time replicating it when he framed her for killing a bunch of cops over eight years ago.

Something Chief Stone never found out about. That was good, because it was the first time Antonio broke the deal he'd made about not touching cops.

Holding the cleaver in one hand, he opened the freezer door with the other. Light flooded the dark space, and Mariana recoiled like a vampire in the sun.

The filthy woman no longer looked like the barbarous demon she was known to be.

Crouched in the corner, she squinted into the light.

Antonio walked into the freezer, keeping the door open.

The smell of urine and feces hung in the air, and he pulled out his handkerchief, putting it over his mouth. A bucket in the corner was the source of the stench.

There was blood on the floor too, from when his men beat her several times to get intel on the Vega brothers. Even from inside the House of the Devil, she had connections that would have given her access to such information. But through the torture, she hadn't said a word.

That was okay. He didn't need her to give the location, anyway. She was now the bait.

Antonio bent down and ripped the tape from her mouth. As she winced in pain, he put a finger to his mouth and held up the cleaver.

"Don't scream, or you'll make things even more unpleasant," he said.

She bared her teeth like a dog, then seemed to cower.

"The time has come to send you back into the wild," Antonio said.

Mariana licked her lips and spoke in Spanish.

He picked up a few words. Something about war and a king. Probably something about how he would never be king.

I'll be king, all right, and you will help crown me.

He held up the cleaver, and she pulled away. For a moment, he considered hacking her up and sending her to Miguel in separate boxes, one a day for a week, until he left his underground dungeon and came to Antonio.

But keeping her alive was the better option.

Antonio brought his hand down in a gesture of peace.

"It's okay," he said. "Miguel bought your freedom."

Mariana tilted her head.

"That's right, he still loves you," Antonio said. "I've made a deal with Esteban and Miguel—a deal with new borders. And with the Nevsky family wiped out and the Bloods on the defensive, it will be just the Vegas and Morettis now."

"Lies," she growled. "Esteban and Miguel haven't spoken for months."

Antonio didn't react, unsure whether this was truth. It was the most she had said about the brothers since they brought her here.

"They have reconciled," Antonio said. "Right after we freed you, actually. But the plan was always to sell you to Miguel, and now that time has come."

He reached down again, fingering the air, when a shadow loomed across the floor.

"Who's she?" said a female voice.

Antonio turned toward his wife's voice. "A special guest," he replied.

Lucia stepped up closer, just shy of the doorway. When the putrid air hit her, she buried her nose in the crook of her elbow.

Mariana snorted. "So you're the guinea queen?"

Before Antonio could stop her, Lucia walked inside, her eyes slits.

"What's your name?" she asked.

Mariana didn't respond.

"I asked you a *question*," Lucia hissed.

Antonio raised a brow, interested to see how this would play out.

"Is this the sister of the Vega brothers?" Lucia asked Antonio.

"More like a mistress," Antonio replied.

Lucia stepped up to his side to study Mariana. "Want to tell me why we are keeping a whore in our kitchen freezer?"

"The same reason we had Isao Yamazaki in a hospital bed. Mariana is a means to an end."

"Cowards, both of you," Mariana said. "You will never win this war, because you don't have the heart or the guts to fight your battles."

"And Miguel does?" Antonio said, laughing. "He's been hiding like a worm in the mud for months."

Another voice echoed through the kitchen. Christopher came scrambling through the maze of tables.

"Brother, I need to talk to you," he said.

"Not now," Antonio said. "I'm . . . we're busy."

"You're both going to want to hear this," Christopher said, panting. "It's Marco. He went to the city."

Lucia whirled. "*What?*"

"What do you mean, he went to the city?" Antonio practically shouted. "How did he get out of the compound?"

"He jumped on a Ducati and sped off," Christopher replied. "I sent Vinny after him."

"You got to be fucking kidding me," Antonio said. "Do you know how dangerous it is out there? Get a fucking crew together and go after them!"

"I have. We're ready to go."

Antonio shut the door to the freezer, locking Mariana back inside. Then he followed his wife and Christopher back upstairs.

When they got to the lobby, a group of armed men was gathering outside.

"Bring me my gear and a rifle," Antonio said.

"You should stay here," Christopher said. "It's not safe out there with the Vegas on the attack. I'll bring them home. I'm leaving Yellowtail and Lino here to protect you and Lucia."

Antonio hesitated. He wanted nothing more than to run out there and grab his son, but leaving the compound now would put him at risk like never before. And it could also leave Lucia exposed to an attack.

In a single act, Marco had jeopardized not only his own life, but the entire organization as well.

He turned to his wife, who was glaring at him with bloodshot eyes.

"I told you I didn't want this life for him," Lucia said. "I told you he wasn't ready!"

The other men paused at this outburst.

But she was right, of course. She was *always* right.

He swallowed hard, considering the implications. He never got played, but this time, he had played himself by giving Marco a chance for a seat at the table.

Antonio had tried to force him to be a man in the desert, but that had only made things worse.

It seemed you couldn't *force* someone to become a man.

Christopher reached up as he was tossed a submachine gun. They circled around Antonio, awaiting orders.

"Get the word out as fast as possible to Miguel and Esteban," Antonio said. "We have Mariana López, and if Vinny or Marco is harmed, we will send her back to Miguel—in boxes."

"Go and find our son," Lucia said to the soldiers.

The men hurried away. As she watched them go, Antonio reached out to her, but she pulled away from him.

"Don't touch me," she snapped. "You better pray nothing has happened to our son, or . . ."

She left the thought hanging and hurried away. But Antonio knew what she had left unsaid. If Marco died, their love would die. And he couldn't blame his wife for that.

-25-

Vinny cranked the throttle of his black Ducati Diavel, the red glow of the speedometer ticking over a hundred miles an hour.

You got a death wish, cuz.

Marco was flying on his bright-red Ducati Panigale. Boasting 290 horsepower and 11,000 rpm, the sport bike lived up to the term "crotch rocket."

If Marco crashed the Panigale, there wouldn't be much of him left to scrape off the pavement. He weaved in and out of the sporadic traffic en route to west Los Angeles. Vinny was right—he knew exactly where his cousin was going: the Goldilocks Zone.

Over the past twenty minutes, Vinny had closed the gap, but Marco was pulling ahead again now that he saw he had a tail.

The chances of him making it to the bars in one piece were getting worse by the second. Driving 110 miles an hour while drunk and angry was about the dumbest thing he could be doing.

Especially on these shitty roads.

The Diavel's wider tire jolted, and Vinny gritted his teeth. His bike handled better, but it was still dicey at these speeds.

"Marco, you dumb, dumb fuck," he said.

Grit and dust pecked at his visor.

Vinny passed a pickup truck with a bed made of boards. Next came an old school bus with drapes covering the windows. Several cars blocked the road ahead, and someone was poking along in the left lane. He eased off the throttle.

"Move over!" he yelled.

The beam from Marco's bike continued to speed away, and if he didn't get past this road hog, he was going to lose any chance of catching up with the faster Panigale.

"Come on, you asshole," Vinny said, pulling behind the car in the fast lane. The lights from his bike hit the face of a kid in the back seat looking out the window.

The driver finally merged right, and Vinny gunned the engine, passing at a cool eighty miles an hour. The boy in the back seat moved to the left window for a glance at him, but Vinny kept his eyes forward, reading the view in his headlights as fast as his brain could process the changing terrain.

Another crack snaked across the road, but he was moving so fast, he didn't have time to do more than hold the bike steady. The tires thumped over the depression and found purchase on the road again.

Vinny about swallowed his heart when he hit a pothole a moment later.

The bike caught several inches of air, or so it felt. The tires hit the asphalt, and his cell phone and a magazine for his Glock flew out of his suit jacket.

"Shit!" he yelled.

Vinny considered backing off and returning home.

Why should he die for his stupid cousin?

Because you made your uncle and aunt a promise.

While debating the question, he maneuvered around a semi hauling a trailer of cattle, then gunned the bike over parallel cracks in the road.

Thump-thump, thump-thump.

Vinny still had his cousin in sight. They were nearing the off-ramp for the Goldilocks Zone, and Marco appeared to be picking up speed again.

He checked the speedometer for a split second: 105 miles per hour.

He gave the bike a final push, gaining ground on Marco over the next mile. Vinny navigated the final stretch by carefully weaving in and out of the light traffic. A pickup traveling under the speed limit on the right lane flashed by, and the workers in the back all screamed and waved their arms.

As Vinny crested the hill, he saw his cousin's taillight in the distance, but he also saw a second slow pickup, moving over into the right lane.

Now he understood the urgency in the workers' waving and yelling—they were warning him.

He had only a split second to steer the bike gently to the left.

Vinny had always heard that when his life flashed before his mind's eye, he would see the ones he loved most. But for some reason, all he saw were the faces of the men he had killed.

The images vanished as he passed the truck. His right handlebar came so close, if the truck had had a regulation mirror on the left side, it would have been the end of Vinny Moretti.

He managed to keep the bike steady down the hill, feeling the engine's vibration right through his bones. The flashing lights of his destination came into focus, the neon glow giving color to a drab, gray city. He thought of Adriana, who was probably serving cocktails at the Golden Oyster. The casino dazzled in the distance, tempting the lucky few who had money to drop.

Not far ahead, the prince of the Moretti family had already driven off the exit ramp. Marco had miraculously made it through the gauntlet alive, but he was about to get a serious ass-kicking.

Vinny eased off the gas and drove toward the lights of the main strip. He had caught his breath, but his heart continued to pound as he searched for the Bling Factory, one of the only places here he had never been before.

Vettes and Lamborghinis and Porsches were parked outside the clubs. The wealthy often flocked here, and tonight it was bumping, which made Vinny even more nervous for himself and his cousin.

Don Antonio's orders had been clear: stay in the compound until they figured out what the LAPD was going to do, if anything, and until the Vegas were weak.

Aside from Vito, who had been given permission to watch his son fight at the Diamond Arena, the only Moretti men on the streets were dealers and lookouts. The boss couldn't afford to lose any more soldiers or captains after losing Frankie and Rush. Of course, Marco was the biggest target besides his dad. Plenty of gangsters would love nothing more than a chance to take out the heir to the Moretti empire.

Vinny passed a row of crotch rockets. Some of the owners stood on the sidewalk, drinking beers and smoking joints. These weren't your average gangbangers.

Vega sicarios.

One of the men had a bandage on his right arm, with fresh blood soaking through. It looked as if they had come straight from a fight. If they were out tonight, it meant they were here to celebrate a victory.

Vinny suddenly felt naked. If these were Miguel's men, they might see a golden opportunity to take out a Moretti, and if they were Esteban's, they still might try something—he didn't trust that narco bastard.

Marco wasn't the only target tonight. Vinny now had crosshairs on his back too, and he had only his Glock and one spare magazine to defend himself. That wouldn't do much if these guys made him and decided to take him out.

He kept his helmet forward, hoping the tinted glass would hide his features, although not many people in the city owned high-end Ducatis. He wished he had Doberman with him.

Several of the sicarios watched him from the curb as he passed. He finally saw the glaring green and orange neon for the Bling Factory around the next corner. Vinny rode the bike around the block. Once he was clear, he glanced over his shoulder for any sign that the Vegas had made him. Seeing none, he put down the kickstand.

He had to make this quick, but he would have to show his face to get in the club. He considered waiting for reinforcements.

Don Antonio would have a small army en route now that they knew Marco wasn't just out for a joy ride. The question was whether they would get to Marco before he got into trouble or maybe even killed.

Vinny decided there wasn't time to wait. He left his helmet on the bike and ran toward the line outside the door, where he pushed his way to the front. Right through the entitled rich pricks just like Marco.

"Hey, wait your turn," a tall towheaded guy snapped.

Vinny ignored him.

Someone grabbed his shoulder, but he shrugged loose, knocking a girl aside. The two bouncers stopped him at the rope.

"Get the fuck out of here," the big man on the right said.

The other guy held up a hand. "Oh shit, you're . . ."

"Vinny Moretti," he replied.

The first guy blanched. "Sorry, bro, go on in."

"Hey, why does he get to go?" someone else said.

Vinny turned to see Towhead again. He was about to tell the guy to fuck off when he saw three Vegas rounding the corner.

He turned and hurried through the open rope, then into the club. The place was jam-packed with bodies. Vinny sidled his way through, scanning faces in the flashing lights.

The place certainly lived up to its name. Prism chandeliers hung from the ceilings, casting a million little rainbows around the room. Even the bar was blinged out with mirrors, crystal lamps, and silver trim.

But he didn't see his cousin anywhere. Glancing over his shoulder, he saw the Vegas arguing with the bouncers out front. They would be able to hold them back for only a few seconds or risk a bullet.

Vinny had to find his cousin fast.

He continued past several leather-upholstered booths and glass tables with crystal lamps, heading toward the VIP lounge. At the bar, a familiar face caught his attention.

Jenny, the skinny blonde Marco had been chasing, was sipping a martini on a stool. And Marco was leaning against the bar right beside her.

Several of his friends were crowded around. Nick, Giovanni, and the twins Alex and Pietro. None of these guys could fight, and unlike Vinny, Marco didn't have a Doberman watching his six.

Shit, I'm *Marco's Doberman.*

In his haste, Vinny slammed into a girl, knocking her to the floor.

"Hey!" shouted her boyfriend, who was a foot taller than Vinny.

"I'm sorry," he said. "Didn't mean to."

The hulking guy wasn't ready to let it go.

By the time the guy reached out to put hands on him, Vinny had a gun muzzle pressed underneath his jaw.

"Back the fuck off, shithead, and help your lady up, or I'll blow your fucking throat out," Vinny snapped.

The guy let go of Vinny's collar and bent down to help up his lady friend.

"Sorry," Vinny repeated to her.

He beelined for Marco.

"Hey, it's Vinny!" Alex yelled.

"Vin!" Nick shouted, smiling and raising a beer.

Vinny ignored them and grabbed Marco.

"We need to leave, *now*," he said.

Marco pulled away from his grip and gave Vinny the once-over.

"Dude, fuck off," Marco said.

"You dumb motherfucker, I should knock you out," Vinny said through clenched teeth. "But we don't have time for that."

"You better watch it," Marco whined. "You can't talk to me like that."

Vinny scanned the crowd. "The Vegas are here, asshole," he said. "They saw me on the way in. We have to get out of here now!"

Marco's gaze flitted to the entrance. "So what? Esteban has a deal with my dad. They can't touch—"

Any supposed deal went up in smoke as bullets pounded the bar. Nick dropped his beer and gripped his chest, where a neat round hole was squirting blood.

"Nick!" Marco yelled.

He reached out to his friend, but Vinny grabbed him and pulled him to the floor. Bullets shattered mirrors and racks of bottles, showering glass all over the seats. Chandeliers rained broken prisms on frightened patrons.

Screams and shouts rang out, and people trampled one another in their panic to escape.

Vinny pointed his Glock at a target, but a girl ran in front of him.

Five Vega sicarios ran into the club, some of them firing submachine guns at the ceiling to clear the room.

Marco had crawled over to Nick, who was choking on his own blood.

"Marco, we have to go!" Vinny shouted. He fired off several shots, taking down a Vega moving toward them.

More gunfire hit the bar.

"Come on!" Marco yelled. His friends all took off, with Vinny leading them.

There was nothing they could do for Nick.

Sirens flashed outside, but the cops wouldn't deter the Vegas. The bloodthirsty killers had the Moretti heir in their sights, along with the son of the second in command.

Vinny made a run for the exit, passing people cowering behind leather booths. His shoes slapped through spilled booze mixing with blood.

Pietro cried out as a bullet hit his leg. His twin, Alex, grabbed him, helping him up and into a back hallway where the bathrooms and offices were. Marco was with Jenny now, and Giovanni.

"You guys hide in the bathroom!" Vinny yelled. "You're safer without us."

Marco, in an apparent moment of clarity, nodded at Giovanni. "Get her somewhere safe."

Giovanni and the twins parted ways, taking Jenny down the opposite hall while Vinny and Marco bolted for the back exit.

Marco stopped halfway down the hall and turned with his gun.

"Vinny!" he yelled.

"Go! I'm right behind you!"

Vinny moved his finger to the trigger and pulled it twice as soon as a man with a dagger tattoo on his neck came around the corner. The rounds hit him in the shoulder and right above the ruby in the dagger's hilt.

Vinny had just killed a soldier. Maybe even the Vega equivalent of a captain.

He took off running for the exit, where Marco was waiting with the door open. They moved into a parking lot, looking around for the best escape.

Cars were racing away.

Vinny pointed his gun at one. "Get out!"

But the driver had other ideas and squealed past, nearly running over his foot.

"What do we do?" Marco asked, his voice shaking. He had a revolver in his hand and fear in his eyes. He wasn't just drunk; he was terrified.

"Follow me," Vinny said. He ran across the parking lot, looking for a car they could jack. But there wasn't time.

Bullets punched into the truck next to Vinny. He hunched down as the windows shattered.

Pop, pop, pop.

The return fire hurt Vinny's ears, because it was coming from right beside him. Marco stood, closed one eye, and fired at two sicarios in the parking lot. Both men dropped on the pavement.

Marco lowered the smoking revolver. "I got 'em!" he said. "I fucking got 'em!"

Vinny grabbed his cousin, yanking him away. He eyed the slums in the distance, a thought crossing his mind.

No, you can't put her at risk.

But they had no other good option.

"Come on," Vinny said. "I know a place we can hide."

-26-

Two hours after fleeing the basketball courts at Long Beach with Sammy, Dom arrived at the Diamond Arena, where the Dodgers once played.

Moose had dropped Sammy off at his house after the kid told them about the next Moretti shipment. But more important things were happening. The military had sent a chopper to the city.

Dom crossed the stadium parking lot with Moose, pondering the implications. If the Executive Council in Norfolk had sent troops, then the city was in bigger trouble than Dom had thought. And some of it, maybe *most* of it, was his fault.

It would be the first time in eight years that a soldier set foot in Los Angeles, and it had to be for a compelling reason. He just hoped it was to help fight the crime families.

The roar of the crowd in the Diamond Arena snapped him from his thoughts. Someone was getting their ass beat on the former baseball field.

Of all the sporting events that used to be popular in Los Angeles, the only one to survive the apocalypse was violent. Fighting would never go out of style.

But this wasn't the cage fighting or boxing that Dom had grown up with. It wasn't even like the fights the Vegas used to put on when Dom battled Rattlesnake and Apache.

The athletes about to emerge from the dugouts and onto the dirt followed few rules. One, actually: no guns.

The only shootings that ever occurred here were in the stands, between fans who drank too much and had poor self-control. Angelenos took fighting seriously.

But the spectators weren't all here for the fights.

Rocky, Camilla, and Bettis sat waiting for Moose and Dom, who joined them in the stands. It didn't take Dom long to spot his target.

Vito Moretti was only four rows below, right behind home plate. The fat soldier stuffed his mouth with candy. Bodyguards stood in the stairwells with arms crossed, one hand inside their jackets.

"Did I do good?" Rocky asked, proud of having discovered Vito Jr. on the fighting roster. Dom had bet the big guy would be here to watch his son.

But the only person who knew why Dom wanted Vito Moretti was Moose. The others had no idea.

Tooth and Pork Chop didn't know, either. They were back at the safe house with Cayenne, prepping the Tahoe, and Namid was at home with his family.

But Dom wasn't going to pass up the opportunity to kill Vito.

"Get into position," he said to Moose. He moved to the concession pavilion, where vendors served hot dogs, beer, and burgers.

Dom pulled up his face mask as wind gusted through the stadium and over the dirt field.

The arena looked far different from the days when Dom's father brought him to watch the Dodgers. It smelled different too, the scent of newly mown grass and salted peanuts replaced by that of alkaline dust.

The wavy roof atop the right outfield pavilion and most of the top-deck seating was gone, blown out by an aerial bomb. The blast had taken out the electronic scoreboards too.

Industrial lighting installed after the war spread a glow over the cracked dirt. The checkered green infield and the bases were gone, leaving just a diamond of dirt in the ground.

Razor-wire fences surrounded the arena where fighters battled before a crowd of thousands. Only a tenth of the original seats remained, most of them behind home plate and under the club levels.

Dom always found the postwar advertisements odd. Banners of sponsors hung across the field: Golden Oyster, Tipsy Flamingo, Catalina, Pig's Ear, Flying Crow, and Horizon Bio-Limited, the Chinese company that manufactured RX-4.

He looked over to Vito. The hardest part was having to sit within fifty feet of the guy who took Monica and do nothing until the tub of shit went to the bathroom.

He wanted to gut the man right now as he stuffed his face with a hot dog.

Hundreds of people got up to cheer the female announcer in a green dress as she stepped out onto the dirt. Dom saw why everyone was so excited. It was Regina Díaz.

"Hello, you beautiful angels!" she yelled.

Rocky stood on his tiptoes for a better look.

"Good Lord, look at that turd shooter," he said.

"Really?" Camilla said. "*Turd shooter?*"

"Her ass, Cam," Rocky said quite seriously. "I could bounce on that thing like a trampoline."

Regina introduced the fighters as they came out of the dugouts and met where the pitcher's mound would be. On the left side were two bald, shirtless gangbangers with more ink than all the Saints combined had.

On the right was Vito Jr., a tall twenty-year-old with slicked-back hair, and muscles that rivaled Rocky's. His team partner was Patrick, an African American guy the size of Moose.

"I bet I could take all those fools," Rocky said. "Maybe I should sign up."

Bettis, sitting to Rocky's right, shook his head. "You got a death wish, kid?

Rocky frowned. "You don't have much faith in me."

"I have plenty of faith—just not in your boxing skills."

"I kicked Tooth's ass last week, and he doesn't suck."

"Quiet," Dom said.

Regina brought the mike back to her collagen-enhanced lips. "Tonight, we're adding something special to the Diamond." She gestured toward an umpire wearing white and black stripes, his features covered by a skull face mask. He carried two baseball bats wrapped with razor wire.

"Tonight, we're bringing back baseball!" Regina yelled.

Bettis shook his head wearily as the crowd erupted in cheers. He hated gratuitous violence more than anyone.

The umpire handed a bat to Vito Jr., who twirled it twice. The other bat went to the shorter gangbanger. He swung like a ball player.

The fans screamed their approval.

Regina blew a kiss to the crowd as she walked off, through the gate in the diamond-shaped fences. The umpire locked the gate and stayed in the arena.

He rang a bell, and the two pairs strode toward each other. The crowd fell silent, waiting to see who would strike first.

The shorter guy with the bat didn't keep them waiting. He charged and swung at Patrick, who deflected the blow, taking a razor-wire cut to his forearm. He grabbed the weapon, yanking it from the banger's hand while Vito Jr. swung at the other guy, knocking him to the ground. He let out a scream of agony and scrambled away as Vito Jr. pursued with the bat upraised.

"This is going to be fast," Rocky said with a frown.

Vito Jr. brought the bat over his head just as the man he had hit spun and kicked him in the groin.

Dom smiled as Vito Jr. dropped to the dirt. The opponent scrambled for the bat, but Patrick kicked it away and grabbed the man by the throat, lifting him up.

The shorter gangbanger jumped onto Patrick's back, wrapping a tattooed arm around his thick neck. Vito Jr. finally got back to his feet, with the crowd roaring.

Dom checked Vito in the stands below. He brought his hands to his mouth to amplify his shouting. On the field, Patrick dropped the guy he was holding, then bucked the other guy off his back.

Vito Jr. had a bat again. He staggered a few steps, then ended the fight with a tight swing into the face of the bucked rider.

The crowd roared.

The final opponent smacked Patrick with the other bat, bringing the big man to his knees. Then he turned it on Vito Jr.

Perhaps this wasn't over, Dom thought.

The two men lunged with their bats, holding them like broadswords. The inked gangster got a shot in at Vito Jr., hitting him in the thigh, but Vito Jr. didn't go down. He didn't even grab the wound.

Instead, he let out a scream and swung again, hitting the bat from his opponent's hand. Then Vito Jr. dropped his bat and lunged at the man, knocking him to the ground.

He straddled the downed fighter, and then Vito Moretti Jr. went to work, punching his face into the dirt. Over and over, to the immense pleasure of the crowd and his father, who cheered with both fists pumping in the air.

The referee walked over, calling the fight before Vito Jr. could kill the guy—although, judging from his limp body, the ref may have been a little late.

Regina returned to the field to declare the winners and announce a break before the next match.

Vito got up, and Dom felt the most excitement of the night. He watched as Vito squeezed his fat belly down the row to the stairs, where his bodyguards escorted him up toward the pavilion.

Dom and Camilla followed, leaving Rocky and Bettis in the stands to watch for Moretti backup.

At the top of the stairs, Dom melted into the hundred-person crowd, his eye still on Vito. He was headed for the bathroom, just as Dom had hoped. Unlike with Max Sammartino, Dom wouldn't have a cell where he could interrogate Vito. In fact, he was probably going to get only a few minutes with him, maybe less.

Dom pulled a knife from his pocket, keeping it concealed in his long sleeve.

One of the Moretti guards took up position outside the door, but the other man went inside. Moose also waited outside and followed Dom into the bathroom. Twenty men were pissing in the long white trough and the urinals, and it took Dom a second to find Vito.

He wasn't alone.

Vito was standing behind a four-year-old kid. His youngest son, who Dom hadn't seen earlier. The kid peed in the trough while Vito looked over his shoulder, locking eyes with Dom for a second.

"What you looking at, you sick fuck?" Vito said.

Dom went over to a urinal, swallowing hard. Killing him in front of his young son seemed . . . *like karma.*

No, it's evil.

And exactly what Lieutenant Marks had warned Dom about. Embracing evil had changed his father. But Dom wasn't his father, and he had to make his own decisions. He had to avenge Monica and Ronaldo.

Dom knew that he had just seconds to act. It was either kill the fat slug in front of his four-year-old son or wait for a better opportunity.

The kid pulled up his pants, and Vito stepped up to the trough. Dom nodded again at Moose, his mind made up. Moose walked over to the bodyguard, who was in the process of zipping up his pants. He punched the guy in the back of the head, cracking the tiled wall with his forehead.

The other people all backed away, some of them scattering with their business not entirely finished. Vito's son was at the sinks when Dom jammed the knife in his father's back, then into his gut.

By the time anyone looked in their direction, he had stabbed Vito four times. He slumped against the wall, eyes locked on Dom.

Moose shut the door and pulled out a gun, waving with his other hand. "Come here, kid."

Vito's son wailed as his dad reached up with a bloody hand and put it on Dom's face, pulling down his mask.

"You took my sister, you sick fuck!" Dom yelled.

Vito choked and tried to talk, but Dom cut him off by grabbing his hand and pushing the blade through his palm. Another scream filled the bathroom.

"You took her, and you sold her into slavery!" Dom yelled. Vito tried to grab Dom with his other hand, but Dom punched him in the gut, where he had stabbed him twice.

Vito threw up onto the floor and tried to pull his impaled hand away, but Dom held the grip steady.

"Tell me where you took those kids," Dom said. "Tell me or *your* kid dies."

It was a lie. Dom wouldn't hurt a kid, but Vito didn't know that.

"Where did you take those kids!" he shouted.

"Vegas!" Vito cried out. "We took them almost all to Vegas. If your sister is alive, she's there!"

Dom wanted to puke now. With all the searching, he had never found Monica there.

"Please . . . please don't hurt my son," Vito groaned.

The irony wasn't lost on Dom, but unlike this fiend, Dom wasn't a monster. Yanking the knife free, he plunged it into Vito's gut as he fell forward against Dom.

Using all his strength, Dom pulled up, opening up a gash. Guts spilled out onto the floor.

Vito glared at Dom for a moment before Dom backed away and let him slide down the wall to the floor. He fell on his side, intestines slithering out.

Dom bent down and traced the knife across his throat, wiped the blade on his shirt, and put it back in the sheath.

Shouting filled the room as Moose opened the door, pointing the gun at the people outside.

"Move!" he shouted. "Out of the way!"

Dom pulled the face mask back over his mouth and looked at the boy, who had scrambled over to his father.

"I'm sorry, kid," Dom said.

* * *

"We still don't know where he is, Don Antonio," said Yellowtail. "Vinny isn't answering his phone."

Antonio clenched his jaw and looked at his two most trusted soldiers. Lino and Yellowtail stood guard, protecting the king and queen just in case this was a ploy to bait him out, as he was trying to do to Miguel.

"We'll find them, don't worry," Lino said.

Lucia, standing in the entryway of his office, put a hand over her mouth in shock. Unlike his wife, Antonio wasn't shocked at all. He was enraged.

He picked up the closest thing, a maple chair, and bounced it off the bulletproof window. Adrenaline and rage rushed through his veins. Even the dogs could smell it.

A German shepherd, sitting on its haunches in the hallway next to a guard, jumped to its feet and barked viciously. Maybe the order to starve the dogs wasn't the best idea.

"Get that *animal* out of here," Antonio growled.

Yellowtail shut the door and stood in front of it, next to Lino, awaiting orders.

Antonio picked up the wooden chair and righted it. Then he stepped to the window and looked out over the city. The power was back on in the slums tonight, but that hadn't slowed the bloodshed. Despite the recent purge of his enemies, many were still prowling in the radioactive darkness—animals that would jump at the chance to take out Marco and Vinny.

Esteban Vega had used the opportunity to attack the Bloods and take the Nevsky territory. It was supposed to be part of Antonio's master plan, but he never anticipated his son screwing it all up. To get drunk, break orders, and then race off on his motorcycle with zero protection when the city was at war . . .

Maybe it was time to send him to the wastes, finally teach him how to be a man.

And on top of it all, the military had shown up after eight years of letting the crime families and LAPD run the city.

The gentle touch of a hand on his shoulder reined him back in.

"We must stay strong for the sake of our son," Lucia murmured. "We must not—"

"Our son just put the entire family at risk," Antonio said, "and now we have a new threat. Our very future depends on whether Vinny can protect him out there."

The darkness took him, and before he could hold it back, he slammed his fist down on the table, shattering the mirrored surface.

He brought his aching hand up, gripping it with his other hand. The pain felt good.

Lucia took several steps back. He hadn't seen that fearful gaze for years. This time, it wasn't just because of his temper. She was terrified they would lose Marco.

"We have to find him before our enemies do," she said. "If you won't do anything, I'll go out there."

She moved to the doorway, but both Lino and Yellowtail blocked her way.

"Move," she snapped.

Yellowtail massaged the gold cross hanging over his tattooed chest—his nervous tic. Lino just stood stiffly, waiting for orders.

"Lucia, come here," Antonio said.

A tear rolled down her face—the first he had seen her cry in ages. Her weakness—the only significant weakness—was the way she raised their son, coddling and babying him since infancy.

This is your fault too.

He should have been tougher on the boy. Sent him to a military school instead of spending a small fortune on his business education.

And now Marco had potentially flushed it all down the drain.

Yellowtail put his cell phone to his ear. "What you got, Chrissy?" he asked.

Antonio gripped his wife's hand.

This time, she didn't pull away or make any threats. She was scared, and fear softened her heart. The two couldn't have been more opposite. Fear only hardened his heart and turned him into a monster.

"Got it," Yellowtail said.

He put the phone back in his pocket.

"Christopher found Marco's friends in the Goldilocks Zone," Yellowtail reported. "He's bringing them here now."

"But where are Vinny and Marco?" Lucia asked.

"Vega sicarios attacked them," Yellowtail said.

Lucia tightened her grip on Antonio's hand.

"I fucking knew we couldn't trust them," Lino said, touching the scar on his chin and neck.

"You're *sure*?" Antonio asked Yellowtail. If this was true, Esteban had already broken his promise, or Miguel had found out they had Mariana. But if that was true, then why go after Marco and Vinny? "Have we confirmed that Miguel or Esteban know about Mariana yet?" he asked Lino.

"No. We just put the word out."

"Then this is unrelated. One or both of the brothers ordered the hit on Marco and Vinny."

He paused to think, trying to take it all in and understand how this could have happened. "Tell me everything," Antonio said.

"The sicarios were celebrating their victory over the Bloods when they must have seen Marco and Vinny," Yellowtail said. "They killed Nick and shot Pietro. The twins made it out with Giovanni but were separated from Vinny and Marco. Christopher is on his way back with them right now."

Antonio let go of Lucia's hand, fearful he might squeeze too hard. If Esteban had killed or taken his son hostage, the dark city would soon be glowing with flames a second time.

Lucia took a seat in front of his desk, and the other two men stood at the door while Antonio watched the city—his city.

They waited in silence for thirty minutes before a rap finally came.

One of the wooden double doors opened, admitting Christopher, three boys, and a girl.

"Who's this?" Lucia asked, rising from her seat.

Antonio scrutinized the young woman. Long blond hair curled slightly at the bottom, defined cheekbones with a touch of blush, dark brown eyes.

"I'm Jennifer, Marco's girlfriend," she replied in a soft voice, extending her hand.

"Girlfriend?" Lucia asked, folding her arms over her chest.

"Yes."

"Interesting. Marco's never mentioned you," Lucia said coldly.

The young woman stared back defiantly.

"Pleased to meet you, Jennifer," Antonio said. "Why don't you have a seat, and we'll bring you some water."

The boys also moved toward the chairs, but Antonio shook his head. "You three stay put."

Lucia, still aiming a hawkish gaze at Jenny, finally walked away to get a glass of water. When she returned, she held it out to the girl, who was shaking as if from cold.

"Tell us what happened," Antonio said quietly. He knew better than to ask the drunk boys. If he wanted a fanciful story, he would have asked them over the phone.

"It was the Vegas," Jenny said. "They followed Vinny into the club and then just started shooting."

Christopher's hard eyes narrowed. "Don't try and pin this shit on Vinny just because you're fucking Marco."

"I'm . . ." She let out a huff. "First off, I'm not sleeping with him. Second, I'm just explaining."

Lucia turned her hawkish gaze on Christopher. "Let her talk."

Apparently, she had a change of heart about the girl after hearing she hadn't slept with her son yet. Antonio had a hard time believing that. And if she was lying about one thing, she would lie about another.

Christopher muttered under his breath and backed off.

"After Nick got shot, we took off for the exit," Jenny said. "Vinny and Marco told us to hide, then went the other way down the hall. I saw Vinny shoot one guy there before we went into the bathroom."

"Then what?" Antonio asked.

"We hid, but we only heard rumors after that," she said.

Antonio moved on to the boys. "Your turn. Did you see or hear anything else?"

All three kids kept their eyes on the floor out of respect or fear, or both. Yellowtail, Lino, and Christopher loomed in silence around the boys. Tension filled the room.

"I heard Marco and Vinny ran out to the parking lot, and Marco shot a sicario there," Giovanni said. "I saw the body, so I know someone shot the asshole."

Antonio drank in the information. So his son had killed one of the men. That was good, but it didn't excuse his behavior. No, that would take nothing short of a miracle—like catching the goddamn Saints.

"What happened next?" Lucia asked.

Giovanni shook his wavy hair side to side. "I heard they ran, but that's all I know. No idea what happened to them after."

Antonio looked to Christopher, who had taken out the chewed butt of his cigar and was looking at it as if unsure what to do with it.

"We have to send out everyone," Lucia said. "Yellowtail, Chrissy, Lino, you guys need to get out there."

The men hesitated, looking to their leader for orders.

"Tell them, Antonio!" Lucia exclaimed.

The kids studied him for a reaction.

Antonio massaged his eyebrows. "If they got away, they will hunker down until it's safe. But if Esteban or Miguel got them . . ."

Lucia wiped a tear from her eye. "If the Vegas have them, then you get them back, Tony. You do everything in your power—*everything*—to bring my son and my nephew home. And then you kill every last one of those pieces of coyote shit."

"Send out everyone we have," Antonio said. "I only want a skeleton crew back here."

"Brother, this could be what they want," Christopher said. "Trust me, I want to send everyone to save my son and yours, but it could be a trap."

"Send *everyone* you can spare," Antonio said. "I'll handle security back here. We're ready for an attack."

Barking and screaming suddenly came from outside the door. Antonio backed up on the Persian rug to stand beside Lucia while Christopher, Lino, and Yellowtail pulled guns and moved to the door.

"Get back," Antonio said to the kids.

They all huddled behind the war table.

The barking stopped, but the screaming turned into a wail.

The female voice sounded oddly familiar.

"Open the doors," Antonio said.

Christopher pulled the right door open, and a large woman came inside, sobbing, her hair frizzled. It took Antonio a second to recognize Vito's wife. She lived two floors down and never came up here.

"Giuliana, what's wrong?" Lucia asked, reaching out.

"It's Vito," Giuliana said, sobbing. "Someone killed him."

-27-

Ray punched Namid in the jaw. The crack echoed through the abandoned garage, but the Mojave warrior didn't cry out in pain. After an hour of taking hits, he was still silent.

"Son of a bitch," Ray said.

He backed away, gripping his bloody knuckles, bumping into his Audi parked in the garage.

"That all you got?" Namid said, spitting blood.

He twisted and squirmed against his restraints on the metal chair, but he wasn't going anywhere. Ray had tied him well, and no one was around to hear him scream if it came to that.

Judging by the abuse Namid had already taken, it might well come down to that. He was a tough bastard, and Ray respected him for that.

"Bro, trust me, it's going to be a lot worse if I turn you over to the Morettis," Ray said. "All you got to do is tell me who the Saints are, and I'll let you go. Simple as that."

Namid blinked away blood dripping from a cut above his right eye, then focused intently on Ray.

"You aren't a cop, you piece of shit. You are . . ." Namid spat blood on the floor before adding what Ray already knew.

"You're a fucking gangster," Namid said. "No better than the Morettis, the Vegas, the Russians, or the bangers."

Ray bent down in front of him.

"Look, bro, I already know you're a Saint. Remember the night at the hospital when you dropped off that RX-Four?"

Namid glared at Ray, rage burning in his brown eyes.

"I know it was you there," Ray said with a shrug. "I know for a fact, so no use lying."

"You don't know shit, because I wasn't—"

Ray pulled out his P320 and hammered him in the knee with the butt. Then he jammed the barrel under his chin.

"You remember Dr. Hogan, right?" Ray asked.

Namid avoided his gaze, his chest heaving as he tried to manage the pain with deep breaths.

"Abdul?" Ray said. "He told me you were there that night. He told me right before I killed him."

"You son of a bitch," Namid slurred. "You killed one of the only guys in the city who are actually trying to help people."

"I did what I had to, to save a lot more people, man."

"I was wrong. You're *worse* than the gangsters." Namid spat again, this time in Ray's face.

Closing one eye, Ray wiped the bloody spittle away. Then he stood and holstered the pistol.

"I also know my brother was with you," Ray said. "And I have a feeling I know who the other Saints are too." He studied Namid, trying to gauge some sort of reaction.

"No?" Ray asked. "Keep lying, but I know everything. I know you guys have been operating under the guise of sheriff's deputies. I know Abdul was your contact at the hospital for the RX-Four. I know there's a contact at the LAPD feeding you funds, weapons, and support. I know you guys have contacts in the refugee camps and the city council."

Namid looked at his boots.

"Yeah, I know everything, man." He pulled out a knife and held up the saw-edged blade, turning it from side to side.

"If I'm just as bad or worse than the gangsters, then I should have no problem cutting off your ears or nose, right?"

Namid looked at the knife, then at Ray.

"You'd turn over your own brother?" he said quietly, as if he couldn't quite believe his ears. "You'd really turn your own flesh and blood over to those bastards?"

"Dude, I'm not the one playing vigilante hero out there. I do what I have to do for my family."

"Believe what you want, you corrupt piece of human garbage."

Ray sliced Namid's cheek, drawing a line that instantly started to bleed.

Namid shook in his chair, raging.

"I'm going to kill you!" he shouted.

"Next time, it's your neck," Ray said. "Admit you and my brother and Dom are Saints, and tell me who the other Saints are. I know it's more than that dude with the ponytail and the guy with the beaver teeth. Oh, and what's her name . . . Carmen?"

Namid clenched his jaw and looked down.

"Brah, I saw you all at that barbecue at my brother's place," Ray said. "I just can't believe I didn't put this together sooner. I guess maybe I didn't want to. Maybe I wanted to believe my brother was just tracking down raiders, but instead he's been hunting gangsters."

Ray crouched in front of his prisoner.

"You're starting to really piss me off," he said. "But I'll be honest with you. If you tell me the truth, I'll let you go. You don't *all* have to die. We can just turn over a few Saints to the Morettis."

That got Namid's attention. He glanced up. "You think I'd trust you? You just want those two-million-dollar bounties. Either that, or you're trying to save your own skin."

The guy was smart, Ray would give him that. But smart didn't mean shit when you were tied to a chair in the middle of nowhere.

"You're a greedy asshole rat," Namid said. "A disgrace to good cops like your brother."

Ray put the knife to his throat. He could smell Namid's breath, and it reeked of fear.

"You think I'm greedy, but you're the greedy assholes that caused this entire mess," Ray said. He leaned in even closer until their noses were almost touching and the knife was pressed against Namid's neck.

"What you don't realize is that the Morettis have helped restore order in this city," Ray said.

"They restored slavery, and you're one of their slaves," Namid said.

Ray pushed the knife even harder, forcing Namid to rear his head back.

"You're wrong," he said.

Namid looked at him in the eyes. "That's where you and your brother are different. He sees the potential of a Los Angeles without the mob, a Los Angeles protected by an uncorrupted police force. A Los Angeles run by the *people*, not the gangsters. A place where everyone benefits from the utilities and the farms."

Ray chuckled. "Maybe you're not as smart as I thought."

He pulled the knife away from Namid's throat and took a step back.

"It will happen. That's what I have been fighting for. That's what your brother has been fighting for. You can help. You can join us."

Even though Ray already knew the truth, something about hearing this admission aloud chilled him to the core.

"Do what's right, Ray," Namid said. "Let me go, and if you can't do that, at least make sure nothing happens to my family. Please. I'm begging you. Tell your brother to go pick them up and take care of them."

Ray took another step back, his mind racing.

Since he left the hospital, his gut had told him that Andre was a Saint, but he hadn't wanted to believe it. He still didn't want to believe it.

Namid looked at the floor as Ray swapped the knife for his P320 and pointed the barrel at the widow's peak on the Saint's forehead.

"Don't let them hurt my family, Ray," Namid pleaded.

An image of the pregnant woman and little boy surfaced in Ray's mind, followed by images of Alicia when she was pregnant with Lolo.

"Please, promise me," Namid said.

You have to do this for your family and to protect Moose.

Ray fingered the trigger, gritting his teeth as he stared at Namid. Could he really kill a cop? A good cop and a good father?

Another image surfaced. This time, it was his partner, Tommy. Ray had gotten the kid killed. Chewed up in a goddamn garbage compactor.

And for what? How many other innocent people had died because of the Morettis and the Vegas and all the others? How many kids were orphaned after their parents were either gunned down or poisoned by the drugs?

Namid's words played in his mind.

A Los Angeles protected by an uncorrupted police force . . . a Los Angeles run by the people, not the gangsters.

"Fuck," Ray said, lowering the gun.

Namid let out a sigh of relief.

Ray pulled out his cell phone and saw several missed calls. He stared at the screen for a moment, knowing who they were from. Then he did what he had to do.

Bringing the phone to his ear, he waited for the cannibal psycho to answer.

"Ray, my brother," Mikey answered. "Where the FUCK you been?"

"I've got one of them."

Namid looked up, his eyes widening. "No," he said. "Please, man . . ."

Ray gave Mikey directions to the garage and hung up. He bent down in front of Namid.

"I'm turning you over. Sorry, but I got no choice. They'll kill my family if I don't."

Namid seemed to consider his fate. Ray fully expected him to beg for his life, but he calmly said, "Do the right thing and make sure my family is taken care of."

"Don't tell them about my brother, and I will," Ray said.

Namid nodded.

"They're going to hurt you, man," Ray said. "Hurt you bad."

"I know." The calmness in his words amazed Ray. Smart, brave, and honorable—all the things Ray was not.

He pulled out a pack of smokes and wedged one in his mouth. He offered one to Namid, who accepted it between his lips.

"We could fight them," Namid said as Ray bent down to light the cigarette. "You and me."

Ray had considered an ambush, but he couldn't without knowing that his wife and kids were safe. If Mikey's people really did know where they were, well, he couldn't risk that.

He had used up all his outs.

There was only one thing he could do: turn the Saint over to the real wolves.

A few minutes later, several headlights burst through the windows in the side of the garage. Ray finished his cigarette and walked over to open the garage door.

Mikey and his right-hand man, Richard Ontiveros, a.k.a. the Chef, got out of a truck. Two other men, carrying automatic rifles, walked away from a car with tinted windows and spinner rims.

"Who do we have here?" Mikey asked, pausing to hike up his pants.

"One of the Saints," Ray said. He stepped aside and let Mikey and his men into the garage. The Chef pulled his machete off his belt and twirled it several times, flecking the concrete floor with blood.

"Been a busy night," Mikey said with his trademark shit-eating grin.

Namid looked over, and Ray saw that one last ray of hope in his gaze. But Ray looked away, unable to watch. He knew what was coming next, and he didn't have the stomach to watch a good man get tortured.

"Namid," Mikey said. "You have a fine-looking family, you know that?"

Ray turned slightly, seeing Namid struggle in his chair.

"Don't you touch them!" he yelled.

The Chef twirled the blade again, flinging more droplets of blood. The light from Ray's battery-powered lamp captured the blood spatter on the butcher's apron around his waist.

No, they wouldn't kill Namid's family, Ray thought. His gut knotted as realization set in. There was *nothing* Mikey wouldn't do. He was a fucking cannibal, for God's sake.

Namid twisted and fought against the restraints, toppling over with the chair.

"Don't hurt my family!" he screamed.

Ray looked at the bloody blade, his heart pounding.

"What did you do, Mikey?" he asked, anger rising in his voice.

"Don't worry about it, Detective." Mikey turned to the side, his burned face twisting into a macabre grin.

"What did you do?" Ray demanded.

"I had a little fun," Mikey said with a shrug. "And now I'm going to find out who all the other Saints are, so I can go to Don Antonio and collect my reward."

He jerked his chin at the Chef, who moved over to pick Namid up and reposition his chair.

"NO!" Namid yelled, his voice an inhuman howl of rage and pain. He choked and sobbed between screams.

"Don't worry, they ain't all dead," Mikey said. "But we—"

Ray pulled out his P320 and fired three shots into Mikey's chest. He shot the man next to Mikey twice in the head and had the gun aimed at the other guy with a rifle before Mikey hit the ground.

But he wasn't fast enough, and the man fired off a burst. Ray dived for cover and fired twice.

A flurry of gunshots ricocheted off the floor as he rolled up behind his Audi. Getting up, he crouch-walked to the other side and shot out the headlights of the two vehicles outside and the lamp.

The room went dark and silent.

Muffled breathing and a gasping sound came from the other side of the garage. He hoped it was Mikey. He wanted the scum to suffer.

Hearing soft footfalls, Ray got down on his belly. He saw a shadow move—the guy with the automatic rifle walking over to the car. Ray aimed at the reflective logo on the tennis shoes and pulled the trigger.

Blood spattered the ground as the guy fell screaming. Ray put a bullet in the side of his chest. Then he moved to the other side of the Audi and peeked over to see the Chef, with Namid upright in the chair, and the machete pressed against his throat.

"Drop your gun, *gabacho*, or I give him a second smile," he said.

"Kill him," Namid croaked.

Ray aimed at the guy's head, but before he could pull the trigger, the garbageman dug the machete into Namid's neck and began tracing it across his throat. A squeeze of the trigger stopped him halfway, and he stumbled backward, dropping the blade to grip his arm.

"Time's up, asshole," Ray said. He pulled the trigger again, but the slide had locked open, the magazine empty.

The Chef grinned. He picked up his machete as Ray grabbed his knife. They ran at each other while Namid squirmed on the ground, bleeding from his neck. He was trying to speak, but Ray could make out only a few words. Something about saving his family.

Everything seemed to happen in slow motion, but also lightning fast.

Ray ducked as the Chef swiped the air with the machete. Lunging, he thrust his knife in the center of the butcher apron, pulled it out, and then jammed it into his chest, where he left it.

The Chef fell to his knees, holding the knife's hilt. Ray crouched next to Namid. He was still alive, blood pooling around him.

There was too much of it.

Ray put his hand on his neck.

"It's okay, man," Ray said. He had said the same thing to Tommy not long before he died.

Namid tried to speak, but all that came out was a gurgling noise.

Ray closed his eyes for a fleeting second. When he opened them again, Namid was gone.

He pulled his hand away, then fell to his butt when something hot slammed into his side and knocked him over.

The echo from the gunshot lingered as Ray crawled for cover.

Two more shots followed, one of them pinging off the ground next to him. He scrambled for cover behind his car again and pulled a fresh magazine.

Reaching down, he felt his side, right below the vest.

Blood came away on his fingers.

The same raspy breathing from before sounded over the silence.

He forced himself up to look over the side of the car. Across the garage, Mikey held up a pistol, raking it back and forth in the darkness.

The fucking trash man was still alive.

"You got more lives than a mutant cat," Ray said.

He aimed the P320 at Mikey's wrist. The bullet ripped through bone, gristle, and muscle. The screams that followed were music to his ears. Ray moved around the car, kicked the gun away, and holstered his pistol.

"You cocksucker," Mikey grumbled.

Ray went to retrieve his knife, then saw the bloody machete. It was time to give Mikey a taste of his own medicine.

Time to do what the Saints had failed to do at the port.

He brought the blade up in the dim lamplight and watched Mikey's eyes widen.

"No," he wailed. "NO!"

"You sound like a little girl," Ray said, echoing the words they had used on him the night they killed Tommy. He swung the blade down on the edges of Mikey's bulletproof vest, cutting into blubber and flesh.

For the next few minutes, he went to work on the demon, methodically hacking him to pieces. By the time he was done, Ray was drenched in the blood of a man who had terrorized the city for too long.

But it wasn't just Mikey's blood. The flow from Ray's gut was bad, and cutting Mikey up hadn't helped. And it wouldn't make up for his sins. He looked over at the still-warm body of the Saint he had gotten killed.

First Tommy, now Namid.

Namid was right about Ray. He was no better than the gangsters. In some ways, he was worse.

With no more outs, there was only one thing left for Ray Clarke to do—only one way for a dirty cop to make up for a dark past.

-28-

Camilla got back to the safe house an hour after Dom killed Vito at the Diamond Arena. Her heart was still pounding at the chaotic scene that followed, and she still didn't know exactly what had happened in that bathroom—only that Dom had more blood on him than a trauma surgeon.

For the past hour, she had been with Bettis and Tooth, busy making final preparations at the safe house. Loading gear and guns and getting the Tahoe ready to roll.

The team was now listening to the police-band radio on the card table while Dom spent time in the office. Camilla worried about what he had planned.

She was no coward, but after the attack on the Morettis and after killing Vito, it was time to lie low or to flee, and she was leaning toward the latter.

If she knew Dom, he wasn't going anywhere, especially after Sammy told them about a new shipment coming in for the Morettis. He saw it as the Saints' next chance to hurt their operation.

She saw it as a suicide pact.

"Any deal the Vegas had with the Morettis is off now," Bettis said.

"It's all-out war," Rocky said. "I can't believe this . . ."

Camilla couldn't believe it, either.

"Honestly," said Tooth, "I'm surprised Vinny and Marco were dumb enough to be outside their fortress."

"Either way, shit's about to fly," Pork Chop said.

"At least, we aren't the main targets anymore," Tooth said. "Not after tonight. Antonio is going to shit grenades and throw them at every Vega-controlled corner."

Rocky threw an uppercut into the air as if this were a victory. But the youngster had no idea what any of this meant. Camilla did, and so did Pork Chop, Bettis, Moose, Tooth, and their leader.

Dom stood in the open door of the garage, Cayenne at his side.

"Where's Namid?" he asked.

"I thought he was still at home," Pork Chop said.

Dom went to the table, still deep in thought. He had changed out of his bloody clothes but still had a carmine smear on his cheek.

The other Saints gathered around, waiting to hear his next orders.

"Most of the Nevskys and most of the Bloods were wiped out, leaving just the Vegas and the Morettis," he said. "What happens next will determine the fate of the city and the people who call this place home."

He held up his cell phone. "I got a text from Lieutenant Marks. He wants to meet, and I'm going to arrange a sit-down with him tomorrow."

Rocky shook his head. "That sounds like a bad idea, boss. How do we know if—"

"We've been through this before," Dom said. "I'll go alone if I have to."

"No way," Moose said. "We're coming."

"Yup," Tooth said.

Bettis nodded.

Camilla wasn't sure what to say. She knew that Dom was close to Marks, but what if this was a trap?

"That's all I have to say," Dom said. "Now, get some rest." He grabbed his gear and walked out of the room, heading toward the roof with Cayenne.

Camilla followed them into the hallway. "Want some company?"

He turned, and the glow of a lantern flickered across his handsome features.

"I really need some time to think."

"Okay."

She turned to go back into the garage.

"On second thought, I do want to talk to you," Dom said.

They went up to the roof, with Cayenne hopping up the stairs after them.

A dazzling sky filled with stars greeted them there. On another occasion, it would have been romantic if not for the blue and red lights flashing in the distance—a reminder of the war still raging in the heart of the city.

The door clicked shut behind them, and Dom walked to the center of the roof and set his gear down. For a moment, he looked out over the city. Then he turned to face her.

"What are we going to do?" she asked.

"Now's the time to strike the Morettis again," Dom said. "They're weak. So are the Vegas. We are no longer their main targets."

Camilla let out a discreet sigh.

"What?" Dom asked.

She looked him in the eye, wondering whether he was high on speed again. The man she had fought beside all these years—a man she loved—was changing.

"I'm really worried about you, Dominic," she said. "Moose is too, and . . ."

Dom shook his head. "And I'm worried about *you*. You haven't been yourself and have been pulling some crazy shit."

"I'm fine. I admit I took a bit of a risk the other night, but I swear, this wasn't my fault." She pointed at the cut on her freckled nose. "Some guys jumped me at the Pig's Ear."

"*Jumped* you?" Dom raised a brow.

"I lost my temper with some assholes, and they jumped me . . . or tried to."

Dom looked back toward the city. "Maybe you should talk to Bettis."

And maybe you should talk to someone about the uppers you've been popping like jelly beans.

"I talked to him the other day," Dom said. "Nothing wrong with asking for help. Bettis gave me some good advice."

"Oh." Camilla suddenly felt bad.

Dom scratched his five o'clock shadow. "We're the same, you know. We both harbor anger from the loss of a sibling. And it motivates us to keep fighting. It also has resulted in some risks that we shouldn't have taken."

He was right, and Camilla realized now more than ever that they both were acting a little crazy these past few weeks. Taking one step closer to the edge in an effort to get revenge and soothe the pain inside them.

"I think of Monica every day," Dom said. "I think about the men who took her, and the domino effect that followed. My mom going crazy, my dad going out to look for my sis and never coming back."

He closed his eyes, took in a breath, and opened them to meet her gaze. The sadness there pricked her broken heart. They had more in common than the loss of their siblings and parents.

"But tonight, I killed one of the bastards responsible," Dom said. "With Vito Moretti and Max Sammartino dead, I can now focus on the snake, Don Antonio."

Camilla narrowed her eyes. "Vito and Max took your sister?"

He bowed his head, but Camilla knew he wasn't praying. He was remembering some awful event.

"Marks was the one that led me to Max, and Max led me to Vito," Dom said. "I didn't want the team to know, because of all the other stuff going on."

She moved over and brushed her hand against his.

"I'm so sorry, Dom," she said. "I had no idea."

"The weird thing is, I don't feel much better. Marks warned me about this. He told me that by embracing evil, we become evil. Maybe this is what happened to my father out there."

Camilla had thought about how she might feel when she killed the Vega brothers. Would it relieve any of her pain?

"Revenge works only if we don't become evil in the process," she said. "And that part's tricky."

Dom didn't reply right away.

"What is it?" she asked.

He was having a hard time meeting her gaze.

"I killed Vito in front of his kid," Dom said. "Gutted him like a fish while his son watched."

Camilla held in a breath. Now she knew what had happened in that bathroom and why Moose seemed so disturbed.

Dom reached out and wrapped his arms around Camilla as Cayenne looked up at them, tail wagging.

At his callused touch, everything came crashing down. All the emotions she had been holding in came rushing out. Dom also seemed to soften and his walls seemed to come down in her embrace. Cayenne's tail whipped faster, and she nudged up between them.

Dom chuckled, and so did Camilla.

"Jealous," Dom said.

"I guess so."

Camilla gave Cayenne a kiss on the head and got a juicy face lick back.

Dom stopped smiling and drew in a deep breath.

"Everything's going to be okay," Camilla said.

"I can't take back what I've done. I can't . . ." He gave his head a weary shake. "I've sinned. I've embraced evil in the pursuit of revenge."

"We all have," Cam replied. She hugged him again and kissed him on his cheek as she pulled away. "You have to stay strong. You can't let this poison your heart more."

"I've numbed my mind and heart with alcohol and used speed to keep me going when I needed to step back and rest." Dom ran a hand through his hair. "This is what happened to my dad in some ways, in his search to find Mon. It's exactly the thing Marks warned me about."

"It's going to be okay, though," she said. "You're a good man, Dom. Kick the speed, stop drinking, and focus. I'll be here at your side."

Dom lowered his hand and nodded. "Thank you for sticking with me, Cam."

"Always."

He looked out over the city.

"I once heard that evil arrives faster than it departs," he said. "This war is only going to get worse."

"I know."

Dom coughed and turned away, wheezing.

The door swung open, and Moose stepped out. He panted, as if he couldn't catch his breath.

"What's wrong?" Camilla asked.

Moose tried to speak. His lips quivered in the moonlight. Camilla had never seen the big guy like this before.

"Andre, what's wrong?" Dom asked.

"It's my brother," Moose finally managed to say. "He . . . he did something terrible."

* * *

"You can't tell your dad or Carmen about her," Vinny said in a whisper.

"Yeah, yeah, I get it," Marco said. He had slumped in a tattered armchair with his forehead in his hands.

"Nick's dead, and it's because of me, isn't it, Vin?" He looked up as if hoping for some sort of absolution, or at least reassurance.

Vinny didn't want to give either, but his cousin looked like shit and was an emotional mess. He sat on the edge of the couch and sighed.

"Nick is dead because of the Vegas," Vinny said.

He glanced into the kitchen, making sure Adriana couldn't hear them. She stood in front of the coffeepot, waiting for it to finish brewing.

Outside, the sirens continued to wail, along with a half-dozen dogs.

"I fucked up," Marco said. "God, I really did it this time. My dad's going to hang my balls in his office, isn't he?"

Vinny couldn't help but chuckle. "Nah, probably just put 'em under a bell jar on the mantel."

"Real funny, Vin," Marco moaned. "I don't understand how this could have happened. The Goldilocks Zone is supposed to be neutral territory, and Dad has a truce with Esteban Vega."

"It could have been Miguel's guys, or Esteban could have broken his promise after we took out the Nevskys."

Marco groaned and slouched in the chair, bumping the suit coat draped over the edge. Specks of Nick's blood had spattered the front of the metallic-colored fabric.

"Drink that water," Vinny said.

Marco picked up a bottle and sipped it. He had sobered up, and with sobriety came anxiety.

"Are you sure Nick was dead when we ran?" Marco asked.

Vinny wasn't sure whether the question was rhetorical, but he nodded anyway. "He's gone, man, but this isn't your fault. You got that?" He reached out and put a hand on Marco's shoulder, but Marco reared back like a frightened dog.

"Calm down, man. It's okay. We're safe, and we'll go home as soon as things calm down. And then, when they do, we'll strike back hard. Harder than they hit us."

Adriana walked into the room holding two steaming mugs of coffee.

"Hope you like honey," she said.

He stood and took the mug from his girlfriend. She couldn't even afford decent coffee beans, but despite the hardships, she seemed content and happy. Unlike his wife, who was never either.

Adriana sat next to Vinny on the couch, and he put his hand on her leg.

She seemed unfazed by the evening's events, but he hadn't told her everything. If she knew that the Vegas were hunting them . . .

"Thanks," Marco said, taking a sip. "This is pretty good."

She watched him drink, then whispered into Vinny's ear when Marco moved over to the window. "Is he going to be okay?"

Marco reached for the drapes, and Vinny shot up. "Don't touch those."

After a slight hesitation, Marco pulled his hand away.

At least we don't have to worry about the Nevskys or the Bloods anymore, Vinny mused.

He put an arm around Adriana, and she leaned her head on his shoulder.

"I'm glad you're here," she said quietly.

Marco turned around, raised a brow, but didn't say anything.

It was nearly two in the morning, and the kid looked like hammered shit. He needed water and sleep, not coffee.

"Marco, why don't you come sit down," Vinny said.

"I want to go home, Vin. Can't we just try calling your dad?"

"With what phone? I lost mine on the bike, and you lost yours in the club."

Marco started to pace, eyes on the floor, deep in thought.

"Dude, sit down and relax," Vinny said.

"You're not my fucking boss."

Vinny took his hand off Adriana and stood. "I get you're upset about Nick and your other friends," he said, "but I risked my ass for you tonight."

"I didn't ask you to do that." Marco ran his fingers through his wavy hair. "And you must be forgetting it was *you*, not me, that led the Vegas to the Bling Factory. It was *you* that got Nick killed."

Dumb little shit . . .

"Vegas?" Adriana asked.

Vinny felt her hand on his forearm, but he pulled it away as he walked toward Marco, stopping directly in front of his slightly shorter cousin.

"You're testing my patience," Vinny said. He was close enough to smell the coffee and vodka on Marco's breath.

They locked eyes.

Even though they had the same Moretti blood in their veins, their hearts and minds couldn't have been further apart.

"You're always showing me up, Vin. Have been since I was a kid. You know how that feels?"

Vinny listened, struggling against the urge to slap the smell of booze out of his young cousin's mouth.

"Do you know how it feels to *always* be walking four steps behind my older cousin when I'm supposed to be strong and smart like my dad?"

"You've made your own choices, Marco, and if you keep acting like this, I'm done trying to help you."

For a fleeting moment, he thought his cousin might do something else he would regret. But Marco finally backed down and walked over to the chair, where he sat down and held the coffee mug in both hands.

"Don't worry, Vin, I won't tell anyone about you and your lady friend here," Marco said with a condescending snort. "When I get home, I'm going to work. I'm going to focus on finding and killing the Vegas *and* the Saints."

Vinny stood next to the chair, looking down at his cousin. "And I'll be there to help you—as long as you start thinking with *this*." He pointed to his head.

Walking over to Adriana, Vinny grabbed her hand, and led her to the single bedroom, where he planned on relieving some stress.

"Get some sleep, Marco," Vinny said. "'Cause if you're serious about changing, you're going to need it."

-29-

Dom floored the Chevy Tahoe away from the City of Industry, taking one last look at the place they had called home for the past year. Abandoning the safe house was an easy call. He should have done it days ago, when they learned of the bounty on their heads.

Hell, maybe he should have gotten his team out of the city. Left with Camilla's uncle's convoy to the Midwest when they still had a chance.

But there was no time to think about that now. All he could do was try to save everyone he could.

An explosion bloomed behind them, a fireball poofing up into the night, erasing all evidence of the safe house. Camilla and Bettis both turned in the back seat to look at the blast, and Dom watched the glow in the review mirror.

Dom looked over at Moose, who stared blankly ahead.

"What else did your brother say?"

Moose kept staring out the windshield.

"*Moose*," Dom said, louder this time.

He looked over. "Yeah?"

"What else did Ray say?"

"He said he knows everything about us, and that the Morettis got Namid. He said something about taking out Abdul to protect us."

"Abdul?" Dom said.

"Your brother killed Abdul to protect us?" Camilla asked. "What the hell does that *mean*?"

Moose shook his head. "I . . . I don't . . ."

"Abdul didn't even know Namid's name, so how did . . ." Dom's words trailed off as a memory from the hospital shootout surfaced.

"Oh no," Dom said. "Fuck me . . ."

"What?" Camilla asked.

"I . . . I shouted Namid's name in the parking lot the night we dropped off the RX-Four. Abdul would have heard it. If your brother got to Abdul, then that's how he knew who Namid was."

"No," Moose said. "Ray wouldn't do that. He wouldn't kill a doctor. Or one of us."

"I don't want to believe it, either," said Dom, "but if it is true, your family is at risk. Ray's been to your apartment countless times."

"He just stopped by the barbecue a few nights ago," Camilla said.

"Oh God," Bettis said.

"The Morettis could be waiting for you at your apartment," Camilla said.

Moose looked incredulous. "No way," he said, shaking his head. "Ray wouldn't do me like that, man. He's an asshole, but not a murderer."

"Did you call Yolanda?" Camilla asked.

"Her cell's off," Moose said. He put his head in his hands and moaned. "This shit isn't happening. It can't be. It's a fucking nightmare, man."

Dom had never seen his friend like this. They both were shocked by the potential of such a lethal betrayal. If Ray did know everything, then they were all fucked.

He mashed the pedal.

"If Namid is dead, chances are, they already got to his family," Bettis said. He reached into his pocket and pulled out his rosary. "All we can do right now is pray."

Dom was too mad to pray. Gritting his teeth, he looked over at the pickup truck pulling up behind them. The other Saints were inside, heading to check on Namid's family.

Family was everything, and Dom would die to save their wives and kids.

"Don't worry, man," Dom said. "We're going to get your family out of there and somewhere safe. We planned for this."

His heart pounded. If the Morettis did know his identity, then what about his mom? What would stop them from going after her in the hospital?

Focus.

He had to stay positive, but he also had to plan for the worst.

Rocky drove the pickup alongside the Tahoe. The bed of the truck was loaded with weapons, ammunition, and all the gear they could throw inside in five minutes. Tooth rolled down the passenger window.

"Good luck!" he yelled.

"You too!" Dom shouted back.

The truck pulled away. Pork Chop was in the back, wearing black fatigues, a ballistic vest, and a black face mask and holding an M4 carbine. He threw up a hand, then ducked back down to avoid the dust.

Rocky turned left onto the highway, toward the Goldilocks Zone. Dom took a right, toward the Angel Pyramids.

Dom decided to pray.

Please, God. Let Moose's family be okay.

"All right, here's how this is going to go down," he said after a breath. "We're parking on the street, and Moose and I are going to head up to his apartment. Bettis, you and Cam guard our ride and provide backup. You hear shots, you come in hot.

Bettis and Camilla nodded.

"Moose, I need you frosty, man," Dom said. "Are you good to go?"

"Frosty," Moose said with a firm nod.

Sweat dripped down his forehead, but he wiped it away and pulled his baseball cap down.

The pointed tips of the Angel Pyramids winked red in the distance. Moose seemed to be praying in the passenger seat.

Dom took a left and sped toward the slums. Pedestrians were out and about tonight, enjoying the lights for the first time in days. He parked under a canopy of trees and killed the engine.

Cayenne looked up as Dom grabbed the door handle.

"Be good, girl," he said, reaching back to pat her head.

Bettis finished pushing shells into his shotgun, and Camilla palmed a magazine into her rifle. Moose grabbed both his submachine guns, and Dom took his M1A SOCOM 16 from the back seat.

They set off across the sidewalk, moving quickly and keeping to the shadows. The way into the courtyard was empty, but several teenagers were at the next corner, hanging out and smoking.

Dom followed Moose toward the front gate and into the open space beyond. Sleeping bums occupied several of the benches.

They both scanned the balconies for contacts as they moved. But Dom saw no evidence of Moretti soldiers in the area.

Could be in the windows or waiting in Moose's apartment. That's the chance you have to take.

Dom flashed the signal to advance. They made a run for the stairs and then loped up the outside stairwell, clearing the first three landings quickly.

On the fourth floor, Dom raised his fist. Then he moved past Moose and went up the stairs first. A cracking noise sounded from the courtyard, and he looked down over the railing. Normally, a few teenagers would still be up at this hour, trying to score a blow job or smoke one last joint before the sun rose on another day.

But he saw no sign of activity in the shadows—only the junkies sleeping on the benches in the moonlight.

He glanced at the other buildings, including the Angel Pyramids. All were dark but for the red aircraft warning lights blinking at the top. The entire grid for zone 2 had been shut down in another energy curtailment.

Moose continued up the stairs, and Dom followed. On the fifth floor, the big man raised a submachine gun. Dom shouldered his rifle, heart thumping as he scanned the darkness to see what had spooked his friend.

They both lowered their weapons when they saw that it was just Leyland, a twelve-year-old neighbor kid. The moonlight partially illuminated a young face already pocked by acne.

"Get back inside," Moose said.

Leyland looked at their guns, then their face masks. He gave him the soulless glare of a boy who feared nothing and no one.

Dom continued past the kid. Chances were good he'd end up like half the youth in the City of Angels: in jail or dead.

Moose and Dom made their way down the final stretch of balcony, passing Dom's apartment. He wanted to stop inside and grab the only tangible item he cared about—a picture of his family—but there wasn't time.

Dom's heart jackhammered as they approached Moose's apartment. He took up position left of the door and shouldered his rifle at the balcony across the way.

Moose crouched down. "What?" he whispered.

Dom lowered his rifle when he realized it was just another teenager entering an apartment.

"Let's go," Moose said. He pulled out his keys and unlocked the door. Then he slowly twisted the knob and pushed it open.

Dom went inside first, with his rifle barrel pointed into the darkness. He held a breath in his lungs, terrified he would find a scene of carnage.

Moose followed him inside.

"Daddy?" came an adolescent voice.

Dom twisted to the kitchen, where Bryon stood with a glass of water. At the sight of their guns, he dropped it to the floor.

"Bryon!" shouted Yolanda. She came rushing down the hallway, with Tamara right behind her.

"Be quiet," Dom said, holding a finger up to his face mask. Then he lowered the mask so Yolanda could see him.

"Dom?" she said. "Andre? What the hell is going on?"

"Grab your stuff, baby," Moose said. "We got to go." He slung his guns and helped Bryon skirt around the broken glass.

"What do you mean, *go*?" Yolanda said. "Go where?"

"Just get your stuff," Moose said.

She rushed back into the bedroom with the kids. Dom stayed at the front door, guarding it while they packed. He pulled back the drapes and scanned the balconies, listening to Moose and his wife talking quietly in the bedroom.

"Does this have something to do with your brother?" she asked.

"Why?" Moose said.

"He stopped by earlier, gave me a letter to give to you."

"Hurry up," Dom whispered. He moved to the other window on the left side of the door. He could hear both Bryon and Tamara sobbing.

"It's going to be okay," Moose said. "We're going on a trip."

They finished packing in a matter of minutes and brought the kids back into the living room.

"Don't cry, baby," Yolanda whispered to Tamara.

Dom moved to help them with their bags, when he heard footfalls on the balcony. He cracked the drape and saw two figures moving furtively in the shadows.

"Back, back!" Dom said, waving. "Two contacts. Get the kids into the bedrooms."

Moose crouched down and unslung his weapons while Yolanda herded the kids away. Dom aimed his rifle at the window, holding back the drape in one hand.

He checked the balconies across the way but saw no movement there. Whoever these two were, they appeared to be alone.

Dom moved his finger to the trigger and aimed at the first figure. The person moved into the moonlight, and he realized in time that it was Camilla.

"Hold your fire," Dom said. "It's just Cam and Bettis."

Moose slung the straps over his shoulders and hurried back to the bedrooms. "Come on, kids, we got to go."

Dom opened the door. Tears streamed down Camilla's face, soaking into the mask.

"I told you to stay put," he whispered.

She wiped a tear away. "I know, but Rocky called. He said there's a crime van at Namid's apartment. They brought out a stretcher with one victim. All we know is, it was an adult female."

Dom's guts churned at the news. He walked over to the railing and slowed his breath.

Keep it together. You have to keep control . . .

Camilla put a hand on his back.

"We need to move," Bettis said. "Come on, guys."

Dom turned from the view of the courtyard, his mind on fire. He cradled his rifle, letting the anger turn to fuel.

Moose emerged in the doorway, holding a letter.

"What the hell are you doing?" Dom said. "Come on, let's go."

Moose held the note up. "It's from my bro. He wasn't trying to sell us out. He was trying to save us."

-30-

Neither Antonio nor Lucia had slept much. He was still fully clothed and lying on the couch in their living room. For a fifteen-thousand-dollar piece of furniture, it sure wasn't very comfortable, but that wasn't the reason for his lack of sleep.

Everything he had worked so hard for was starting to fall apart. First, the military showing up—something he had told Lucia would never happen—then Marco driving drunk to the clubs and getting in a shoot-out. Then came the news that masked men had stabbed Vito to death at the Diamond Arena in front of his youngest son.

But Antonio still had outs, even if the Vegas did have his son and nephew. He had Mariana to trade for them.

In the faint glow of daybreak, he opened the sliding door quietly to avoid disturbing his wife. Soon the destroyed skyscrapers downtown would stand out like the bones of monstrous robots.

The city, still reeling from last night's battle between the Vegas and the Bloods, was already alive with predawn workers. The faint wail of sirens and the whine of traffic from miles away drifted into the Moretti compound.

A brown haze drifted over the skyline. Guards patrolled with German shepherds, but most of his associates and soldiers were still in the city, looking for Marco and Vinny, leaving the compound exposed.

But would Esteban or his brother really have the balls for that?

As he stepped closer to the exposed balcony, their recent meeting surfaced in his mind. He was too angry to be fearful.

Esteban had been clear: *They were amigos until the barriers were crossed.*

On the road beyond the walls, dust swirled from an approaching vehicle. A single black Mercedes—one of his. The gates cracked open.

Part of him was disappointed. Deep down, he wanted to see the Vega brothers try to attack him.

But neither brother had responded yet to the news that Mariana was in his basement, shitting in a can.

Still, he scanned the wastes beyond his walls, his heart kicking at the thought of a battle. Not because he missed the thrill, but because he felt like a coward sitting here while his men searched for his son and nephew.

Maybe Mariana was right.

"No," he mumbled. "I am no coward."

He used to think the Saints were cowards, but now he realized they were much like the Morettis. Underdogs who wore masks and who ambushed their enemies and framed others.

The same playbook Antonio had used to climb to the top of the food chain and build his empire.

He had upped the bounty on their heads to three million each, because there was one thing underdogs couldn't fight: money.

Soon, he would have the head of every Saint on a pike—a warning to other vigilantes who threatened his operation. He cursed himself for letting Vito leave the compound last night, and he cursed himself for making a deal with Esteban.

Just like Antonio, the narco had his eyes on the prize. And Esteban had struck first, seizing an opportunity to take out his rival's only heir.

But only one contender would come out on top. Only one would control the drug trade and the lights, the food, and most importantly, the water.

His wife's Neapolitan accent pulled him from thoughts of war and grandeur.

"Have you heard anything yet?" She stepped just outside the open door, arms folded, shivering in the cool predawn breeze. He walked over to her and wrapped his arms around her, kissing her forehead.

She had calmed down since threatening him earlier. Deep down, Lucia had to know this wasn't his fault. Marco had made choices that put their family at risk.

"One team has just returned," he said. "Maybe they'll have news. Everyone else is still looking."

"*We're* not."

Antonio closed the bulletproof glass behind them. He held her cheeks in his hands, looking her square in her dark eyes. "I will bring our son home, and then I will rip the hearts out of the men who did this."

"No . . ." She paused but held his gaze. "*I* will rip their hearts out."

The living room door opened, and Carmine walked inside with an ARX160 slung over his shoulder.

"Sorry to disturb you, Don Antonio," he said.

Lucia stepped up. "Did you find Marco and Vin?"

Carmine sighed. "Not yet."

"Then what are you doing here?" Antonio asked.

He gestured to the hallway, where a dark-skinned man wearing a leather jacket walked into the open doorway. Antonio didn't have his glasses on and couldn't make the guy out until he stepped under the crystal chandelier.

"Detective Clarke," Antonio said. "I wasn't expecting to see you this morning."

"That makes two of us," Ray said.

"Mikey says you have some information for me."

"I do."

"Hearing you were involved with the port attack was a real disappointment. But I'm assuming, if you're standing here, that you know the Saints' identities and have brought that info to redeem yourself."

"That's correct, Don Antonio."

Carmine lurched a few steps into the living room. The soldier had been a mess since Christopher whacked Frankie. But Carmine wasn't the only one fucked up tonight.

Ray staggered slightly. Sweat dripped down his forehead, and his skin looked pale. He was either high or really nervous. And that made Antonio nervous.

He narrowed his eyes. "So where is Mikey?"

Ray slowly opened his leather jacket, grimacing as he revealed a blood-soaked bandage on the right side of his belly—the true reason for the sweat and the ashen skin.

"Your two-million-dollar bounty is what happened," Ray grunted. He pulled his jacket back over the wound.

"Mikey decided to try and clip me so he could keep the bounty for himself," Ray said. "Long story short, they ended up killing the Saint I captured, and then they came for me."

Antonio looked to Carmine.

"I saw it. Ray's telling the truth. He brought Mikey one of the Saints."

"Mikey's dead?" Antonio asked.

A nod from Carmine.

"Guess he used up all his lives," Antonio said. He shrugged it off. "I never liked that asshole, but his expertise did come in handy from time to time."

"Expertise?" Ray said. "The sick fuck butchered women and children. Not to mention he's a freaking cannibal."

Antonio glared at Ray.

"I don't like your tone, Detective. Remember where you are. This is my house, and you will show some fucking respect."

"I'm sorry, Don Antonio," Ray said. "My apologies."

Antonio turned to his wife. "Lucia, why don't you give us the room."

"I'd rather stay," she replied. "I want to hear who the Saints are, from the mouth of someone who knows."

Antonio looked back to Ray. "You heard her. Speak."

"Namid, a sheriff's deputy, was one of them," Ray said.

Antonio had never heard the name.

"He's dead?" Lucia asked.

"Mikey's men cut his throat before he could tell me who the others are," Ray said. "But I think I know."

Carmine nodded.

"Well?" Antonio asked, growing impatient. "Who are the other Saints?"

Ray opened his leather jacket again and pulled out a SIG Sauer. It took Antonio a microsecond to process what was happening.

He reached for the .45 in the back of his waistband, then remembered it was under a pillow on the couch.

"Carmine!" he yelled.

The soldier struggled to unsling his rifle.

"I'm a Saint," Ray said calmly. He directed the gun at Antonio, who moved to shield his wife with his body. He made it two steps before Ray stopped him.

"Don't fucking move or I'll put one in your dome," he growled.

Carmine finally unslung his rifle, but instead of pointing it at Ray, he turned it on Lucia, a few steps away from Antonio.

"Go watch the hall, Ray," Carmine slurred. "I got this. If any of the guys I sent out return, blast 'em."

Ray glared at Antonio, then moved out of the room, pistol out.

Antonio knew the chill of betrayal all too well. Some men would have frozen, but instinct took over as Ray stepped out.

Carmine looked toward Lucia, giving Antonio a split second to grab a chair and fling it at the captain looking to usurp the throne.

Gunfire shattered prisms from a chandelier.

Antonio dived for the couch. He grabbed his pistol as bullets blew through the expensive cushions.

"Don't!" Carmine yelled.

Antonio knew that by the time he fired, he would be dead. The only chance was to make a deal with his old friend and this . . . Saint.

"This has been a long motherfucking time coming," Carmine said. "Now, drop it or I'll put one in your whore's face."

Antonio gritted his teeth, tempted to sacrifice his life just to kill these two pieces of trash, but that would only get his bride killed.

What he needed was time to make a deal, and time for his loyal men to return.

This was partly his fault. He had left himself lightly guarded—a rookie mistake that had cost so many of his enemies their lives. But what choice did he have now?

He dropped the gun on the couch as the glow of a new day brightened the room.

Was this the last one he would see? The last time he would see his wife?

"You good?" Ray asked from the doorway.

Carmine kept his gaze on Antonio. "Stay in the fucking hallway, Ray, or our deal's off."

Antonio put his hands up and stared into the pinned eyes of his betrayer.

Carmine stared right back.

"Get this shit over with," Ray said. He gripped his side and walked back to stand guard in the hallway.

Antonio checked his wife. She stood against the other wall, breathing hard, a hand over her pounding heart.

"Why?" Antonio asked Carmine.

He laughed and then switched to Italian. "Your prick of a brother killed Frankie in cold blood. Gunned him down over a stupid kid."

Antonio waited for the real reason.

"But most importantly, you two have lost your way. Our product is dried up from the disaster at the port. We're hemorrhaging money. You made a deal with the pigs, then broke it. Now I've made my own deal."

Antonio shook his head but let his old friend continue spewing bullshit.

"Even worse, you've taken on the entire city, and now the military is here. You created more enemies than we can fight. Your reign has come to an end."

"My enemies are wiping one another out," Antonio said, also in Italian. "Soon there will just be me and Esteban Vega."

Carmine laughed again. "You crazy bastard. I believed in your vision long ago, but you've lost your way. This family needs new leadership, and once I kill you and your brother—"

"You kill us, and you're a dead man. No one will follow you."

Had Carmine ever considered what he was going to do? Perhaps not, judging by his tiny pupils. Being high made him even more dangerous.

"I'll give you Frankie's spot at the Four Diamonds," Antonio said. "It will make you a rich man, and we will forget this ever happened."

Carmine grinned. "You're offering me something that I will already own once I kill you. I'd rather be Don Carmine Barese."

"The men will hunt you," Lucia said. "You don't know what you're doing, Carmine."

"The men can't even find your dumbass son, and no one will be hunting me. You've lost their respect. Everyone knows Marco is your weakness. Everyone knows he won't ever be able to run this family."

Carmine jerked his gun muzzle at Lucia.

"Don't do this," Antonio said.

The barrel moved back to his face.

"The Moretti family is doomed from your leadership and your blind love for Marco. If he's still alive, I'll kill the little bitch after I'm done wi—"

A gunshot echoed, and blood spurted from just above Carmine's heart. He was so focused on Antonio, he never saw Lucia grab a pistol from the drawer.

A scream of pain rang out, followed by the crack of return gunfire. Bullets sprayed the wall above Antonio. He scooped his pistol back up as Lucia put another round into Carmine.

The second .45 bullet still didn't bring him down. The rat was wearing a vest.

Antonio fired two more shots, one in each leg. Carmine wailed in pain and crashed to the floor.

Ray fired into the room, forcing Antonio down. The detective moved the barrel of his gun to Antonio's right and fired.

A cry rang out; a body slumped to the floor.

"NO!" Antonio yelled.

He fired several shots, hitting Ray twice. Ray stumbled back through the open doorway and around the corner as Antonio fired shots into the wall.

"You rat motherfucker!" Antonio yelled. He backed away, the gun still on the open doorway.

He backpedaled past Carmine, who squirmed on the floor, bleeding out.

"Tony," came a faint voice.

Antonio rushed back to Lucia. She lay on her back, still holding the nickel-plated .45, a present he had given her for her forty-second birthday.

He gently moved her hand away from the wound. The bullet had hit her in the stomach.

"Help!" Antonio screamed, putting pressure on the wound. "Someone, fucking help!"

"Tony," she whispered.

Antonio met her gaze. The dark eyes he had fallen in love with seemed dimmer as life faded away.

"It's going to be okay, my love. Going to be okay. Just hold on."

Her eyes fluttered, and he gripped her hand.

"Stay with me, Lucia."

She grabbed his wrist and looked him square in the eye as she gasped for air.

"Marco," she said, her voice weak.

Blood bubbled from her lips, and she choked, flecking him with red.

"No," Antonio said. He gripped her hand tighter. "Don't leave me, Lucia. Don't . . ."

In a moment of clarity, she said the last words Antonio would ever hear her speak.

"Save Marco, and tell him I'll always love him."

* * *

Ray stumbled down the stairwell, blinking away the stars. He had snorted some cocaine with Carmine on the ride in to keep focused, and though it was already wearing off, his heart continued to kick.

He could feel it thumping in his chest and singing in his ears.

His arms and back were soaked with blood, but he didn't feel much pain. Probably a combination of the shock from having bullets tear through his left biceps and shoulder, and the drugs in his system.

Dizzy and numb, he wouldn't be conscious for long.

He kept his left arm elevated, and the pistol up in his right hand.

Fueled by thoughts of his family, he kept going down the stairs, dripping blood on each step. He had come here to kill Don Antonio, and while he had failed to take out the don, he had nailed the matriarch.

Perhaps, losing his wife would help Antonio realize the terror he had inflicted on the city. Sometimes the only way to see the light was through trauma.

For Ray, it was the wave of violence after the port that finally helped him understand. The Saints weren't the cancer in the City of Angels—it was the gangs, like the Morettis, that were spreading the disease.

For his final acts, he had protected his brother and the rest of the Saints by calling Carmine and making a deal. After being in their pocket for years, Ray had known that Frankie and Carmine were going to make a move on Antonio Moretti, and had decided to take the gamble and ask Carmine for help.

The bet had paid off, but not for Carmine.

The identities of the other Saints would die with Namid, and with Ray if he didn't make it out of here.

It wasn't redemption, but it was a start.

He stopped on the next landing and palmed the wall, smearing blood. Taking in a breath, then another.

The oxygen helped. Feeling less light-headed, he opened the door and cleared the hallway.

Keep going, Ray. Keep breathing . . .

Crimson drips followed him on the tile floor. He was almost to the lobby and didn't see the guards posted there. Carmine had told the few men to leave their posts and wait outside for Marco and Vinny.

The plan was working.

Ray hugged the wall as he moved, keeping his gun trained on the open doorway to the marble lobby. Several closed doors separated him from the rotunda. Offices and apartments where the family members lived.

He paused to listen for voices or footfalls, knowing that even one of the wives could give him up. But there was only the distant hum of mechanical equipment, and the air-conditioning pumping cold air into the expensive apartments.

The Morettis did live like kings. And he had just capped the queen.

Ray stopped a few feet from the lobby. He listened again. Hearing nothing, he moved out across the marble, clearing the open rotunda with two passes of his gun. He limped to the exit doors and shouldered them open.

A second pair of glass doors led outside, providing a view of the circular drive, courtyard, and gardens inside the walled compound. He bent down when he saw the headlights moving down the road. Several vehicles pulled through the open gate in the distance. Range Rovers, Suburbans, and an Escalade.

Shit, shit, shit.

He checked his last magazine. Only five bullets left—not nearly enough to shoot his way out of this.

The thought filled him with dread. He had hoped that just maybe he could make it to the Mercedes and drive to meet his family and say goodbye.

But none of that was going to happen. He had already lost too much blood.

This was the end of the road for Detective Ray Clarke.

He locked the front doors and sat with his back to the wood doors leading to the lobby. A wave of pain ripped down his left arm. After it eased enough for him to move his hand, he pulled his cell phone from his jacket.

He wiped the blood off the screen with his coat and squinted to make out the missed calls from Alicia and Moose.

Headlights lit up the front entrance as vehicles pulled into the driveway. He slouched and dialed his brother, fumbling with the phone as he brought it to his ear.

"Ray, where the hell are you?" Moose said.

"The Moretti compound."

A beat passed before Moose replied.

"What the hell are you—"

"Long story, but I took down the queen."

"You got to get out of there, man," Moose said, panic rising in his voice.

"Don't worry about me, bro," Ray said. "Did you find Namid's family?"

"His wife is gone," Moose said. "But Isaac escaped. LAPD picked him up."

Ray closed his eyes. "I'm sorry, man. I swear I never meant for that to happen. I didn't realize Mikey would go after his family."

"What about Abdul? Did you really kill him?"

Ray felt a tear streak down his face. Or maybe that was sweat, or blood, or all those things. He was a mess, his heart thumping in his chest as if it wanted out.

"I killed him to protect you. Made it look like a Vega—"

"Jesus," Moose said. "You killed an innocent man. A guy who served this city and represented everything that's still good about it."

"That's why I'm going to hell."

"Ray, why . . . why didn't you come to me for help?"

Voices sounded outside the front door, and Ray bent lower to stay out of view.

"I'm out of time, bro. And I know nothing I say will wash away my sins, but I tried to do you right . . ."

"Ray, don't hang up!"

"Promise me you'll look after my family, Andre. They're at Alicia's aunt's house. You remember where she lives, right?"

"Yeah."

"Promise me," Ray said—the same words Namid had used.

"I promise."

"I love you, Andre. I'm sorry I wasn't a better cop, and a better man."

Ray hung up the phone before Moose could try to talk him out of it.

There was no time to call Alicia, but maybe that was for the best. She knew he loved her, and the kids knew he loved them.

Calling would just make things worse. He would rather take thirty more bullets than hear the pain in their voices.

Shouting continued outside, and more voices came from the lobby behind the closed doors. Ray crushed the phone under his boot, stomping on it several times. Then he drew in a breath, exhaled, and opened the doors, bringing up his gun.

He shot two Morettis running across the marble, dropping them both. He lowered his gun and clutched the injured arm against his chest. With only three bullets left, he moved back to the glass doors and stepped out onto the staircase looking over the Moretti compound.

Dozens of soldiers moved away from the vehicles, weapons shouldered and aimed at Ray. He smiled when he saw Christopher Moretti. The man had brought back the prince of the family, Marco, and his cousin Vinny.

"Drop your gun!" Christopher shouted.

Ray's grin widened as he saw an opportunity to fuck the Morettis up even more. He raised his pistol at Marco. "For the Saints!" he yelled.

Muzzle flashes lit up the night like exploding fireworks before he could pull the trigger. Bullets ripped into his vest and his muscular body.

He hit the ground on his side, the air in his lungs gone. The gunshots continued, more rounds cracking into the steps around him. He felt another flash of pain so bad that he tried to scream. Nothing came out besides a tear.

He blinked it away and watched as Christopher Moretti raised his hand into the air.

"Hold your fire!" he shouted.

Ray fought for breath, thinking of his wife and kids as he struggled for a few more seconds of life. In the end, he would never be a good cop or a good man like his brother, but he had given some of those good men a fighting chance to save the city from the darkness of the sinners fanned out below him.

Red encroached on his vision, and Ray looked down as Christopher walked up the steps. He smirked at the thought of that asshole finding his brother upstairs with his dead wife.

The Morettis' second in command and a group of soldiers moved past Ray as he lay bleeding out. As the other men stepped away from the vehicles, he saw someone he hadn't seen earlier—a man sitting in a wheelchair, wearing a suit.

A crack sounded above Ray, and the darkness consumed him.

-31-

Camilla hardly recognized the woman in the sun visor's mirror. Between her injuries and all the crying, she looked like a raccoon. There was plenty to be upset about. They had lost Namid and his wife. Moose had lost his brother, and the violence was spreading throughout the city.

She flipped the sun visor back up as the convoy of three vehicles pulled into the hidden section of Canoga Park just before midnight. Two days had passed since Mikey the Mutant killed Namid, but in that time, they had managed to get his son, Isaac, out of police protection with the help of Lieutenant Marks.

That was the easy part.

None of the Saints knew whether the Morettis had figured out any of their identities besides Namid's, and Dom had decided not to take any chances. He made the call to get their families out of the city.

"This is the right move," Camilla said. "We can trust my uncle."

Dom steered the truck to the left as the Chevy Tahoe ahead moved down a ramp leading to the dry riverbed. It stopped halfway down, and Moose jumped out with Rocky. Both men ran over to a gated fence and pushed it open.

The trucks rolled along the concrete gorge, toward the tunnel her uncle had marked on a map as the pickup point.

"I hope you're right about Álvaro," Dom said. He kept his eyes on the road, both hands on the steering wheel. He hadn't said much over the past few days, and she still didn't know what he had planned other than sending the families to a safe zone somewhere in the Midwest.

They had a lot of people to take care of. Moose had Yolanda and their two kids, Tamara and Bryon. And Ray's wife, Alicia, had Jamal, Will, Lolo, and Maddie. And with Namid and Victoria gone, little Isaac was now alone in the world.

To further complicate things, Lolo required daily shots of RX-4. But Ray had prepared before his death, leaving Moose the address to a stockpile of RX-4 and silver just in case anything ever happened to him.

Camilla would never forgive Ray for betraying Namid and killing Abdul. But in the end, Ray had tried to make things right by sacrificing himself for the team and his family.

The convoy slowed as they drove into a dark tunnel. Drops of water splatted on the windshield.

Camilla pulled out her Smith & Wesson. She was nervous—not because she didn't trust her uncle, but because they were being hunted. Antonio would burn the city down and kill everyone in his path to find those connected with the death of his wife.

Every life in all three trucks, young and old, was at risk.

The Tahoe stopped ahead, and Moose hopped out. He turned on a flashlight as the convoy shut off all headlights.

"Everyone, hurry," Dom said. He picked Cayenne up and set her on the ground. She hopped over to the kids as they got out of the enclosed delivery truck.

"Where's your uncle?" Dom asked her.

"He'll be here soon."

The other Saints helped the families unload their belongings: Suitcases, backpacks, blankets, and pillows. It reminded Camilla of the days during the Second Civil War when people were fleeing for their lives.

"Set up a perimeter," Dom said.

Pork Chop, Tooth, and Rocky took off running with their rifles, leaving Bettis and Camilla behind with Dom and Moose.

Thunder boomed a few seconds behind a slash of lightning as a light rain fell outside the tunnel. The first in weeks.

Another lightning bolt forked across the dark skyline, illuminating the faces of the kids and their parents as they stood waiting under the lip of the tunnel. Camilla walked over to Isaac.

She knew what it was like to be an orphan, and she knew that there was nothing she could say to this young boy that would take away his pain.

He shivered at the crack of thunder, and Camilla bent down next to him. Isaac had his dad's intensity and his mother's light eyes.

"Where are we going?" he asked.

"Somewhere safe."

"Will my mom and dad be there?"

Camilla looked up at Dom.

"Your parents had to go to another place," he said. "A better place."

"Why didn't they take me?" Isaac asked.

Camilla and Dom exchanged a glance, and she let him take over as he crouched and pulled his face mask away from his beard.

"Sometimes, our moms and dads leave us and can't take us with them. But that doesn't mean they don't love us or that they aren't still with us. In fact, it's because they love us more," he said. "Your mom and dad love you very much, and they will always remain with you here . . . and here."

Dom pointed to his head and his heart.

"But I want to be with them," Isaac said. "I don't want to be alone."

Dom gestured for Cayenne. She hopped over and nudged up against Isaac. Petting the dog cheered the boy up.

"You're never going to be alone," Yolanda said. "You're going to be with me and all these other people."

"We're going to take care of you, sweetie," Camilla said.

The growl of diesel engines sounded in the distance, and Camilla unslung her AR-15.

"Everyone, back," Dom said. He herded the wives and children to the left side of the tunnel, and Camilla moved to the right with Bettis.

The rumble of motorcycles rose after another crack of thunder.

"Get ready," Dom said.

Camilla squinted at the approaching vehicles. If something went wrong, this would be on her. Then again, if something went *really* wrong, no one would be alive to blame her.

She moved her finger to the trigger guard, praying her uncle hadn't been compromised.

Truck headlights dazzled her, forcing her back into the shadows. When her vision cleared, she saw multiple vehicles approaching. A tractor-trailer led the convoy down the wide river passage. Barbed wire festooned the front grille guard, and metal bars protected the windshield.

She caught a glimpse of a gold cross surrounded by roses, painted on the hood.

"It's him," Camilla said.

The truck drove in and kept rolling, stopping a few hundred yards from the tunnel entrance. Motorcycles squeezed by on both sides, the riders armed with compact submachine guns.

The big rig's passenger door opened, and a man stepped down from the cab. She heard the click of a cane on pavement as her uncle walked into view.

"You all ready, or what, *mis amigos*?" he called out.

Camilla felt her face stretch into the first smile in days.

"It's okay," she said, gesturing for the team to lower their weapons.

Dom slung his rifle and joined her out in the rain to meet her uncle.

"How many you got?" Álvaro asked.

"Seven kids and two adults," Dom replied.

Álvaro looked over their shoulders at the women and children behind them.

"Where are you taking them?" Moose asked.

"Place in northeastern Iowa," Álvaro said. "Green fields, clear water, and best of all, it's safe. One of my crews just got back from a trip a few weeks ago. Long drive, but worth it."

Moose lowered his head slightly. Camilla had a feeling this was going to be hardest on the big guy. After losing his brother, he was now being wrenched away from his family.

But at least, they were still alive.

"All right, let's get moving," Dom said.

Rocky, Tooth, and Pork Chop returned to help load up the vehicles. A few minutes later, they had everyone rounded up outside the trailer.

The convoy was an impressive setup that included an escort of four cars, six motorcycles, and two semis. One of the crew unlocked the steel doors to the back of the first trailer to reveal a large living space inside.

"Welcome to your new casa for the next few days or a week," Álvaro said.

"Wow, cool," Bryon said.

Tamara stepped up and looked inside, then turned back to Moose.

"Dad, I don't want to go," she said. "I want to stay with you."

Camilla walked away, leaving the families to say goodbye as she scanned for hostiles. This would make the perfect place for an ambush.

But her uncle was prepared.

At the front of the convoy, the six men on motorcycles watched the sloping concrete riverbank for trouble. Behind them, the first truck's railings and bumpers were wrapped with barbed wire, and men wearing armor and gas masks stood inside two turrets on top, sweeping the .50-caliber machine guns over the riverbank for hostiles.

Camilla walked back to check the other vehicles. Four supporting cars were decked out with armored plates, brush guards, off-road tires, and turbocharged engines.

Finally, there was a second semi, loaded with gear, gasoline, and more soldiers.

Able to relax now, Camilla returned to her team for goodbyes.

Moose kissed Yolanda and then wrapped her in a hug. After they parted, he bent down to scoop up Bryon and Tamara in his massive arms.

"I'll see you kids soon," he said.

"Why can't you come?" Bryon asked.

"I got to stay here, but I'll be with you in a little while," he said.

Yolanda walked over to Dom.

"Make sure you keep that promise," she said.

Dom gave her a hug, then unslung his backpack. He waited for Moose to finish saying goodbye to his brother's family. When he parted, Dom walked over and handed the bag to Moose.

"What's this?" he asked, unzipping the bag.

"Satellite phone, some extra coin, and a little something I wanted you to have," Dom said.

Moose ruffled through the contents and pulled out a SIG Sauer 1911 Nightmare.

"What's this?" he asked, looking up.

"A parting gift."

"I don't understand. This was your dad's."

"And now it's yours, brother," Dom said. He put a hand on his friend's shoulder. "It's already brought me luck, and now I hope it'll bring you luck on the journey east."

Moose lowered the gun and shook his head. "I'm staying."

"Your family needs you, Andre. We'll be fine here."

Camilla and the other Saints gathered around.

"We'll take good care of Dom," Rocky said.

"Be careful out there, big guy," Tooth said.

Moose sniffled, then drew in a deep breath. He embraced them each in turn, stopping on Dom last.

"Call me on the sat phone if you run into trouble."

Moose nodded. "Once I get my family there safe, I'll come back."

"Let's go, amigos," Álvaro said, tapping his cane on the concrete. "This train is leaving in *cinco minutos*."

The team said their final goodbyes, and Camilla went to Isaac.

"I hear there are *fish* where you're going!" she said, bending down. "Catch me one, okay?"

Isaac looked up, his eyes searching hers.

She ruffled his hair and helped him into the back of the truck with the other passengers. Moose took one of the M4s from the back of a pickup truck and climbed in after his family, holding a hand up to his friends.

"Good luck, boss," he said.

"You too, brother."

"That it, or do we have any other last-minute guests?" Álvaro asked, turning his eye to Camilla. "Last chance, Cam."

She shook her head and looked over to Dom. "We got unfinished business here."

He coughed into his mask and pulled it down to pop a pill as the convoy rumbled to life.

Camilla glanced at him as he forced the fat pill down.

"I thought you were done with that junk," she said.

He licked his lips, hesitating.

"It's not a rush pill," he said. "It's RX-Four."

* * *

The morning after the families left the city, Dom was headed for a face-to-face with Lieutenant Marks at the solar farm. It felt odd having Rocky and Tooth by his side instead of Moose, but he had done the right thing by sending his old friend to be with his family, and he still had the rest of the surviving Saints.

Pork Chop and Bettis were camped out in rock outcroppings in the distance, and Camilla waited in a vehicle just in case this was an ambush. But if it was, the team could do little more than make their enemies pay dearly.

Storm clouds lingered over the solar panels sponging up whatever meager rays penetrated. Wind turbines sliced the air, feeding energy to a city on the verge of collapse.

And Dom blamed himself.

He walked down the dusty path between rows of solar panels, contemplating the past few weeks. It all had started the night of the port raid. He should have backed off when the cops arrived.

Embracing evil had gotten Namid, his wife, and their unborn child killed. It had gotten Abdul killed. Jason and Lenny were dead. And how many others?

The night at the port had started a chain reaction that Dom couldn't stop. He looked over at Rocky and Tooth. The tan shemaghs and fatigues, body armor, and automatic rifles didn't help him relax.

He had a bad feeling about the first face-to-face meeting with Marks in months. A lot had changed in that time, including his health.

But the truth was out now.

Dom was sick with radiation poisoning. Abdul had diagnosed him a month ago, and he could no longer lie to the team. It wasn't just radiation poisoning. He had chemical toxins in his blood from inhaling alkaline dust. According to the late doctor, the condition would worsen and even kill him if left unchecked.

That didn't scare Dom. He wasn't afraid of dying from a disease or a bullet. He was afraid of dying before he could finish his mission of cleansing Los Angeles of Don Antonio Moretti.

He wiped the sweat from his forehead and stopped to scan the buildings in the distance with his binos. Despite the side effects of RX-4, he actually felt better now that he had slept a full night.

He centered the binos on the buildings at the eastern edge of the solar farm. This was where Marks had asked them to meet, only a few miles from the seawater desalination plant where Dom first met Councilman Castle.

"Got a bad feelin' about this," Rocky said.

"Marks won't betray me, and he hasn't let us down yet," Tooth said.

"I didn't think Ray would screw his own brother, either," Rocky said. "Goes to show, you can't trust anyone in this world."

Dom looked at him.

"Well, except us, obviously," Rocky said.

"Just shut up already, Rock," Tooth said.

Dom led the way, noticing a glint of light from the third-story window of an adjacent building—Pork Chop's signal that the coast was clear.

Aside from Bettis, the young deputy was their best marksman, and Dom had positioned him there with a M107 .50-caliber sniper rifle.

Dom, Rocky, and Tooth took another path through the maze of solar panels until they got to their target, a one-story structure with a metal roof that looked more like a hangar than a warehouse.

Windows wrapped around the structure, providing firing zones inside. Dom checked the rock outcroppings on a distant hill where Bettis was set up with his M107.

Another flash of light told him it was clear.

"Let's go," Dom said.

Rocky was first to the door and took up position on the right side. Tooth waited behind Dom, rifle up.

Dom opened the door, revealing a long space furnished only with stacks of crates. In the middle of the room stood Lieutenant Marks. He looked as though he had aged several years in the past few weeks. Dark bags hung under his eyes, and his regrown mustache was almost entirely gray.

The captain wasn't alone.

Six men shouldered their weapons at the Saints. Marks was the only one who didn't raise a weapon.

"Whoa, whoa!" he called out, holding up his hands.

"What the fuck is this?" Dom shouted. He moved his barrel over each masked face in turn. The soldiers were all armed with the newest M4A1 models and wore camouflage fatigues and body armor.

"Tell them to stand down or this gets ugly, fast!" Dom shouted.

Marks held up his hands and stepped in front of the other men.

"Stand down," he ordered.

One of the soldiers stepped out from the group and said, "This is just precautionary."

"So's this," Tooth said. He took a step forward, but Rocky and Dom held their ground. They were outgunned inside, but if bullets started flying, his men would take these guys down.

Although it would be certain death for the Saints.

Dom had to play it cool.

"You said you were coming alone," he said. "Who are these guys?'

"I'm sorry, but I knew you wouldn't come if I told you the truth," Marks said calmly.

"Fuck this," Rocky said. "Let's bounce, boss."

"Hold on," Dom said. "Let him explain first."

"These men are friends from Naval Station Norfolk in Virginia," he said. Marks gestured toward the tall middle-aged man with short-cropped hair dusted by gray. "This is Captain Rick Sanns of the United States Navy."

"I'd appreciate it if your men lowered their guns, Captain," Dom said. He had no idea what the military wanted with his team, but if they didn't get their shit together, the Saints were going to drop them.

"*Friends* don't point guns at one another," Rocky said.

"Like I said, this is just precautionary," said Sanns.

"So's that little dot on your chest," Dom said.

The captain showed them his salt-and-pepper buzz cut as he looked down at the red spot jiggling in the square inch over the center of his heart. The other men looked around and raised their rifles at the windows.

"Well, I can see why you guys have survived this long," the captain said.

"We're very careful," Dom said. He kept his rifle aimed at one of the men.

"I'm sorry," Marks said. "This was the only way."

"Sorry for lying to us?" Rocky said.

"I'm sorry to hear about Namid and Victoria. We've taken quite a few of our own losses, as you well know."

He walked toward Dom with his palms up. "You're more like your dad than I realized. You know how to piss off your enemies."

"We wouldn't have to do what we do if the LAPD did their job," Rocky said.

Dom glanced over, silencing the kid.

Marks stopped when he got to Dom, and stuck out his hand. Dom relaxed enough to shake but kept his weapon up with the other hand.

"I'm really sorry to meet under these conditions," Marks said.

"Me too."

Marks looked back at Captain Sanns, who stepped forward, chest out and chin up. He filled out his uniform well, reflecting a warrior who cared about his own ability to keep up with those under his command.

"I'm here on behalf of the Executive Council of the United States of America," Sanns said. "The Council has had a hopeful eye on Los Angeles for several years now. Unfortunately, things have gotten worse here."

"Not going to disagree with you there," Dom said.

"With the recent fall of several major cities, we can't afford to lose any more," Sanns said.

Dom recalled the rumors, but he was so focused on Los Angeles, those places may as well be foreign countries.

"I've heard a lot about your team, and I respect your efforts. That's why I wanted to do this in person," Sanns continued. "When I was a much younger man, I was assigned to SEAL Team Seven. We worked with the DEA and South American governments to fight the narcos, and later we took the fight to the Mexican cartel. Things have changed considerably since the war that left our country in ruins."

Dom scrutinized the veteran captain. Goddamn, it would be good to have these guys in the fight, but he knew that wasn't going to happen.

"I know better than most what you're up against," Sanns continued. "But your vigilante and guerrilla tactics have made the situation in Los Angeles worse."

Marks looked down.

"The government has already invested hundreds of millions in housing, food, and other supplies to keep the citizens alive here," Sanns said. "Now there is a new deal with Mayor Buren."

"What deal?" Dom narrowed his brows.

"A recent deal to keep this city from falling into anarchy," Sanns said.

"Did you know about this, Lieutenant?" Dom asked.

Marks was silent.

"*What* deal?" Dom asked again.

"A deal that allows the crime families to keep their power as long as they don't kill innocent civilians or cops," Sanns said.

"The same deal that was in place before?" Dom asked.

"Not exactly."

"A line was crossed at the port, and my hands are tied," Marks said. "Follow me. There's something I need you to see."

Dom and Rocky stood their ground.

"I'm not asking," Marks said. "This is an order."

"Let's go," Dom said to Rocky, finally lowering his weapon. They did the same and followed the soldiers out of the warehouse. The sun peeked out through the clouds, spreading over the solar farms.

"It's not far," Marks said. "You can tell your team to stand down and join us. They're going to want to see this too."

"They stay where they are," Dom said.

Marks looked over his shoulder but didn't reply. They walked through another section of the farm before Dom saw their destination. He swallowed hard when he realized what he was being led toward.

The soldiers fanned out around a pickup truck parked near a hill that had hidden them from view earlier. Several other vehicles were there too.

Marks walked over to the back of the pickup and dropped the gate. Then he motioned for Dom. He walked over to the bed, and Marks pulled a sheet off a naked, broken body still tied to a solar panel.

"We found him like this," Marks said. "Going to need a fucking mortician to properly remove him from the panel. The sons of bitches burned his back and stuck him to it, then let him suffer in the sun."

Dom forced himself to look at the twisted face of Councilman Tom Castle.

"Jesus," Rocky said, crossing his chest.

"Mayor Buren handed him over to the Morettis as part of the deal he made with the government," Marks continued. "Now you see what we're up against. There's no use fighting the Morettis."

Dom held a breath in his chest, the evil on display seizing the air from his diseased lungs.

"You poked the hornets' nest and you lost," Sanns said. "We're here to shut you down." He motioned for his men, who fanned out.

"What the actual fuck," Rocky said. "You're shutting us down? We're not the enemy! The fucking Morettis—"

"Quiet, Rock," Dom said. He held up a hand to stop the kid from doing anything stupid. He knew there was nothing they could say to stop this. They were here on orders from people across the country who had no idea what was happening here.

Rocky stuttered and then shook his head. "I don't fucking believe this shit. Do you not see what they did to Castle?"

Sanns looked at the body and then nodded at Marks, who covered it back up with the sheet.

"It's over," Marks said. "Hand over your badges and promise you will stop your vigilante attacks. It's the only way. They wanted to take you in, but I made a deal too. You get to stay in the city, as long as you give your word—"

"That we will stop fighting evil?" Dom said. "The men who took my sister and killed and tortured your friend here? The men poisoning these streets with drugs and death?"

He looked his father's former best friend in the eye. Dom fully understood now what had happened to his father in the hunt for Monica. The darkness and evil of the war and its aftermath had eaten his heart and soul as it was doing to Dom, but his father hadn't given up fighting.

"I'm sorry," Marks said ruefully. "I didn't want this."

"Did he give us up?" Dom asked, jerking his chin toward the pickup.

Marks shook his head. "Your identities are still safe, or you'd already be dead."

Sanns stepped over. "I don't like having to do this, but the Executive Council wants things to calm down here. From this point forward, the Saints are over."

Dom reached into his vest and pulled out his deputy sheriff's badge. He gripped it in his gloved hand, remembering how he had felt the day he first held his LAPD badge.

Those days seemed a lifetime ago.

He tossed the badge in the dirt by the captain's boots, then turned to walk away with Rocky. Marks followed him away from the truck.

"Hold up," he said.

Dom turned halfway, one eye on the soldiers, who watched them like hawks.

"If you think I'm going to stand down and listen to these assholes, you're wrong," Dom said, his lip curling beneath his mask. "I'm not going to stop fighting even if I don't have any bullets to fire."

"I know, and I was wrong," Marks said. He leaned in closer, as if to keep the others from hearing, and said, "Your father was right—what he said about embracing evil."

Captain Sanns walked over, listening.

Marks put a hand on Dom's shoulder. "I'm sorry. I failed you, Dominic. I failed Castle too, and your dad, and Monica."

Dom wanted to reply, wanted to say he was wrong, but Marks wasn't wrong. He had spent so much time following the rules that he had let the lawless win.

"I'm sorry too," Dom said. He walked away with Rocky, leaving Marks behind with the soldiers and the mutilated corpse of the man who should have been mayor.

"Wait," Marks called out. When Dom turned, he shouted, "Use evil to defeat evil!"

-32-

Rain pelted the umbrellas of those who had gathered to pay final respects to Lucia Moretti.

Antonio had left his in the car. That way, he could cry in the rain, with no one the wiser. He led the way up the twisting path.

The little cemetery stood on a bluff overlooking the ocean. Today, he couldn't hear the waves breaking below or feel the warm coastal breeze rustling through the eucalyptus and cypress trees. Instead, there was thunder and howling wind.

Lucia had once told him she wanted to be buried by the ocean. Long ago, when they were young lovers in Naples. Back when his empire was just a dream. The conversation surrounding death had come up several times during their marriage, as she realized more and more just how dangerous his chosen line of work was.

But she had accepted this life after he promised to take care of her always.

I'm so sorry, my bride. I'm sorry I failed you.

Wet pebbles crunched under his Italian leather shoes. Tears streamed down his face, along with the cold rain. The twenty people here today weren't looking at him, anyway. They had avoided his gaze since they left the compound.

This wasn't solely out of respect. It was also out of fear.

All his men knew what had changed after Carmine betrayed him, and the traitor cop Ray shot Lucia. That bullet had shattered everything, throwing wide the floodgates that would bring a tsunami of death crashing down on the enemies of the Moretti family.

What was left of it, anyway. Raphael was dead. Vito was dead. Frankie, dead. And Carmine was dead after a betrayal that Antonio hadn't seen coming. It was his gravest mistake, costing him Lucia.

He turned to see the men still left in his inner circle. Vinny, Christopher, Yellowtail, and Lino were all he had left. In the span of a few weeks, three of his captains had been wiped out, along with his head of security, the former AMP soldier Sergeant Rush.

The Moretti family wasn't running low on muscle, but it was running low on Italian blood. Soon he would promote Doberman to soldier. The seemingly unkillable young man had more than earned it. And perhaps soon, Marco would earn his button as well.

Antonio crested the hill and spotted the tent they had constructed in the center of the little graveyard. He stayed put as his men walked past him and gathered under the awning, where a priest and two attendants stood facing a dozen white chairs set up at the graveside.

For security purposes, his team had already brought the casket up here, without pallbearers. Just as they'd had to do at the funeral for Antonio's father, on one of the two worst days in the history of the Moretti family.

A day that he had promised would never happen again. Antonio had learned from his grief. His family would never suffer another ambush like the one on that fateful day in Naples.

He scanned the cemetery. The former military special-ops soldiers on his payroll were patrolling at the other end of the graveyard and near the bluff overlooking the beach. And though Antonio couldn't see them, he knew that several snipers were hidden in the surrounding thick sumac and willow scrub.

Another team of ten men stood guard in the parking lot at the bottom of the hill, watching for any vehicles that might take the back road. The women were still inside the new fleet of armored Chevy Tahoes, waiting for the all clear.

Antonio wiped his eyes and walked over to his soldiers under the tent. Christopher met him at the entrance.

"It's all clear up here," he said, putting a hand on Antonio's shoulder. "Are you ready, brother?"

"Yes. Bring up the families."

Antonio walked over to his place in front of the casket, where the priest and two attendants stood in preparation for the ceremony.

"Father Ricci," he said with a nod.

The priest, holding a leather-bound Bible against his black robe, nodded back. He was a tall man, whose neat white beard contrasted with heavy black brows. His eyes stayed on Antonio for a long moment.

Normally, Antonio wouldn't take direction from another man, but this holy man was making him bow his head in prayer. He closed his eyes and managed to ask for forgiveness before his thoughts relapsed back into vengeance, rage, and despair.

The hardest part of losing Lucia was knowing that he would never join her in heaven. When Antonio was done with this world, he would enter one of fury and fire, never to see his precious bride again.

More tears fell at the thought of life without her.

You will find a way to see her again. Even if you have to fight your way out of the pits of hell.

He took solace in the thought, burying the despair. For the next hour, he would honor Lucia. Then he would bury all his enemies.

Alive.

The Saints, the Vegas, and every wannabe gangbanger still looking for turf in Los Angeles would be breathing dirt in the coming days.

Seeing the women arrive in their black dresses snapped him back to the present. Carmen, Vinny's wife, led the way with a beautiful bundle of red and white roses. As she approached the casket, a heavy boom of thunder shook the ground.

Antonio glanced at the ocean. Over the drumming of the rain, he could hear the white noise of the crashing waves. Lucia had loved that sound.

Again he thought about his failure to protect his wife. He had also failed to keep Marco out of the family business—another promise broken.

Marco stood beside him. He glanced over, his eyes swollen from crying. Normally, Antonio might have been rougher with the lad, reminding him that men didn't cry. And most of the time, they shouldn't. But a man who didn't cry over the death of his mother wasn't a man.

The women all moved to the chairs. Vito's widow, Giuliana, sat, eliciting a groan from the folding chair. Vinny's wife sat beside her, then Lino's sister Angela. There weren't many others. Carmine's and Frankie's wives had been exiled from the compound for the sins of their men.

As soon as Carmen and the others took a seat, Antonio nodded at Father Ricci.

"We are gathered here today to celebrate the life of a beautiful soul taken far too early from this world," Ricci said. "I did not know Lucia Moretti as well as you did, but in the short time I knew her, I saw that she was a wonderful mother, a devoted wife, and a soul that shone brighter than most."

Marco lowered his head and wiped his nose with his wrist.

"As many of you know, Lucia Moretti was born in Naples, Italy. There, she worked as a barmaid before meeting and falling in love with her soul mate, Don Antonio Moretti."

Lightning sizzled over the beach, and the thunderclap made people flinch. The wind picked up, rippling their clothing and peppering them with rain. A rose fell off the casket, and Antonio bent down to pick it up.

He didn't believe in the paranormal. Nor did he believe that souls had power on earth in the afterlife, but it sure seemed as if Lucia was trying to send a message today.

"Lucia was a connoisseur of the arts, fashion, and decorating," Ricci said. "If anyone could make a room sparkle, it was Lucia Moretti. I'm told she oversaw the remodeling of the Moretti compound, and from what I've seen of the inside, it's one of a kind, much as she was one of a kind."

Some of the women nodded. Others smiled.

"Let's take a moment to think of other memories, and what we loved about Lucia," Ricci said.

Everyone bowed their head, except Antonio and Christopher. His brother seemed to hear the same faint noise coming over the wind.

It was barely perceptible at first—a whooshing that gradually resolved itself into a rhythmic, percussive beating. Antonio scanned the horizon as Father Ricci went on.

"Lucia Moretti loved her son and husband more than anything, and she lived her life for both of them. In the end, she showed just how much she loved them, by giving her life trying to save them."

The image flashed through Antonio's mind: her pulling out the pistol he had bought her, using it to save his life while sacrificing her own.

The anger emerged again, rage filling his veins just in time.

Father Ricci looked up at the sky with the rest of the men, who were already reaching under their suit jackets. The priest flipped open his oversize Bible. But instead of reading a prayer, he pulled a scope-mounted handgun from the hollowed-out book.

Both his attendants pulled MP5 submachine guns from under their raincoats as a Black Hawk helicopter came up over the cliffs to the south.

Antonio's heart skipped. Here was the moment he had hoped and planned for.

He hurried to the casket, took the roses off, and set them on the grass. Then he pushed the lid open as the helicopter bore down on the group of mourners.

"Everyone, get down!" Christopher shouted.

The bark of heavy machine-gun fire rose over a crack of thunder. One of the special-ops guards Antonio had posted near the edge of the cliffs went down.

Antonio hadn't expected them to bring a chopper to the ambush he had set up, but if that was the death they chose, he would oblige. Reaching inside the casket, he came up with an RPG launcher.

He hefted the weapon to his shoulder and strode out into the rain with Father Ricci. The priest made the sign of the cross, then started shooting with the rest of the men.

The door gunner jerked from a dozen rounds, then dangled halfway out, held in by his retaining strap.

The helicopter hovered less than a hundred feet away, over the other end of the graveyard. A dozen Vega soldiers, wearing their colorful skull masks, started fast-roping down four lines. Easy target.

Antonio lined up the sights and pulled the trigger on the launcher.

"*Hasta la vista, pendejos*," he said.

The rocket streaked away, veering slightly and hitting the tail section in a burst of metal and fire. The explosion sent the bird spinning over the side of the cliff as the soldiers fell from their ropes, crashing to the ground thirty feet below.

Others, who hadn't clipped in, jumped from the troop hold as the bird spun out of control, their bodies landing all across the graveyard.

Antonio reached out, and Christopher tossed him a ballistic mask and then an M4 from the casket. Lino and Marco fastened on their masks and ran for cover behind two big granite headstones. Antonio did the same, keeping low.

At the other end of the graveyard, several sicarios writhed and screamed in pain, their bodies broken on gravestones after falling off the rope. But the ones who had been lower on the ropes managed to find cover and shoot despite their injuries.

Antonio fired a burst and took cover behind a headstone. As his men laid down suppressing fire, he turned to check on the women.

"Stay down!" he yelled. Father Ricci and his attendants stood guard with their weapons aimed out over the cemetery.

But not all the women were quite so passive. Vito's widow had a sawed-off Mossberg shotgun in hand, and a few graves over from Antonio, Lino's sister Angela joined her brother with an Uzi.

Back at the head of the path overlooking the parking lot, Yellowtail, Vinny, and Doberman provided support to the guards at the parked SUVs.

"Four trucks, twenty men!" Vinny called out.

Gunfire was already cracking from the parking lot and road, where a second group of narcos had shown up in pickup trucks that looked loaded to the brim with sicarios.

Yellowtail hefted up a second RPG while Vinny and Doberman opened fire from their vantage above.

Antonio fired another burst, then jumped up and ran to the next gravestone with bullets zipping past. Glancing over the side, he counted at least seven sicarios who could still fight.

Bullets forced him down. He rolled away, crawled a few feet, then got up and ran for Christopher and Marco, who were hiding behind a family crypt much like the one where they had already buried Lucia back at the compound.

"Cover me," Antonio said.

Christopher nodded. The only Moretti man without a mask was chewing on a cigar. He stepped around the stone wall and fired.

"Go, go, go!" he said.

Antonio and Marco both ran out, weapons shouldered and blazing away at the sicario positions. Two of the special-ops soldiers were crumpled on the grass, bleeding out from devastating 7.62 mm rounds to their bodies.

Three sicarios lay nearby, only one of them moving. Antonio put a bullet through his skull. Four more had taken position behind a row of stones. Antonio prayed Esteban and Miguel were among those still alive.

Only a *bastardo cattivo* would ambush a family during a funeral. Of course, only a *bastardo cattivo* would use his own wife's funeral to ambush his enemies. But it was too perfect an opportunity to pass up. Lucia would have approved.

Marco had welcomed the idea when, for maybe the first time ever, Antonio asked his son's opinion.

The boy fired his pistol into the mask of a Vega soldier with telescoped legs, blowing out the back of his skull before moving on to the next target, lying behind another gravestone, his back broken. He pulled out a knife and slit his throat.

Antonio held back a grin of satisfaction. Revenge was a sweet thing, even when it was this easy.

He had selected the site because he knew it would draw out his enemies. It probably looked easy to the Vegas as well and would therefor arouse their suspicions. So Antonio had brought enough security to make them seem ready for an attack, but not enough that they seemed to be *expecting* it.

His plan had worked beautifully.

He fired again as the ground rumbled from more explosions. Chatter from automatic gunfire came from across the cemetery, where three sicarios were holed up behind a mausoleum.

One of them fired from the side at Christopher, who was finishing off a crippled soldier with his knife. As he stabbed the man, a bullet hit him in the arm.

"Christopher!" Antonio yelled.

Another bullet hit him in the chest, knocking him off the dead sicario.

"NO!" Antonio lined up the sights on the shooter behind the wall. He squeezed off a burst, the rounds clipping the stone and forcing the man back.

Christopher squirmed in pain on the ground as Antonio ran over to him. He fired several bursts for cover, then bent down to check his brother. Blood ran from the wound on his arm, but the vest had stopped the one to his chest.

Chest heaving, he gasped for air and spat the cigar out.

Lino and Marco fired at the mausoleum, giving Antonio a chance to pull his brother behind a grave.

"Waste of a good cigar," Christopher muttered.

"Stay down," Antonio said. He got up and ran over with Marco and Lino to flank the sicarios' last bastion. They closed in around the mausoleum, firing bursts to keep the fighters back.

Then Lino ran around the other side and unloaded a magazine on them. Howls of pain rose over the automatic staccato.

"Over here!" Angela shouted. She stood behind a grave near the edge of the bluff, pointing her Uzi at a man Antonio couldn't see.

As he made his way over, he spotted cowboy boots.

He had given the order to kill Miguel and take Esteban alive, but the narco king didn't appear to be long for this world.

Both his legs were splintered, the pointed bone shards protruding through his jeans. Blood bubbled around his lips as he sputtered, gasping for air.

Antonio motioned for Angela and everyone else to fan out—except for Marco, whom he waved over. He wanted the two of them to be alone with his enemy.

The crack of gunfire dissipated as the last sicarios in the cemetery and the parking lot were slaughtered.

This was it. Antonio had finally won.

Esteban blinked, clearly trying to keep his eyelids open.

Antonio waited a moment for him to catch his breath.

"Where's Miguel?" Antonio asked.

Esteban shook his head. To focus his mind, Marco stepped on a splinter of shinbone, breaking it off and prompting a scream of agony.

"You can still have an honorable death," Antonio said. "Or we can make you shit and piss yourself like a senile dog."

He gave Esteban a few seconds to consider it.

"Where's your brother?" he asked.

"*Las Pirámides Diamantes*," he said. "The Diamond Pyramids."

"You're lying," Antonio said.

He aimed his rifle just below the silver belt buckle the narco had worn the night they made their peace treaty.

"No, I swear it," Esteban said. He choked and gasped.

It was odd, seeing such a powerful, proud man fighting for his last breaths, and for a moment, Antonio wondered how he himself would use his final moments.

Not like this, he thought. He would go out cursing and screaming.

"Miguel's there, I swear. Floor forty."

"How many men?" Marco asked.

That was good, Antonio thought. It was his next question.

"Fifty, maybe more. I don't know . . ." Esteban reached up. "Please, spare me. I will give you my entire kingdom. And I'll bring you Miguel."

Antonio looked at Marco.

Sometimes, money was more important than revenge, but he would let his boy decide. Marco reached down and grabbed the narco by the boots, then started dragging him by his broken legs.

Esteban wailed in pain.

"Good decision, son," Antonio said.

He helped pick up the man and carry him across the cemetery. By the time they got back to the tent, he was unconscious.

The downpour had stopped, and the sun broke through gray lint. The rest of his men surrounded the area. It appeared they had done well—not a single Moretti casualty except for two of the four special-ops guards, according to Yellowtail.

With over fifty sicarios dead, it had been a slaughter.

Christopher was already sitting in a chair, a hand on his arm, glaring at Esteban.

After the women were safely back in the SUVs, Antonio motioned for his soldiers to join him around the freshly dug grave. Father Ricci stood in front of it.

"Wake him up," Antonio said.

Vinny pulled out his knife and cut Esteban's ear off. He jerked upward, shrieking in pain, eyes bouncing back and forth from one enemy to another.

Father Ricci made the sign of the cross and stepped back from the hole.

"No! Please, NO!" Esteban yelled.

Antonio nodded at Yellowtail and Vinny, who grabbed the man and tossed him into the hole. He landed with a thud and another scream of pain.

Antonio handed his son a shovel.

"Today, you earned your name—and your button," he said. "From here on out, you will be known as the Narco Slayer."

The other men nodded their respect. Even Vinny patted Marco on the back.

Esteban reached up, whimpering until they could no longer hear him through the dirt that covered him. Antonio looked down, then walked away.

"Get the word out," he said. "The Morettis are coming after Miguel Vega next, and then the Saints."

Instead of walking back to the parking lot, he walked to the edge of the cliff. He looked out over the Pacific, thinking of Lucia. Without her, he had nothing to lose.

Now he could build his empire without fear. And a man without fear was the most dangerous thing. Together with his brother, nephew, and son, he would kill the rest of their enemies and expand their empire far beyond the City of Angels.

Antonio no longer had a queen by his side, but he was the unrivaled king.

Lightning forked over the horizon as the storm moved out to sea.

Meanwhile, a new storm was brewing—a Moretti storm, with no regard for anyone or anything in its path of devastation. And this storm the Saints would not escape.

Dear Reader,

The Sons of War series is one of the most exciting and rewarding projects I've had the privilege of writing, and you have my sincere gratitude for reading all three books. I would love to continue writing this story and explore what the future has in store for the Salvatore and Moretti families, but I need your help.

Unfortunately, the Sons of War series struggled to take off as it launched in the very beginning stages of the COVID-19 pandemic. A fourth and final book now depends on factors outside of my control. One way to help as a reader is by sharing these books with your friends and family and posting links on social media. The other helpful thing you could do is take a few minutes to leave honest reviews on Amazon for each of the three books.

Hopefully, with enough word of mouth and the incredibly important reviews, I will have the opportunity to write a fourth book and bring this series to a close the way I had planned.

As always, you have my thanks. It is an honor to bring stories to life for you.

Stay safe, and be well,
Nicholas

ABOUT THE AUTHOR

Nicholas Sansbury Smith is the *New York Times* and *USA Today* bestselling author of the Hell Divers series, the Orbs series, the Trackers series, the Extinction Cycle series, and the new Sons of War series. He worked for Iowa Homeland Security and Emergency Management in disaster mitigation before switching careers to focus on storytelling. When he isn't writing or daydreaming about the apocalypse, he enjoys running, biking, spending time with his family, and traveling the world. He is an Ironman triathlete and lives in Iowa with his wife, their dogs, and a house full of books.

Join Nicholas on social media:
Facebook: Nicholas Sansbury Smith
Website: www.NicholasSansburySmith.com